PRAISE FOR LUCINDA BRANT

'Brant has carved a niche for herself in this particular patch of history and she is gifted in weaving both story and history into a compelling read.'
Fiona Ingram, *Readers Favorite*

'Witty prose and well-researched context, skillfully drawn characters you'll be captivated by, are the main features in her style.'
Maria Grazia Spila, *Fly High*

'True talent is when an author creates an in-depth backstory of intricately woven together complicated characters and events and yet the reader starts on page one, right in the middle of the action and is none the wiser to the author's machinations, only having eyes for what is happening on each and every page, eagerly turning to the next.'
Eliza Knight, *History Undressed*

'Brant has a deft palette for historical detail which contributes to a strong backbone for the narrative. The characters are larger than life and its not hard to read with a visual image in mind. Brant's writing is filled with freshness and wit... highly recommended.'
Prudence J. Batten, *Mesmered's Blog*

'Once again I am in awe of Lucinda's originality to go outside of the norm and use historical moments to create an elaborate story.'
Crystal, *For Your Amusement: My Life*

'Grab a glass of wine, a quiet corner and plan to read the night away. The intricate web that Lucinda Brant constructs with a most amazing cast of characters is sure to keep you mesmerized.'
SWurman, *Night Owl Reviews*

Noble Satyr

A GEORGIAN HISTORICAL ROMANCE

Roxton Series Book 1

LUCINDA BRANT

FOR BJB

One

Part One: the France of Louis XV

The Comte de Salvan stood at the end of the canopied bed in red high heels and pacified his offended nostrils with a lace handkerchief scented with bergamot. He was dressed to attend a music recital in stiff gold frock, close-fitting silk breeches with diamond knee buckles, and a cascade of fine white lace at his wrists that covered soft hands with their rings of precious stones. His face was painted, patched and devoid of the disgust and discomfort his quivering nostrils dared display at the stench of the ill, and the smell that came from the latrines that flowed just beyond the closed door to this small apartment below the tiles of the palace of Versailles.

Its occupant, one Chevalier de Charmond, gentleman usher to the King, languished amongst feather pillows, his shaved head without its wig and in its place a Chinese cap. He was suffering from *la grippe*, but being a committed hypochondriac was convinced he had inflammation of the lungs. His physician could not tell him otherwise. He blew his nose constantly and coughed up phlegm into a bowl his long-suffering manservant emptied at irregular intervals. He had been bled twice that day but nothing relieved his discomfort. The presence of the Comte de Salvan promised a relapse.

The Comte listened to the Chevalier's platitudes without a smile and waved aside the man's apologies with a weary hand. "Yes it is a great honor I do you to descend into this stinking hole.

How can you bear it? I am glad it is you and not I who must exist like a sewer rat. No wonder you are unwell. If you left that bed and went about your duties you would feel better in an instant. But it is your lot," Salvan said in his peculiar nasal voice. He shrugged. "It is most inconvenient of you to take to your bed when a certain matter of great importance to me is left unfinished. If I thought you incapable of carrying out my wishes…"

"M'sieur le Comte! I—"

"To the benefit of us both, remember, dear Charmond, to the benefit of us both. I could have given Arnaud or Paul-René the privilege of doing this small favor for me. Indeed, does not Arnaud owe his alliance with the de Rohan family all because I made the effort to whisper in l'Majesty's ear? One cannot have one's relatives, however removed, married to inferior objects." He proceeded to take snuff up one thin nostril. "And Paul-René would still be scraping dung off Monsieur's boots if I had not put in a good word on his behalf to have him promoted from the kennels to the Petite Écuries. And now you dare lie there when you are well aware my dearest wish must be fulfilled forthwith. I will certainly go mad if something is not done soon!"

The Chevalier attempted to sit up and look all concern with the first rise in the Comte's voice. He schooled his features into an expression of sympathy and shook his head solemnly. "You cannot know what agonies, what nightmares, I have suffered on your behalf, M'sieur le Comte. Every night I have lain here not sleeping, my head pounding with the megrim, unable to breath, and I have thought of you, my dearest Comte, and only you. How best to serve you. How to successfully bring about a resolution to your torments. It has been a constant worry for poor Charmond."

"Then why can you not do this small thing for me?" screeched the Comte. "Do you believe you are the only one I can trust? Do you? You promised me three days at the most and I have waited *seven*. And time is even more important now because the old General is dying; of a surety this time. And nothing is signed. Nothing is in writing. Nothing is fixed until you get me what I want! I must have what I want and I will. I *will!* Whether *you* get it for me or I go elsewhere—Why do you smile, eh?"

The Chevalier blew his nose and tossed the soiled handkerchief to the floor. "I offer my humble apologies, M'sieur le Comte, if you thought I smiled at you," he said quietly. "I was not smiling at you but for you. I have a picture of the beautiful mademoiselle in my mind's eye and I am indeed happy for you. I congratulate you on your good fortune. It is not every day a man comes across one as she. You are a lucky man, M'sieur le Comte."

The anger left Salvan's eyes and he smiled crookedly, a picture of the girl in his mind's eye. Some of the heat cooled in his rouged cheeks and he swaggered. Another pinch of snuff was inhaled, leisurely and long. "She is a beauty, is she not, eh, Charmond? Such round, firm breasts. A rosebud for a mouth. Hair shot with gold and eyes that slant ever so slightly, like a cat's. Most unusual. And to think her delights are all untouched. Ah, it makes me hard just thinking about her! But I tell you, Charmond, I do her a great honor, a great honor indeed. I am lucky, yes, but she doubly so to even have a second look from Jean-Honoré Gabriel de Salvan. When she learns of the honor done her she will surely embrace me all the more sincerely and devotedly. Oh, Charmond, I cannot wait until she—"

"—becomes your son's wife?" interrupted the Chevalier smoothly, which brought the color flooding back into the Comte's face and caused his eyes to narrow to slits. "What a joyous day for the house of Salvan!" declared the Chevalier. "But an even more joyous day for the beautiful mademoiselle. Who would have thought the old Jacobite General's granddaughter would be done such a great honor? Not she, I wager. She cannot but be grateful to you, my dear Salvan. She will embrace you! And show her gratitude? Of a certainty. She will repay you the way you desire her to do so."

"I do not doubt that but..."

"But?" The Chevalier shrugged expressively. "What can go wrong?"

"Idiot!" snarled the Comte. "If you do not get me that *lettre de cachet* my plans, they will be ruined!"

The Chevalier threw the last of his handkerchiefs on the floor and rang the small hand-bell at his bedside for a lackey. "I am doing all I can to do just that, my dear good Comte. Even as we speak I am certain it is being attended to. Poor Charmond may be bedridden, on the point of pneumonia, but still he thinks only of you, my dear M'sieur le Comte, and your ever so desperate predicament. Poor Charmond only hopes, humbly hopes, M'sieur le Comte has not forgotten his own—not quite so desperate— predicament? After all, and I beg your pardon for even mentioning it to you because I know you would not disappoint me, a favor for a favor is what you promised."

The lackey came into the room with clean handkerchiefs and the Chevalier boxed his ears and felt better for having done so. He settled back on the pillows and pretended to show an interest in his hands, but he was watching Salvan and he trembled inwardly at the black look on the man's hideously painted face; the lead paint thick and white to cover pitted cheeks and chin. He thanked God he had never had the smallpox to such a disfiguring degree. He cleared his throat and the Comte looked at him.

"Forgive me for recalling to your memory our agreement, M'sieur le Comte," said the Chevalier. "You shall have your *lettre de cachet*. I hope it brings your son into line. Why he does not want to wed a beautiful virgin is not for me to understand. He must be a little mad, eh, Salvan?" When the Comte did not laugh he dropped the smile into a frown. "Should he still not do as you wish once the *letter de cachet* is waved under his nose, and you clap him up in the Bastille or Bicêtre until he sees reason, you still owe Charmond his favor. I hope M'sieur le Comte intends to honor his bargain."

"Honor it?" shouted Salvan. He went up to the bed, causing the Chevalier to cower, and lowered his voice, for he knew the walls between the apartments to be thin. "How dare you question my honor!" he hissed. "A Salvan's word is never in question! You tell me I will have my *lettre de cachet*, and so I tell you I am doing all I can to steer Roxton away from Madame de La Tournelle's orbit! Your task is the infinitely easier one, Charmond. Have you any suggestions on how to oust a consummate lover from an eager woman's bed? Have you? No! I thought as much. And do not spout drivel at me that it is you who wants this favor. It is Richelieu who directs you, is it not?"

"M'sieur le Duc de Richelieu?" blinked the Chevalier.

"Very well! Play out your game!" spat the Comte. "I know you have little interest in the de la Tournelle. Or to put it correctly she is not the sort of female to interest herself with an insignificant worm such as your—"

"M'sieur le Comte! I object most strongly to your tone. Have I been of insignificance to you? No! Charmond he has been most valuable to M'sieur le Comte!" The Chevalier blew his nose vigorously and looked offended.

The Comte sighed. "As you wish, Charmond." He went to the looking glass in the corner and critically surveyed himself from powdered campaign wig to the sparkle of his over-sized diamond shoe-buckles. Ever the conceited nobleman, he was well-pleased with himself and this improved his mood, as did the thought of seeing the beautiful mademoiselle at the recital. "I grant you have been helpful to me. But do not tell me you are interested in Marie-Anne de Mailly de La Tournelle. That I will not believe! It is Richelieu who wants her, or wants her for the King, and hopes to rule Louis through her. So he thinks. Whatever! His gyrations do not interest me." He glanced at the Chevalier. "I will tell you why you want Roxton tumbled out of Marie-Anne's bed: jealousy."

"Jeal-ous-y?" It was the Chevalier's turn to screech. Instead he coughed and wheezed until his face turned the color of blood. When he could speak again he said, "How can you say so? What do I care for Roxton's conquests? I admit, my dear Salvan, I find it unbelievable that such a one as he is so sought after in the bedchambers of Versailles and Paris. Yet, he is! His reputation equals Richelieu's. Some say it surpasses his conquests. What female has not thrown back the covers for M'sieur le Duc de Roxton? And which ones does he disdain from favoring? Only the ugly and the virtuous. And as they are one and the same, my dear Comte, the number is small indeed!"

The Chevalier pulled a face of loathing and thumped his fist into the coverlet. "Why? Why do our women receive this Englishman with open arms who dares wear his own hair down his back like some Viking conqueror? He has a great beak for a nose, shoulders that are too broad and legs as thick as tree trunks! And as if to goad us all beyond permission, what does he do?" he continued in a thin voice. "He does not keep beagles or wolf-hounds or greyhounds. No! He-he keeps *whippets*. A woman's toy!

He could very well parade about with two kittens in diamond collars as have those ill-looking animals at his heels. Ugh! I will say no more." He collapsed against the pillows and wiped sweat from his florid face. "You must excuse me, M'sieur le Comte. I must be bled..."

Salvan came away from the looking glass and stood over the Chevalier, his eyes bright with a private humor. "You lie in that bed sweating like a pig, pouring scorn on my English cousin, when it is what he does with this," he grabbed his own genitals, "and this," stuck out his tongue and wiggled it, "is why your heart's delight prefers the attentions of M'sieur le Duc d'Roxton."

"You defend him only because his mother was a Salvan," the Chevalier said sulkily.

"As it should be," the Comte replied haughtily, adjusting himself. "I cannot answer for his English ancestry, except it is an ancient lineage. An English dukedom is no small thing. And his mother, my aunt, was of impeccable virtue and of a most noble character, and a Salvan by birth. Enough said! Do not try my patience to its limit, my dear Charmond." He flicked open his gold snuffbox and took a pinch. "Your observations of Roxton amuse me because they are quite to the life, but when you dig beneath the muck you lose your footing!"

"Forgive me, my dear M'sieur le Comte," said the Chevalier with excessive politeness. "I admit I harbored expectations that Felice would grant me certain liberties. That was until she caught the eye of your cousin at the Comédie Française. Yet I do not despair of having her, knowing Roxton tires so quickly of such easy prey. But resentment was not the only reason which prompted my outburst. Perhaps I will not voice my concerns at this time. It is late. You have a recital to attend, and I, I am tired. It is only—well, no, I shall not open my mouth—"

"Open it! Open it!" ordered the Comte. "Do not goad me, Charmond! You have wasted enough of my evening and still I am no nearer to having what I want in my hands!"

"Has not M'sieur le Comte considered the alternative?" asked the Chevalier smugly. "It would be infinitely simpler if you were to bed the beautiful mademoiselle without consideration for the formalities. Why must you wed her to your son before you take her as your mistress? Is not your son's marriage to the beautiful mademoiselle the bone that sticks in your throat? Remove it! Touché. All is as it should be."

The Comte de Salvan had a great desire to choke the life out of the Chevalier de Charmond yet he restrained this murderous instinct. Instead he clapped an open palm to his powdered forehead and groaned aloud. "Why do I endure this imbecile? *Mon Dieu*. I am surrounded by fools and scoundrels!" He stuck his face up close to the startled Chevalier. "Do you think I did not think of that? Ah! You are too stupid. I will not explain. Do you think me a man of no honor? I, a Salvan? I do not go about as M'sieur le Duc de Richelieu seducing unwed females. Preposterous! There is my unsullied reputation to think of. There is what I owe my name. That fever, it has entered what little brain you possess. I am done with you!" He turned on a heel to go to the door. "I will have the *lettre de cachet* by the end of this week—"

"Your so English cousin has turned his satyr's eye on the beautiful mademoiselle."

The Comte stood still. He did not turn or speak so the Chevalier continued after a pause and a blow of his red nose. "You think me a dolt and a scoundrel for advising you to cut through the formalities, but I tell you, my dear Salvan, if you do not, the girl will no longer be worth all the energies you expend to have her in your bed—wed or unwed. Roxton has noticed her and so it is only a matter of time before his tongue—"

"By the end of the week," Salvan said without turning and slammed the door.

Had the Chevalier the benefit of seeing the Comte's face he would have revelled in the effect of his words. As he did not he gave himself up to complex musings, and into the hands of his physician to be bled. He ordered his servant to scuttle across the palace to a particular suite of rooms to report all that had transpired between he and his visitor.

The Comte de Salvan repaired to the upper levels of the palace. Leaving the stench behind he forced himself to put aside the Chevalier's warning and to wear his most gay public face. He tottered up the Grand Escalier to the first floor, crossed the Hercules drawing room, bowing and waving his handkerchief to all who acknowledged his existence. The opulence of this large ornate marbled room was a comfort to him and he breathed easier. He stopped to take snuff with two cronies who lounged by a Sarrancolin column and searched for his son amongst the crowd of powdered and beribboned nobles moving into the Appartement. Unsuccessful, he dismissed the moody boy from his thoughts hoping to catch sight of the one beautiful face amongst a hundred he desired to make his own. Alas, she had yet to appear.

He was one of the last to enter the Appartement. It was crowded and he could hear the orchestra but had no chance of seeing its members from the back of the room. He spied the Duc de Richelieu, newly returned from exile in Languedoc, and close by his side, languidly fanning herself, was Madame de La Tournelle. She was resplendent in petticoats of blue damask, embroidered with large sprays of flowers, and showed a pretty wrist covered with milky strands of pearls. For a long time he did not notice the Duke of Roxton standing by his side.

"You will not find what you are looking for," drawled the Duke of Roxton, quizzing-glass fixed on Madame de La Tournelle. "That which you desire is not here."

Salvan spun about and stared up at the impassive aquiline profile.

"Continue to gawp and I will go elsewhere," murmured the Duke. "Mademoiselle Claude has been beckoning with her fan this past half hour. Sitting next to that frost-piece is preferable to being scrutinised by you, dearest cousin."

Salvan snapped open a fan of painted chicken-skin and fluttered it like a woman, searching gaze returning to the sea of silk and lace. "To be abandoned for that hag would be an insult I could not endure, mon cousin. You merely startled me."

"I repeat, your search is fruitless."

"Ah! You see me scanning faces. I always do so. It is nothing," Salvan said lightly. "Did you think me looking for someone in particular? No! Who—Who did you think I was looking for?"

"My dear Salvan," drawled the Duke, "your son, your most obedient son."

"D'Ambert? Yes-yes of course my son!" Salvan said with relief.

He turned back to the performance in time for the final round of polite applause. When the King had taken his leave Salvan drew his arm through that of his cousin. They walked a little way off to a corner of the room that was less crowded to better observe the audience disperse. "That ghastly noise is at an end, thank God. Were you as bored as I? Don't answer. I know it! Where have you been, mon cousin? I have missed you in the corridors of the palace this past week. Do not tell me you are fatigued with us and stay in Paris? Or are you weary with what is on offer?"

They bowed to a passing beauty, her hair dressed in an eye-catching creation of plumes and pearls and her lips painted a delicious red.

"She tries to catch your attention, Roxton. Now there is one who could cure your ennui."

"Madame is not worth the effort."

"*Parbleu!* How fortunate are those who can afford to choose."

Roxton took snuff and flicked a speck of the fine mixture from a wide velvet cuff. He shrugged. "It is obvious M'sieur le Comte has not had the—er—privilege of madame without her skilful paint and uplifting bodice. You are welcome to her if that is to your taste."

"No. Not I!"

"No. Your tastes lean toward the—er—*uninitiated*, do they not, my dear cousin?"

There was the slightest pause before the Comte let out a forced brittle laugh. He tapped the Duke's velvet sleeve with the silver sticks of his fan. "That is as well or our paths would cross, and that would not amuse me at all!"

"You may rest easy, my dear," said the Duke smoothly, quiz-zing-glass allowed to dangle on its silk riband. "I have never yet had the urge to play nursery maid."

Salvan flushed in spite of himself. He changed the topic immediately. "You saw Richelieu? He has been back at court this past week. They say he and the Tournelle plan to oust the dull sister as soon as it can be contrived. De Mailly is ignorant of the whole! She will see herself banished before she knows what she is about and—"

"My dear, this is old news," interrupted the Duke. "But perhaps it is new to you? You need to spend less time lurking in corridors and a good deal more between the sheets—"

"As you do?" Salvan snapped before he could help himself.

Roxton swept him a magnificent bow. "As I do," he confirmed.

"Ha! A novel approach. Do not tell me you expend any energy in conversation."

"I was not about to tell you anything of the sort, my dear," came the insolent reply. The Duke's black eyes watched a storm cross his cousin's ravaged face and he laughed softly and changed the subject. "Madame sends her regards," he said politely. "She asks when next you intend to visit Paris. She longs to hear the latest gossip of court which I cannot bring myself to repeat. I said I would petition you on her behalf and beg you go to her. I beg and have done my duty. I leave it in your hands. Sisters weary me."

The mention of the Duke's lovely sister instantly transformed the Comte de Salvan, as Roxton knew it would. He clapped his hands in delight. "Estée has asked to see me? You do not jest?" he said expectantly, and fell in beside the Duke as he walked out of the Appartement and crossed the Hercules Room and went down the staircase. "Is she in good health? Does she pine away in that dreary hôtel of yours? You are most cruel to her, Roxton! Such beauty deserves to be admired, to be fawned over, and cherished. She has not been to court now in seven years or more. She the widow of Jean-Claude de Montbrail, the most decorated of Louis' Generals. If he had not been cut down in his prime Estée would now be at court."

"Yes, I forbid her the court. That is my right."

"Even in the face of Louis' displeasure?" whispered the Comte de Salvan, taking a quick, nervous look over his padded shoulder. "I cannot forget your private audience," he continued with a shudder. "Me, I fainted. I expected a *lettre de cachet* at the very least. I praise God it did not happen so. You are still barely tolerated by l'Majesty. He never forgives or forgets such slights, mon cousin. He might relent a little if you were to allow your sister to return to court—"

"I have not the least interest in Louis' opinion of me."

"M'sieur le Duc! Please!" Salvan gasped in a broken voice. "Not so loud. I beg you!"

The Duke paused in the vestibule that led out into the Marble courtyard to permit a lackey to assist him into his many-capped roquelaure. "I repeat, what your king thinks of me or my actions is of supreme indifference. You forget I am of mixed blood. Only half is French, and that my mother's. My allegiance is to a German-born King who sits on the English throne. Regrettable as that circumstance may be to many, it serves a purpose. And as I am a peer of that realm, and not this, I need not hold my actions accountable to your liege lord and master. If my presence at this court unnerves you, my dear cousin, I am happy for you to disassociate yourself with my family." He bowed politely. "Versailles is no place for those of noble character, such as my sister."

The Comte de Salvan tottered outside after him, a servant with a flambeau quick to follow on his heels. "And what of the rest of us?"

"Those of us of noble birth and no character amuse ourselves as best we can. I bid you a good night."

Halfway across the courtyard two figures moving in shadow caught Salvan's eye and he drew in a quick breath. Instantly, he tried to divert the Duke with some inconsequential tale about a notorious female and her present lover, all the while conscious of the raised voices travelling across the expanse of open air from the dark recesses of the Royal courtyard. But the Duke of Roxton was not diverted. He listened to his cousin's chatterings as he slipped on a pair of black kid gloves then abruptly changed direction and sauntered toward the voices. His cousin made a protesting sound in the back of his throat and followed as best he could in red high heels.

A slim youth, richly clad in puce satin under a heavy coat thrown carelessly about his shoulders, and a girl, her gown concealed under a shabby wool cloak too large for her small frame and allowed to trail in the mud, were huddled under a red brick archway. In the light cast by a flickering flambeau, they were in heated discussion, the youth with an arm out-stretched to the opposite wall to block the girl's exit.

The Duke did not go so near as to disturb them, yet he showed enough interest to put up his quizzing-glass. He was soon joined by the Comte de Salvan, who had hobbled across the pebbles in his high red heels, was chilled to the bone for having left his cloak indoors, and was mentally heaping curses upon his father's memory for having permitted his name to be forever allied with a family of heretical Englishmen whom he blamed for all his past and present misfortunes.

"Permit me to explain," Salvan rasped, catching his breath.

"Explain?" purred the Duke. "There is no need. Your so devoted son is of an age to defend his own actions."

The Vicomte d'Ambert despaired of making Antonia see reason. He gave an impatient grunt and looked away into the black night. "I tell you it is impossible!" he declared. "What do you not understand? The moment you leave the palace I cannot protect you. You have managed to avoid him until now. I say we wait for word from St. Germain. When we know how your Grandfather fairs something will be contrived. I promise you."

"It is you who do not understand, Étienne!"

"Antonia, I—"

"My grandfather is dying," Antonia announced flatly. "He has gone to St. Germain to die, not to hunt or debauch but to die. He is old and infirm and his time has come. So be it. You think me unfeeling to speak the truth? Well, it is best I understand how it is and not allow silly expectations to fill my head. And do not tell me otherwise! Do not say I must hope because I know you only say so because I am a female and think to shield me from the truth. Such gallantry is wasted on me, Étienne." When he kept his silence and refused to look at her she tried to rally him. "Do not sulk. You know what I say is the tr—"

"—the truth?" he repeated angrily. "Yes, it is the truth. I wish it was not so!"

"If you would convey me to Paris then I know I could make my own way to London. Your father will not find me in Paris, it is too big a city, and I have the money Grandfather gave me—"

"—to what?" The Vicomte threw up a hand in a gesture of hopelessness. "It is madness, Antonia. You, a pretty girl alone in

Paris with not even a maid as chaperone? God grant me patience! You would not survive a day."

"So you think? I am not afraid of a big city. Father and I lived in many strange cities and we enjoyed ourselves hugely."

D'Ambert laughed. "Only an ignorant child would give me such an answer."

"You are eighteen years old, does that not make *you* a child?" retorted Antonia.

He ignored the truth of this. "Have you been to Paris?"

"What does that signify?"

"Have you ever taken a diligence on your own?"

"No. But I am not so spiritless as to shy away from using public conveyances."

"And once you took the diligence to Calais and by some miracle boarded a packet for Dover, what then? Assuming none of these journeys put you in the slightest danger—another miracle—what then? You have never visited England. I doubt you can speak the barbaric English tongue."

"Wrong! I can," Antonia announced proudly. The Vicomte's sneer made her blush. "It is a very long time since I used the English tongue with Maman, but—but—I can *read* Grandfather's English newssheets. And it is not as if I do not understand what is being said. That is the least little problem."

"That is very true for no sooner set down in a Parisian street than one of a thousand scoundrels would abduct you. Before nightfall you would be clapped up in a brothel and your favors sold to the highest bidder by a fat bawd. Is that what you want?"

"No worse a fate than will befall me should I remain here."

The Vicomte's mouth dropped open at this statement, but there was nothing he could say in answer to it. He knew very well his father's scheme and it sickened him. He blamed the Earl of Strathsay for all his present troubles. The old man should have left Antonia in Rome with a strict governess until his return. A convent better befitted girls of her breeding, where they were safe from lechers such as his father. But what convent school would take her when she stubbornly refused, in the face of her grandfather's wrath, to embrace the one true faith?

He wished his hands would stop shaking. He felt hot and

damp in his coat despite a bitter cold wind whistling through the archway. His manservant held a taper closer to cast light on his pockets whilst he rummaged for a snuffbox. Two pinches of the mixture and in a short while the shaking would cease and he would feel calmer, better able to think what to do next. But what could he do? What was he to do? Never mind Antonia was beautiful and young; there were many such girls at court. Why couldn't his father find another diversion to occupy his time? But the Vicomte knew the answer. Antonia's great beauty was equalled by a strong will and a naïve exuberance for life. And she was a virgin. A rare commodity in a place like Versailles. Strong attractions indeed for such a jaded roué as his father. And his was not the only jaundice eye that had been cast in Antonia's direction, thought d'Ambert with a growing depression.

Antonia touched his arm. "So you will take me to Paris?"

"You know why I cannot. My father has threatened a *lettre de cachet*."

"That I will not believe. He is your father, not your jailer. Why should he do such a thing? You are his only son. It is unbelievable."

"Would I lie to you?" he demanded.

Antonia looked at him frankly, clear green eyes searching his damp face and shook her head. "No. You would not lie to me, Étienne. He is quite abominable to threaten such a thing. Would it mean the Bastille?"

"Or any other fortress so named in the warrant. The stinking subterranean dungeons of Castle Bicêtre, if it suited his purpose. There everything is complete darkness. A living death! And at the King's pleasure. I could not endure it."

"He would never send you there," Antonia said with confidence, though the thought of such places of torture made her inwardly shudder.

"Salvan will stop at nothing until he has what he wants," said the Vicomte discouragingly. "He wants you and he says I must marry you. Mayhap—"

Antonia blinked. "But I do not want to marry you at all."

"You could do worse than marry into my family!" Étienne flared up.

14

Antonia chuckled. "Oh, do not look so offended. When you pull that face you remind me of the Archbishop of Paris."

He blushed and smiled. "I am sorry. It is just—If it was not for my father's schemes perhaps you would consider?"

"No," she stated. "I do not love you, Étienne. I am sorry. When I marry it will be for love. My father and mother married for love and I will not settle for less."

The Vicomte bowed mockingly. "M'sieur d'Ambert thanks mademoiselle for her frankness. Mademoiselle has a most novel approach to marriage. Perhaps it is my person which offends? I am not tall enough? Too young? Do you prefer brown eyes to blue? Or does mademoiselle look higher? My name and lineage are impeccable, but I will only inherit the title of Comte. Perhaps it is a tabouret you crave? Yes! It is a Duke you want! Eh?"

"Now you are being childish," said Antonia without heat. "It is when you are like this I dislike you." She went to walk off but he blocked her exit. "Let me pass, Étienne. It is late and Maria will scold me if I do not return before she goes to mass."

"Childish, am I?" he demanded and caught at her arm under the cloak. "You, who go at the beg and call of a whore—"

"Maria is no such thing!"

"No? She is your grandfather's mistress?"

"Yes..."

"Yes?"

"She loves him, Étienne."

"You are a child. A whore is a whore. Maria Caspartti is a whore! A Venetian *whore*."

"Let me go! You are hurting me!"

"Perhaps little Antonia has a particular nobleman in mind?" taunted the Vicomte with a sneering smile, twisting her arm. "Is that why she so easily dismisses me? Let me think who might take your fancy…"

"You do not even care for me," said Antonia in exasperation. "Only three weeks ago you were ears over toes in love with Pauline Alexandre de Rohan. She is a very beautiful and accomplished girl and I know if you had pursued her your father could not have objected to such a match. She cared for you too—"

"Perhaps mademoiselle prefers men to boys? Is it my age you

cavil at?" goaded the Vicomte. "Someone of my English cousin's vintage and reputation intrigues you, does he not? Once you asked many questions about him and I know you sneak off to watch him fence cork-tipped in the Princes' courtyard. I have had you followed. My English cousin is very good with his sword. He has one of the best wrists in France. He has also slept in every woman's bed in this palace!"

"What of that? So have three-quarters of the gentlemen at court!"

"I am not of that number," stated the Vicomte haughtily.

Antonia smiled up at him. "Foolish Étienne. That is what I most admired in you from the first. Now please let me go. I am certain you have bruised my wrist."

He gave an embarrassed laugh and squeezed her wrist before releasing her. "My temper is very bad," he said with a shrug. "Do not anger me and I will not hurt you, foolish Antonia. If you have a bruise I am sorry for it. Mayhap tomorrow we will hear from St. Germain. Unlike you I do not despair of good news— What is it?"

Antonia had heard the echo of high heels across the deserted courtyard and seen the Vicomte's manservant give a start. She scooped up the cloak which had fallen from her shoulders at d'Ambert's rough treatment and hastily threw it over her gown, not caring that the mud and grime of the cobbles splashed her petticoats.

"Listen, Étienne," she whispered. "If we are caught—"

"Too late," he answered and stepped into the pale orange light.

The Vicomte watched the glow of a flambeau brighten as it crossed the courtyard, and three figures emerged out of the darkness. His whole being stiffened and he pulled Antonia behind him as he greeted the intruders with a stiff bow. He dared not look at his father who stood at the Duke of Roxton's shoulder. "Good evening, M'sieur le Duc," he said politely.

Before the salutation could be returned the Comte de Salvan jumped at his son. "What are you doing here?" he demanded in a falsetto whisper. "Did I not warn you? Do not meddle in my affairs! You will ruin everything! Everything."

"M'sieur, let me explain—"

"*Taisez-vous!*" snarled the Comte and instantly transformed himself into the gay courtier for Antonia's benefit. "Mademoiselle Moran, allow me to apologise for my unthinking son's behavior. To bring you out-of-doors on such a cold night is unforgivable. He is a clod! An inconsiderate dolt! I would be thrown into a thousand agonies if I thought a worthless piece of my flesh had caused you the slightest inconvenience."

He took a step closer but Antonia shrunk from him, causing his son to stand taller. This incensed the little man but his painted face remained fixed in a coaxing smile. "Come now, you must not be frightened of Salvan. He thinks of little else but your well-being and how best to serve you." He glared at his son's unblinking countenance. "What has my son said to make you have a dread of poor Salvan?"

"Pardon, M'sieur le Comte, but what I discuss with M'sieur d'Ambert is not your concern."

Salvan's smile tightened. "Pardon, mademoiselle, but when my son takes it into his head to conduct clandestine meetings with unattended and very pretty females, it is very much my concern." He bowed with formality.

Antonia was a little unnerved that the Duke of Roxton continued to stare at her in a leisurely fashion through his quizzing-glass, but she did not allow this to stop her answering the Comte. "Pardon, M'sieur le Comte, I had not realised M'sieur le Comte's life was of such a boredom he needs spy on his son's."

Far from taking offence the Comte de Salvan threw his hands together with delight. "Is she not refreshing, Roxton? What spirit! And in one so young! Mademoiselle is divine. Do you not agree, mon cousin? What next will she say?"

The Duke ignored his cousin's exuberance and let fall his eye-glass. The girl's haughty upward tilt of her chin and the insolent sparkle in her green eyes annoyed him. "You lack manners," he said to Antonia and turned away into the darkness. "Walk me to my carriage, Salvan," he ordered. "The boy can escort the girl back to the nursery."

Salvan's face fell and his shoulders slumped. "But, mon cousin…"

17

"Excuse me, M'sieur le Duc," retorted Antonia, "but as you refuse to own our connection, you have no right to comment on my manners."

"Antonia, *no*," whispered the Vicomte and felt his knees buckle with nervousness when the Duke of Roxton, who had not gone more than two strides, turned and came back to stand before Antonia. The Vicomte tugged at the girl's sleeve to get her behind him but she would not go. She stood bravely beside him, the tinge of color in her cold, pale cheeks the only sign of her nervousness. "M'sieur le Duc, I beg you to forgive Mademoiselle, she—"

"Be quiet, d'Ambert!" the Comte de Salvan hissed. "If anyone is to beg on Mademoiselle's behalf it is I, you dolt!"

Father and son were ignored.

"Unlike my good cousin, I do not find Mademoiselle amusing," the Duke enunciated icily, suppressed anger reflected in black eyes that stared down at the girl unblinkingly. "You mistake insolence for wit. A few more years in the schoolroom may correct the defect."

Antonia pretended to demure and lowered her lashes with a sigh of resignation. "Sadly, I may not be given the opportunity for such correction, M'sieur le Duc," she answered despondently, a fleeting glance at the Comte de Salvan, "that is…unless M'sieur le Duc he will own me as his kinswoman…"

The Duke caught the significance in her glance but he was not fooled by her veneer of humility. He saw the dimple in her left cheek and he knew what she was trying to do. It annoyed him more than it should have. He would not have his hand forced, not by anyone, certainly not by an impertinent chit whose disordered hair and ill-fitting clothes were more befitting a street urchin than the granddaughter of a much decorated General Earl. He gritted his teeth. "You are not my responsibility."

"Of course she is not," the Comte de Salvan proclaimed with a forced laugh of light-heartedness, his scented handkerchief up to his thin nostrils, yet a wary eye on the Duke's implacable features. "Mademoiselle has a grandfather who has only her best interests at heart. *Infin.* That said, let me see you to your carriage, mon cousin, before we all catch our deaths out in this night air."

"My grandfather's interests do not accord with my father's last will and testament," Antonia stated to the Duke, ignoring the

Comte. "My father he sent M'sieur le Duc a copy of his will from Florence, before his final illness."

If Frederick Moran had sent him a copy of his will, it was news to the Duke, and surprise registered in his black eyes. Yet the girl continued to regard him with her clear green eyes, eyes that were accusatory; as if he had read and deliberately ignored her father's last wishes and should account for his actions to her. Insolent creature. He would not give her the satisfaction of a response, and with a small nod at the Vicomte d'Ambert, he turned on a heel, beckoning the Comte to fall in beside him.

With a small, knowing smile, Antonia watched the Duke stride off into the darkness, deaf to the Vicomte's monologue about how her ill-mannered behavior would get them both into trouble. The Duke might be angry with her, indeed the look on his face suggested he had washed his hands of her once and for all time, yet, Antonia was satisfied that this late-night encounter, unlike the half dozen letters she had written him about her predicament, had finally pricked at his conscience.

Confident she would soon be leaving Versailles, there was no time to lose. She must ensure her portmanteaux were packed and ready for the flight from this Palace and the Comte de Salvan's menacing orbit. At the Galerie des Glaces masquerade in two days time, that's when she would force the Duke of Roxton's hand. She smiled at her own cleverness and, gathering the over-large cloak about her small frame, she ran off across the Marble courtyard towards the Palace buildings, calling out to the Vicomte that she was a very good runner and would beat him to Maria Caspartti's apartment.

Two

An hour later, the Duke of Roxton's town chariot swung through the black iron gates to his hôtel on the Rue St. Honoré. The four chestnuts glistened with sweat, their heads rearing up, curls of hot breath expelled through wide nostrils into a black night. Grooms ran to the horses heads; liveried footmen scattered across the courtyard; the porter opened wide the massive studded door and bowed low; everywhere was ordered chaos. The driver jumped down from his box with a grunt and stripped off leather gloves. When a lackey hastened to his side with an expectant look he jerked a thumb at the chariot and lifted his thick eyebrows.

"He's in a rare one," muttered Baptiste the driver. "Tell Duvalier. Two wagons overturned on the Pont de Sèvres and a near miss with a coucou on the Quai de Passy. The devil was in it tonight!"

"What is so unusual?" chuckled his fellow. "It is always the same with him."

Two whippets, one grey, one spotted white and tan, both dressed in diamond studded collars, greeted their master in the marble foyer with a nuzzle of his gloved hand and frenzied wags of their whip-like tails. The Duke's butler Duvalier stepped forward, careful not to come between master and devoted animals, and relieved the Duke of roquelaure, gloves and sword. He was informed Madame de Montbrail and Lord Vallentine waited in the salon and went up to the second floor, whippets following happily at his heels.

He entered the room quietly and found his sister seated by the fire working at a tapestry screen. Lord Vallentine, legs sprawled out in front of him, frockcoat unbuttoned, wig slightly askew, and square chin resting on his lace cravat, was comfortably situated in a deep chair, reading aloud from an English newssheet. His progress was slow and deliberate. Translation made all the more difficult by Madame's constant interruptions.

"I do not understand at all," she interjected, her head of shining black curls bent closely over her stitchery. "Why does your King listen to this minister at all? I would not sign a bill I did not like. Why should he? Is he not King?"

"Listen, Estée," said Lord Vallentine patiently. "England ain't France. I keep telling you that. I've explained it a hundred times. The House of Commons votes on a bill, it goes to the Lords. Then if it has a majority vote it is presented to the King for signature to pass it into law. If he don't like it he can return it to the House and—"

"It is all too tedious," she sighed. "But please, read me more about this Cambric bill."

"Well, I'm parched," said his lordship and stretched out a hand for the small silver hand-bell. "More coffee, Estée?"

"For three, my dear," said the Duke stepping further into the warm room.

"Hey! Hey! Look what the night has brought us! It's Roxton!" declared Vallentine with a huge grin and leapt up to grasp the outstretched hand of his closest friend.

"As always, my dear Vallentine, you are omniscient," said Roxton with a rare smile. He snapped his fingers and the dogs came to heel, waiting expectantly, not moving as Madame in a rustle of voluminous silk petticoats swept across the room and into her brother's arms.

"Didn't I tell you this morning Vallentine would be in Paris by supper time?" she scolded playfully and received a kiss on both cheeks. "And you not here to greet him!"

"How was your crossing?" asked the Duke and sat in the chair opposite his friend, the whippets quick to curl up at his feet. "I trust it was calm?"

"I wish. Damme! Sick as a goat!" laughed his lordship,

stretching out again. "But a good supper at your table and you see me back to full health." He looked his friend over with a critical eye. "Not unlike yourself. You don't get any older. I declare I've more lines on my face than you. And you're still looking the cleric," he said, commenting on the Duke's stiff black velvet frockcoat and raven hair, pulled severely off the stark face and plaited in a que that reached to the middle of his wide back. "I can't understand it. A man in your position could do much better. Have a wardrobe of fine frocks in any color, material and adornments you desired. Not that I'm saying the black and white don't suit. Far from it. It does. Mighty finely too!"

"I try not to disappoint you, Vallentine," said the Duke. "But I see I have dropped in your estimation. On your last visit you branded me a—er—magpie."

"Did I by Jove? Well, and that too!" said his friend unabashed.

"It is useless to go on at him," complained Estée. "I am forever saying the same and he is deaf to all my entreaties. Oh, Duvalier, fresh coffee and clean dishes." When the butler had closed the door she said to her brother, "I expected you home much earlier. You stayed for the recital?"

"Recital?" repeated the Duke absently, his eyes on the large square-cut emerald he wore on a finger of a long white hand. It was his only piece of jewellery. "Recital? Yes. I don't remember the pieces played, only that the whole was insipid."

"Is it true the Duc de Richelieu has returned?" she asked.

"Armand has returned," he answered. "Madame du Charolais took him instantly to her bosom, and Mademoiselle de Vintimille to her bed as soon as he was out from under Madame de Flavacourt's covers. As always one smells him before one sees him. His habits and his perfume remain unchanged."

"Was he pleased to see you?" she asked.

"Armand is always pleased to see me," the Duke replied with a thin smile. "He remarked he missed the competition in Languedoc. I assured him I would do my best to keep him guessing."

Estée laughed. "And does he know about Marie-Anne de La Tournelle?"

The Duke showed her a neutral expression and this made her frown.

Lord Vallentine understood immediately and gave a low whistle for which he received the same treatment as the sister. "Leave it be, Estée," he cautioned.

"Why should I not say something about Marie-Anne?" she bristled. "Most men would boast of such a conquest. Why, even here in Paris, it is whispered she will soon oust the de Mailly—that so ugly sister of hers—as Louis' next mistress. Thus I am interested. You play a dangerous game, dearest brother. I don't care for it."

"I do not ask you to care. It is none of your business."

Estée de Montbrail's beautiful face quivered and she bustled back to her tapestry frame and sat in silence without taking up needle and thread. Lord Vallentine hated to see her in any distress but he knew his friend to be right so he kept his mouth shut. The silence was only broken when Duvalier returned with a footman and the coffee things. Estée absorbed herself in pouring out and her brother watched her, saying as he accepted a dish of coffee,

"I passed on your compliments to Salvan. He has promised to come to Paris as soon as his duties at court permit. Soon you will be up on all the gossip at Versailles. He always has a store of scandal at the ready."

"Still hanging about is he?" grumbled Lord Vallentine.

"Why do you pull a face?" asked Estée. "Salvan is our cousin and often visits when he can."

"I don't like the fellow. His paints and powders annoy me, as do his pleasantries. Damned overbearing!"

"You have a personal grudge against M'sieur le Comte de Salvan?" enquired the Duke, putting the dish back on its saucer. "I assure you, my dear, he never seeks to interfere in another man's gallantries. Unlike the Duc de Richelieu, unless, of course, the—er—lady permits."

"Is that not gentlemanly of him?" Estée teased Lord Vallentine.

"He hasn't done me any harm—yet," replied his lordship darkly, and in English.

The Duke offered him snuff. "Nor is he ever likely to, my dear Vallentine," he answered in his native tongue. "You either lack the necessary confidence or you are casting—er—aspersions upon the virtue of a lady. The former I can do nothing about.

The latter, if it be so, is an insult, and that I am quite capable of dealing with."

"You have a nice turn of phrase."

Roxton bowed his head. "I aim to please."

"Accept my apologies."

"As always."

Lord Vallentine smiled at Madame and reverted to the French tongue. "Forgive us, Estée. There are some things I find too difficult to explain in French."

"No?" she said and sipped at her coffee. "When you speak in English with my brother it is because you do not want me to understand at all. Me, I find that very unfair! You will have all the time in the world to do so when I retire. But, if you were talking about the court please tell me. If it was politics, I do not care in the least to know."

"They are one and the same, eh, Roxton? Though I prefer the halls of Westminster to the stifled intrigues of Versailles. There is something far more sinister about that place. Too much muck-raking under all that glitters! Don't know why you bother with it, Roxton. Plenty to do in Paris without getting mixed up in the goings-on out there."

The Duke looked up from admiring his emerald ring. "It can't be helped. It is in the blood."

"A poor excuse!" scoffed his lordship. "You're an English-man to the marrow. Eton schooled and Oxford educated thanks to your grandfather's influence. 'tis a pity your sister wasn't sent to England with you."

"And leave Maman?" said Estée with alarm. "It was horrid enough when my brother was wrenched from Maman's arms when Papa died. He belonged here with us. This was where he was born and raised. This is what Papa wanted for us. He did not like England. He wanted us to be French, just like Maman. I am French. My brother is too."

Vallentine sat bolt upright, spilling coffee over into the saucer. "Roxton ain't French! He ain't even a papist! His father wasn't either, whatever you say."

"It is a great shame," sighed Madame, a twinkle at her brother.

"Shame? Now listen, Estée—"

"Something is troubling you, Roxton," said Madame, ignoring his lordship's heated outburst. "You are constantly looking at Papa's ring. Why?"

"Tell me, Vallentine. What color are the Lady Strathsay's eyes?"

Lord Vallentine looked puzzled. He shrugged. "No idea."

"Lady Strathsay?" asked Estée. "I do not know in the least. I have not seen her in many years. The old Earl, her husband, he is finally dying. *Malheur!* It is quite an occasion, this event. Has he been moved to St. Germain? Tante Victoire says he has gone there to die."

The Duke shrugged. "Possibly."

"Tante says he refuses the confessional until he has had word from the true English King, and he has sent his mistress of fifteen years away. I feel sorry for the woman. Tante says she was more devoted to him than any wife. Not that Lady Strathsay has the right to be called his wife, never living with him these past thirty years." Madame gave a long sigh. "Poor man, to have such a wife. And she our cousin! I am glad she does not visit. I would not wish to play hostess to one such as she."

"The old man must be close to eighty," put in Vallentine. "Will you have done fidgeting with that damme ring, Roxton! You're blinding me. Strathsay dying? Well, well! That will soon put another nail in the Stuart coffin. He's the last of Charles's bastards, and the last of the Pretender's Generals. He must be close to eighty."

"So you have said. He is four and seventy and it is not age that is killing him, but the pox," the Duke informed them. "A fitting end for the Merry Monarch and that shrew Jane Strathsay's bastard. Tell me, Estée, what is the color of Augusta Strathsay's eyes?"

His sister glanced suspiciously at Lord Vallentine, but when his lordship could only shrug she looked back at her brother. "I think they are green," she said with impatience. "Yes, they are green."

"And why do you remember them so particularly?"

"I wish I knew what you are thinking!" she said. "I don't remember them so particularly. It is just that they are green."

"Is that all?"

"Yes! That is all!" said Estée with a pout. She poured out a second dish of coffee for each of them. "They are green. Val-lentine would know better than I."

"Grass-green? Sea green? A jade, perhaps?" persisted the Duke.

"I wonder how Lady Strathsay will take the news of the Earl's death?" asked Lord Vallentine, hoping to turn the subject from his friend's newly found obsession with the color green.

"Augusta will hate going into mourning. Black and white does not suit her," answered Roxton and stretched out his hand so the emerald caught the light from the chandelier. "You think mayhap a pea-green?"

Estée rose with a flounce. "You are being insufferable! Sometimes I do not understand you at all! You were in London just four months ago, so you can tell us what shade of green are Cousin Augusta's eyes."

"I would like you to tell me," he said softly.

Madame went back to her tapestry. "Augusta is, or was, but I dare say still is, a very beautiful woman. So. Her eyes are beautiful also. If I remember at all correctly she has unusual eyes—slightly oblique, like a cat's. Most unusual. And with long dark lashes, which is also unusual for someone with a head of flaming curls."

"Don't recall 'em myself," mumbled Lord Vallentine out of his depth. He was restless and stood to stretch his legs. "Prefer blue eyes m'self. What is it with her eyes? She ain't going blind, is she?"

"Of course not," responded Estée, her cheeks tinged with color at Lord Vallentine's guarded compliment.

"I'll be blinded if you don't leave off turning that emerald into the light," announced his lordship with a squint. "Hey! Emerald! Emerald green!"

The Duke sighed. "At last Vallentine's brain turns a cog. I am aghast."

His lordship's face darkened. "I'm right, ain't I?"

"You shall collect a sweetmeat from Duvalier for your efforts, my dear Vallentine," said Roxton and flicked the grey whippet's ear with a careless finger. He kissed his sister's forehead and said goodnight. "Come, my children," he commanded the dogs. "You too, dearest," he said to his friend. "I'm off to Rossard's. Shall you join me?"

"Certainly. But only if you leave off about eyes and emeralds!"

"I won't tax your brain further, only your skill at table."

There was a scratch at the door before the gentlemen departed. It was the butler, very apologetic, and with the news the Vicomte d'Ambert wished to speak to Monseigneur on a most urgent matter that could not wait until morning.

"The library, Duvalier. Vallentine, will you wait?"

"I'll sit a little longer with Estée."

"What is the matter?" Madame asked the Duke. "Not Salvan? Or Tante Victoire?"

"I don't believe so," replied Roxton with an expression Estée always found so infuriatingly hard to read. "Yet, I should have guessed he would follow hot-foot from Versailles. No doubt the street urchin sent him to do her bidding." And he left the room before his sister and Lord Vallentine could question him further.

There was a fire in the library but little light. Only one chandelier cast a glow over the long room of leather-bound volumes and heavy furniture. The rich burgundy curtains of velvet were drawn across the windows that had a view of the inner courtyard with its small garden and stables. One window was not draped, and it was at this the Vicomte d'Ambert, booted and spurred, had positioned himself when a footman opened the door to admit the Duke.

"You wished to speak to me on a—er—urgent matter?" asked the Duke in his characteristic soft voice.

The youth gave a start and came away from the window to meet the Duke in the middle of the room. His bow was stiffly formal and betrayed a nervousness his pale face tried hard to disguise. "I apologise for disturbing you, M'sieur le Duc. But I thought an explanation due you regarding what occurred this evening. I came as soon as I could, before-before—As soon as I could."

Roxton perched on a corner of his massive writing table and swung a leg casually. He fixed the young man with an unblinking stare. "Before I had the story from your father?" he enquired.

Color flooded the Vicomte's lean cheeks and he faltered. "It is not supposed I would be believed above my father. I must tell you about Mademoiselle Moran and—"

"Excuse me, d'Ambert," interrupted the Duke. "I have not the slightest interest in Mademoiselle Moran. Your father's interest in her or yours."

"B-but, M'sieur le Duc," stammered d'Ambert. "It is important you know!"

"Why?"

"W-why? Because—because you saw Mademoiselle Moran and I together. And you are my father's closest cousin. He must confide in you at times and—"

"I would greatly object to Salvan confiding anything in me," responded the Duke evenly. He offered his snuffbox.

"N-no, I thank you. I—I prefer my own mix."

Roxton took snuff. "As you wish."

There were several moments of silence, then the Vicomte could no longer control himself. "You must listen to me, M'sieur le Duc! It is important. My father, he is your cousin. I am your cousin. I have no one else I can talk to about this matter. No one who will not think my father right and I wrong. He will not see reason. He is a man possessed. A madman! He threatens me with a *lettre de cachet*. Me, his son! Is that not a hideous abuse? Is it not?" He broke off to take a deep breath and realised he had been shouting at his host. "You do not believe me, do you? Who would believe a father capable of such an action against a son?"

"It is not a novel solution to a problem, my boy. Fathers have clapped up their sons for less."

The youth's shoulders slumped. He had to admit this was true. There was a dozen or more of the nobility's most ancient names he could think of who at one time or another had had a member of their family—and that usually an errant son—shut away in the Bastille for an undisclosed reason. Even that hearty libertine the Duc de Richelieu had spent time in the Bastille for refusing to marry his family's choice of bride. D'Ambert's blue eyes surveyed the older man's face. It was as inscrutable as ever.

"And what of a father who wishes to marry his son to an innocent girl to make her his mistress? His mistress with honor. Ha! It disgusts me!" spat out the Vicomte. "That is what he intends with Mademoiselle Moran. You know her grandfather is too ill to oppose my father's wishes? I tell you she must leave

Versailles—at once! I will have her away from him. You will help me?"

"With what?" asked the Duke calmly.

The Vicomte was incredulous. "To have my father desist with his putrid designs! He must abandon this absurd notion to have her wedded to me and then—If you would only talk to him, make him see reason. He listens to you. I think also he is a little afraid of you."

"You do not want to marry her?"

"I—I am a Salvan," he said with a haughty air. "She is a Protestant. Her father was one generation removed from Huguenot silk merchants."

"Salvan in need of funds?"

The Vicomte stiffened.

"Yes, it is an impolite question," drawled the Duke. "Is he in expectation of Strathsay leaving the girl his fortune?"

"Yes, M'sieur le Duc. The Salvan estates are greatly in need of repair. My grandfather was a great player of all games of chance, as is my father," admitted the youth. "He does not have M'sieur le Duc's great luck nor his good fortune."

"The fact that I am—to be quite vulgar—exceedingly wealthy, is a constant running sore for your father. Then, so is my—er—uncanny luck at table. I can do little about either."

"You will help Mademoiselle Moran?"

Roxton shook out his lace ruffles as he stood. He regarded the youth's eager face with indifference. "No."

"N-no?" uttered the Vicomte. He did not understand. "Why-why not, M'sieur le Duc?"

"I make a habit of never helping anyone."

"B-but I am your cousin! She-she is your cousin!"

"I have many cousins. It is too tedious."

The Vicomte d'Ambert was stunned. He was unable to find the words to answer such a flat reply. He watched the Duke prod the burning logs in the grate with a poker, the prominent aquiline profile silhouetted in the orange glow, and wondered why he thought this consummate libertine would offer to help him. The man's reputation was as sinister as it was notorious.

"Forgive the intrusion, M'sieur le Duc," he said finally and with a sullenness that did not go undetected. "One forgets that although M'sieur le Duc is our cousin and his mother a Salvan he is not, nor is he French. If he was he would understand."

Roxton replaced the poker on its stand. "Yes, one must remember that."

"Why indeed should you care what happens to me. Or to a girl not quite twenty!"

"Twenty?" The Duke paused at the door. "Are you certain?"

"Yes, M'sieur le Duc."

"And your age? Remind me, d'Ambert."

"I am eighteen years and two months old, M'sieur le Duc."

For a fleeting moment, the Duke looked startled. "*You* have turned eighteen?"

"Y-yes, M'sieur le Duc."

"Do you want her?" asked the Duke, and smiled crookedly when the Vicomte hesitated. "Salvan could have had his way with her before now had he wanted to."

"That would be rape. She loathes him."

"And you. You do not—er—desire her?"

"Must all men want to seduce a pretty girl?" asked the Vicomte with disdain. When the older man merely raised an eyebrow in reply he colored painfully. "Pardon, Monseigneur," he said quietly and went out of the room, his host holding wide the door.

Lord Vallentine met them in the hall. He greeted the young man with a warm smile and gripped his hand. The Vicomte was polite but showed no desire to linger in conversation with his lordship although he liked him well enough. His horse was called for and he quickly excused himself.

"Got a serious disposition that lad," said Vallentine with a frown, a footman helping him into a wool overcoat. "Not much like old Salvan, is he?"

The Duke collected a pair of black deerskin gloves from the hall table and took his sword and sash from the butler. He declined for his carriage to be called saying he would walk. "He is his mother's son," was his only comment as they stepped out into the courtyard.

"Handsome lad," remarked Lord Vallentine. "I seem to recall his mother was a beautiful woman. Small blonde blue-eyed thing. Fidgety, though. Ain't she the one who hanged herself?"

"Poison," stated Roxton.

Lord Vallentine failed to hear the edge to his friend's voice. "That's right," he said as they set off at a good pace up the Rue St. Honoré. "Whatever the means, she did away with herself as I remember it. Caused a scandal, didn't it? D'Ambert must've been only a boy."

"He was twelve."

"Remarkable memory you've got, Roxton."

"Quite as remarkable as yours is lamentable."

Lord Vallentine sidestepped a street sweeper. "So I said hanged and not poisoned. What of it? Suicide is suicide, ain't it? Why did she do it?"

"I have not the least notion," said the Duke and turned down a dark side-street.

His companion kept his silence, hands dug deep in the pockets of his coat and square chin tucked in the folds of a silk stock. It was an unusually cold night for the first days of autumn and so he commented but the Duke did not hear him, or did not want to hear. Rossard's, the fashionable gaming house of the Parisian nobility, was at the end of the avenue, flambeaux lighting up the elegant entrance.

"I know why," stated his lordship.

"Know what, my dear?" asked the Duke, waving aside a persistent link-boy.

"Why she killed herself," said his friend. "It was rumored at the time she overdosed. Well, she was an addict. One supposes opium or some derivative an apothecary can concoct. She wasn't a very stable creature at the best of times. I remember on one occasion when I was at the embassy and—Well, that don't matter now. I didn't believe then she overdosed for no reason, neither did many people."

"Did they not?"

"No! She had a lover."

"What lady of fashion does not?"

They went up the steps to the front door and were admitted by two liveried footmen.

In the small gilt hall, ablaze with light and bustling with activity, two more footmen met them. Lord Vallentine considered it prudent, after handing over his coat, cane and gloves, to continue in English, confident none present would understand the run of conversation. He followed the Duke up the narrow staircase to a suite of gaming rooms on the second floor, their progress consistently interrupted by the greetings of friends and acquaintances.

"I know all fashionable ladies take a lover," whispered his lordship with annoyance. He watched his friend sweep the crowded and noisy room with his quizzing-glass. "But she wasn't discreet about it at all, was she?"

"Must you pester Claudine-Alexandre beyond the grave, my dear Vallentine?" asked the Duke, a slight rigidity in the deep voice. He swept a magnificent leg to a gentleman in a blue powdered toupee who had hailed him with a wave of a scented handkerchief and lounged on the back of a spindle-legged chair at the far side of the room. "There is no need to exert yourself on her behalf."

"Thing is," confided his lordship, close to the Duke's ear, "I seem to recall her lover is someone we know intimately. Damme if I can remember his name! Must've put it out of my mind. Don't know why. It would be unforgivable if I happened to be chattering away to Salvan and mentioned the wretched fellow's name. I mean, it might evoke unsavoury memories for him. It wasn't so long ago as to be completely forgotten. And if he loved his wife—Did he love her?" he asked.

He accepted the glass of burgundy being offered by a blank-faced waiter and drank to his friend's good health. "This is the reason I come to this over-priced establishment with you, Roxton. The wine is always first-rate! Can't complain. I don't think he did love her all that much. Salvan's as cold as a snake. It was quite a scandal all the same. Her letters strewn all over the place. Jesus! And leaving that note when she died, heaping all the blame on that poor fellow for ending the affair. Naming his long list of conquests, past and present. That circulated the salons faster than any political pamphlet. Well I don't blame him for being rid of her, I can tell you that." Vallentine shook himself. "Damned dreadful business." He broke off, seeing the Duke absorbed in the play at the table closest them. "Who was he?"

Roxton did not take his eyes from the players. "Who was whom, my dear?"

Lord Vallentine frowned. "Not listening, aye?"

Cards were returned to the bank, the rubber concluded. Gentlemen began to shift in their seats and more wine was called for before the next deal.

"The lover. Surely you know his name."

The Duke turned his quizzing-glass on his lordship with a grin of his perfect white teeth.

Lord Vallentine blinked, breathed in, and gulped a mouthful of burgundy at one and the same time. "Jesus!" It took him several seconds to control a fit of coughing. A waiter and his fellow hurried to his assistance with profuse apologies and a cloth to sponge down his lordship's exquisitely embroidered waistcoat of gold thread. The hum of conversation descended to a murmur then started up again almost at once. Play resumed. The Duke did not stir. He continued to observe the deal at the table closest him, oblivious to one and all.

It was the following afternoon before the Vicomte d'Ambert departed Paris and returned to Versailles. He had spent a restless night at the residence of his grandmother, Madame de Salvan, in the Place Royale. Had he not looked pale and troubled and more fidgety than usual when he went to take his leave of her she may well have asked him nothing out of the ordinary. That his father was just as frightened of her as he was the Duc de Roxton gave him hope and he poured forth his visit to the English Duke. He also told her something of his father's mad schemes. The old dowager Comtesse loved her grandson more than she loved her son, and hating to see him in any distress, assured him that she would do everything she could to set matters to rights.

What an infirm old lady of sixty years could do to help his predicament he had not the slightest idea but he did not let that bother him. Her reassurances were enough to put a spring back in his step, and as soon as he was within the palace grounds he went in search of Antonia.

His scratch on her door was answered by Maria Caspartti's

tire-woman, a fat jolly woman of Italian-French origin. With a wide smile she ushered him into the small cluttered room and asked him to wait while she enquired if mademoiselle was able to receive him.

D'Ambert looked about with distaste. There were portmanteaux, band boxes, and upturned trunks all bursting with various articles of clothing. A half-eaten supper covered the table, and chairs were piled with hats, shoes and jewellery boxes. Pannier frames and discarded tissue paper were shoved in a dark corner, along with dyed plumes, crumpled capes and mounds of silk ribands. The room was unaired and stank of overpowering perfume and dog urine. He prayed Signora Caspartti was not in.

The fat tire-woman beckoned him into the second room, which was smaller than the first and served as a bedchamber. It was in the same state of disarray but the offensive odour was not present, possibly because this room had a tiny window and it was open. The fire had died in the grate so it was cold within these walls, whereas the day had been warmer than it had been in weeks. The Vicomte shivered despite his wool cloak and went to pull the sash.

The tire-woman made a protesting sound which brought Antonia's head out from behind an ornate dressing screen.

"If you close the window it will be as bad in this room as the next," she said and disappeared again.

The Vicomte pulled the sash but left a tiny gap between it and the sill. "It is a wonder you have not turned blue," he called out. "And gone numb! What are you doing back there?"

"Do not be impertinent, Étienne. I cannot very well dress before you! A few more minutes and I will be done. I need only to be laced up. Then I will make you one of Maria's special coffees and you will forget the cold."

D'Ambert looked about for a chair. He found one over by the canopied bed piled high with soiled stockings and garters. He threw these off and sat down in the middle of room. He took out his snuffbox. "How can you tolerate this pig sty?" he asked with a grimace. "It is disgusting. Why does the fat woman not clean it up?"

"She does. But what is the use when Maria will only destroy

her good work when searching for a particular thing? I don't think she can function except in chaos and grime. At least her temper is not so bad when the rooms are this way. Besides I am only too grateful for a place to sleep. You heard Grandfather's apartments have been given to the Marquise de Durfort's third cousin?"

"No. I am sorry to hear it," said the Vicomte quietly, for he knew such an action would not have been taken by the King, who was known to be fond of the old Jacobite General, unless all hope of recovery had been given up. "Where is the Caspartti?"

"Where do you think. In the chapel where she has been this past week."

"Why are you dressing at this hour?" he enquired and became suspicious when Antonia laughed in response. "Why has that woman taken a powder cone and dusting jacket behind the screen? What are you up to, Antonia?"

"M'sieur le Vicomte is of a sudden inquisitive," she scolded playfully. "Be patient. You shall see. Where have you been? I sent a note to your room this morning. If you had been there to receive it you would know what I am about."

He took another pinch of snuff and watched a fine dust of loose powder rise in a cloud above the screen. There was another, then the tire-woman came out to fetch a looking glass and a jar of something from the cluttered dressing table. She disappeared behind the screen again. He shifted uneasily on the upholstered chair and pulled at the points of his damask waistcoat. There was more movement from behind the screen then the tire-woman left the room to make the coffee.

"I went to Paris," he confessed. "I stayed the night at my grandmother's house. I only came back today because I am expected to attend this wretched masquerade. I know it is going to be tedious. I wish I did not have to attend but Salvan will note my absence," he said gloomily. "Why should he care when the place will be overrun with all sorts of riffraff, and in dominoes and masks and the like. He will be too intent on catching the eye of some whore to worry if I am there or not."

"Have you considered entering a monastery, Étienne?" asked Antonia as she came out from behind the screen fluttering a fan of gouache painted chicken-skin at her bare bosom. "Most youths of your age would be eager for the chance to dance attendance at one of the King's masques. Think of the fun of it! No female recognised until the unmasking at midnight. All guessing who the other is. And everyone able to talk as freely as they wish without fear of detection. I am going to enjoy myself hugely!" She poked a tiny silk shoe out from under her wide hooped petticoats of salmon-pink silk and shimmering silver tissue. "Do you like these buckles? They are Maria's. They are not paste, but diamonds. Grandfather gave them to her many years ago. It took me two days to convince her to let me wear them. They compliment my earrings, do you not think?"

While she had been chattering, moving about the small room, picking up a looking glass to inspect her upswept powdered curls, and then to assure herself in the long mirror behind the door her hem was straight, her shoes just showing under the petticoats, a tiny bow on the bodice not crooked, the Vicomte stared at her open-mouthed, unconvinced it was Antonia. Her face was painted. Her lovely honey curls were powdered out of all recognition and there was a mouche at the corner of her eye and one placed above the outward curve of her cherry-red mouth. When he dared to permit his eyes to stray to her décolletage he was unable to find the words to express his profound shock. Her lovely breasts were almost bare. In spite of himself he flushed up to his ears.

"Oh good!" she said with a nervous laugh. "You do think I look like the whore." She gazed at herself in the mirror and sighed. "I confess I did not recognise myself either. When I put on this gown, and before I applied Maria's cosmetics and powdered my curls, I was very ashamed of myself. I never expected the bodice to be cut so low as to reveal practically all of me! If it is any consolation it is very uncomfortable."

Étienne rolled his eyes heavenward and seeing this in the mirror's reflection Antonia laughed. It caused him to leap off the chair and grab her by the wrist and pull her to him. "Was this that whore's idea?" he demanded.

"Maria? No! Let me go! She knows nothing about it. I do not want her to know. I do not want anyone to recognise me but you."

He let her go at that but he was still angry. He searched a pocket for his snuffbox. "You must think me a great jobbernowl if you believe I will allow you out of this room dressed—dressed so every man can ogle at your-your—at you!"

"I have a domino," she explained. "With that draped over my gown what does it matter? I am only dressed in such a way should my domino accidentally be removed and—"

"You must be the most naïve female at court!"

"—catches under a heel, or on a door knob and falls off," argued Antonia. "I would at least look the part I hope to play."

"What if it is removed by some lecher with or without your permission?" he retorted. "What do you think goes on at masquerades, in the great crush of revellers, after a goodly quantity of wine has been guzzled with the rooms hot and close. Will a noble merely say 'goodnight', 'pardon madame, I have enjoyed the evening immensely, may I kiss your fingertips?' As if! He will be three parts drunk and manoeuvre you to an alcove or behind one of the curtains. Before you know what is happening, whether you be flustered or not, your domino will be about your ankles and your petticoats up around your ears!"

"Étienne," gasped Antonia.

"If you have the sauciness to dress the bona roba you need not be shocked by the truth. Go and change. You will not be attending."

Anger sparked in Antonia's eyes but she kept her silence because the fat tire-woman came back into the room carrying a tray with two dishes of sweet coffee upon it. She set this down on the vacated chair and slipped behind the screen to collect Antonia's discarded clothes. She showed no desire to go about her business with any speed so Antonia and the Vicomte drank their coffee in tense silence, neither looking at the other.

"It is unlike you to go to a masquerade dressed as a whore for the mere sport," d'Ambert said at last. "There have been other occasions, other masquerades that you did not attend."

"Grandfather would not permit it."

"Why the sudden desire to go now? It is hardly the time to be making merry."

"That is unfair!" Antonia whispered angrily.

"The Caspartti is a whore but at least she shows the old General proper respect. You should go to chapel and pray once in a while."

"I am not a Papist, Étienne. I won't enter that chapel. My father would be very upset with me," she said. "Besides, what do I need fear tonight when you will be there and know my costume?"

He was not to be diverted. "Why do you attend this particular occasion? Tell me!" he ordered. "Tell me or I will lock you in this room until you do!"

"What is wrong with enjoying one's self?" she answered airily and picked up the black scarlet-lined domino from the bed and put it about her shoulders. "Will you ask me to dance?"

"Yes—No! You will not be attending!"

"Will many people from Paris be here tonight?"

"Paris? Yes, many. Why?" he asked and followed her into the next room. He watched her keenly as she searched the contents of a band box and found a half-mask of white dove's plumes. "You have some wild scheme planned," he said and snatched the mask and threw it across the room. "I will not let you go dressed like that!"

She ignored his anger and calmly picked up the mask. "If you do not change your clothes you will be late," she said, and herded him to the door. "You must leave before I do or we shall be seen together and my disguise will be uncovered. And when you ask me to dance pretend you do not know me. Oh, Étienne, we are going to have a prodigious time this evening!"

Three

The Vicomte did not think so and as he hovered at the bottom of the stairs watching the hordes of merrymakers in their plumed and beribboned outfits strung with jewels and studded with precious stones, every lady's face masked, he remonstrated with himself for being so weak as to allow Antonia to attend. Not that he thought himself capable of stopping her had he locked her up. She would have found a way out, or cajoled a servant to break in the door. He had caught sight of her once, in the Galerie des Glaces where the orchestra competed with the noise of the revellers. Before he could go to her an aging dowager, daughter in tow, trapped him in conversation and he lost sight of her

The ornate drawing rooms off the Galerie des Glaces were open to the revellers, one leading off the other, their painted and gilt furniture pushed to the walls, window sashes shut tight against the autumn evening and every chandelier blazing with light. Gentlemen and nobles alike brushed shoulders and tried to guess the identities of the masked beauties. D'Ambert found himself pushed along with the flow moving through the rooms in a steady stream, and as he jostled with the next man he searched about for a small black domino with a dove feather mask.

He did not trust Antonia to leave the cape about her shoulders. It was stifling hot and many a lady had discarded them. And if a gentleman did approach her to dance she would remove it regardless because it was two sizes too big and dragged on the floor. Not finding her in the Diana drawing room he turned a heel to retrace his steps. He would stand vigil at the dance floor and hope she found him. He had just walked back to the Galerie des Glaces when an arm was thrust in his path. He spun about and came face to face with his father.

"A word, d'Ambert," ordered the Comte de Salvan.

He had his son follow him to an alcove by a long window. A gentleman watching the dancers removed himself as the Comte approached and he bowed to both with a flourish. The Comte turned an altogether different face on his son.

"Where did you go last evening?" he demanded. "Your sniveling valet vowed he did not know! You did not sleep in your bed and your horse and groom were seen returning to the stables after dinner. Have I not warned you enough? Never leave the palace without first informing me. Where did you go?"

"F-father—I-I—"

"Never mind! Ugh! Can you not say something to me without stuttering like an oaf from the field?" The Comte broke off to exchange pleasantries with two masked females who glided past fluttering their fans on their bosoms and smiling invitingly. He laughed at the wit of one and bowed at the silent invitation of the other, then returned to his son who stood woodenly at his side. "Étienne, do not lie to me. You went to Paris."

"I stayed with Grandma Salvan."

"Do you think I do not know that? You think me an imbecile? You are the imbecile!" hissed Salvan. "I expend my energies to contrive a suitable match for you—"

"I do not want—"

"What you want is of no importance. You are my son. A Salvan. You will do what is best for the name."

"To marry this bourgeois heretic is best for the name, Father?" the Vicomte stammered haughtily.

"It is expedient," said the Comte with finality.

"Why must I marry to—to end our financial difficulties at the cost of making myself the laughing stock of our friends? Listen to me, Father—"

"I am done arguing with you. You will do as I tell you or you know what will happen."

"The Bastille does not strike dread in my heart."

The Comte looked his son over and laughed. "No? We shall see, my son. Cut off from the world and your comforts you would soon change your mind. Snuff, d'Ambert?"

The Vicomte's eyes widened and he went pale. "N-no I—I prefer my own mix, thank you."

"Precisely," sniggered Salvan and shut his box with a snap. He turned his attention to the dancing couples. His son continued to stare out of the window. "Go away, Étienne. Your morbidity offends me. Wait! Tell me. Who is the little dove flirting with Richelieu? *Parbleu!* she has pretty ankles."

The Duc de Richelieu and his partner pirouetted after their fellow dancers and stepped lightly back into line, dancing the length of the floor toward a crowd of onlookers who chattered and laughed at the edge of the circle. The Comte's mouth quivered as he watched the couple dance toward him.

"Oho! Richelieu has all the luck! Not only pretty ankles but magnificent breasts also!" Salvan shook his son's arm without taking his eyes from the dance floor. "Étienne, look! Is she not delicious? I must find Charmond. He will know if she is from Paris. Ha! Now what goes on? A raven swoops on the dove! Étienne, will you attend to me?" he demanded.

The Vicomte came away from the window and followed his father's gaze out across the glittering sea of silks.

"See!" continued the Comte. "It is the end of the dance and he is forced to hand her to her next partner. Oho! She curtseys prettily enough but he saunters off, not at all happy. Richelieu gives himself away I think." He chuckled into a scented handkerchief, eyes glinting at the small drama being played out before him. "Poor M'sieur le Duc de Richelieu! He hoped for better things and now he takes refuge with Madame Duras-Valfons. I can tell it is she. Her mask cannot hide such a graceful carriage. What will Roxton care for Richelieu's petty moves on his mistress when he has the upper hand in the game? And if he does?" Salvan shrugged. "Mon cousin is a consummate performer! He will feign indifference merely to pique Richelieu. He has a fine leg, does he not, Étienne?"

The Vicomte gave no answer. He stared as if transfixed on some point on the opposite wall of mirrors. The Comte wondered if had heard any of his monologue. He sighed in irritation at having spawned such a son who cared nothing for court intrigue and was of a melancholy disposition. He dismissed his presence with a grunt and a view of his back, turning to watch the Duke of Roxton and his partner in the dove feather mask.

A crony in canary-yellow silk breeches and a stiff frock of purple flowered velvet minced up to Salvan and bowed with a flourish.

"Salvan! You see too?" he whispered loudly in the Comte's ear. "This little one makes a spectacle of herself. The rumor is she is from the Maison Clermont. Can you believe it? It is a thing most shocking! A c-common whore dancing at court behind a mask! We will know at midnight. Charmond has wagered it is the daring English Duke who has put her up to it. Can you believe it?"

"No," said Salvan sticking out his bottom lip. "That is too crude even for him. Mon cousin is notorious but he knows how to play the game. He goes to Clermont's to taste the talent not to procure dancers for court masquerades. And this one, something tells me she is not so practised in her movements."

"Mayhap, Salvan, but your cousin was at Clermont's last night with a new female, an accomplished Oriental."

"So? He is curious," said the Comte with a shrug. "You cannot make me believe this one is the Oriental. René, you are full of wine! If she is anything she is an actress. Would Roxton dance openly with a common whore? Preposterous!"

"*Hélas*, it is hot in here," murmured René, and with a bow minced off to join a lady who beckoned him with a subtle movement of her fan.

Salvan saw that his son still stood at his elbow and like a statue cast of alabaster. "You are interested, eh, Étienne? You pretend to be shocked but I see through you! M'sieur le Duc de Roxton's movements intrigue you too?"

"Yes, Father," answered d'Ambert, a shaking hand carrying a pinch of snuff to one nostril. He inhaled deeply.

"Why do you look down your nose at Roxton's games of seduction? These females want it. They enjoy it. And it is well known that mon cousin is very talented in bed. He more than satisfies them. In that we are the same, he and I," Salvan bragged. "If you were more my son you would understand the ways of women better."

The Vicomte started to laugh hysterically.

The Comte de Salvan's chest swelled. "I offer you advice and you dare to laugh at me?"

"No, Father, no!" tittered the Vicomte. "While you and I stand here he—he—Roxton wins all! From under our very noses he wins all! You are impotent; impotent to stop him!"

"*Taisez-vous!* Shut up I tell you! People stare at us! You are deranged!"

"What if I am?" said d'Ambert, trying to control himself. But his mouth twitched and he suddenly burst into another fit of wild laughter. "The little—the little dove—she-she has flown her cage! She has flown away with the raven!"

Salvan swung about on a heel and his little eyes searched the dancers and onlookers. Roxton had disappeared, so had his dance partner.

"Is that so amazing? So laughable?" he asked. "There is something to be learned from our cousin, eh? If you had not waylaid me, diverted me from my revels, it would have been I, and not he, who darts off behind a curtain to taste the little dove's delights! Is that why you laugh like a great buffoon? You think your father outwitted? Ha! She cannot be all that enticing for she gave in too easily. There is no sport in that! But when next I see mon cousin I will ask if she was worth his while."

The Vicomte wiped his moist eyes on the back of a silk sleeve. There was something oddly mechanical about his bow and the smile he gave his father. "Do that, Father. Roxton has just departed with Mademoiselle Moran."

The Duke of Roxton had decided to attend the palace masquerade in the hopes of curing his boredom. Had Lord Vallentine accepted his invitation to accompany him there was little doubt that watching his friend's gyrations amongst the French nobility and their sycophants would have offered him some amusement.

Lord Vallentine preferred to stay at home and spend a quiet evening with the Duke's sister. He said he loathed Versailles and all its excesses. Roxton had called him old. He teased him about his declining ability at the art of seduction, to which his lordship floundered for a reply under the penetrating gaze of Estée de Montbrail.

The Duke was not fooled into believing his friend had made the harrowing (for him) voyage across the Channel for the pleasure of his company. Nor by the indifferent face his sister presented on learning Lucian Vallentine was to visit them. He wondered how long it would take one or the other to confide the truth of their feelings to him. Watching them play cat and mouse with their affections was diverting but it did nothing to cure his ennui.

He was not at the palace over an hour before he decided he had had enough of the crowds, the perfumed heat, and the incessant din of high-pitched voices. He ignored several invitations to disappear behind a curtain with a willing masked female. The wine on offer was insipid to his sensitive palate. Observing the frustrated gyrations of youths and their drunken companions did not amuse him. And his latest mistress was intent on making a spectacle of herself with the young Prince de Bouvallies. No doubt to illicit a jealous response from him, but he hated such banal behavior, and he did not care that much for her to exert himself.

As he stood to one side of a mirrored archway in the Galerie des Glaces observing the dancers through his quizzing-glass, he wondered if he, and not his friend, was declining into his dotage. He scanned the multitudes with a sigh, was about to turn on a heel to depart, then spied the Comte de Salvan and his son. What interested him was the Vicomte's stance and stony-faced gaze out to the dancers. A gaze he followed to the Duc de Richelieu and his dance partner, a small female in an absurd mask of feathers which sat crookedly on her laughing face.

He conceded that she could dance and possessed dainty hands and feet. But she appeared awkward in a gown that was several seasons outgrown. The bodice pulled too tightly across her breasts, making the whole unattractive, when a different cut would have show such a voluptuous figure off to full advantage.

The female must have the worst dresser in all France. That, or she was a charity case on the lookout for a fat-pursed lover, possibly a husband if she could catch one. Whomever she was, she was very much out of her depth...

It did not take him many minutes to disentangle Antonia from the Duc de Richelieu's slimy clasp. In fact she was only too willing to exchange dance partners. A circumstance which did not please Richelieu's fragile ego and he went off to console himself with Thérèse Duras-Valfons. Roxton laughed to himself at such a spiteful manoeuvre but thought it typical of Armand.

He danced a quadrille with Antonia and if she was aware that he knew her identity she was shrewd enough to keep up the pretence of her disguise. She chatted prettily on inconsequential topics, contrived to smile and be gay when he returned mono-syllabic answers and did not look at her, but out across the dazzling multitudes for the closest and most convenient exit.

With the last chord struck by the orchestra he made as if to return her to the crowd, but once engulfed by the masses he kept on walking. When the firm cool pressure of his hand on her upper arm tightened she glanced up at him swiftly.

"Do not think I am amused by your antics," he hissed, striding through one drawing room and on through the next and then the next. "All the paint and feathers in the world can't hide you from me."

"No, Monseigneur," she replied respectfully, but hung her head so he would not see her spreading smile.

He said nothing further until they were standing in the court-yard awaiting his carriage. One of his lackeys came running through the traffic of carriages and horses with a roquelaure and black gloves. Another darted forward between two coaches and stood waiting instructions. A moment later an elegant chaise and four pulled up before them and two liveried footmen jumped off the box to let down the steps.

"Give the boy direction to your rooms," ordered the Duke. "I presume you have—er—things?"

"Nothing of great importance," Antonia answered cheerfully, but obediently gave the servant directions to Maria Caspartti's rooms and what he should collect. There was only one small portmanteau and it was by the door, and he was not to alarm the fat tire-woman who would answer his scratching. When he ran off into the night she turned to the Duke expectantly.

He watched her as he stretched on his gloves and at her shiver of excitement, thinking her feeling the cold, handed her up into the well-sprung vehicle. "There is a wrap in the corner. Put it across your shoulders."

"May I take off this silly mask now?"

"By all means," he said and snapped his fingers for a lackey to attend him. "You are not at all distressed?" he asked her from under hooded eyes.

"Why should I be, Monseigneur?" she said from the window. "You are taking me to Paris!"

"Your confidence is misplaced. I do so for my own reasons, not yours."

"Yes, of course. But we are going to Paris, are we not?"

"Yes," he said with a sigh of exasperation. "Now put that wrap about you before you catch your death and sit still until I return."

Antonia did as she was told but immediately came back to the window. "You are not going to leave me?" she asked in a small voice. "What if—What if someone comes while you are gone?"

"I would not worry yourself unnecessarily," he said caustically. "Now that you are under my—er—protection your reputation is in shreds and no gentleman would dare risk offending me by attempting to rescue you."

"Then I will not worry, Monseigneur," she said happily and disappeared inside, to snuggle up in a velvet upholstered corner under the cashmere wrap.

Roxton expected a wholly different response to his quip. Antonia's unquestioning faith pushed him off-balance. So did her use of the courtesy title *Monseigneur* rather than the more formal *M'sieur le Duc*. It sounded intimate when spoken by her and he did not like it; it unnerved him and put him on edge. He wondered if she was being facetious. Thus when his valet, who had been standing at his side listening to this odd exchange between his master and the small painted female, asked for direction, the Duke was slow to respond. He continued to stare absently at the open window of his chaise, as if waiting for Antonia to reappear, until his valet coughed into his gloved fist.

Finally, he called for a standish and after scrawling a note and affixing it with his seal (wax and light provided by a link-boy's flambeaux), he ordered his valet to take one of the horses and ride post-haste to the Hôtel de Roxton and deliver the missive to Madame de Montbrail. And if Madame was abed to get her out of it. A circumstance the valet did not look forward to because he was all too well aware of Madame's temper. But he showed his master a blank face and within ten minutes galloped off, the missive tucked securely in an inner lining of his worsted wool coat.

The Duke did not step up into the chariot until his servant returned with Antonia's portmanteaux, then the order was given and the horses set to. The chaise swept out along the tree-lined boulevard, past a line of waiting coaches and carriages and onto the Versailles road for Paris, the Duke seated opposite Antonia who leaned from the window, the cold night air in her face, taking a last glimpse of the palace.

"Put up the window," he ordered in his soft drawl.

Antonia obeyed and sat back in her corner. Her powdered hair was dishevelled and wind-blown and fell in a tangled mass about her bare shoulders. The carefully applied cosmetics were smudged and her dress was so crumpled that no amount of pressing would take out the creases. She did not care and it did not worry her the Duke kept watchful silence. She was free of Versailles and the Comte de Salvan, closer to London and the grandmother she had yet to meet.

"Aren't you curious to know where I am taking you?" he asked.

"I know. To the Hôtel de Roxton on the Rue St. Honoré," she said confidently and smiled when there was a flicker of surprise in his black eyes. "It is the largest privately owned mansion in all Paris and you keep an army of servants and there is a good library on the second—"

"I know my own house!" he snapped. "What if I told you I was not taking you to that particular house?"

"Monseigneur has another?" she asked, curiosity sparked, and pulled the wrap closer, a bump in the road causing it to slide off one shoulder. "I would prefer the one on the Rue St. Honoré, because I wish to see the library, but if you want to take me to this other one—Does it have a library too?"

"You are either an exceedingly good actress or rather dull-witted—"

"I am not dull-witted!" retorted Antonia. "Papa gave me a very good education in classics and history and taught me to speak—"

"He failed to teach you to be polite to your elders," the Duke said coldly. "If we are to go on in a tolerable fashion know this: There are three things I abhor: lack of manners, slovenliness, and stupidity."

"Yes, Monseigneur," she answered meekly but could not hide her dimples. When she saw his jaw set hard she lowered her gaze. "I apologise. I do try to behave as I should but it is very difficult when one has been taught to speak one's mind to suddenly not do so."

"Your father was a fool to give you a boy's education. Yes, I know all about that. Just as you know all about my house and my servants, my library and, no doubt, my—er—habits. So now we will dispense with the charade. I am going to ask you a few questions to which I want truthful—"

"I do not lie!"

"To which I want truthful answers," he enunciated.

"Yes, Monseigneur," she answered softly. She brushed the hair off her face and shifted to be more comfortable on the cushions, and when she was completely settled she showed him an obedient face full of expectation. "I am ready now."

"Thank-you," he said patiently and took out his snuffbox. "Why did Strathsay leave you behind at the palace?"

"I don't know, Monseigneur. He was very ill. Mayhap he did not think about it? He would not let Maria go with him either."

"Maria?"

"His whore."

"His mistress?"

"That is what I said. His whore."

"It is more polite to call her his mistress."

"I said so, too, but Étienne will have it she is a whore," Antonia told him. "Are they not one and the same?"

"Yes and no. A woman who is kept by a gentleman in comfort,

her wants and needs attended to in exchange for her—er—favors, that is a mistress. A whore is something else entirely."

"Yes, Monseigneur?" asked Antonia, head tilted to one side.

Roxton looked up from contemplating the engraving on his gold snuffbox and was not deceived by her expression of polite enquiry. Her clear green eyes sparkled mischief. For the first time in his life he felt an embarrassing discomfort in the presence of a female. It annoyed him; an uncanny ability she had made all her own. As if reading his thoughts she was the one to break the silence between them.

"I am sorry. I did not mean to embarrass you," she said frankly. In the next breath she was at the window and had pulled the curtain back. "Monseigneur," she hissed. "Did you hear that? It sounded like a shot! And we are slowing down! Do you think there are bandits on this road? *Mon Dieu*, but this is exciting!"

She pressed her little nose to the glass but not satisfied with this view started to push down the window. A firm hand threw her back against the seat and a gloved finger was pressed to her lips.

"Quiet," whispered the Duke and when she nodded he removed his hand. He felt in a pocket for his silver mounted pistol and cocked it.

Another report, louder than the first and from a blunderbuss, and the chaise came to a standstill in the middle of the road. The driver had been struck in the arm, he was certain the bone was shattered and he lurched forward in pain. There were no other immediate casualties. The rest of the Duke's men stayed at their posts, not daring to move. Only the horses pulled at their bits and stamped their hooves in fear. Across the path of the chaise were three men on horseback, hats pulled low on their brow to keep their faces shaded from the moonlight. A carriage and a carabas travelling in the opposite direction were halted fifty yards up the road. The occupants were made to stand in a huddle and kept under watch by two men dressed like their fellows and brandishing pistols at their captives. All was bathed in eerie moonlight. The surrounding countryside was forested and dark.

The Duke did not alight until rudely requested by a thump with the end of a blunderbuss on the chaise door bearing his coat of arms. He was leisurely in his movements, maddeningly so, and proceeded to take snuff. All the while he took stock of the situation; the position of the two horsemen, the large scruffy bandit who stood close by, and the hold up in the flow of traffic up the road. His apparent nonchalance confused the brute closest him for he looked to his accomplices for direction.

"Search the carriage," was the order.

"I would not," said the Duke haughtily, and dusted off a coat sleeve with a lace handkerchief.

The large brute hesitated. He was solid and tall and good with his fists but this nobleman with his lean aristocratic features and finery under the well-cut coat was the taller. He also knew the voice of command.

"Do it, Pierre!" came the command.

The brute grunted, angry at his weakness. What could this nobleman do to stop him in the face of his companions? He had his orders. He had also been told not to harm this nobleman. That remained to be seen; he itched to bruise such delicate skin. He took a step closer but the nobleman stood between him and the carriage door.

"If you touch my property I will be forced to stop you," said the Duke calmly.

"We want the girl," called the bandit who had earlier barked out orders. "When we have the girl you are free to go on your way!"

"Girl? There is some mistake."

The leader's voice became harsh. "There is no mistake! You have abducted my master's property! He wants it returned."

The Duke appeared indignant. His fingers curled about the pistol's trigger. The other hand held up a scented handkerchief to his thin nostrils and he breathed in luxuriantly. Although his attention did not waiver from the large brute who hovered in front of him he spoke to the leader on horseback. "Your master's property?" he replied coldly. "The minx! You may certainly have her. She assured me she had had no other lover."

All three men chuckled at this, and a lewd private joke passed between the two on horseback. The leader with the laughter still in his throat looked back at the Duke.

"'tis a pity to bring your delicious interlude to a halt, M'sieur le Duc. But you see, you would not get very far with that one. Her virtue is as well guarded as the Bastille. You've been well and truly duped!"

His companions began to snigger and the large brute with the blunderbuss strode forward and shoved the Duke aside with his shoulder. He grabbed the door and wrenched it open and had a boot on the fold-down step when there was a deafening report. He lost his footing, staggered backwards, the blunderbuss dropped from his hand, and he fell lifeless into the mud.

"No, my friends," said the Duke, "it is you who have been bamboozled. I have just had her."

The leader who was momentarily stunned into inaction by the death of his accomplice glared at the Duke. "What?!" he thundered and kicked his mount to canter forward. He did not know what to do next, but a movement at the carriage door swept aside his hesitation. "Come down from there!"

The sound of a shot so close to the chaise had Antonia instantly in the doorway, frightened the Duke had been struck. Seeing him standing very still near to her, a smoking pistol in his hand brought a smile of relief and she was no longer afraid. She turned to see the results of his handiwork and her eyes widened at the dead man lying face up in a muddy pool.

Thus, when the bandit on horseback charged up to the carriage shouting and waving a pistol she was slow to respond. What followed happened quickly. Later she was unsure of the precise sequence of events—only of the blur of movement all about her, of shouting, and the offensive smell of gunpowder; falling in the mud, then being dragged to her feet; looking for the Duke and seeing him safe; he calling out to her but she not hearing his words because of a last deafening report; a searing pain which would not go away; and finally, collapsing into the Duke's arms.

All was blackness.

❧

Lord Vallentine returned from supper at the house of a friend and enquired of Duvalier if Madame had retired for the night. The butler, an exceptionally discreet and haughty man of his vocation who had been with the Duke since his master was a young man and thus considered himself above all others, was not accustomed to being greeted with a 'hey-ho' and a cheerful grin. It disconcerted him. Lord Vallentine always did so and it affected Duvalier to the extent that his face froze over. Tonight was an exception. The butler was worried and it showed on his thawed features. His lordship saw this and frowned.

"What's to do?" asked Lord Vallentine bluntly. "Has M'sieur le Duc returned from Versailles?"

"No. That is to say, Monseigneur has not returned from Versailles as yet, m'sieur."

"He's late, ain't he?"

"He is sometimes so," answered the butler stiffly.

"All right! All right! I'm not some ignorant oaf."

"M'sieur, I was not implying—"

"No need. I know what you were implying! Did he say he would return at a specified hour?"

"Yes, m'sieur."

"So he is late!"

"Two hours—"

"Two hours, eh?" murmured Vallentine. He took the butler aside, away from the ears of the porter and a lingering footman. "Any word?"

"Monseigneur's valet returned on horseback with a note for Madame," confided Duvalier.

"He with her now?" he asked and at the butler's shake of the head rubbed his cleft chin. "I think I'll see Madame."

"Very well, m'sieur," answered the butler and would have said more but Lord Vallentine dashed up the stairs without further ado. Duvalier watched him go with a small smile, knowing what awaited him. Seeing the porter gaping at him his features froze over once more and he retired to the pantry to await developments.

Madame's maid admitted his lordship to the decidedly feminine boudoir which smelled heavily of Madame's perfume. The furniture was gilt and upholstered in palest blue flowered damask. Estée reclined on a chaise longue, a heavy silk robe over her night chemise and kid slippers on her stockinged feet. She had an arm across her brow and clenched in her hand was a crumpled piece of paper. The light was dim and cast shadows up the fabric wallpaper.

Lord Vallentine had to squint to see.

"What's amiss?" he asked.

Estée saw him, burst into fresh tears, and buried her face in a chintz cushion. Vallentine hurried forward and knelt at her side. He sent the maid away with a jerk of his head. She scurried off, but only to the other side of the door, leaving it slightly ajar so she could clearly hear the conversation.

"Look at me, love," he said soothingly and patted her hand. "It is no use talking into that pillow, it don't understand, and I can't if you don't look at me."

Madame sniffed. "You are horrid to come up here when I must look dreadful! My face has run and-and my eyes are red and—Oh! Lucian!" she burst out and threw herself into his lordship's arms.

He was happy to hold her, in fact had she not been crying he would have kissed her. But she was crying into his shoulder staining a perfectly good silver-threaded waistcoat, and that he could not abide. Besides, he felt rather stupid not knowing how to stem the flow so he sat with her in this way for several minutes until her hysterics finished of their own accord, then he gave her his dry handkerchief.

"Thank you," she said in a tiny voice. "Please call Hélène to fetch up some burgundy." When he came back she was sitting up, away from the candelabra where the shadows were kinder on her blotchy face. "Read this," she commanded and thrust the crumpled paper in his hand. "It's from Roxton. I don't know what devil has possessed him! He has not been himself this past month or more, and now this! I know one can never gauge his moods and he can be insufferable and contemptuous, but of late I know he has been brooding. Now I know why!"

Lord Vallentine smoothed out the paper over one silken knee as she spoke and read the familiar script. Frankly he could not understand why Estée was making such a fuss. "Who's the guest?" he asked casually.

"Guest? *Guest.* You are as shameless as he!"

"Steady, Estée," cautioned his lordship. "I object to being put in a box with your brother. He is my closest friend but that don't mean I care for the way he lives. But then I'm not judging him either. As far as being shameless—"

"Don't pretend to be such a blockhead, Lucian! You know perfectly well what I mean."

"Be that as it may," stated his lordship," I don't know what you see to object to. He only asks that you prepare a room and engage one of the chambermaids as tire-woman until a more suitable arrangement can be organised."

"Suitable arrangement!" scoffed Madame. "He has finally dallied with the wrong sort of female and is being brought to account for it! That will teach him to rape and pillage—"

"Estée!" gasped his lordship. "May the burgundy arrive pronto! You're in need of it! Roxton don't go about rapin' and pillagin', and you know it! And he is an altogether too slippery fish to be caught by any feminine hook dangled in front of him, however tempting. Why are you so upset? He says it will be only for a day or two—"

"Then why does he write in the next sentence I am to engage Maurice—*Maurice.* Paris's finest mantua-maker no less."

Lord Vallentine shrugged. "No idea. Still it can't be that much of an inconvenience, surely?"

Madame was about to tell him exactly what sort of inconvenience it was when Duvalier came into the room with a bottle of wine and two glasses and set them in front of his mistress. He poured out then left with a bow and the merest of glances at his mistress who ignored his existence.

"I will not have a room prepared and I will not engage one of the maids to act as tire-woman! And I refuse to summons Maurice to dance attendance on one of Roxton's whores! Do not gape at me, Lucian! You know perfectly well that is what she must be or she would not be in my brother's company without benefit of chaperone and a decent cloth to her back! And do not think you will get any sense out of his servant. They are all the same! Sly closed-mouthed barbarians!"

"Ellicott ain't a barbarian. He's an Englishman who can

speak damn good French."

"Precisely! A barbarian!"

Lord Vallentine held his tongue, knowing it was useless to argue with Madame when she was in one of her passions. He sipped his wine and wondered what could be keeping his friend. He was beginning to feel uneasy so sent for the Duke's valet hoping the servant could put his mind at ease.

"Tell me about this female my brother has ensnared himself with," said Estée sullenly.

"Listen, Estée," said his lordship soothingly, "would your brother bring one of his-his—one of those females here, to a house he shares with his sister? He may be lax, damned lax, but he knows what is due his name. If she was that sort of female he'd take her to—to…"

Madame raised perfectly arched brows. "Yes?"

Vallentine sighed. "You might as well know as not. One more sordid detail about your brother's lifestyle can't make you blush. He has a petite maison on the south side of the Seine for the purposes of—um—entertaining."

"Indeed!" snapped Estée. "Then one wonders why he must needs also visit the Maison Clermont!"

His lordship smiled sheepishly. "You know Roxton. He becomes bored so easily."

There was a scratch on the door and Hélène admitted the Duke's valet Ellicott. He bowed to his lordship, face devoid of expression, although only half an hour earlier he had received a severe tongue-lashing from Madame.

Vallentine knew him to be devoted to Roxton, to have shared in many an amorous adventure with his master and never to have whispered to servant or friend about Roxton's female excesses. Thus he was unlikely to divulge the slightest shred of information upon this occasion. Vallentine only hoped Ellicott would tell him what the Duke was not up to. He decided to interrogate the man in his own tongue, which would undoubtedly bring Madame's wrath down upon him but hoped it would make the valet more at ease and inclined to confidences.

"You look fagged unto death, Ellicott. What's amiss?"

The valet glanced fleetingly at Madame de Montbrail who sat

bolt upright at his lordship's use of English, points of color in both her cheeks.

"I could not say, my lord," he said cautiously.

"Who or what is his Grace's guest?"

"His Grace did not take me into his confidence, my lord."

Lord Vallentine decided a bolder approach. "Is she some whore he picked up at the masquerade?"

"As I explained, my lord," said Ellicott woodenly, "I could not say."

"Cagey bird, ain't you? Look, Ellicott. You know me. I'm the Duke's closest friend. I'm worried. His sister is worried."

"You are stupid to even try and talk to this barbarian!" Estée flung at Vallentine. "He will tell you nothing! All Roxton's servants are the same. Sly and insolent and-and baboons; all of them! He has trained them too well. I am leaving to attend to my face and hair but I will return and you will be good enough to tell me everything this barbarian tells you."

Lord Vallentine watched her flounce from the room then turned expressionless to the valet. "Out with it. What's the old fox up to?"

"I do not know precisely, my lord," said the valet truthfully. "If your lordship would permit? I am concerned for his Grace's well-being. The journey from Versailles normally is not over an hour and usually less with such horses as his Grace stables."

"Don't think he has stopped off at that petite maison on the Rue St. Dominique, do you?"

Ellicott held Lord Vallentine's enquiring look without a blink of recognition. "I have prepared the Duke's rooms here, my lord, as he requested."

"And you can't tell me anything about this female who is with him, eh? Hey! What's this?" he said going to the window.

He heard a carriage over the cobbles in the courtyard below and flung back the heavy curtains. It was the Duke's carriage and the usual commotion and activity which accompanied its arrival was taking place. His lordship noticed nothing out of the ordinary in the scene presented him and was about to let the curtain fall but Madame came rushing up at him and demanded to know what was going on. It was then that he noticed the absence of the Duke's usual driver.

"Did Baptiste drive Roxton tonight?" Vallentine asked Ellicott in French.

"He always does, m'sieur."

Lord Vallentine's noble brow furrowed. "That's odd. He ain't up on the box."

The valet gave a start. "May I—"

"Go! Go!" said Vallentine with a wave of his hand, his nose pressed against the window pane. "He's not come down yet, Estée. The door is open—Well, that's odd—"

"What? *What?*" demanded Estée clinging to his lordship's shirt sleeve and not daring to look over his shoulder.

"I think I best get down there," said Vallentine. "One of the footman jumped up into the carriage and hasn't come down. Now another has followed and this one's out and running like a rabbit and shouting for a horse. Duvalier's come outside onto the step—"

"*Mon Dieu!*" groaned Madame de Montbrail and fled the room, Lord Vallentine close behind.

Four

The Duke came into the foyer just as his sister and Lord Vallentine bounded down the curved staircase to greet him. That he was deathly pale and carried close to his chest a bundle wrapped in his roquelaure, a bundle from which protruded two small muddied, stockinged feet, did not seem to register in the minds of sister or friend. They were just glad to see him alive and unharmed. But Estée was not blind to the fact her brother was in his shirt sleeves, and that the white lace ruffles at his wrists were stained with blood and mud. She ran up to him, blocking his path, chattering away, half-crying, half-laughing with relief.

"Where have you been?" she scolded. "We were so worried. You are never usually late and when your valet came with a note, and then you did not come and—Oh! There is blood on your hands! Are you hurt? Are you—"

Vallentine disengaged sister from brother. "Let him pass, love," he said softly, taking in the whole at once. "The physician been called?" he asked the Duke, following him to a drawing room where a servant was already attending to the grate and another had arrived with pillow and coverlet.

"He's been sent for," said the Duke.

"Physician?" demanded Estée looking up at his lordship. "Why does my brother require a—" and shut her mouth tight as the Duke gently deposited the bundle on a sofa and put out a hand for the pillow and coverlet.

"Send the servants away," ordered the Duke. "Are you comfortable?" he asked Antonia, who nodded, her eyes wide and looking about her with interest despite the unbearable throbbing in her shoulder. He watched a spasm of pain cross her dirty face and said sharply, "Do not try to move. Stay still until the physician arrives."

"This is indeed an elegant mansion, Monseigneur," she observed. "It is just as Papa described it to me. May I please have a drink of water?"

"Estée. Water," the Duke commanded over his shoulder. "I am pleased mademoiselle approves and is not disappointed," he said with a bow. "The doctor will be here very soon."

"Good. The pain, it is very bad," said Antonia and closed her eyes.

The Duke stood up and faced his sister who had not moved. She was staring fixedly at the female wrapped in her brother's cloak. She did not like at all what she saw. The girl—for she was not a woman whatever the heavy cosmetics on cheeks and lips proclaimed to the contrary—the girl's hair was a tangled mess of powder and mud and blood, the small oval face smeared with the same. Despite the little nose, high forehead, and beautiful curve to the full lips, Estée could draw but one conclusion as to the girl's vocation. Thus she recoiled from the sight of her and confronted the Duke with a face of furious outrage. None of this was lost on Lord Vallentine and he mumbled something about fetching a pitcher of water and seeing to other liquid refreshment and left the room.

"You are wrong, Estée," the Duke said wearily.

"You should not have brought the creature to this house," his sister answered curtly. "Remove her. Take her—take her to that petite maison you keep as well stocked as any fish pond!"

The Duke's face hardened. "I remind Madame that this is my house."

"Then I shall leave if that," and she pointed a long well-manicured nail at Antonia, "is not removed at once. I do not know what is wrong with it—"

"She has been shot."

Madame laughed bitterly. "The company one does keep!" But she cowered when the Duke took a stride toward her. "Do you wish to strike me? Dear me, M'sieur le Duc! The creature obviously means more to you than your own flesh and blood!"

Lord Vallentine entered upon this scene with a tray holding a pitcher of water and a decanter of brandy, and almost overset the lot when he looked up. "Jesus! Roxton! The girl!"

The Duke swung about to find Antonia swaying on her feet. With a supreme effort of will she had forced herself to stand. The pain in her shoulder was blinding as she attempted to cover the makeshift bandage and her naked breasts with the remnants of her tight bodice the Duke had torn to her waist in his haste to staunch the blood.

"You little fool!" hissed Roxton as he scooped her up and dumped her back on the sofa. He threw the coverlet over her. "Move again and not only will your shoulder hurt!"

"Shall I not sit down for a week?" asked Antonia with a chuckle that totally disconcerted him and he moved aside to allow Vallentine to administer a shot of brandy. The fiery liquid burned her throat but warmed her stomach and she thanked the handsome gentleman. "M'sieur hopes to get me drunk, Monseigneur," she said and pushed the glass away. "That is not such a bad idea but burgundy would be better. I like burgundy."

"Do you, by Jove!" smiled Vallentine. "You're too young for either, I'll wager."

"I am not! I am—I will be—*twenty* in a month's time!"

"Oho! Such a great age!" laughed Vallentine and looked up at his friend to find him frowning down at Antonia. "She'll live. There is too much spirit in her."

"Of course I will live," retorted Antonia and grimaced. She was close to fainting with the pain and opened her eyes with an effort. "I-I am not so badly wounded as Baptiste. He is Monseigneur's driver and his arm is broken, we think. Don't we, Monseigneur?"

"Yes, we do," he said with an unconscious smile and looked at his sister who stood immobile by the fireplace.

Antonia followed his gaze and spoke to Lord Vallentine. "That is M'sieur le Duc's sister? I am sorry to be such a nuisance."

"Don't you worry about her," whispered his lordship and patted her small grubby hand. "She'll come about, you'll see."

Estée heard this exchange and went to the door with her

nose in the air. "If it was because of you that she was shot then I am truly sorry for her," she said coldly. "Still, you should never have brought her to this respectable house." With that she swept from the room and almost collided with Duvalier who came to announce the arrival of the physician and his assistant.

The fat little physician in bob-wig and black, his assistant following with a large black bag full of instruments and medicines, hurried into the room and bowed to all. He clicked his fingers and immediately the assistant opened the bag and began to arrange ominous looking surgical instruments on a low table by the sofa. He then issued several orders to Duvalier and went to Antonia's side and smiled down at her.

"So this is the Chevalier Frederick Moran's little daughter?" he cooed, not a blink at her odd clothes and heavy cosmetics. "Your papa, he was a great doctor of medicine. But you have nothing to fear in my hands for I am just as great. Gentlemen, if you will permit...?"

Lord Vallentine and the Duke made to leave but Antonia caught at the Duke's hand. "You will stay?" she asked in a small fearful voice.

"I will only be in the way," muttered the Duke looking at the fingers that clung to his.

The physician glanced up from contemplating the table laden with the tools of his trade and gave the Duke to understand by a gesture that the decision was his. Antonia smiled and closed her eyes but she did not slacken her hold.

"If the sight of me offends you, M'sieur le Duc, then by all means take your leave of me."

The physician patted her dirty cheek and then turned his mind to the task of extracting the bullet from her flesh. He did not leave the hôtel until some two hours later, when the house was in complete quiet, and with Antonia tucked up between clean sheets; her shoulder expertly bandaged and a large dose of laudanum administered to dull her sufferings and allow her to get a decent night's sleep. He informed the Duke his patient was not to be moved for at least three weeks and that he would visit every day to follow her progress. With that the fat little man took his leave, tired and satisfied he had performed another surgical miracle.

Lord Vallentine, a Chinese silk banyan over his nightshirt and a cap of similar cloth covering his shaved head, slipped into the library where a fire and chandelier still blazed. The Duke of Roxton sat at his writing desk in fresh white shirt and ruffles composing a letter.

"There is coffee on the sideboard," the Duke said without looking up. He dipped his quill in ink and began a clean sheet of paper.

"Couldn't sleep," confessed his lordship with a grin. He refilled the Duke's dish and poured out a dish for himself. "Tried to but tossed about for an hour. Damned awful business," he muttered and settled himself in a deep chair adjacent to the ornate mantle. He sat watching the flames for several minutes before he said, "How is she, Roxton? That physician took his time about it! I hope he lived up to his reputation and his pocket. I mean, she is young and—Damme! Must you go on writing?"

"Yes, my dear. I need only sign my mark and then I will be with you."

Vallentine gazed back into the flames and waited. The Duke took longer and when he finally came to the fire Lord Vallentine looked at him sharply.

"Well? Ain't you going to tell me what happened?" he asked. "How is the girl? It's been a shocking night's work! My nerves are shredded, I can tell you. It took me forever to coax Estée down from one of her passions—"

"Lucian the Martyr," the Duke teased caustically. "I don't know why you bothered. She deserved to be left to her ill humors."

Vallentine squirmed uncomfortably under the Duke's steady gaze. "I know she don't behave as she should but she was over-wrought when you didn't come home on time. She'd filled her head with all sorts of imaginings. So, when she saw you safe I think it was relief which prompted her to act so damned foolishly. You understand how she is, Roxton."

"I understand Estée's sensibilities were far more bruised than any feelings of compassion she may have exhibited on my behalf."

His lordship nodded and kept his eyes on the dark liquid in his dish. "I admit when I first saw the girl I thought as Estée did. It was only natural we would! You ain't exactly a-a saint. I mean, you've done some pretty sordid things in your time and well, you've kept Estée sheltered. Although she's heard the whisperings she's never been a party to any of it and coming face to face with that girl dressed as a—"

"And if I said she is my latest whore?"

Lord Vallentine's mouth dropped open. "That girl? No! I don't believe you." When the Duke smiled crookedly he was made to feel more uncomfortable. "You're shamming me, by Jove!"

"Yes I am," the Duke answered in a flat voice. "I could be her father."

"Hardly!" said Vallentine with a snort. "She said she was going on twenty and you're three years my senior, and I'm six years older than Estée but you're two years younger than that snivelling cousin of yours Salvan. So that makes you... Well! I guess you could be!"

The Duke sighed at his friend's complicated mathematical musings. "Yes, I could be. I admit she was dressed atrociously," he mused. "Her idea of what the worst of whores must look like—idiot girl. It only served to get her Richelieu's unwanted attentions and those of every lecherous dog at court. My suspicion is she did so to force my hand, which I—er—felt compelled to do, under the circumstances. And it only served to have my carriage held up by a herd of ignorant cattle."

Much of what the Duke said was lost on his friend but the mention of highwayman made him sit up and set his nightcap to rights. "What! Taking a chance on the Versailles road weren't they? What happened?"

"Happened, Vallentine?" said Roxton, slowly looking up from contemplating his emerald ring. "Two peasants lie dead on the Versailles road, both by my hand. The leader failed to take the girl from me and escaped. We were shot at—"

"You? Who would dare?"

Roxton shrugged. "A mystery, my dear. Two shots came from the forest. The second found its mark. Mademoiselle Moran lives because the bullet shattered the carriage door before it entered her, thus lessening the impact. The ball lodged shallow in her upper shoulder just missing collar-bone and rib. She was extremely fortunate."

"Damned fortunate!" stated his lordship. "She will mend soon enough?"

"She is out of danger," said the Duke calmly. "But she has lost a great deal of blood and is very weak. At least four weeks in bed and then we shall see. The scar will not be pretty."

"Poor babe," muttered Vallentine. "What did the ruffians want besides the usual pretties?"

"They demanded I hand over the girl; nothing more. A singularly stupid expectation."

"That's damned odd."

"Yes. My friends were not highwaymen at all but men in the employ of someone—someone I am yet to identify. Although, I have my suspicions."

"Yes?" Vallentine asked eagerly.

The Duke sipped cold coffee. "It is much too early in the game to voice my theories, Vallentine. You must be patient."

"Any witnesses?"

"A carriage and a carabas headed for the palace pulled over by my friend's accomplices. Their occupants were standing in full view of the drama acted out by a silvery moon. They had excellent seats."

"Then they saw you mur—kill those two men?"

"I am reasonably confident of receiving a visit from the lieutenant of police tomorrow."

"Benyer wouldn't dare touch you!"

Roxton shook back a ruffle and took snuff. "God forbid," he drawled. "I am hardly a nobody."

"I didn't mean—of course not," said his lordship awkwardly. "But won't there be a lot of questions?"

"Probably. He can ask all he likes."

"But you ain't going to tell him a whit are you?" said Vallentine with a laugh.

"My dear, Vallentine," said the Duke with a raise of his eyebrows, "are you implying I, the most noble Duke of Roxton, would deliberately obstruct the course of French justice?"

Lord Vallentine grinned. "You've already dispensed your own as it is! And they deserved it! Murderous dogs to want to abduct a-a—Mademoiselle—Moran...?"

"Your so charming face betrays you, Vallentine," said the Duke. "Her name is Antonia Diane Moran, daughter of the famous physician, one Chevalier Frederick Moran—"

"The fellow who killed the Prince de Parvelle's heir in child-bed?" said his lordship sitting up straight. "Jesus!"

"I commend your excellent memory, Vallentine. Not—er—killed precisely. Let us say it was a bad—er—delivery," answered the Duke quietly. "It was never proved but it certainly ruined his reputation in Paris thereafter. He sought refuge in England and subsequently eloped with the Earl of Strathsay's young daughter."

"Adventurous character, ain't he!"

Roxton declined to comment on Lord Vallentine's smirk and continued. "Lady Jane died when Antonia was about five or six-years-old and her father less than a year ago in Genoa. She has no one in the world save a dying grandfather—Yes, Vallentine, do calm yourself. The Earl of Strathsay and his estranged wife—"

"Your cousin Augusta is that girl's grandmother?" blurted out his friend. "What a lineage! The notorious Lady Strathsay's grandchild. Well! Well! Wait until Estée hears about this!"

"Do you think that will further endear her to the girl?" sneered the Duke. "To continue. She has one uncle, Theophilus Fitzstuart, the Earl's son—"

"But the old man don't acknowledge that connection."

"Must you continually interrupt?"

"Sorry."

"What the Earl continues to announce to the world and what is absolute fact are not necessarily one and the same," the Duke answered crushingly. "Theophilus is his son whatever Strathsay says to the contrary. Augusta's morals are decidedly unsavoury but there is no disputing that boy's sire. It is my belief the dear old Earl will come to his senses on that score with his last breath. After all, he is a papist and frightened for his soul. He will make amends be sure."

"You think it was Strathsay who tried to have the girl abduct-ed?" asked Vallentine standing at the sideboard refilling his dish, the Duke declining more coffee. "He couldn't have been pleased to know you had abducted her. Did you abduct her?"

"Let me ruminate on the speculations. I have my own reasons. But no, I do not believe it was the dear old Earl's men." Roxton looked levelly at his friend and smiled thinly. "And no I did not abduct her. My sordid reputation has magnified itself tenfold, even in your tiny mind." He gave a weary sigh. "There is no further hope for my declining prestige. Thus it is no use telling you she is well aware I am her grandmother's cousin and that she wrote to me some months back asking me to—er—extricate her from an unpleasant situation. She is under the misguided belief that her father's will left her in my care—"

"What? *You?* Guardian to a girl not quite twenty years of age?" Lord Vallentine scoffed. "The man must've had rocks in his head!"

"Your confidence in me is unswerving," sneered the Duke. "As I was going to add, in my care to see her safely to England to her grandmother."

"The knight errant! Bravo for you, Roxton," exclaimed his lordship. "But is it wise to send the girl to a woman of your cousin's morals? I mean, you have a reputation, that's certain, but Augusta Strathsay doesn't have a moral bone in her body!"

The Duke had gone to the fireplace and was absently poking a log with the toe of a black leather shoe. He had his back to Lord Vallentine denying him a view of his features, but his lordship thought he detected a wisp of emotion in the normally placid voice.

"The girl cannot remain in France," he said. "Her grandfather has—or is in the process, we await to see if he lives a little longer— of contracting a match between his granddaughter and the Vicomte d'Ambert. Wait, Vallentine, before you tell me such a union does not seem unreasonable, for I would agree with you but for two reasons. First: the Vicomte is loath to marry her because she is beneath his touch. I do not know her feelings for him. And second: no sooner will Salvan wed his son to her than he will take the girl himself—"

"Good—God. That's disgusting!" declared his lordship with a tug to his mouth. "Salvan and that girl?"

"Quite, my dear. Nonetheless that is Salvan's intention," said the Duke, resting his wide shoulders against the mantle. "I admit

I found the tale rather fantastical but I had to give it an ounce of credence given my cousin's penchant for virgins straight from the nunnery."

"I've always thought your cousin a disgusting little worm," grumbled his lordship and pulled a face.

"Yet," reflected the Duke, "observing my cousin's behavior of late, and Antonia's aversion for him, I was not totally disbelieving. Then, through a fortuitous accident, I learned there is a *lettre de cachet* in d'Ambert's name. And let us not forget the state of my cousin's finances. He needs his son to make an advantageous match. Antonia will be an heiress when her grandfather dies. He will leave what is not entailed to her. What price the family name if Salvan can bag an innocent heiress for his son whom he wishes to bed?" He watched his friend's face cloud over. "Go to bed, Vallentine. Your brain has passed the limits of its comprehension."

Yet when the Duke announced his intention to visit Rossard's his lordship summoned up all his reserves of energy and dashed off to change clothes, declaring his wish to accompany the Duke. He said he would be down in the foyer within ten minutes. It took him considerably longer to make himself presentable. Roxton patiently waited, great-coated and gloved, one hand scratching the ear of his grey whippet, its companion content to lie at his master's feet.

"Do you think it wise to show your face at Rossard's tonight of all nights?" asked Vallentine as he was helped into coat and gloves. "There's bound to be a stir. All Paris must know by now what happened on the Versailles road and well, as you said, two men are dead and—"

"—there is blood on my hands?" Roxton shrugged. "Ridding the world of such *canaille* is of supreme indifference to me, my dear. But if you feel…"

"No, not I! I couldn't agree more!" Vallentine responded quickly and waited for the Duke to pass out under the hôtel portico before him, the whippets close at their heels. "But there's bound to be talk. And not a few who won't condemn your actions. For no other reason than it was you who killed those swine. I just hope it ain't an unpleasant reception."

67

"Not for me, my dear," said the Duke, a hand to the jewelled hilt of his sword, "but for my friend who dared to mutilate a beautiful young girl, it will be unpleasant, deliciously unpleasant."

<hr />

"How can you be certain he will show his face after what has happened?" asked the Chevalier de Charmond, contemplating the cards dealt him. "It is your lead, Gustave," he said to a fat nobleman with large red painted lips that twitched annoyingly.

"All of Paris is here tonight. Of course he will show up," muttered the Comte de Salvan and picked up the pile of cards in front of him. He did not look at them immediately. Again his small black eyes scanned the crowded and noisy gaming tables and then went to the door. There were more than the usual number of faces and not one belonged to his English cousin. "*Mon Dieu* it is close in here."

The Chevalier chuckled. "I sympathise, M'sieur le Comte. I truly do. It is very bad for you I think. What will you discard?"

"I do not know why you came to Paris! It is not bad, not bad at all! You will see how Salvan makes the most of this situation." He discarded recklessly and his gaze went back to the door. "I admit he has an advantage. But I will have the girl returned to me."

"How do you know the girl is still with him?" asked the Chevalier. "Mayhap she ran away into the Paris night after he—"

"Absurd!" declared the Comte. He snatched up a glass of wine off a tray a waiter offered him. "What time did he have to seduce her and kill three—or was it four?—men who held up his carriage? Eh? None I tell you!"

Charmond fanned out his cards and took time to discard. "He may be with her now. Think of it, Salvan! While we sit here your cousin he is mounting the little mademoiselle for a third time!"

"It was two men," said the fat nobleman, one Gustave, Marquis de Chesnay. "I know. Marguerite had me stop the driver so she could take a look at them. She not the only one. There was quite a crowd gathered. The police, they questioned everyone! They even questioned Marguerite. Imagine that!" He looked about the table with wide expressive eyes. "She lied to them of course. She always does. What an absolute angel! I wish my wife was half as clever—"

"—and half as talented," murmured a gentleman to De Chesnay's right. He made a rude gesture with his tongue which sent the men into great guffaws of uncontrolled laughter.

De Chesnay smiled broadly and waited for the laughter to subside. "Marguerite, she said those two bodies afforded more interest than a visit to the morgue! Have you ever heard the like of her? Ah! She truly is an angel! Fabrice, I believe it is our rubber."

"One was shot through the heart," said a gentleman in a powdered-blue bob wig who leaned on the round back of the Chevalier de Charmond's chair. "The other in the temple. I would have done the same. Filthy vermin!"

"Why hold up Roxton's carriage and no other?" asked the Marquis de Chesnay. "And so I asked Marguerite. You must agree, gentleman, that that is a very odd circumstance. She said it must have something to do with a female."

"Who said?" asked the Comte de Salvan too quickly. "Who was the female?"

The Marquis shrugged and licked his fat lips. "Marguerite, she said it must be a female. It always is with our friend Roxton. Depend upon it! If there is trouble with a woman Roxton can be counted to be involved! Who can forget, only a month back that absurd actor challenged M'sieur le Duc de Roxton to a duel. An actor. All because of that actress Felice. The audacity of the man! That Felice, well, she is of a softness, and it is said her talents with her—"

"M'sieur le Marquis need not elaborate!" cut in Charmond and threw down his hand. He stood up, pushing the gentleman in the bob wig off-balance. "Unless, Gustave, this Felice has given you the pleasure of her company?"

"No," said the Marquis and blinked. "I don't like actresses."

The Chevalier bowed. "No. M'sieur le Marquis prefers other—"

"Leave him be!" growled the Comte de Salvan and pushed the fat nobleman back in his chair. "I apologise a thousandfold for Fabrice. He is not himself. He aches for Felice, oh, how he aches! But alas, my friends, it is Roxton who makes the divine Felice ache over and over again!"

Those gentleman at and about the table laughed loudly at this, each nudging the other; even De Chesnay smiled. The Comte de Salvan sauntered off, well-pleased with his quip. He found the Chevalier in the adjoining room filling a plate high with food from a buffet set out on a long table against one wall. Salvan selected an oyster and let it slide down the back of his throat. He took another and waited until the Chevalier's plate was full and they were comfortably situated at a table by the window before he took out his snuffbox and returned to the topic uppermost in his thoughts.

"You brought it with you?" he asked in a low voice.

The Chevalier stuffed his mouth with a slice of pigeon pie and nodded. He put down his napkin and reached in a deep pocket of his puce velvet frockcoat. He dumped the contents on the table: two snuffboxes, an etui, a wad of folded bills, a handful of papers and a scatter of livres. He handed the Comte what he so desperately wanted and went back to eating.

"Keep it safe, Salvan," he said between mouthfuls. "There will not be another. You do not know what trouble poor Fabrice took to—"

"I know, I know," answered the Comte impatiently, his be-jewelled fingers caressing the royal seal lovingly. It was only for a moment, then he quickly slid the *lettre de cachet* in an inner pocket of his flowered waistcoat. "I will not forget your exertions on my behalf, Fabrice." He held up his wine glass in a toast. "Let us drink to our good fortunes. I have heard the soft Felice is not at all happy with her lover."

"Yes?" whispered the Chevalier, hardly daring to breathe.

The Comte drank deeply. "It has come to her attention M'sieur le Duc contents himself with what is on offer at the Maison Clermont, one blossom in particular, rather than spend his evenings in the arms of Felice. Your actress, she does not like to be upstaged, especially by an Oriental."

Charmond's watery eyes glowed. He bit ravenously into a cooked onion.

"Oriental? It was you who told Felice? Ah, M'sieur le Comte, you have lifted a great burden from poor Fabrice's shoulders! I shall go to her tomorrow with gifts and a mouth of sympathies!

Yes, that is what I shall do! She will not be able to resist me. I must have a new wig and my tailor, he must run up a pair of velvet breeches. Perhaps new diamond knee buckles—"

"It pleases me you are happy, but close your mouth! The contents, they disgust me!" The Comte pulled a face and called a waiter to bring another bottle of wine. "You eat like a pig! It is too hot in here. Open the window. Where is that wine?"

"You are worried, very worried. I, Charmond, can tell it," said the Chevalier sympathetically. "I do not blame you. I would be very worried were I in your heels, my dear Comte. It is very bad for you I think. This situation, it is very bad. The little mademoiselle, she is in the satyr's skilful hands and you, you are powerless to act, to go to her, to spirit her away! Why even with the *lettre de cachet* now in your possession, what is the good of it? What can you do with it? Your son, he is not the problem any longer. You can thrust it under his nose but to what end? Your plans, they are all in a ruin. All your efforts, they are wasted.

"Best find another female. She can't be the only one. To tell you a truth, Salvan, I did not like the slant of her eyes; like a cat's! And their color, a green! It does not do well to bed females with green eyes. And now? The pitcher, it is broken. Roxton, he is probably between her soft thighs as we speak. My friend, you can do better than she."

"I don't want another! I won't have another! I will have her! I *will!*" screeched the Comte like a nasty spoiled child. He was up on his heels and pounding the table with a clenched fist, sending the silver and crockery clattering, drops of wine spilling from his glass and the noise in the room hushed. Salvan was oblivious to it all. The white's of his eyes were all that Charmond dared look at. "Imbecile! Idiot! Great fool! Do you think it is only her virtue I crave? Ah! Why do I try to explain these things to you?"

He sat down again and drank a great gulp of wine. A minute's quiet reflection helped to restore his calm. The Chevalier dared not eat or drink or look away from the little man's pitted face.

"I am a flea's hair from signing a marriage contract with Strathsay," said the Comte in a quiet voice. "It is being drawn up as we speak. My lawyers, they are working night and day to see it is done. Time, it is of the essence! The old man is dying. His insides, they rot I think. I tell you, Charmond, every time I visit him I almost vomit in his face. The stench, it is unbelievable! But what do you think will happen if he hears the slightest whisper of this night's work, eh? What?"

The Chevalier did not speak. He did not even shrug.

"All of it! Everything in ruins!" said Salvan dramatically. "It will kill the old buzzard! And he will hear of it soon enough because although it has taken all my genius to keep that Italian whore from his bedside, she will contrive to get to him. I am in Paris and not at court and so cannot watch her every move. She thinks he does not want her, but he does, oh how he wants her! It is pathetic, Fabrice, truly pathetic. Such a great General and he reduced to calling out for a whore like a child for its nanny!"

He washed the distaste from his mouth with more wine. "Caspartti will tell him everything if she gets to him before he dies. He thinks the girl wants to marry my son. I have made him think it. He desires to see her well cared for before he dies. That is what keeps him alive. He likes the idea of her marrying into a noble French family. But if that whore tells him otherwise? Ah! He will hesitate, call the girl to his bedside and ask her! A disaster! I must make certain that does not happen."

"Salvan, you are a genius," whispered the wide-eyed Chevalier.

The Comte smiled smugly. "Yes, I am, Fabrice."

"Such a mind as yours shall conceive of a solution to this difficult—but I am certain not insoluble—problem. Mayhap the little mademoiselle will come to no harm? Especially if Roxton took her to his hôtel. Does not he live with his widowed sister? Estée de Montbrail is a most respectable and beautiful creature. One look at the little mademoiselle and she will take her under her wing."

"You are not such a great fool as I thought," conceded Salvan. He leaned across the table and the Chevalier followed his example; their long noses almost touched. "About this business on the Versailles road. I will tell you something. I came upon the scene moments after it happened. Naturally I did not show myself. I was pursuing the girl. I see her leave the masquerade in company with my cousin. I follow with all speed. Yet, I have my driver stay at a distance. And then! He is held up!

"I stop my driver and wait. Another carriage behind stops. It is some bourgeois lawyer I do not know and care not to remember. We wait together. I send a lackey closer under cover of darkness. He hides in the forest. He comes back all white. Roxton he fires without hesitation, he says. There was too much confusion to unravel the rest. We wait, this lawyer and I, until all is quiet and a carriage flies past in the opposite direction. We know it is safe now. We go on. This lawyer continues on his way. He is cowardly and fears for his reputation to stop.

"But I, I send a lackey with a flambeau to inspect the carnage. One of the canaille, he is still alive! Shot in the lung and going fast! But he tells my man with great glee one of his companions found his mark and struck the girl—"

"Great God! But this is hideous!" gasped the Chevalier. "To fire on an innocent—it is a thing that is most shocking in the world!"

Salvan sat back in his chair, an arm hanging loose over its ornate frame. "I do not believe it," he said with a wave of a ruffled hand. "That piece of scum, he lied. Had he said Roxton was struck perhaps I believe it. But not the girl. That is too fantastic."

"But—Salvan," said Charmond confused, "why should a dying man lie? That too is unbelievable!"

"How should I know," snarled Salvan. "Am I his confessor? Do I care if his soul is in hell? Now we wait. Wait for mon cousin. He has the girl. I admit I am no longer master of the game. This worries me a little. But I wait. And when the marriage contract it is signed I shall retrieve what is mine. He will be forced to concede my win. He will. He must. He is a man of honor is mon cousin, thus I am only a little worried."

Both men were diverted by a buzz of voices in the doorway. The crowd seemed to part down its center and there stood the Duke of Roxton, dressed in his customary black and white raiments, snuffbox and lace handkerchief in one hand, and quizzing-glass held up by the other to the stark handsome face. Oblivious to the stares and whispers, he peered about him with one magnified eye. Close at his shoulder was Lord Vallentine, deeply conscious of the stir caused by his friend's entrance and wary of any who might dare say a word out of place.

Roxton saw his cousin and the Chevalier at once and sauntered over to their table by a window. He made each man a magnificent bow. Salvan and Charmond stood staring at him like two school-boys caught out by their master for some unspeakable indiscretion.

"Charmond, what a delight to see you," purred the Duke. "We thought you languishing in your bed with a terminal complaint of the lungs, or was it of the——er——heart? It is of no consequence. You have risen! What, may I enquire, brought you back to the land of the living?"

"I am well, thank you, M'sieur le Duc," said Charmond stiffly and returned the formal bow with reluctance. "My cold, it has gone. You, as always, are the picture of good health."

"Thank you, Fabrice," replied the Duke with an uncustomarily broad smile Vallentine considered dangerous. "I am blessed with unnaturally good health. I can say I have never——er——languished in a bed in my life."

The Comte laughed at this quip and Charmond bristled. But the Chevalier held his tongue and was polite when Roxton made him known to Lord Vallentine. The Duke was still smiling, perhaps a little broader then before, and a glitter came into the black eyes his friend did not care for when he turned his attention exclusively to Salvan.

"I thought you still at the masquerade, Cousin," he said. "The field is left to our dear friend Richelieu. What is it at Rossard's that drags you away?"

"As you do, mon cousin," said the Comte expressively. "It was quite shocking behavior, his flirting with Thérèse. And right un-der your nose! I do not blame you for spiriting away that so charming lady in the dove mask just to pique the beautiful Thérèse. I asked myself: how could she prefer Richelieu's charms to your own? It is incredible! Ah, the minds of women, they are a mystery. So fickle and of a jealousy incomprehensible."

He accepted a pinch of the Duke's snuff and inhaled luxuri-antly. "You have the most exquisite blend of snuff in France and still you refuse to tell me its secret."

Roxton shut the small gold box with a snap but the smile was no less broad. "There are——er——treasures——in this world, my dear, which are best left untouched."

"How so?" enquired Salvan.

"You desire to know the secret of my blend of snuff. It is exquisite, I agree. But would it remain so desirable, so exquisite, its powers to attract just as potent, were you to learn its secret? And once you had had your fill, what then?"

"I see your point, mon cousin," said the Comte with a thoughtful nod, a suspicious glance up at the black eyes. "But can one become satiated by exquisite and desirable treasures? It would seem to me the more logical outcome is that once one knows its secret and has had one's fill, the only action is to improve, to go forward, to put all one's own experience into achieving an even greater blend."

"And yet that which was given you pure, uncorrupted and exquisite, the effort of years of careful nurturing, you would seek to corrupt because once you have had your fill it no longer holds you?" said the Duke with feigned surprise. "That is why I do not give you my secret, dearest cousin. You would only turn it into a husk of its former self. You fail to appreciate the essential essence. And you would not cherish, as I cherish, its unadulterated purity."

"Claret?" asked Vallentine, breaking a long pause between the cousins.

The Comte looked unusually thin-lipped and pale and the Chevalier moved from foot to foot, an eye to the gentlemen who hovered close-by. Roxton was still smiling, an unnerving and rare circumstance, and it put his friend on his guard.

"Best keep to your own blend, M'sieur le Comte," advised Lord Vallentine. "Roxton's rather particular about holding on to what he considers his. Aye, Chevalier. We aren't men to cavil."

The Chevalier de Charmond shrugged. "I am sorry, M'sieur Vallentine. I was not attending," he said with a weak smile. He had no wish to be drawn into a discussion between the cousins. "Snuff you say?"

The Comte eyed him with contempt but showed the Duke a sweet smile. "Mayhap I will contrive to take the treasure from you, Cousin."

"By force?" said the Duke with interest.

"Oh no, that is too crude," answered the Comte. "I am not such a fool as to cross swords with one who is considered a premier swordsman of France."

"You flatter me. My friend here is the premier swordsman of France and England. I am merely his pupil."

"Thank you, Roxton," Lord Vallentine said beaming a smile.

"Yet," continued the Duke, who still held his cousin's gaze, "I could easily run you through. But no, such a method is too crude and affords either of us little satisfaction. Thus to wrest from me what you so desperately desire will require a more skilful and intelligent plan. Do you have one?"

The Comte paused while a waiter distributed glasses of wine amongst the small group by the table. His attention did not leave the Duke's face though he appeared to be contemplating those helping themselves to the buffet.

"If I do have a plan I will not tell you!" he declared with a laugh. "It is a little game you and I play, eh, mon cousin?"

Lord Vallentine puffed out his cheeks and shook his head. He was sceptical. "Pardon, Salvan, but you ain't got a hope of outwitting Roxton. Take the advice I gave you."

The Comte's ears turned red but before he could retort the Marquis de Chesnay had minced up to them and stuck his fat person between the Chevalier and the Duke of Roxton. He touched the Duke's arm with the sticks of his ivory fan.

"*Mon Dieu*! It's Roxton!" he exclaimed. "And unharmed! Tell us what happened, cher. All Paris awaits to hear the story from your lips, M'sieur le Duc."

"There is nothing to tell, Gustave," answered the Duke, the smile gone and his face devoid of emotion. "My carriage was held up. Two worthless cattle are dead. I am untouched. There is the story."

"Ah! You wish to humble your efforts in this drama," said De Chesnay. "But you were brave, very brave to take on such cut-throats. You may have been shot. I shudder at the thought! Yet, you ended their designs so expertly without a mark to your person, or a casualty on your side. Indeed, we are all grateful that our roads are made a little safer by your actions. Now mayhap the canaille will think again before attempting to steal from their betters. Do we not applaud M'sieur le Duc de Roxton, gentlemen?" he said looking about the room to receive nods and exclamations of agreement. He licked his fat lips and smiled spreading wide his hands. "You see! There is not one amongst us who disagrees!"

"Did I omit casualties on my side?" said Roxton lightly. "How lax. Yes, there were casualties."

"Marguerite was right," gasped De Chesnay. "There is a woman! I told you so, Salvan. Marguerite, she is never wrong."

"Not difficult to guess that when Roxton's involved," murmured Vallentine, avoiding the Duke's eye.

"My driver, a most excellent whip, was shot through the arm shattering a bone," the Duke told them. "I was forced to leave him in the care of the closest innkeeper. He will never handle the ribbons again." He scanned the faces of the group about him. The Comte was the only one who appeared disinterested in the tale for he drank from a glass and looked about the room distractedly. "Gustave, I commend Marguerite. There is a—er—female involved…"

"Yes? Yes?" uttered the Chevalier in spite of himself.

"I knew!" announced Gustave. "Marguerite, she is never wrong."

"Upon this occasion I wish to Christ she had been, damme!" said Vallentine angrily. "It ain't anything to crow about when a young girl—an innocent—is brutally cut down by a pack of worthless dogs!" He glared at the Comte whose painted face quivered. "Sorry, Roxton, it couldn't be helped. I need a refill," he said and walked off, the crowd now gathered about the Duke parting to let him pass to the buffet tables.

"Is this true?" whispered De Chesnay. "An innocent girl? It seems incredible!"

"That she be innocent?" sniggered someone in the crowd.

No one else dared comment under the Duke's disdainful gaze.

"Tell us what happened," said the Comte in a steady voice. He took snuff with a barely controlled wrist, the powder falling in a sprinkle over one great upturned cuff. "A girl you say? This is most interesting."

"Quite interesting indeed, Salvan," said Roxton coldly. "You will be surprised to learn my companion was the said mademoiselle in the dove mask."

"No!" demanded the Chevalier in exaggerated surprise.

"A girl. An innocent, coldly and brutally fired upon—"

"No! No! It is not true!"

The anguished cry came from the back of the crowded room, and all powdered heads turned as one to see to whom the voice belonged. One of their number pushed through to the Duke's side.

"She must not be hurt! Tell me she is not hurt!"

"What are you doing here?" the Comte demanded in a choked whisper. "How dare you set foot in Rossard's dressed like that! You are a disgrace. A disgrace to your name!"

The Vicomte d'Ambert stood panting. He ignored his father and looked only at the Duke. His face was smeared with dirt and mud caked his jockey-boots. He had not bothered to remove greatcoat, sword, nor gloves. He had bounded up the staircase without a word to the porter and footmen in the vestibule, and searched all the rooms for his father and the Duke, two of the servants hot on his heels.

"I have just come from your hôtel, M'sieur le Duc," he explained breathlessly. "I was turned away without word if she be there or not. Tell me of this hold-up! I knew nothing, nothing of it until now! I swear it to you! Tell me she is unharmed! Please, I beg it of you!"

De Chesnay turned to the Chevalier. "Another player in the game," he murmured. "It becomes complicated. What is this boy to this girl?"

"I wish I might do so, my dear d'Ambert," said Roxton softly. "It would be a lie."

The words had hardly died on the Duke's lips when the Vicomte spun about to glare at his father with uncontrolled anger. "It is your fault!" he raged. "You and your mad schemes! She would not now be lying with a hideous wound if you had let her be! She'd not have run off if you hadn't pursued her like a hound to a deer!" He broke into an hysterical laugh. "When I think of what you've done to her—"

The sharp stinging slap across the face was quick and unexpected. It served its purpose. The youth was instantly deflated. A chair was pushed under his legs and a hand pressed his shoulder to keep him seated. Lord Vallentine thrust a goblet of claret under his nose and made him drink. When the Vicomte dared to glance up from under his brows he found the room was empty of spectators and the door was closed. Two discreet footmen guarded the entrance either side of the doorway. The Comte had his back to his son and stood in the window nursing his hand which still smarted from the blow he had inflicted.

"Father—forgive me," murmured Étienne and hung his head when the Comte did not answer him.

"My boy," said the Duke, and held out a silver snuffbox to the Vicomte, "you dropped this."

"Thank you," said d'Ambert and pocketed the box. "I ask your forgiveness, M'sieur le Duc. I-I was overwrought. I did not mean what I said—I—Is she—is she badly hurt?"

"Yes."

The Vicomte put his head in his hands.

"He's taking it a bit hard," whispered Vallentine in the Duke's ear. "Knew her did he?"

"I shudder at your use of tense, Vallentine. He knows her. I find I am wanting my bed. Today and tonight have exhausted even I." He put a hand on the Vicomte's shoulder. "She will be a month abed, perhaps longer. When she is well enough to receive visitors you are welcome."

"Thank you, M'sieur le Duc," said the Vicomte with a shy smile. "I want to see her very much."

"I forbid you Roxton's house!" declared the Comte. "Now go home and await me!"

"As it is my house, my dear, it is hardly your place to forbid even the street-sweeper should I wish it," drawled the Duke.

"Allow me to deal with my son as I see fit," said the Comte frigidly. When his cousin swept him a low bow, one he could only interpret as insolent, he willed himself to remain in control. "Pardon, M'sieur le Duc."

"Please, my dear," said Roxton with a quick unsympathetic smile which caused Lord Vallentine to choke back a laugh, "you need not explain. The episode is one which has caused you—er—deep anxiety. Rest assured the villain will be brought to account. Justice will be served. As for the girl, she will mend, given plenty of rest and every attention."

"You go to a good deal of trouble on her behalf, mon cousin," said Salvan. "I do not seek to interfere in her convalescence but should she not be with her people at such a time?"

"It is no trouble at all to help a young and very beautiful girl. You of all men know that, Salvan," replied the Duke. "And, rest assured, she is with her—er—*people*. Good night, gentlemen." He bowed to all, satisfied his cousin was on the brink of a demented rage and the son close to nervous collapse. He was half-way across the room when he heard the Chevalier hiss loudly,

"He knows! Your plans, they are a great pile of ruins! She is too divine to be wasted on that raven-locked icicle, but he'll have her. Take heed of my words, Salvan! He can hardly wait until she's mended to mount her, I see that! And when he's had his fill she'll be worthless—"

"Shut up! Shut up!" screeched the Comte, and would have gone on but his cousin turned on a heel and came back to them.

Lord Vallentine followed. He had a hand to the hilt of his sword and itched to use it. An insult to his friend was not to be tolerated. But a look from the Duke and he obediently retreated to stand by the door.

"I go to Fontainebleau next week as a guest of the King and—er—Madame de La Tournelle," Roxton informed the Comte, an eye on the Chevalier's blank face. "I do not suppose I will see you there, having as you do your own little diversion here in the city?"

Salvan gave a start. "What?"

"You need not fear my interference," continued Roxton. "It is a wise man who knows when to beat a retreat. I congratulate you. She is one of the more accomplished of her kind."

"Who?" the Chevalier asked the Comte, but that gentleman stood rigid, so he looked to the Duke with a sly smile. "Our friend here has a new diversion? A pretty object of dalliance? He is too shy to admit it!" He peered at the Comte. "Come, Salvan," he laughed, "tell poor Fabrice the name of this latest object of your desire. Then I too can offer up my congratulations."

"She is of no importance," grumbled the Comte. He walked away from the Chevalier who stood too close and smelled of onions.

"Oho! You humble yourself, M'sieur le Comte. This one, she must be quite a catch for M'sieur le Duc to comment upon it."

The Comte glared at his son who was still slumped mute on a chair. "I told you to go home!"

The Chevalier minced over to Roxton.

"Tell me, M'sieur le Duc," he said. "I beg of you! Do not keep poor Fabrice in suspense. It is this Oriental I have heard much about, eh? This blossom from the East?"

"Hardly, Charmond," said the Duke quietly. "My cousin is not one to indulge in exotic fruits."

The Chevalier's eyes danced. "Parbleu! He is not as adventurous as you, M'sieur le Duc!"

"Nor does he have such a way with words," quipped Lord Vallentine, which sent the Chevalier into another spasm of laughter his lordship found irritating. "I'm for home, Roxton. And you?"

"And I. But I cannot leave Charmond in suspense. Although, perhaps I shall," said the Duke and glanced at his cousin who seemed transfixed, as if willing him not to speak. "It is Salvan's place to tell. And—yet. No. He will not say because he is modest in his little victory." He bent to the Chevalier's ear and whispered the name Felice.

Five

$\mathscr{A}$ntonia sat huddled on the window seat peering out of a window that was partially frosted with ice. She dared not push up the sash. It was bitterly cold outside and snow had been predicted. She was supposed to be seated by the warmth of the fire, with a coverlet over her knees and a cashmere wrap across her shoulders, but she could not sit still waiting and waiting for her hair to dry. That could take hours and ever since her bath, when the shouts from the courtyard had echoed up the walls, she had wanted to run to the windows to see if it really was the Duke of Roxton returned home.

Madame de Montbrail had made her stand by the fire in her chemise and stockings to be dressed: to be laced into a tight bodice of cream silk, an embroidered stomacher hooked into place; layers of petticoats of tissue thrown over panniers and pulled tight about her waist; and finally, expertly slipped over the whole, an open-robed gown of the palest shell-pink embroidered with tiny flowers and vines. Then her waist-length hair had been towel-dried, combed free of tangles, scented, and left to dry down her back, a cashmere shawl folded about her shoulders to keep the damp off her gown. Satisfied, Madame had then departed with strict instructions to Antonia's maid, Gabrielle, to see to it her mistress did not stray from the fireside.

No sooner had the door closed than Antonia flew to the window seat. She ignored Gabrielle's pleas, intent on knowing what was happening in the courtyard below. She heard shouts and male laughter and the clash and scrape of steel on steel. Yet the only persons in view were two lackeys, each with a frockcoat over an arm and holding a goblet of wine.

Her patience was soon rewarded when the two swordsmen came into view. They traversed the courtyard from corner to corner. Elegant of wrist, they were strong and quick in their art. There was the hiss and sing of blades as each fought for mastery over the other. First the Duke was pushed back by Lord Vallentine, then he proved stronger of wrist and forced his lordship against the low stone wall which separated the garden from the stables. They were stripped to their white shirt sleeves, oblivious to the cold and not caring.

"Come look, Gabrielle!" insisted Antonia, forehead pressed against cold glass. "M'sieur le Duc and M'sieur Vallentine are fencing cork-tipped. This is the first time I have been up to see them. Always I could hear their carryings-on and always I was confined to that wretched bed! Is it not exciting? They are very good I think. Perhaps Vallentine is the quicker but M'sieur le Duc is the stronger. He looks very fine in white shirt and breeches, and his hair just so. Poor Vallentine! If he is not careful he will lose his wig! Oh! He has slipped on the icy cobbles!"

She laughed and turned too quickly. A pain shot down her arm to her fingertips; a grim reminder that she was not as mended as she would like to believe. Gabrielle had gone to fetch her mistress's breakfast so Antonia looked out of the window again and discovered the battle over. The two gentlemen leaned against the garden wall catching their breath and drinking wine. She wondered if they could see her and was sure of it when Lord Vallentine looked up and said something to the Duke. Antonia waved and Vallentine responded in kind. The Duke did not even glance up, not even when they passed under the window to go inside some five minutes later.

She sank back down on the cushions and frowned. This was how Estée found her and was not at all pleased her patient had left the warmth of the fire. She scolded Gabrielle who had followed her into the room with a breakfast tray. The girl took the abuse good-naturedly and disappeared to complete her other duties.

"Did I not tell you to sit by the fire?" demanded Madame.

"You think just because that fat physician says you are allowed out of your rooms you are strong enough to do as you please? Catch a cold amongst other things? You try my patience, Antoinette—"

"Antonia. My name is An-tonia! I do not like the French form. You must remember that, Madame."

Madame de Montbrail sighed and propelled her charge to the chair by the fireplace.

"I will strive to remember if you will do as I ask," she said picking up the cashmere shawl and fussing with it. "Why you should mind the name Antoinette is beyond me. It is the prettier and it is French. Antonia is merely a Latin corruption—"

"Antonia was name of the mother of the Roman General Germanicus. He was a very good soldier who fought the Germans and she was a devoted and pious—"

"Where do you pick up such trivia? No, I know. Your papa."

Antonia accepted a mug of hot chocolate and drank gratefully of the bitter-sweet brew. "It is not trivia," she said defiantly. "It is history and Papa said—"

"Enough! Drink your chocolate and eat those rolls and give me a minute's peace, wretched girl."

Antonia chuckled into her chocolate and was silent, but not for long. "I am a great trial on you, am I not, Madame? I am sorry. Indeed, I do not mean to be. Sometimes I cannot help it. As when you call me Antoinette, which I loath more than I loath any other name. You understand, yes?"

"I understand you a good deal recovered, mon petite," smiled Estée. "There was a time when you had not the strength to argue with me."

"How long have I been here?"

"One month and one week to the day," she answered and picked up a hair brush from the dressing table and set to brushing the girl's long curls. "It is not so damp that your hair cannot be dressed. La! You have such hair and of a color I adore. You make me envious, child. It would have been a great pity had it been cut off."

"Cut off?" Antonia almost spilled her chocolate. "I will not have it cut! I am very vain about my hair, Madame. It is a fault, I know… Why must it be cut off?"

"Anyone would think it was your neck for the chopping block!" said Madame with a click of her tongue. "Sit still. I have not finished. I said it was to be, not that it is going to be! The physician, he suggested it be cut off because it was such a great tangle. Even I thought it impossible to put to rights. But my brother he would not hear of it. He can be very obstinate. And men, they don't like a woman's hair to be short, not even a few inches cut." She gave a sigh as she pinned up the girl's hair and threaded ribands through the weight of clustered curls. "My brother he was right in the end. It would have been a great pity to see such hair for the cutting floor. It is as well, is it not, my dear?"

"Yes, Madame," answered Antonia, glad Estée had a view of her back and could not see her inflamed cheeks. She was patient while her hair was fussed over but after a long silence she said in a small voice: "Why has M'sieur le Duc not visited me? M'sieur Vallentine, he comes every day to play at backgammon and at reversi. Sometimes he reads to me from the newssheets. But M'sieur le Duc never comes. I find that strange."

So did Estée but she was not about to say so to Antonia. "Mayhap he has a disgust of the sick-room? Persons who are never ill always do."

"No, I do not think that can be the reason," argued Antonia. "When I was shot it was he who tended to my wound and bound it up. And he stayed with me the whole time of the operation. Not once did he show a disgust or was repulsed at the sight of my injury. He said I was very brave."

"And so you were. Very brave."

"So why does he not come?" Antonia persisted. "I have been out of bed for almost a week now."

"There, I have finished," said Estée cheerfully. She gave Antonia the hand-mirror but the girl did not look at her handiwork.

"Madame, why has he not visited?"

"He has been very busy," answered Estée in an off-hand manner she did not feel in the least. "He went to Fontainebleau for a fortnight to hunt with the King, and after he was a good deal at court. And just three days ago he returned from a stay at Marly, or was it Choisy? La! I cannot remember where! He has been away so much recently it is difficult for me to keep up with all his comings and goings. So you see how it is. He has not been in Paris at all while you've been confined to your rooms."

"But he has been here in Paris," persisted Antonia with that streak of obstinacy Estée found beyond her endurance to deal with. "I have heard Vallentine and he fencing under my window most days this week. And Vallentine said only yesterday he and Monseigneur went riding in the forests of St. Germain. And I know when he is home because Grey and Tan visit me and he always has them with him when he is away for more than a day."

Madame de Montbrail threw up her hands in exasperation. "Enough! He does not keep me informed of his movements! I am not his keeper! He is home today. That is all I know. Does that satisfy you? He may come and see you today."

"I do not think he will."

"*Eh bien!* I will not have you frown at me! Now see what I have done with your hair and if it is to your liking."

Antonia went over to the long looking glass and dutifully peered at herself. "I look very well I think, Madame. Thank you. Oh! And you have affixed a nice clasp to hold up my curls. They are diamonds and emeralds, not paste?"

"*Parbleu!* What next will you say? Do not let my brother hear you call his gift paste!"

"It is not yours, this pin? It is a gift you say? For—for *me*?"

"Of course it is not my hair clasp. Emeralds do not suit me. Sapphires and rubies yes, but never emeralds. Come here, I have something else for you."

"What are those, Madame?" asked Antonia when Estée dropped two diamond and emerald encrusted shoe buckles into the palm of her hand. When Madame rolled her beautiful eyes Antonia smiled shyly. "I know what they are. But—they are not for me, too? I mean, you did not have to give them to me. I have Maria's and you have given me so many lovely things already."

"They are yours, Antonia. And also from my brother. I was instructed not to give them to you until you were well enough to leave your rooms. So. You are pleased with his gifts?"

"Very much. They are beautiful and he is very generous," said Antonia in a small voice, a finger tracing the pattern of one of the shoe-buckles. "And now I have so many petticoats and gowns and bonnets, oh, and shoes too! All made for me by this Maurice who is forever telling me he is the best mantua-maker in all Paris. Monseigneur, he spends too much on me. I do not deserve—"

"Good grief, you must not worry your head over mere trifles," said Madame dismissively as she returned the brushes and mirror to the cluttered dressing table. "What is the expense to my brother? He is very rich. And it is better he spends his fortune on you than on one of those vulgar creatures that take his fancy. He lavishes three times as much expense on their wants. And all for nought. So do not worry your pretty head. They are nothing; nothing at all to him."

Antonia put the buckles aside and went to the window seat because she felt hot tears behind her eyes. She knew it was foolish to be upset by Madame's words but she was and she did not know why. "No, Madame," she said flatly. "I will not worry. Where are Maria's buckles?"

"My brother returned them of course. That is what you wanted him to do."

"Did I?"

"Apparently so. In the carriage coming here. You were very adamant that Maria not go without her buckles."

"I am glad he returned them to her . She was very good to me when Grandfather fell ill. He—He is still..."

"He is not better, no worse," said Estée. "Why the tears, *mignonne*? Come dry your eyes. Your grandfather is still alive so you must not cry for him. What if Vallentine or my brother were to visit this minute? You must be happy. Today you can go downstairs and eat your meals with us and later we may go for a drive if you are kept well cosseted and the sun comes out. Here put on your shoes and go stand by the door so I may see the whole. See, the buckles are perfect! Now, turn about, slowly. La! I said slowly! Turn too quickly and you will make yourself sick! Ah, now you are annoying me! Antonia! Stand still!"

"But, Madame, when I twirl about just so you can almost see my garters!" Antonia laughed but she was a little giddy and quickly came to a stop. She saw Madame's frown. "Do not be angry with me. Sometimes I say and do things that others consider outrageous. I am sorry if I offended you."

There was a scratch on the door and both women turned. There were voices in the outer room and Antonia's eyes sparked with expectation. In sauntered Lord Vallentine, hands thrust in the pockets of a Venetian scarlet frockcoat, with a froth of lace at his wrists and a freshly powdered wig snugly atop his head. He was grinning from ear to ear. When Antonia saw who it was her shoulders slumped and the sparkle died.

"It is only Vallentine," she announced with a heavy sigh of resignation.

"Hey! Is that how you care to greet an old friend?" he asked as he kissed Estée's hand. "Good morning, Madame. I trust our impertinent patient is behaving herself? Her tongue is very well if that is any indication of her general well-being."

"See for yourself, Lucian," said Estée smiling up at him. "Then tell me what you think of the miracle I have wrought."

"Well I ain't one for miracles," said his lordship turning to look at Antonia who had hidden herself behind the door. "And if mademoiselle has—Jesus! I mean—well that is—I'll be damned!"

"Lucian! And so you will be if you do not watch your tongue in front of the girl!"

Antonia chuckled at the expression on Lord Vallentine's face. "You look like a fish!"

"Antonia! Is that any way to address M'sieur Vallentine?" demanded Estée. "You must curtsey to him, not make fun of him!"

"I am sorry," said Antonia with no real regret. She curtseyed prettily enough but still smiled brightly. "But Vallentine he still looks like a fish!"

"And by Jove I feel like a fish," confessed his lordship, astounded by the girl's transformation. The last time he had visited the sickroom Antonia's hair was still a mass of unwashed curls and she had still been in undress. With her honey curls freshly washed, scented, and tied up with ribands; and dressed in a froth of petticoats with a low cut bodice that showed to advantage her round firm breasts, he did not know how to adequately express his admiration except by giving a low whistle. "Roxton is in for the shock of his days!"

Antonia frowned. "Why? You do not like these clothes?"

"Far from it!" Vallentine declared. "You, my dear girl, are a little beauty. Estée, I congratulate you. Your brother been up yet?"

"He is coming?" asked Antonia in a rush.

"I don't know, chit. But I hope I'm about when he does set eyes on you! Small wonder why he abducted you. I'd not have run the risk of leaving you at court to be molested by—"

"Lucian!" whispered Madame angrily.

"He did not abduct me!" Antonia declared hotly. "I was very clever in arranging that he should rescue me from the masquerade."

"Oho! So you think!" scoffed his lordship. "I don't suppose he had any say in the matter? I suppose he'd have rescued you had you been a one-eyed hag with no teeth, aye? And I suppose he murdered those would-be kidnappers into the bargain just to oblige you?"

"M'sieur le Duc did not murder anyone! You must not say such horrid things. And you call yourself his friend. He merely defended himself and was forced to fire at them! He did not abduct me and he is not a murderer!"

Antonia's angry distress only made Lord Vallentine laugh harder. "A regular fire-eater, ain't you!"

"Must you goad her?" admonished Estée. "You know she will defend my brother every time. She always does."

"Here am I," said his lordship with a wounded look, "visiting every day, allowing you to win at backgammon, reading from the newspapers, and as soon as I say a word out of place it's come-at-me as quick as you please! That's fine thanks that is!" He slumped in a chair and crossed his long legs. "And not even a word of welcome for Lucian Vallentine!"

"I apologise," Antonia said haughtily. "But you must not say such things about M'sieur le Duc. They are not nice words and it upsets me. I cannot help it."

"I can see that! I ain't blind to it!"

"You are no better than she with your pout," Estée scolded his lordship and beckoned Antonia to her. "Stand still, child, so I can put up your hair again. And you are not to speak to M'sieur Vallentine in such a tone, and with that frown. It is bad manners in a lady."

"Yes, Madame, but he still must not say such things about M'sieur le Duc. I do not like it."

"The Lord save us!" said Lord Vallentine with a heavy sigh and threw up his arms. "You don't give up easily! Wait until Roxton learns he's got himself a chit who defends him right or wrong, sunshine or hail! Don't it amuse you, Estée, to think your brother is defended so vehemently? And he with a character not worth saving. Hey-ho! What the—What are you doing with that pillow, brat? No! Now don't you throw that—"

Madame de Montbrail stamped her foot, her arms akimbo. "Have done! Have done! I will leave you both if you do not behave! Do you want to see me cry, Lucian? Do you? I will! I will if you both do not stop acting like bébés!"

"Now, Estée, there is no cause to be upset," said Vallentine seriously, though it was evident he was enjoying himself hugely. He had sustained a direct hit to the head with a soft cushion, setting his wig outrageously askew. "Antonia and I are only funning. Ain't we, chit?"

Antonia nodded, her eyes full of laughter despite the throb in her arm which she ignored. "A great John Dory fish! That is what you look like, Vallentine."

"I am going out!" announced Estée and bustled to the door. "I am going for a drive to the Tuileries to have some peace, and I do not care how cold it is out of doors!"

"Wait up!" shouted Vallentine and jumped up to follow her. "You can't leave me alone with Mademoiselle Fire-eater. Get your coat, chit," he whispered to Antonia as he strode out of the room, his voice still to be heard on the landing trying to placate Estée as Antonia called for her maid.

"I do not know why I permitted you to persuade me to let you come," said Estée sullenly. She was watching the passing traffic and refused to look at her two travelling companions huddled on the opposite bench. She sensed they were smiling at her and clasped her gloved hands tighter in the huge muff of fox fur. "If Antonia catches a chill you will answer to my brother for it!"

"Fresh air will do her good. And she needs the exercise. Cooped up in that ancient mausoleum for nigh on five weeks would make anyone nauseous."

"It is not an ancient mausoleum," argued Antonia. "M'sieur le Duc has a lovely hôtel."

"That heap of old bricks?" scoffed his lordship, rising to the bait. "You wait until you see Treat. Now there's a lovely house. More a palace really. Then you too would call the hôtel Roxton a heap of old bricks!"

"What is this Treat? It is a palace you say? It belongs to M'sieur le Duc?"

"That's right. His seat in England. His grandfather had the house remodelled and Roxton's been addin' to it and fixin' it ever since," Vallentine told her as he helped her alight.

They waited for Madame de Montbrail to step down. All three pulled their capes closer about their throats and the ladies covered their hair with large hoods. Vallentine offered an arm to each and they set off to stroll the walled tree-lined gardens.

"Madame, why does Vallentine call M'sieur le Duc's house a heap of old bricks when Monseigneur is kind enough to allow him to stay under his roof? Does Vallentine live at the hôtel?"

Despite her belligerent mood Estée could not help a chuckle and she squeezed his lordship's arm. "You had best answer that, Lucian."

"I refuse! Now, both of you, be quiet and let us enjoy our stroll in silence."

It was on their third turn past the newsmongers who lounged under a group of trees and sat at tables arguing and playing at chess, that Antonia gave Lord Vallentine's great cuff a sudden tug. They had come to an intersection of paths running along the boulevard and a cluster of persons stood at its center. Affected displays of greetings were being conducted with much bowing and scraping, curtseying, and elaborate handkerchief waving. Outstretched gloved hands were touched to painted lips, mouches at the corners of eyes and mouths twitched deliciously, and a shrill of idle chatter permeated the serenity of a cold but sunny autumn day.

The scene reminded Antonia of a flock of gathering peacocks. One nobleman was of an altogether different plumage. Her impulse was to run up to the Duke but Vallentine held her in check.

He exchanged a worried glance with Estée. At any other time they would have joined the group for they knew them all. Yet they held their ground only yards away and watched.

"So it is Thérèse who remains his latest diversion," whispered Estée, blue eyes devouring the tall female who clung possessively to the crook of her brother's velvet sleeve. "She has dangled her hook in his direction long enough."

"Just as you say," replied his lordship in low accents.

"I expected no less from him. She must be very amusing or very talented between the sheets."

"Both, is the common report," confirmed his lordship.

"Yes, she must be for he has kept her longer than most. Ah, she looks too well pleased with herself. I wonder if she is aware she shares him with the de La Tournelle and that actress. What is her name? Felice? Yes, Felice!"

"Given those two up."

"What? The actress?" said Estée loudly.

"Hush, love. Both. I said both of 'em. De La Tournelle and Felice."

Madame pulled a face. "No! That I do not believe! If it is true then it is no small wonder Thérèse smiles. She thinks she has him all to herself. She will be impossible next time I meet her at a levee. I wish he would fall in love."

Vallentine gave a snort. "Steady, Estée. You've never been one to disapprove of Roxton's varied interests. And now you're advocating *romance* for one such as your brother?"

Estée's eyes narrowed to slits as she continued to stare at Madame Duras-Valfons with her blonde powdered curls and beautiful laughing face. "I do not want him attached to that woman for too long. She is not good for him. She is vain and stupid and cares for no one save herself. She does not love him."

"Love him? What's that got to do with it? He don't love her either I'll wager."

"Why are you whispering?" asked Antonia coming to stand before them, her chin tilted up at his lordship. "Do you talk about M'sieur le Duc and the Comtesse Duras-Valfons? She is as painted as a doll and at court she parades about thus—" She mimicked the woman's floating walk and got for her pains

Madame's iron grip about her wrist. "Please! That-that is my injured—" A stab of pain crossed her face and she was instantly released. She turned back to the party in time to see the Duke whisper in Madame Duras-Valfons's ear and she laugh and tell her companions what he had said. "They are all as painted as clowns! Pshaw! That woman she is nothing but a *putain*."

"Antonia! Where did you pick up such an expression?" demanded Estée.

The girl smiled angelically. "Why at court of course."

"*Allons!* It is time you were indoors," said Madame de Montbrail and did an about face on her brother and his mistress. "The gnats are always terrible this time of year."

"Vallentine, you will tell me please," said Antonia skipping up to him. "Is Thérèse Duras-Valfons M'sieur le Duc's latest whore?"

This forthright question made his lordship stammer an incoherent reply and Estée's eyes to widen in horror. Antonia repeated the question unabashed at their response but both deigned to ignore her.

"*Parbleu!* Where does she get such notions?" whispered Estée.

"Your brother is hardly one to be discreet. The chit's been at court. She has eyes. And you know what it's like at Versailles. A nest of vipers. Unsavoury company for a young girl, that's certain."

"I shudder to think what vices she has been exposed to left in the care of that whore Maria Caspartti."

"M'sieur le Duc says it is more polite to call Maria Caspartti Grandfather's mistress, not his whore," lectured Antonia with a mischievous twinkle which had Vallentine grinning. "There is a difference, yes?"

Madame de Montbrail only heard her words. She did not see the mischief and stormed off ahead of her companions, remaining silent on the short return journey to the hôtel while Lord Vallentine and Antonia continued their playful banter all the way home. Her mood did not improve once in the relative warmth of the hôtel's foyer and she announced she had the headache so would go to her rooms to rest for an hour or two before dinner. Lord Vallentine offered his escort, but this was bluntly refused, and she left Antonia and his lordship to stare after her in contemplative silence.

When Vallentine suggested Antonia follow Madame's example she declared she was not the slightest bit tired, despite a dull ache in her shoulder which annoyed her when she made a sudden wrong movement. She coaxed his lordship into playing at backgammon. Not only did he acquiesce but allowed her to persuade him they should spend the early afternoon by a fire in the Duke's private sanctum, his library.

And so they spent an enjoyable hour playing at backgammon on the deep carpet in front of the fire. When his lordship declared he was tired of losing he ordered hot chocolate and coffee. And this Duvalier deposited on a heavy silver tray on the carpet before them, taking his time to depart, an ear to Antonia and Vallentine's heated discussion concerning the various merits and demerits of particular Italian states they had visited. When he took his leave he was more than ever convinced the Duke's friend, although closer in age to his master, had a brain well-suited to the companionship of children.

When she had finished her chocolate Antonia curled up on the large leather chair closest the fireplace and settled on the velvet cushions with a slim volume selected from the book-lined shelves. His lordship was quick to point out she was not to sit on that particular chair because it was the Duke's favorite, and that the book she had selected was not fit for a lady's eyes. Besides, it was in Latin and he did not believe for one minute a chit from the schoolroom could read Latin; if so it was scandalous. His entreaties fell on deaf ears and he was forced to concede defeat, and retreated behind the pages of a day-old English newssheet.

The Duke entered the library not an hour later. He found it deserted despite his butler's assurances Lord Vallentine and Mademoiselle Moran were within. Duvalier followed him and placed several dispatches on the desk. He began to tidy the chocolate tray when a rustle of movement caught his attention and he almost overset the silver pot and mugs. Roxton glanced up from the pile of correspondence, instantly saw the reason for this distress and waved his butler away. Only with the door closed on the servant's back did he dare approach his favorite chair.

By the turned leg of the chair was a pair of silk-covered shoes and a leather-bound volume, propped on its spine and with a silk riband tucked between two pages to hold a place. He scooped up a discarded shoe with its large diamond and emerald encrusted buckle and inspected its workmanship. And with it still in his hand he leaned on the high back of the upholstered chair to peer down at its occupant.

Antonia was fast asleep, her face turned away from the dying fire, one arm caught in a quantity of tangled curls, the other resting limp across her bodice. The layers of her silk petticoats surrounded her like a soft pink cloud and exposed her small stockinged feet to the warmth of the fire. He couldn't recall the last time he'd had the leisure to admire the prettily turned ankles of a sleeping beauty. The sensation was new to him and made him smile.

He wondered what would be his next move, now that he had taken possession of the sweetmeat his cousin so desperately craved. The smile broadened. Poor Salvan, he thought without sympathy, he must be going out of his mind that the singular object of all his pent-up lust was recuperating in the house of his noble English cousin whose wealth and way with women he envied to the point of loathsomeness.

Yet, as he continued to watch Antonia sleep, he became absorbed in the rhythm of her breathing, and the smug smile of triumph dropped into a frown on the more sobering thought that now he had the girl what was he to do with her? Whisking her away from the masquerade had been an instinctive reaction, of grabbing the prize out from under his cousin's nose; the consequences ignored.

And then Antonia had totally put him off-balance by not being the least wary of him or his intentions. She seemed to have every confidence that he meant to rescue her from that consummate libertine Richelieu and every other lecherous dog at Court. That she regarded him as some sort of knight in shining armor and not of the same mold as his friend Richelieu completely disconcerted him. As did a niggling doubt that the girl had orchestrated the entire escape, he merely a pawn in *her* plans.

After all, she had pestered him with letters and lingered on the fringes of his social circle at Court for so many weeks that her presence became an unwanted intrusion on his liberty. He was not immune to her striking beauty. He had noticed her on her very first day at Court and been intrigued. But beauty coupled with the inexperience of youth and a lack of sophistication had never appealed to him. He had always preferred seasoned beauties, whose sexual proclivity was equal to his own and who had an understanding husband lurking somewhere in the background ready to offer a padded shoulder to cry on when boredom dictated he move on.

When discreet enquiries about Antonia revealed she was in reality one of his needy, distant relatives out to seek his help, he quickly consigned her to the latrine of annoying liabilities that came with his title and wealth. He went out of his way to ignore her. Yet, why at the first sign she might be out of her depth, attending a masquerade dressed as a whore was certainly way out of a young girl's depth, had he not only exerted himself to snatch her away from Richelieu, but by such action showed the world that she was his responsibility; a circumstance he had spent the previous three months trying to avoid?

And now, as he continued to watch the flicker of the fireplace shadows play upon her lovely profile, it was patently clear that any satisfaction he had derived from having Antonia away from Salvan had evaporated when considered against the responsibility that was now his in seeing the girl fully recovered from her ordeal and safely placed in the care of her grandmother in London.

He was still contemplating the burden of these new found responsibilities when Lord Vallentine strode into the room, a coverlet over one arm, and tapped him lightly on the shoulder.

"She would fall asleep in your chair," he whispered apologetically. "I didn't have the heart to wake her so I thought it best to fetch this myself. Don't want her taking a chill." He arranged the coverlet to his satisfaction and glanced up at the Duke. What he saw gave him a start. "Jesus, Roxton, what's amiss? You've not taken ill? I'll get Duvalier to fetch up a bottle. Hey, Duvalier," he hissed, "a bottle of M'sieur le Duc's finest and be quick about it!"

The butler hurried away and Vallentine followed Roxton to a set of sofas in the middle of the room. The fact his friend still had Antonia's shoe in one hand made him smile. When he commented upon it the smile widened into a grin watching the Duke awkwardly dispose of the article.

"You've got yourself a little minx in that one," said Vallentine in English as he sprawled on a chair opposite the Duke.

"Indeed?" said Roxton, the color back in his cheeks.

"Yes, indeed!" laughed his lordship. "She beats me at back-gammon and reversi every time. I've tried all the tricks. None have helped me! She told me her dear father taught her how to play. I could throttle the man for that alone! And ever since she's been on the mend there's no holding her chatter. And argue? Oho! With me until I'm blue in the face. She's more subdued with Estée, but only because Estée will get in one of her moods and threaten to create a scene if the chit don't behave herself."

"Her manners are atrocious," the Duke said with annoyance.

"Oh, there's no spite in her," Vallentine assured him. "She's just a bundle of mischief. It's refreshing. Sometimes it puts Estée out of all patience. If you ask me that's just feminine jealousy."

"You amaze me."

"I ain't as cotton-headed as you think me. Sometimes I warrant I ain't the most acute observer but when it comes to females, well, I have a fair notion of what does and what don't make 'em irritable. Your sister is a beautiful woman, a damned beautiful woman, but Antonia, well, she's—she's—unusual."

"My dear, your tongue trips you up. Unusual in what way?"

To Lord Vallentine's extreme discomfort he found his face warming. He was relieved when Duvalier sought to interrupt at that moment. A glass of claret helped his color but the Duke awaited his answer with an irritating lift of his black brows.

"You needn't look at me in that way! I ain't in love with the chit if that's what you're thinking," confessed his lordship. "I admit I find her company a delight. And I ain't blind, so don't sneer at me! I can see she's a little beauty. But she don't try and use it on a man either, as most females are want to do. She's just—she's just herself. In fact," he continued belligerently, "I find her adorable! But that don't mean I want her; not in that way. Besides, she don't want me, or that young puppy of Salvan's."

"No?"

"She ain't in love with d'Ambert, that's certain. He's come

calling once or twice and she won't see him. Said she wasn't well enough to receive visitors. Though I think he's fooling himself if he thinks he ain't in love with her."

"So you think?"

"Yes, so I think. And another thing. Any attempt on my part, or Estée's, to say a word against you and the little lovable minx turns into a hellcat."

The Duke frowned. "What have I done to deserve such adoration?"

"You can be indifferent if you like," said Vallentine sarcastically. "I suppose you've done nothing out of the ordinary, except it must seem out of the ordinary to a girl Antonia's age. Quite the hero rescuing her from Salvan's slimy paws and shooting two ruffians dead on the Versailles road, not to mention tending to her hurts with your own fine hands."

"My dear Vallentine, if I did not know you better I would hazard I have inflamed your jealousy."

"A man has the right to be a little envious," admitted his lordship. "After all, I'm the one whose been visiting the sick-room every day, taking her sweetmeats and newssheets, and losing at backgammon! What do I get for my troubles and attentions? An ear-full of you. Damn you! Why, I couldn't take her for a walk in the Tuileries without coming across you with the Comtesse Duras-Valfons, and Antonia asked some damned awkward questions. How am I supposed to answer 'em? She's a mere babe in the woods when compared to the ferocious felines you usually associate with."

Roxton's brows drew sharply across the bridge of his nose. "I hope you were sensible and kept your tongue in your head."

"Didn't have to open m'mouth," said Vallentine primly. "She knew precisely Thérèse's vocation without a word from me."

"My lord has become paternal of a sudden," taunted the Duke. "If the girl was affronted by the company I keep—"

"Affronted?" scoffed his lordship. "Antonia? *Affronted?* Much you know about her! She called Thérèse your *putain*, and had the nerve to ask Estée for confirmation! Aye? What's this?" he asked, turning at the sound of rustling petticoats. "Methinks the minx awakes."

Six

Antonia took a sleepy peek over the chair back and when she saw the Duke her eyes widened and she smiled. She flew out of the chair not caring to smooth down her crumpled petticoats, forgetting to cover her stockinged feet, and ignoring the fact the clasp that held her curls up clattered to the floor. She ran to the sofa and dropped a curtsey at the Duke's feet.

"M'sieur le Duc," she said happily, "it is you! I thought I was dreaming, but when I heard Vallentine's voice I knew that could not be true because why would he be in one of my dreams?"

"See what I mean, Roxton," groaned his lordship. "I believe I will ignore you, chit."

Roxton smiled at his friend's bruised ego but kept his eyes on Antonia. "I do not think mademoiselle is kind to M'sieur Vallentine. He has been very good to you, so he tells me."

Antonia nodded. "He has, Monseigneur. But he is also very easy to bait." She went to his lordship's chair and looked contrite. "I am sorry if I offended you, m'sieur."

"Minx," he grumbled and flicked her under the chin. "Did you sleep well?"

"Yes, thank you," she answered brightly, and invited herself to sit beside the Duke on the sofa. "Do you like this gown, M'sieur le Duc? And thank you for the clasp, and the shoe buckles and my gowns, and the hundred other things you had Maurice make for me. Oh? What is my shoe doing there? Maurice is a very good mantua-maker I think. But he talks too much and fusses like a woman, which I do not like at all. Madame thinks he is amusing but I cannot think a man who wears one pearl drop earring and colors his eyelids anything but laughable, can you? Do you think he is one of those men I have heard about who prefers his own kind? A-a Spartan! Or like M'sieur le Duc de Gesvres who is an expert with his knitting needles?"

Both gentlemen were laughing but at the last name mentioned Vallentine gaped at her.

"Antonia! Where—Where do you pick up—I've never heard—"

"At court," she answered simply and looked to the Duke. "I should not say such things perhaps? Did I shock you?"

"Not in the least," answered Roxton, the hand across the back of the sofa absently fondling a silky lock of her hair. "I have always known him to be of that persuasion. You may have shocked my friend, however."

"Me? I ain't shocked," Vallentine said with a huff. "But you can't go saying such things to the chit. It ain't decent. She's not much more than a child for God's sake."

"You are right, M'sieur le Duc," said Antonia with a sigh of resignation. "I have shocked Vallentine. *Hélas.* He is very easy to shock, and to beat at backgammon."

"Roxton already knows you've defeated me at every encounter. No need to rub that in!"

"Will you play me at backgammon, Monseigneur? And perhaps you will stay home some nights so we four can play at whist and at hazard. And now I am so very much better we can dine together, yes?"

"She's got your days planned!" laughed Vallentine, who found himself ignored by the couple on the sofa.

"If you wish it, *mignonne*," said the Duke. "But I warn you, I am a better player than Vallentine, and I will make you no allowances."

"Then we will have an interesting contest," she said. A sudden thought made her frown. "You are not going away again, are you? You—you do not have to go to court or into the country while I am here, do you?"

He shook his head. "No. I am not going away again. We can do whatever you wish."

Her smile returned and she touched his arm impulsively.

"You see, Vallentine," she said to his lordship, a sparkle in her lovely green eyes, "we shall all enjoy ourselves hugely now that M'sieur le Duc stays in Paris."

Lord Vallentine nodded but he did not hear a word Antonia said because he had made a startling discovery. He should have known how it was from the first, but he had taken the girl's spirited defence of his friend at every opportunity as little more than a means of teasing him. But now watching Antonia in the Duke's company he realised that the girl was in love with the Duke. He wondered if his friend had any idea and guessed he did not. He could not wait to share this interesting turn of events with Madame de Montbrail.

Estée de Montbrail did not share Lord Vallentine's enthusiasm. It was her opinion the girl was not so much in love with her brother as infatuated and it did not please her at all. She reasoned the infatuation stemmed from her brother's rescue of Antonia from kidnappers on the Versailles road and because he had spent a small fortune on clothing her; having all that the best mantua-maker Paris could offer, and the most exquisite fabrics available, for the countless gowns, shoes, bonnets and fineries. As for his gifts of shoe-buckles and clasp? Although exquisite and thought-ful pieces, she had made it clear to Antonia at the time that her brother had lavished trinkets on many a lovely neck and pretty wrist, and so the girl should be under no illusion on that score.

Try as he might Vallentine could not convince Madame that the girl was of an age to know her own mind, that her unadulterated feelings for the Duke might just be the making of *him*. It was about time Roxton realised that not all beautiful females demanded a pirate's treasure in return for their sexual favours. Time spent in Antonia's company might teach him a thing or two about love. After all, wasn't it Madame who suggested her brother fall in love? But Madame argued that Vallentine was not taking into consideration the devastating effect this would have on Antonia, who was, for all her bravado, young and inexperienced in the sexual politics between male and female. It was her belief her brother was merely amusing himself with Antonia as one does with a new and fascinating toy. But what happened when the fascination wore off and the girl had her heart broken?

Estée reminded him of what he had confided to her about the Comte de Salvan's plans for Antonia and her brother's interference in these plans. Estée said it just proved her worst fears: Antonia was just a pawn in an ugly game brother and cousin were playing. Her own misjudged conclusions about Antonia's character on the night of her arrival only served to magnify these fears. She felt a great burden of guilt for having thought the worst of Antonia's character. Her first outright rejection of her weighed heavily. She wanted to make amends and felt it her responsibility to protect her, not only from the likes of the Comte but from her own brother. She trusted his motives little more than she did Salvan's.

Thus, she and Lord Vallentine came to an impasse. They could not talk without Antonia's name being mentioned and Madame's fears being raised that the girl was doomed to have her heart broken by the Duke. She loved her brother unreservedly but she knew him for what he was. She could accept it, live with it even, but she was not about to be convinced that years of habitual depravity could be changed by one simple girl, however beautiful and unusual of personality. His lordship disagreed, as Estée knew he would. They had a falling out. The result was a stinging retort from Madame that he was in love with Antonia himself. Why else would he champion her cause so vehemently? Lord Vallentine's response was to storm out of the room on an oath and slam the door, leaving Estée to weep her eyes dry of tears.

Dinner that evening was a subdued affair. In the hopes of placating her, Lord Vallentine had invited Estée to attend a performance at the Comédie Française after dinner. She still picked at her food and could not be drawn into conversation, as hard as Antonia tried. His lordship merely lifted his brows when applied to by Antonia to explain Estée's moody silence, and the dinner dragged on. The Duke, who was never one for inconsequential chatter at meal times, ate in silence and spoke only when addressed.

"Estée and I are off to the theatre," Vallentine told the Duke when the covers had been removed and the brandy set upon the table. "Will you be there?"

"No. I think not," answered Roxton. He poured brandy of unequal amounts into three glasses and pushed one toward his friend. The smallest drop he offered to Antonia. "This is an excellent brandy. Try it. Tell me what you think."

"She is too young for spirits!" snapped his sister.

"It's the merest drop," smiled Vallentine. "It won't hurt her. Try it, imp."

"Is it better than that horrible drink you had me swallow when I was shot?" asked Antonia, sniffing tentatively at the glass.

"Course it is! You don't think I'd have thrown a good brandy down your throat. Hey! Not so fast with it! Savor it. Savor it. You'll be flustered if you drink it like that."

Brother and sister stared at one another; Madame with a significant haughty raise of her little nose. Vallentine caught the implication and rolled his eyes.

"The chit can't get drunk on a drop," he whispered. "Don't make something out of nothing, Estée. Leave Roxton and the girl be, for Christ's sake.

Estée ignored him. She said in an affected voice, "All Paris goes to the theatre tonight. It is a wonder you do not. After all, the main attraction is that charming actress with the most delightful singing voice. I think her name is Felice."

"She does not bear a repeat performance."

"Come now!" said Estée with a brittle laugh. "She, the toast of all Paris and you brush her off so lightly? Do you recommend Lucian and I to stay at home then?"

"No. You will enjoy the evening much better than I."

"After the performance Thérèse Duras-Valfons is holding a select soirée. Shall you go?" asked Estée.

"I have been invited," was the Duke's flat reply.

Lord Vallentine squirmed on his chair and glanced at Antonia who seemed not to be attending but peering into her glass.

"Lucian and I thought we would stop by," continued Madame in a light conversational tone which contrasted with the hard glint to her blue eyes. "If only to see who puts in an appearance. Richelieu and Salvan may attend. I will scold Salvan I think for not visiting me when he promised he would." She gave a sigh. "Yet, mayhap I will not go to this supper because I am not fond of Thérèse. Especially of late. She is too well pleased with herself, thinking she is the object of a singular devotion."

"Does she?" said Roxton with an expression of bored interest.

Yet, it was obvious to Antonia that underneath the mask of inscrutability the Duke was not pleased with his sister's behavior. She wondered how a sister could be so blind to a brother's moods when she, who was not much more than a stranger in this house, could so easily read his frame of mind.

Perhaps she was more attune to his true state of mind because of an acute observation made about the Duke by her father, one she had remembered if not understood fully at the time. It was when her father had confided in her that he had made their distant cousin, the Duke of Roxton, the executor of his will. Antonia was to remember that fact, and the Duke's name, if ever she found herself in difficulties. Despite the Duke's reputation with women, which was very true, her father judged him to be a man of principle and honor who, as Duke and Head of his Family, took his responsibilities to family and retainers very seriously. Her father adding with a shrewd laugh that the nobleman's blackened shell covered a multitude of decencies.

So when the Duke happened to regard her over the rim of his brandy glass Antonia held his gaze, not at all embarrassed at Madame's brazen mention of his current mistress by name at the dining table.

"Your verdict on my brandy, mademoiselle?"

Antonia put her head to one side, the mischievous dimple making an appearance. "The aroma I find *pleasing*. But although there is a smoothness to the—*palate*, I do not think I will make a habit of drinking brandy after dinner."

Roxton smiled and inclined his head while Lord Vallentine shattered the frigid atmosphere with a whoop of laughter.

"Did you ever hear the like from the mouth of a brat?" exclaimed his lordship. "Heard your father say that, did you, chit?"

"I said it. No one told me. And I wish you would not call me a brat and a chit!" Antonia flared up. "Tomorrow I am—Oh, it does not matter! You should still not call me such names. If I did not like you I would be very angry with you!"

"And you ain't now?"

"You all think me too naïve to know—to know certain—certain things about *life*. But Papa and I saw a great deal on our travels and he never once shielded me from life's brutalities. It is because I have seen much of life's miseries that I like to believe there is some goodness in all creatures, even whores, miscreants and thieves!" She stopped herself and hung her head, the ensuing silence making it all the more difficult for her to regain her composure. "I am sorry," she said flatly.

Estée pushed back her chair and shook out her wide petticoats. "I must change. Antonia, do not stay up late tonight. You need your sleep whatever you think to the contrary. So, we will see you at the soirée, Roxton?"

"No. I stay in tonight."

Antonia looked up swiftly, the light of expectation in her green eyes bringing an indulgent grin to Vallentine's face. "To keep me company?" she asked eagerly.

"To keep you company."

"That pleases me very much," Antonia replied with a smile and pushed back her chair. "May we play at backgammon in the library? And then perhaps I can show you this most interesting book I discovered on your shelves. I tried to talk to Vallentine about it but his knowledge of history is very poor. And I have written a letter to Maria. She cannot read French so I must write in Italian. I thought perhaps you might read it through for me? You are staying home all night? Promise me?"

The Duke gave a sigh. "Promise? My word is not good enough? Very well, I promise. Now run and fetch your letter."

Antonia was out of the room before Estée had a chance to scold her for her lack of manners at leaving the room in such a fashion and without a curtsey to the gentlemen. Hardly had she gone when Madame needled her brother a little more.

"La! Roxton, she's as devoted as one of your wretched dogs. You must give her a diamond collar. Is it not amusing, Lucian?"

Lord Vallentine looked uncomfortable and tugged at the lace of his cravat. "She's just high-spirited, Estée. There's no harm in her."

"No, not in *her*," she flung over a bare shoulder as she swept to the door. She would have gone out but for the quiet command from her brother that she remain and Lord Vallentine and the servants leave them. The tone of the Duke's soft voice caused her to go weak at the knees but she was determined to put a brave face on it. She turned to look at him, chin tilted in defiance.

"Your behavior of late offends me. It will stop," he said coldly. "If we are to go on tolerably together you will do me the courtesy of acting the well-bred hostess you were brought up to be." He ignored her expression of shocked outrage, inspecting the well-manicured nails on one long white hand. "I am surprised and somewhat offended that my own sister does not know me well enough to realise that within the walls of my own home my morals are unquestioningly sound. But I will spell it out for you if it will make you feel less anxious for the girl's well-being: I have not the slightest intention of seducing Antonia. She is a guest in my house and she is our cousin, however distant the connection. Your flagrant disloyalty disappoints me, but I realise it is prompted by your concern for Antonia's well-being, and an unreasonable and stupid jealous spite." When Estée gasped and opened her mouth to argue with him he added with a crooked smile, "Save your dramatics for Vallentine, my dear. He has more patience." He collected his snuffbox from the table and pocketed it. "You may offer my apologies to the delectable Thérèse. Tell her whatever you wish; the truth if it suits your purpose."

Madame's only response was to flounce out of the room and slam the door. Meeting Antonia on the stair she could not help but be curt. She told her to straighten a bow on her bodice and brush the hair from her face, and not to run down the stairs like a hoyden. Antonia was too happy to take offence and quickly made amends for her appearance then skipped off to the library. Madame watched her go with a heavy frown and picking up a handful of her petticoats stomped off to her boudoir.

"I do not think Madame will enjoy the Comédie Française if Vallentine cannot coax her into a better mood," Antonia confided to the Duke. She put aside her letters on the writing desk and sat down on the sofa beside him where a backgammon board was set up for play. The tan and white whippet trotted up and demanded she rub its throat. "I am glad you ordered coffee," she said as she watched Duvalier arrange coffee dishes, plates of sweetmeats and silver service on a low table he positioned before them. "I must confess to needing a dish after the brandy. You—you do not mind me saying so—about the brandy?"

The Duke cast his dice and landed a six.

"It is my opening," he said. "Your quatre cannot beat my six. I would mind if you did not tell me the truth."

She rolled the points trois and ace and made the combination.

"You did not have to stay at home with me if-if you wanted to attend the Comédie and Madame Duras-Valfons's soirée."

He looked up from contemplating the state of play through his quizzing-glass. The hesitancy in her eyes made him smile. "I stay at home because I want to, *mignonne*. Now drink your coffee and concentrate on the game, or you will surely lose."

They played in silence a long time until at the end of the fifth game Antonia scooped up her dice and examined them critically. "You have won a third game," she said not unhappily. "Why can I not throw my combinations, Monseigneur?"

"The luck is not with you," he replied. "You try too hard to win. If you thought more about the game and less on defeating me your luck would turn. Come, show me your letter and we will sit closer the fire where it is warmer." He shifted to his favorite chair and Antonia was content to curl herself up on the uphol-stered stool at his feet. "You shouldn't feed them sweetmeats," he said, watching her give Grey a second morsel of cake. "You spoil them."

"They enjoy being spoiled. Will Maria understand my letter do you think?" she asked when he had come to the end of the second page of script.

"It is a well-written letter, my dear. You had a good teacher methinks."

"Thank you. I had a tutor until Papa's death. But Grandfather would not allow me to continue on with my studies. He said it was wrong that I should be taught boy's lessons. He took my books away. He was a great fool to do such a thing. I cannot un-learn what I already know!"

"Your father was quite the eccentric, *petite*," said Roxton seri-ously, though the corners of his mouth twitched at her tone of studied thoughtfulness. "It was because he was an eccentric and learned physician that he permitted you a tutor. He had no son. Though I wonder if that would have made a difference to your upbringing? I think not. Young ladies of your birth are not indulged in lessons on History and Classics and the study of languages."

"These young ladies, they must be very dull creatures then."

"Listen, Antonia," he said. When she shifted to look at him he tried to appear very grave. "Young ladies are taught to dance and to make polite conversation, and to work at their needlepoint. They learn the clavichord, a little history, and how to dabble in watercolours. They don't speak their mind unless requested, and they never answer back. It is not polite. Do you understand?"

Antonia shook her head.

"I am sorry, M'sieur le Duc," she said. "This way of life you describe, it is inconceivable to me. I would be bored if I was not permitted to read whatever I wanted and so was unable to learn new things. Girls of the bourgeoisie are taught differently. I know because Papa he told me so. He said the parents of such girls are more enlightened than their betters. So it is no small wonder to me why noblemen are attracted to the salons of such women when all they can discuss with their wives is polite conversation and watercolours!"

When she realised he was quietly laughing she blushed and looked away to the fire. "I—You must think me equally as foolish. I—I know conversation and relief from boredom are not the primary reason noblemen seek out the company of such women."

The Duke forced her to look at him, a finger under her chin. "I was not laughing because I thought you foolish. I was laughing because I agree with you and you put the case so well."

"Oh? Do you—Do you think it important I know these silly accomplishments?"

"Let me explain it to you this way," he said patiently. "Your grandfather is concerned lest you appear too different from other young ladies of your station. Females who profess to know subjects that are exclusively a male's domain are not viewed very favorably by our society. It is one thing to *be* Lady Mary Wortley Montague but quite another to simply have her reputation. The English are more tolerant of such eccentricities than their French cousins. In France it is all very well for those of the bourgeoisie to educate their daughters in the new manner; they are not likely to marry into our circle. It is a different proposition for a girl of your birth."

"But Papa disgraced himself with the court. And Maman ran away with him and so disgraced herself too. And I do not care about the court or what is thought of me by this society to which I supposedly belong. I have never contemplated marriage and I do not want to think about it. It would be horrid to be forced into a marriage I do not want in the least! Madame says Étienne will make me a good husband, that he is of a fine noble family, but—but I do not love him. If you hand me over to the Comte de Salvan," she said in a rush, "I will run away!"

"Do you truly believe I will hand you over to Salvan?" he asked, stroking her flushed cheek.

She hung her head, hair hiding her face because she felt the heat in her cheek at his touch. "A month ago you did not care what happened to me. You never answered my letters, or looked my way at Court when I tried to catch your eye—"

"Too many females try to catch my eye," he said flippantly with a sigh of resignation.

"Those females are as stupid as they are superficial!" Antonia retorted and immediately recanted for speaking her mind. "I am sorry, Monseigneur. I understand that a gentleman's feelings do not have to be *engaged* to bed one of these silly females."

He made her look up at him. "Do not discount your own sex in that equation, Antonia," he said seriously, looking into her clear green eyes. "At Versailles, what is good for the rooster is just as good for the hens."

"To make love without engaging one's feelings is incomprehensible to me," Antonia stated, her gaze never wavering from his handsome face. "I could not. That is why I will not marry the Vicomte d'Ambert or any other man my grandfather tries to force on me, whatever Madame says to the contrary."

Roxton looked away from her, suddenly uncomfortable, thinking the run of conversation inappropriate between a nobleman of his years and this girl who was now in his care. "My sister's intentions are good but she is quite stupid. Five minutes in your company should've told her that you are strong willed enough to know your own mind. And thus I owe you an apology…" He turned his emerald ring into the path of the firelight and finally met Antonia's gaze. "I should have treated your predicament at Court seriously and granted you five minutes of my time to plead your case. As it is you forced my hand, did you not?"

Antonia's eyes sparked and she could not help a small smile of triumph. "Yes, Monseigneur. Was I not clever?"

But Antonia was thrown totally off balance when the Duke caught up her wrists and stuck his face in hers.

"No, it was not clever! It was a great piece of stupidity to dress as a whore at a public masquerade. You talk of not making love without first engaging your feelings, but that night you, a naïve girl who doesn't know the first thing about being bedded, were in grave danger of being raped. Idiot child! And where did your scheming get you? Shot on the Versailles road!" He let go of her and sat back, annoyed with himself for allowing Antonia to get under his guard, a circumstance that had occurred on one too many occasions with her. "You will not force my hand again, Antonia, do you hear?"

"Yes, Monseigneur," she answered demurely, a curious glance at the impressions left on her wrists by the pressure of his long fingers.

He shifted his muscular legs to make her more comfortable on the footstool and abruptly changed the topic, a tweak of her curls as he returned her letter to her. "You give Maria the wrong impression, *mignonne*. By your account she will think I single-handedly took on and killed the entire fraternity of highwaymen."

This made Antonia chuckle. "Oh, but you were very brave! And I did not tell her an untruth when I said the odds were against you from the start. And do not forget there was one of their number hiding in the forest close by. He was a coward because he did not show himself and he meant to shoot you. Instead he hit me, which was a good thing because it would have struck you, this bullet, closer the heart. When I think of where we were standing and the angle of—"

"You have spent a good deal of time reconstructing the—er—crime."

"What else is there to do tucked up in bed for a month?"

He frowned. "Will you show me the scar?"

She wondered what she had said to make him angry again so quickly and quietly pulled her sleeve off her injured shoulder and brushed aside the hair that fell forward across her breasts. The wound was not a pretty sight. The flesh was puckered and livid, and still very tender to the touch. He leaned forward to inspect the disfigurement, one hand placed gently on her good shoulder and the long cool fingers of the other barely touching the flesh near the healing wound. Yet when deep colored blotches of embarrassment appeared at her throat he sat back and told her to cover herself.

"In time it will fade," he said gently. "There is a stiffness in your arm still?"

"A little, but less each day," she answered and covered the damaged shoulder with a quantity of hair.

"Does this blemish bother you?"

"It would be a lie if I said no. Only when people stare do I think about it. I caught one of the chambermaids—a silly wench—staring when Gabrielle was dressing me, and it made me feel very ugly. I could see she thought it hideous." She glanced up at him. "Do you find it hideous and ugly?"

The frown instantly disappeared and his black eyes smiled into hers. "Not in the least, *mignonne*," he said gently. "It is but a tiny battle scar."

She put her hands on his crossed knees. "I worry that the bullet it was meant for you. It is a silly worry, but it won't go away. Promise me you will be careful. Promise you will take care."

Her earnest entreaty surprised him and he brushed it aside. "My dear girl, I have done an excellent job of looking after myself all these years—"

"*Promise me*, Monseigneur!"

"—that a promise to you is unlikely to change matters one way or the other," he finished flippantly. Yet as soon as he had said this he realised he had hurt her feelings. "Very well," he said, and playfully chided her under the chin. "I will make you a promise. I will promise to take care, though I am yet to discover the identity of our friend in the forest. Did you happen to see anyone per chance?"

"No," she said quietly. "It happened so quickly, all of it, that there was no time to see much at all. But I thought it strange when one of them should stay in the forest. The others, they all had their faces covered with kerchiefs and their hats pulled down, so why would their friend remain out of sight?"

"A mystery indeed," he murmured. "Let us not think on it any more tonight."

Antonia was ready to comply with this for she was suddenly very tired. She rested her head on her arm against the chair and watched the burning logs in the grate crackle and hiss and occasionally burst into yellow flame. Shadows played up the walls of the vast room making it feel close and comfortable and peaceful. It also made her feel very sleepy. She did not know if she fell asleep or not. It seemed only for an instant that her eyes closed.

She felt content with her life for the first time since her father's death some eleven months ago, curled up on the footstool at the Duke's feet, the whippets stretched out on her flowing petticoats, Grey with his muzzle on one of her discarded shoes. She closed her eyes again and shifted to be more comfortable, the Duke resting a hand on her curls. The gentle touch of his fingers entwined in her hair caused a mixture of sensations and the heat was back in her throat again. She had the oddest feeling of embarrassment and yet of complete happiness and something more, deep within her, that she could not explain but which she knew was inexplicably linked to this man and this man alone. She had felt it the very first time she had set eyes on him.

It was at Versailles and he had been fencing in the Princes courtyard watched by two dozen or more admiring onlookers. Stripped to his shirt sleeves, the white shirt billowed about his wide shoulders and was tucked into the waist of a pair of tight black velvet breeches that showed to advantage muscular thighs matched by strong calves encased in black stockings. His hair, without powder and pulled tight off his starkly handsome face, fell in a plait to the middle of his wide back. Watching him thrust and parry with his opponent as they traversed the courtyard she was caught up in the admiration for two well exercised and very skilled practitioners of their art. But her eyes were all for the Duke whom she considered the most magnificent specimen of maleness she had ever seen.

To think she was curled up on his footstool and he caressing her hair was dreamlike. She wondered if she opened her eyes she would wake to find herself back in Maria Caspartti's claustrophobic filthy rooms at Versailles. But his fingers in her hair assured her that it was not a dream and she wished life to remain just as it was, her and the Duke alone together in the quiet of the library without the interference of others, not the Comte de Salvan, not Madame and Lord Vallentine, and most definitely not the Duke's assortment of mistresses.

The Duke's soft-spoken answer to a scratch on the door ended the peace in the library. He did not move or attempt to turn to see who trespassed on his time with Antonia, and as she did not stir he was content to leave her be. The butler informed him Madame had come home, and before Duvalier had a chance to remove the coffee things Lord Vallentine and Madame de Montbrail shattered the last vestiges of one of the most peaceful evenings he had spent in a very long while.

"Bring a new coffee pot, Duvalier," ordered Lord Vallentine. "And port. If there is any food in your larder to throw together a cold collation that would put the growls to rest." He looked about the room with a squint. "Why is it so damned dark in here? Roxton not economising is he, Estée?" He threw his frockcoat on a sofa. "Glad we didn't stay at Duras-Valfons's little affair. She has a pretty way with her and I admit she is fascinating to look at but she wouldn't suit me! You was right too. Pleased with herself ain't she? Glad you settled her on that score, though your brother may not be finished with her yet. At least there's a fire in here. Hey-ho, Roxton!" He took two paces back and grinned like an idiot to discover the Duke's hard gaze upon him. "Told you were in here but didn't see you, did we, Estée?"

Estée had seen her brother and Antonia well before Lord Vallentine had made the discovery. She also saw the girl's head resting against her brother's crossed legs, with her shoes kicked off, and the whippets curled up on the froth of her petticoats. She stared significantly at him, and at his fingers entwined in the girl's honey curls, and sat down heavily on the sofa opposite.

"How was the theatre?" Roxton asked casually.

"Tolerable," she answered in a clipped voice, not looking at him. Then in a rush, because she could not help herself, "The girl should have been put to bed hours ago!"

"Your motherly concern is lost on me, my dear," answered the Duke.

Lord Vallentine stretched out beside Estée and drew out his snuffbox. "Salvan was at the soirée," he said in a low voice. "He was prancing about in those steepled shoes of his laughing like a damned girl! I don't like the look of him. He's too well pleased with himself. That makes me nervous." He took snuff. "The thing is, Roxton, he was very particular in telling me he is going to make a call on you tomorrow."

"Is he? How disappointing for him that I will not be home."

Lord Vallentine eyed Antonia for a moment. "He's not only giving you the pleasure of his company," he said grimly. "He wants to see the girl. Ugh, he offends me! He positively gloats at the mention of her."

"Calm yourself, my dear. I intend to take Antonia with me. We will go for a drive in the country. The fresh air will do her good. I will leave our cousin in your capable hands, Estée."

"As you wish," said Madame. "Do you want to hear about Thérèse's soirée?"

"Not particularly," answered the Duke. "Richelieu in attendance?"

"No. He has to be sent to Flanders at the head of his regiment," Estée told him. "And it seems de La Tournelle has ensnared Louis, for it is whispered she is to be created a Duchesse! Madame de Mailly will surely be banished to Paris—"

"I can think of a worse fate," quipped his lordship.

"But it is horrible for her, Lucian," argued Madame. "She truly loves the King. I do not think Marie-Anne does."

"Then she'll last longer than most," predicted his lordship and leaned forward to help himself to the cold collation just put on the table before him. "Know what, Roxton, I've been thinking—"

"Spare me, I beg of you."

Vallentine ignored the slight. "I don't think much of the whole Salvan clan," he said, pointing a half-chewed bread roll at his friend. "Grandmother, father or son. That boy—"

"Étienne? *Parbleu*! He is just a boy. What have you against him?" demanded Madame. "Tante Victoire and Salvan I can understand, but not Étienne, he is different from them."

"Different, perhaps. But there's something about that lad that won't wash," said his lordship. "He's pleasant enough to you or I and to Roxton, 'cause he's a little frightened of your brother here. But I don't like the way he's been hauntin' this house after Antonia. It unnerves me. And it's obvious the girl ain't keen to see him."

"Do eat that roll, Vallentine. I can't abide it in my face," complained the Duke, and accepted a dish of coffee from his sister with his free hand, careful not to disturb Antonia's slumber. "But go on. Your—er—nerves interest me."

"How can you possibly have anything against that boy?" asked Madame incredulously and looked from one to the other. "How—"

"Let me finish, Estée, then you can scold me if you wish," said Lord Vallentine. "I've been about these past few weeks when the lad has been visiting and I grant he can be very personable. He's a bit sulky but I'll leave that be. He's a black to his father's white. He takes too much of that mixture, call it snuff if you will, but I've got my own ideas about the contents of M'sieur d'Ambert's snuffbox. You remember how upset he was at Rossard's, Roxton? And every time he's come visiting, the poor girl won't see him. Says she ain't up to it. I'll tell you why she ain't up to it—"

"I am at a loss to know what you are trying to imply against Étienne," said Madame in an agitated voice.

"You can say what you like but I think the lad is queer in his attic," Vallentine stated and jabbed a finger at his temple.

"That is utter nonsense, Lucian," was Madame's response. "The boy has a melancholy disposition because his mother died when he was young. She died under difficult circumstances which were not pleasant for a sensitive child such as Étienne to cope with. He was unnaturally attached to her. Salvan, he has never had time for his son. The way you speak of him, it is as if he was some sort of monster! He is young, that is all. Young men, they sometimes do not know how to express their feelings in an elegant way. And what hope has he with Antonia when she has eyes only for my brother? Is it a wonder the boy sulks with such odds against him?" She gave an embarrassed laugh. "You are merely jealous of him, Lucian."

"Jealous? Of a stripling?" scoffed Vallentine.

"You see! You are!"

"I am not!" shouted his lordship, on his feet and glaring at Estée.

"My dears, if you are intent on a quarrel go elsewhere. You will wake Antonia."

"How-how positively *fatherly* of you," Estée lashed out at her brother.

"Now listen, Estée," his lordship demanded angrily, "you leave Roxton be. He made a perfectly reasonable request and we—"

"How like you! How very like you to defend him," she cried and burst into tears and fled the room.

Lord Vallentine stared after her, jaw swinging. He colored up, mumbled unintelligibly to the Duke, kicked a chair leg to vent his frustration, and strode off in pursuit.

Roxton waited a few seconds then peered down at Antonia, gently brushing the mop of curls off her cheek. "You can wake up now. I don't think they will return."

"Oh, you knew I was not asleep?" she said with a chuckle and struggled to sit up. She stretched her arms and tossed her hair over her shoulders. "Was it wrong of me to pretend? I truly was asleep at first but I did not want to interrupt a lover's quarrel you see."

"So you think?"

"Most certainly, Monseigneur. Can you doubt their feelings for one another?" When he made no immediate reply she peeped up at him from slipping on her shoes. "Why does Madame scold Vallentine when she loves him, and why does he not marry her when it is obvious he loves her?"

"Aha. Now there are two questions that require complicated answers. I don't think I am qualified to answer for them."

"Mayhap Madame is hesitant because Vallentine keeps a mistress and she does not approve?"

The Duke scooped up her crumpled ribbon off the carpet. "Most gentlemen do, petite," he answered softly. "That is not an obstruction to marriage."

Antonia slowly brushed back her waist-length hair, wondering how best to answer him. "If I was Madame," she said quietly, "I would not wish to share Vallentine with any female. I would want to be the object of a singular devotion. It is a foolish thought but that is how I would feel—if I was Madame." She regarded him with knit brows, his aquiline profile to the fire. "Do you mind if Vallentine marries your sister?"

"Not in the least," he stated flatly.

"I must go before Vallentine returns. He will ask for your permission tonight I think. *Bonne nuit*, Monseigneur."

"*Bonne nuit, mignonne*," he answered absently, a hand out-stretched to the mantle. He watched the flickering flames a long time, unaware she had slipped away until his thoughts were inter-rupted by footfall. "Antonia, I—"

Lord Vallentine smiled self-consciously. "Gone," he said coming out of the shadows.

The Duke looked at him keenly and did not miss the smudge of lip paint at the corner of his mouth. He closed his eyes briefly and sighed. "You have come to ask me something of grave importance, my dear Vallentine?"

"Well—yes, I suppose I have," his lordship muttered with hunched shoulders. "That is, I want to ask you—possibly you've not guessed that I—that we—"

"The answer is yes. You are welcome to her."

"Well, stamp me if you didn't know already!" He let out a great sigh of relief. "Glad that's done. Never been more frightened of asking you a thing in my life."

"Understandable. Being in love must be the most frightening thing in the world. Good night and—er—congratulations."

Lord Vallentine's eyes widened but he said nothing and smiled to himself as he watched his friend silently leave the library with one of Antonia's ribbons unconsciously dangling between two fingers.

Seven

$\mathcal{A}$ntonia was in the library searching the shelves for a suitable book to read while she waited for the Duke to return from his early morning ride. As soon as he had changed out of his riding habit he was taking her on the promised drive into the country. She really did not feel she could sit still and read, such was her excitement, but the waiting was worse than anything and she had been up and dressed for an hour.

The door opened and she thought it the Duke, but Duvalier ushered in the Vicomte d'Ambert and left at the youth's insolent wave of dismissal. She gave a start then smiled and put out a hand in greeting as he crossed the room. He frowned at her, and at the whippets curled up on the hearth for they had cocked an ear at his intrusion. He did not like dogs and he liked these two even less. They were a reminder of the Duke; that this was his house and that Antonia was under his protection.

He bowed over her hand and stepped back to look her over. "I meant to be here yesterday but father asked that I wait. He is coming especially to see Madame de Montbrail, and you."

She did not like the way he was regarding her from head to foot but still managed a smile. "Have you no word of greeting, Étienne? It has been a while since last we saw each other, has it not?"

"Yes," he replied mechanically.

There was something about her that annoyed him. It was not her appearance, though he couldn't remember when he had seen her looking so pretty. The day gown of dark red velvet became her figure, and the honey curls tied loosely with a red riband fell caressingly about her bare white shoulders. He was pleased she was finally out of the sick-room and seemingly fully recovered from her injury, but it annoyed him she should look so happy and pretty in the house of his father's cousin. In fact, she looked radiant.

She turned away and continued her search of the shelves. "Can you reach the book third along; the one with the burgundy spine?" she asked pointing to a shelf out of her reach. "No, the next one. Yes, you have it. It is a history of the Julio-Claudian emperors. Have you read Tacitus?"

"Did you hear what I said to you?" he demanded.

"Yes," she said and took the book out of his hand. "Your father is coming to visit Madame—"

"—and you," he stated and took snuff.

"You take too much snuff, Étienne."

"That is not for you to say!"

She smiled hesitantly. "There is no need to shout at me. I thought you would be pleased to see me but it does not seem so when all you do is frown." She brushed the hair off her shoulder. "Look. The scar is not so very bad and my arm is not so stiff. So if you are worried lest you think me still ill—"

"Cover your shoulder," he said, averting his eyes. "I don't want to see it. It is a hideous reminder—a reminder you nearly died. If I had done what I threatened and locked you in your room and not let you go to that masquerade…"

"Hush. You cannot blame yourself," she said. "Tell me what you have been doing whilst I have been ill. Have you joined the Academy? Oh, Étienne, do not look at me in that way! I am re-covered, I assure you. And now I can look at the episode as a great adventure! I have never been held up by highwaymen before, not even travelling with Papa. And M'sieur le Duc was very brave to shoot two dead and now—"

"—you are in his house receiving his hospitality when you have no right to be here!" he flung at her.

Antonia stared at him and bit back a retort. She sat down on a sofa by the fire and pretended to read, but all the while she was conscious of the Vicomte staring at her in mutinous silence.

"You are quite content to remain with the persons under this roof, are you not, Antonia?"

"Madame and Monseigneur have been very good to me," she answered without looking up from the printed page.

"And why do you think that is? Why do you think they have been very good to you, bébé Antonia? Look at me when I address you!"

Antonia still did not look up. She knew he was beside her chair and she heard the familiar snap of his snuffbox. The tan whippet moved to sit at her feet and its mate sat up from the hearth. "Étienne," she said calmly, "if you are about to scold me, or try and warn me against M'sieur le Duc de Roxton, or frighten me with one of your silly tales about your father locking you up, I would rather you did not. I will not believe a word of it. That is to say, I do not think you deliberately lie to me, but that your own fears about your father have made you imagine unreasonable fears for my safety. I know it is only because you are worried for me but—"

The Vicomte burst into laughter and stamped a foot upon the upholstered arm of her chair. "Worried for you?" he snorted and snatched the book out of her hands and tossed it over his shoulder. "Look at me," he ordered. "Yes, I am worried for you. But I have more to worry about than you can ever imagine! You truly have no idea what is afoot, do you? You really are a *bébé*!"

"What is the matter with you?" demanded Antonia. "Why do you goad me? What have I done to deserve your anger? If you cannot speak in a civil tongue please go away. And I hope for your sake you have not ruined that book because it is a rare edition and M'sieur le Duc will be very angry with you."

"What a fine lady thinks mademoiselle!" mocked the Vicomte. "You think because Roxton plays the hero he is one? Wrong! Wrong! Wrong! He is merely playing a game with my father. Do you know what the prize is? Your virtue! Yes, oh so shocked Mademoiselle Moran. It is a game they are playing with you and me. The sooner you realise this the sooner you will learn to trust me and do as I say, or both of us will come out the losers. Your precious Duke laughs behind our backs as surely as you sit there with that expression of outrage on your face. He hates my father and my father him. They hate each other so much that they do not care who is hurt in the process of their revenge. Let me tell you a family secret—a scandal involving Roxton and my father. Mayhap it will convince you he is not the man you believe him to be."

"You will not shock me, Étienne," Antonia said stubbornly. "I know precisely what his life is like. So?"

"So? Have you wondered why my father and Roxton hate each other? They, close in age and raised almost as brothers; they who are first cousins. They were very close as boys and as young men they often debauched together. Grandmother told me all about their adventures when young. I do not love my father, but I pity him. He is a great coward. I would have called Roxton out for what he did to my mother. But my father, he cares more for his name than his honor. So he simpers about pretending to be on the best of terms with cousin Roxton, all for the good of the family name. Ugh! I despise him!"

He pulled a face and dipped into the contents of his snuffbox a third time.

"You think I am raving to say all this but I am not. No. You tell yourself the Vicomte d'Ambert is mad, deranged, a foolish boy, but I am telling you only the truth. He is not a good man, Antonia. My father is not a good man but Roxton, he is much worse. My father can never be branded a filthy murderer—"

"Murderer? All because he dared shoot two villains dead? That is not murder," argued Antonia. She shifted so the Vicomte was not so close but he came around to the other side of the chair and blocked her view of the fire. "Étienne, I do not care if he has shot a dozen villains dead."

"Will you still not care when I tell you he killed my mother?" he said softly and smiled to himself when she looked swiftly up at him. "My father loved her very much and she betrayed him. He shut himself away from the court for six months after she died. He did not know she had had a lover until her letters were found. Her letters and those of her lover! This lover made her elaborate promises, and for these she betrayed my father. Then, when this lover deserted her for some other pretty trinket she could not live with the betrayal. She poisoned herself. Her lover did not even have the decency to leave Paris when his villainy was made known to the world. I know. I was twelve years old and I remember M'sieur le Duc's visits to my mother. It disgusts me even now to think about it!"

"I am truly sorry you lost your maman in such—such awful circumstances," Antonia said gently. "The world can be very cruel at times. But you must try not to dwell on such matters. You were only a young boy and so cannot know the whole truth of the matter. How—how can you be certain it was M'sieur le Duc who was your mother's lover? And your father, mayhap it was his great jealousy of M'sieur le Duc which prompted him to accuse him of such cruelty?"

"You are not shocked? You do not care that I tell you he murdered her? He drove her to her death. She would not have poisoned herself if he had not seduced her with false promises and lies and forced her to be unfaithful to my father who loved her!"

"That is unfair! M'sieur le Duc is no rapist. If your maman had been a chaste woman she would not have taken M'sieur le Duc as her lover. I am sorry if that offends you but that is the way of the world, Étienne."

The Vicomte gaped at her and the anger he felt was uncontrollable. "You cold hearted bitch! I will not have my future wife speak of my mother in such a fashion. What do you know about her? You are not fit to speak her name! Father was right. The sooner you are away from here the better for me."

"What are you talking about? Wife? I am not going to marry you, I told you that. Stop talking nonsense," she said in a level voice though he truly frightened her now. She made to stand but he pushed her back in the chair. "M'sieur le Vicomte forgets himself!"

"It is you who forget," he spat out. "At one time you could not wait to flee to England and now you sit in this house as if you have a claim to it. You do not."

Antonia held up her head defiantly but the Vicomte saw his words had had an effect because she was trembling. "When I am well enough I am going to London to live with my grandmother."

"So you think?" sneered d'Ambert. "Your grandmother wants nothing to do with you. She has agreed that you should be cared for by my grandmother until such time as our wedding takes place."

Antonia was out of the chair in an instant and heading for the discarded book when the Vicomte caught her about the waist and pulled her to him. "I do not believe you! You are lying!" she said and struggled to be free of him. "Let go! How dare you touch me!"

"You think I am lying? Just this week Salvan received a letter from the Comtesse de Strathsay. It is true I tell you! Salvan is coming here today to show it to your precious Duke and his sister. Your grandfather will sign our marriage contract and your grandmother has agreed with his wishes. Stop struggling!" he demanded and kicked out a foot at the grey whippet that pawed at his leg. "Call off these stupid animals!" He kicked out again, connected with the tan whippet's soft under-jaw and sent it sprawling backwards with a yelp.

"Leave them be, Étienne," Antonia whispered fearfully. "They are frightened. They will not bother you if you let me go."

He seemed not to hear. He held her closer, causing her to wince with the pain as her stiff arm was forced behind her back. "Why would this grandmother in London want anything to do with you when she has never seen you in her life?" he argued. "Why should she not think a marriage with the Salvan family in your best interests, eh?" He smiled down at her and laughed. "I will not be going to the Bastille you see, because I mean to marry you."

Antonia stared at him in mute disbelief. When he bent and kissed her full on the mouth she flushed scarlet and jerked her head away, down into the crook of her arm.

"To seal the bargain," he explained and attempted a second kiss.

Lord Vallentine strode into the library. Behind him was the Duke. They had just come from the stables. Dust covered their jockey-boots and their riding frocks were slung over a shoulder.

"I warned De Chesnay that last fence was damned difficult," said Lord Vallentine over his shoulder. "But the silly fellow had to try and jump it anyway. It's a small wonder something other than the whalebone in his corset didn't snap!"

"I seem to recall you only warned the—er—silly fellow as he and animal were in full flight of the attempt. Not the most opportune moment to shout out a warning."

His lordship's smile broadened into a grin. "Damned inconsiderate of me, wasn't it?" He glanced back into the room to discover the Vicomte with his arm about Antonia's waist. He was holding her to his chest and kissing her on the mouth. Vallentine sucked in air through his clenched teeth and pretended an instant of blindness when the young couple sprang apart and stood red-faced and guilty in the middle of the carpet. "Where's Duvalier with that bottle of burgundy?" he demanded in a loud voice. "You sure the man ain't getting on a bit in years to be of use to you, Roxton?" He saw the Vicomte as if for the first time. "Didn't know you'd come to visit, d'Ambert. How goes the Academy? I hear you're top of your fencing class."

The Vicomte mumbled an answer and declined to say more. He was acutely conscious of Roxton's hard gaze upon him and he brought himself to stand up tall, despite the sick feeling in the pit of his stomach. The grey whippet still pawed at his leg and refused to be shaken off.

"I came to visit Mademoiselle Moran," he explained looking straight at Lord Vallentine, his face burning bright with a hot flush. "It has been an age since last we spoke. My father, he is to visit also, in a little while. He has a most important letter for M'sieur le Duc. It is from the Comtesse de Strathsay."

"How dare you take such a liberty," hissed the Duke, a sudden constriction in his throat forcing him to swallow hard. He turned his furious gaze upon Antonia, but when she could not bring herself to look up from the riband in her hand he flung his frockcoat over the back of a chair and strode to the writing desk to sort through several cards and invitations awaiting his attention. "Get out, d'Ambert," he ordered, and with snap of his fingers the two whippets came to heel. "Get out before I whip some manners into you!" And turned away, a gilt-edged invitation crushed in his fist.

The Vicomte took a step forward then thought better of it, an eye on the dogs growling softly at their master's feet. A bow to Lord Vallentine and a glance at Antonia and he was gone. She looked at his lordship not knowing what to say by way of explanation. The Duke had his back to her. It was straight and stiff and very unapproachable. She glanced at the ball of paper he had thrown on his desk and swallowed.

"I did not ask him to kiss me. I made him angry and he just grabbed me," she explained to his lordship who smiled encouragingly. "When he gets angry he does strange things and I think he only kissed me because he knew I did not want him to in the least. I should not have made him angry, I know, but he said some horrid things I did not like at all. So I could not let him say them and get away with it could I? You believe me, do you not?" she asked Vallentine in a whisper and added naïvely, "I am glad you interrupted when you did."

"Never would doubt you, little one," he said kindly and brushed her cheek. "'bout time, Duvalier. Where did you trot off to for that bottle—Bordeaux? I'm parched, and you, Roxton? On the table there, and another glass for mademoiselle."

The butler sniffed and bowed, then startled his lordship by smiling at Antonia in a grandfatherly way. "It will take but one moment to fetch mademoiselle a glass."

"If that don't beat all!" announced Vallentine, the butler not quite out of earshot. "The old devil just smiled at Antonia, Roxton. Fair smiled at her and you missed it! Wait 'til I tell Estée. Never seen the old sober-sides smile, ever."

"Do shut up, Vallentine!" The Duke tossed to one side a card he'd been inspecting through his quizzing-glass and propped himself on a corner of the desk. "In half an hour we leave for our drive," he stated to Antonia, finally meeting her gaze. "I suggest you see to your—your hair. Tie it up."

"Yes, M'sieur le Duc," she murmured and hurriedly threaded the crumpled velvet ribbon through her curls. She could not understand why he was angry with her when it was the Vicomte who had taken unwanted liberties. It should have been evident that she was not a willing participant, besides which it had been a very clumsy kiss. "Monseigneur, you cannot think I wanted Étienne to kiss me?"

"We will talk about this later."

Antonia blinked at him. The heightened color in his cheeks and the hard set of his jaw confused her, as did his continued anger. "No, M'sieur le Duc, we will talk about it now because it is obvious you are angry with me and I do not know why when I explained to you that I—"

"Later," the Duke enunciated through clenched teeth, a quick glance at Lord Vallentine who had discreetly retreated to inspect a row of leather-bound books on one of the library shelves.

But Antonia stood her ground, clear green eyes never wavering from his tight face. "You think because I am a female who barely reaches your shoulder that I am incapable of defending myself? Had you not interrupted when you did I would have slapped his face for his impertinence, or put my knee into his tender male parts as Maria Caspartti showed me is the way to fend off unwanted attentions. How else did M'sieur le Duc think I managed to defend my virtue in a place like Versailles?"

Roxton stared at her for what seemed like minutes. "I did not think about it, Antonia. And for that I am truly sorry," he answered softly. "Now please fetch your cloak and muff, there is a cool breeze today."

"Yes, Monseigneur," she smiled and dropped a quick curtsey before she fled to the door. A glance at Lord Vallentine and she wondered why that gentleman's jaw was swinging.

His lordship was staring open-mouthed at his friend because he had never heard him be contrite. He had to concede that there were depths to the Duke that he had not known existed, depths that were being brought to the surface by a plain spoken girl who was barely out of the schoolroom.

At the door, Antonia chanced to look back into the room and caught the Duke regarding her steadily. Their eyes met. His were the first to look away. For once she was unable to interpret the emotion in his face and that bothered her, as did the Vicomte's declarations concerning Salvan having a signed marriage contract from her grandfather and her grandmother's unconcern for her welfare. But she forced herself to push these fears to the back of her mind. She wanted this day to be special. After all, it was her birthday and she wouldn't allow the Salvans to spoil this of all days.

⁓〜⌒⌒

The Comte de Salvan bowed low over his cousin Estée's plump white hand, brushing it with his wet lips. As he straightened he smiled into her fair face and cursed himself for the hundredth time for not taking his mother's advice. He should have offered for her as soon as she was out of mourning. In the years since the death of her husband he had hinted that it would not be such a bad thing for both families if they were to marry. She had laughed him away and he had joined in her amusement, but was uncertain if she laughed with him or at him. He wondered if he should still make her an offer and if Roxton would be favourable to such a union. He thought not and was not about to try his luck.

Estée rang a small silver hand-bell and to the maid who came at her bidding she ordered the afternoon coffee tray to be brought to her salon. The Comte perched on a dainty chair of gilt and striped silk and flicked out his skirts of stiff gold thread careful not to crush them. He set his walking cane with its polished gold top between his high heeled leather shoes with their enormous tongues and leaned on it in an affected manner.

"It has been an age since last I visited you, Estée," he said with a quick pleasing glance about the decidedly feminine room. "I must try and visit more often, but you know how it is at court. Again I tell you to come to court where your beauty can be appreciated. And I am selfish. I want someone to gossip with. Someone who understands Salvan. Who better than you, Cousin? We would enjoy ourselves. I would enjoy myself if you would only come to court once in a little while." He shrugged his shoulders and sighed dramatically.

"Not even mon cousin visits Versailles these days. His sexual escapades have always amused. I ask myself: what keeps him in Paris? Thérèse, she tells me on her honor—which in itself is amusing, yes?—that he neglects her! Can you believe it? I would not have believed it possible had I not seen with my own eyes that he does not show himself at her soirée. All Paris wonders at his absence. Poor Thérèse, she was most offended, was she not." He sniggered and intended to go on but a footman came in with the coffee things and a large plate of the Comte's favorite gateaux. A compulsive sweet-eater this was enough to divert him from his run of conversation.

"You overwhelm me, Salvan," said Madame with a smile. "I am flattered you think me needed at court, but I have been away so many years now that my interest wanes more and more. There was a time when I, too, could not go a day without knowing the latest on-dits. And so many sleepless nights did I have worrying about what was being said of me behind my back and by whom. Now, I do not care in the least. It is not important to me. I am happier in Paris."

"I wish it was so with Salvan," said the Comte and licked the cream from his lips. "It is a constant worry to me that you do not remarry. You need a man to take care of you. Not as Roxton does; that is a brother's way. That can hardly satisfy a woman of your beauty. No, a man who can appreciate you. This cake, it is delicious. I must have its recipe. Will you part with it?"

"I will have Jacques write it out for you," she promised. "Though I warn you he does not like giving away his little secrets. Another slice, Salvan?"

Salvan put out his plate. "What is it about you, Estée, that intrigues me today. Last night that sparkle was not in your so lovely eyes. Ah, you blush! Tell, Salvan. You have a new lover?"

"There is no secret," she said. "I am betrothed to the Vicomte Vallentine. You are the first in Paris to know. Are you pleased for me? Shall you congratulate your cousin?"

It was only for a matter of a moment that the Comte's total surprise showed itself in a heavy frown but almost instantly he set aside his dish and threw up his hands. "So sudden," he said with forced gaiety. "It is a most interesting piece of news. All Paris must be told. It must be shouted from all points. *Bon Dieu*, but I cannot believe it! And here was Salvan always ready to offer his name and rank to no other, and you, you take another in his place!" He kissed his fingertips. "Just so! I am devastated. But I will rejoice for you. This M'sieur Vallentine is a good sort of man I think. Very handsome and tall and of the English complexion. A most exceptional swordsman. I envy him. I congratulate him too. Tell me your plans. When do you marry? Will you invite Salvan to the festivities?"

"It will be soon. That is all I can tell you. Lucian only spoke to my brother last evening so there is much that still needs to be finalised. We have not discussed where we will live permanently. We will of course have a house here in Paris but mayhap we will spend a good deal of our time in London."

"London! *Parbleu*, but that is another world away. You cannot be serious. London? It is not Paris. I must persuade this Vallentine to keep you in Paris. Let him return to London by all means but, Estée, you will wilt in London."

"It will not be as bad as you think," she said defensively. "London is Lucian's home. That is where his family is."

The Comte was not to be convinced. "Where will you shop? What will you eat? Where will you get a decent chef? It is a horror you cannot imagine, Estée. Love has blinded you. You cannot even speak the Englishman's barbaric tongue."

"La! Salvan! You think me going into exile. You forget I am half English. My Papa, he was an Englishman. Lucian assures me all well-bred Englishmen speak our tongue. So, these problems they solve themselves." Madame poured out more coffee into the Comte's dish. "And I need not concern myself with these trifles immediately. Lucian is taking me into the Italian States for our honeymoon. He has a cousin with a villa in some quaint little town I cannot remember the name of, but it will be wonderful."

Salvan shrugged one shoulder in a gesture of finality. He smiled. "I wish you joy. My mother, she will be delighted. For years she has lamented your continued widowhood. And now! What a surprise for her."

"Thank you, Cousin. I could not face Tante Victoire with the news so soon. She-she does not know Lucian and she loathes all things English with a passion I find incomprehensible."

"I understand. Salvan, he will arrange it all." He shifted to sit next to her on the damask covered sofa, his smile no less broad. "It is as well I visited today," he said in a low voice, "so that arrangements can be made post-haste for the little mademoiselle's future. I will applaud your sensibility in this matter. It is for the best. I know you cannot but agree with me. Everything arranges itself. The last thing you need is to watch over a girl when you have so many preparations of your own to consider. She will only be under your feet."

"We-we have grown very fond of her," said Madame quietly. "She is not the least burden to us. In fact I will miss her very much when she leaves to go to her grandmother in England."

The Comte let fall his gay façade. "But she is not going to England," he stated bluntly. He produced a letter from a flowered waistcoat pocket. "Read this. It is of enormous interest. It is from the girl's grandmother." He smiled to himself when Estée snatched the papers from his hand and he sat back and watched her scan the lines of scrawl, enjoying her look of growing outrage and discomfort with an expression of sympathetic superiority.

"As you see, the Comtesse is happy indeed to have the child placed in the care of my mother until my son's wedding," he said. "A double nuptial for the Salvans! Madame Strathsay, she wants what is best for the child. And what is best for the child is to be married to my son without delay. Are you not pleased for us? And the little mademoiselle, she is done a great honor to be chosen to be my son's bride. Her grandmother recognises this fact and wishes the union joy."

All Estée's usual buoyancy drained from her. She did not know why she should feel a sudden dread at the prospect of Antonia's marriage to the Vicomte d'Ambert because she had been in favor of the match from the beginning. Perhaps it was her own recent betrothal that had put everything into perspective and she could more readily see Vallentine's point of view. Besides it was basic female intuition that told her to be wary of her cousin the Comte and his motives and she would trust in this instinct before anything else.

"I am not at all convinced the girl is well enough to leave the hôtel so soon," she said, grabbing at straws. "Mayhap in a couple of weeks…"

"Oh no, dearest cousin," stated Salvan with a sweet smile and pocketed the letter. There was a flat note of anger in the nasal voice which put Estée on the alert. "The girl has had ample time to recover under this roof. Tomorrow I will come to collect what is mine." He placed his hand over hers and squeezed. "Think, Estée. The child cannot possibly remain here once you are married. One shudders at the thought of her here, without you, without a proper chaperone, and with only mon cousin in residence."

Madame withdrew her hand. "Roxton looks on Antonia as one would one's own child, as a father would a daughter. I will not allow you to make anything more of the situation. It is ridiculous that you should do so to me, his sister."

"No? You know your brother better than I," said the Comte and took snuff. "You do not believe the past dozen or more years attest to a reputation most disreputable? What is one pretty female compared to another? They all serve to satisfy an enormous appetite. Is he not *au fai* in such matters?"

"Antonia is different. She does not play the coquette with him and he—he has become very protective of her."

"I do not believe you can be so easily duped by his many techniques of seduction?" said the Comte incredulously. "I admire his ingenuity in orchestrating these little affairs of the heart. Such resourcefulness! Not even that consummate player of such games, the Duc de Richelieu, could think up a more complete way to capture the heart of a young and impressionable girl."

Estée brought herself to sit up tall and she glared at the Comte de Salvan with large blue eyes full of alarm. "What are you suggesting, Salvan?"

"You have not heard the latest rumor concerning your brother?" asked the Comte affecting surprise. "Me, I do not know if I believe the whole. But there are those who do, a great many who do. They applaud M'sieur le Duc his tactics on the one hand, and on the other?" He shrugged. "They deplore such vulgar use of an innocent. I say the girl's injury was an accident. Not even he would dare stoop so low. No. That is too much even for Salvan to believe. He hired one too many scum. That two died is no matter. We are well rid of them. The one who shot at the carriage, he disappeared, and mayhap he feared he was the next for the bullet? Roxton will find him, have no fear of that. To shoot your accomplices dead is very ingenious. There can be no tales. Then who can say it was anything but truly a hold-up on the Versailles road?"

"That is what happened," Madame declared angrily. "These highwaymen they are everywhere. We are not safe, our carriages are never safe from attack. It is a daily occurrence. I do not understand at all what you are implying. What is this rumor?"

"Do not alarm yourself, my dearest cousin," soothed the Comte. "As I said, me, I do not believe it. But if for one moment let us pretend we do believe it. Why! M'sieur le Duc your brother is a genius. He spirits away the little mademoiselle to Paris where she will be safe from unwanted attentions. And then? They are held up by these men who call themselves highwaymen. M'sieur le Duc is very brave and mur—kills two of them who dare to offend his person and his property. The little mademoiselle, she is hurt. An unfortunate circumstance he did not account for, but she will recover. So! What has mon cousin achieved? He has the girl and her total devotion for his daring deeds. He must wait out her recovery but what is that to him? He has the prize! His plan worked, and my son's life it is made miserable! I tell you, Estée, what am I to do to restore my—my *son's* happiness?"

Estée was appalled. "This rumor circulating Paris, who dared to start it? It is a monstrous piece of villainy. I knew Roxton was envied and disliked by those who do not know him well but this, this rumor, it disgusts me! Can he be so hated that it is dared whispered he staged a hold-up of his own carriage all to impress a girl not quite twenty years old? It is so ludicrous as to be laughable!" she scoffed.

The more she thought on the idea the broader her smile became until the laughter bubbled up in her throat and she giggled. The Comte stared at her not knowing whether to join in her laughter or continue to appear grave-faced as he thought the situation deserved.

"Oh, Salvan, you must tell Roxton all about this rumor," she said dabbing at her watery eyes with a small lace handkerchief. "If only he was home now. It will amuse him, I know it will. The person who started this ludicrous tale should write for the Comédie Française. It is obvious this person is insanely jealous of my brother. Does he think my brother needs impress a female by going to such lengths? Ridiculous! Only M'sieur le Duc de Richelieu contrives such ridiculous schemes in order to bed a female. Do you not think it all one big joke?"

"Joke?" whispered the Comte. When he realised his cousin was in earnest he forced himself to laugh too. "A joke! Yes, a joke! Ludicrous! As I said, I do not believe it for one moment. A tale put about by an-an idiot! A jealous idiot!"

Madame glanced at him over the rim of her porcelain dish and smiled slyly. The laughter had vanished from her eyes leaving them hard and cold. "Roxton will be amused at first but then I think he will want to know the name of the person who dared to try slander his good name. He will seek to teach this jealous idiot a lesson. You would do the same in such circumstances, would you not, Salvan?"

"Call the man out?" stammered the Comte. "Yes, yes of course I would! It is the only response to such slanders, I agree."

"Another slice of cake perhaps?" asked Madame sweetly. "And let me refill your dish. You have gulped down all your coffee."

"You are too good to Salvan. This Vallentine, this scoundrel who has taken you from me, it is he who should be called out for ruining your cousin's happiness."

"I ain't adverse to the idea," said his lordship who lounged in the doorway picking at his teeth with a gold toothpick.

The Comte almost leapt from the sofa with fright as Lord Vallentine came further into the room. His lordship kissed his betrothed's forehead and said casually,

"I trust the good Comte hasn't been filling your little ear with idle gossip, my love?"

"Never idle gossip, m'sieur," said the Comte with a bow. "I congratulate you on your betrothal. You are a lucky man, M'sieur Vallentine. You find me speechless that she is taken from me! I am envious beyond words. I cannot tell you what this has done to me. Now it is too late for Salvan. Ah! But that is the way of the world is it not, m'sieur?"

"For a man who's speechless you can still manage a mouthful," observed Vallentine. "But I thank you for your congratulations, if that's what you meant by that mouthful of platitudes."

Madame handed him a dish of coffee. "Salvan has just been telling me the latest most interesting whisper circulating the salons. It involves Roxton, naturally."

"Naturally! When don't it?" said his lordship with a grunt.

"It is nothing, nothing at all," responded the Comte expansively. "I tell Estée only to amuse her. A rumor. Nothing but a rumor put about by an idiot—a jealous idiot. We will please forget all about it."

"No, Salvan, you must tell Lucian. It is most interesting. Especially now that Lucian is to be a member of our family. As

Roxton's brother-in-law he has a right to know what is being said."

Salvan made a noise in his throat similar to that of a startled pheasant and gulped down cold coffee.

"I'm ready for an interesting tale," said Lord Vallentine sitting forward. "And any tale about Roxton is bound to make me laugh because it always distorts the truth. And if you say this particular rumor was put about by a jealous idiot then I'm all ears. And when ain't a rumor about Roxton spread by such numbskulls?" His lordship sat back and smiled. "Though, I wouldn't like to perpetuate slander 'bout the Duke. He's rather sensitive to it, y'see. For that matter, so am I about me and my own. He's mighty handy with a pistol but give him a foil and he's just as deadly. And there's more sport in a good cut and thrust, ain't there, Comte?"

"Yes that is so," agreed the Comte with a nervous laugh. He looked at the pearl face of his pocket-watch. "The porter informed me M'sieur le Duc had gone out. He disappoints me by his absence. And the little mademoiselle?"

"Gone for a drive in the country with Roxton," Vallentine informed him. "Can't say when they'll return. I'll give him your regards. Dare say you've got other calls to make in Paris before you return to Versailles."

"Not at all," said the Comte. "I do not return to court until the morrow so I can keep you both company all the afternoon."

"The son in the morning and the downpour in the afternoon," murmured his lordship with annoyance. "Listen, Comte. Estée and I don't know when they'll be back. You might have a long wait."

"But it is soon the dinner hour. He will be home to dinner? It would be too bad for him if he was not."

"What do you mean?" growled his lordship. "He'll be here. He's got to be—"

"Lucian!"

Salvan smiled and bowed to both. "Thank you. I must speak to mon cousin on a matter of great importance. Immediately."

"Salvan has a letter from the little one's grandmamma," burst out Estée. "She-she does not want her. She has given permission for the girl to be—"

"Hush, love," ordered Lord Vallentine with a meaningful stare. "This ain't the time to discuss such matters. Leave it to Roxton.

He'll know what's to be done—"

"To be done?" echoed the Comte. "But it is obvious what *must* be done! She must come with me. Everything is arranged. She is betrothed to my son. As I said to Estée all that is needed is the old Earl's signature—"

"Well, we'll wait for that," interrupted his lordship. "Until the old man puts ink to parchment I don't think you've got a right to demand anything."

"Pardon, m'sieur," said the Comte sweetly, "as you say it is a matter betwixt mon cousin and I."

"Lucian, please, you must sit down," pleaded Estée and grabbed at his hand.

A commotion in the adjoining antechamber diverted them and Lord Vallentine sat down again. Madame fumbled with the porcelain dishes and stacked plates onto a tray for want of something to do to break the heavy silence in the salon. His lordship fidgeted at her side and rummaged for a snuffbox while the Comte sat forward, expectant, for he recognised the deep smooth voice of the Duke and the tinkle of female laughter. He was not to be disappointed.

$\mathcal{E}$ight

$\mathcal{T}$he salon door burst open and Antonia swept in divested of warm cloak, muff and bonnet. She was laughing over her shoulder in response to something the Duke had said as he followed her into the room. She almost collided with Madame, who had jumped up off the sofa to greet them, but the Duke, whose face was tinged with color and uncustomarily all smiles, steered her clear and she turned to Estée with bright eyes and a happy smile.

"We have had such a day, Madame!" Antonia said breathlessly, kissing Estée's cheeks. "There was no hint of bad weather and the sunshine made it seem not so cold. We saw plenty of deer in the forest and Grey and Tan had the most wonderful time chasing them about the wood. It exhausted them I think." She stripped off her gloves and threw them on a small table by the door. "Monseigneur took me to this quaint little village with a water wheel where we had our nuncheon and visited a fête. There were so many, many stalls, and wait until I tell you about the—"

She broke off abruptly, aware Madame de Montbrail looked anything but happy. There were tears in the woman's blue eyes which she was quick to dab away but Antonia saw them and frowned. "What is the matter?" she asked softly and looked over Madame's shoulder. She saw Lord Vallentine and the Comte and glanced swiftly up at the Duke for guidance.

Roxton had spied the Comte de Salvan immediately upon entering the room. He heard Antonia's stammered apology but when she shrank toward him he propelled her forward with a hand firmly in the small of her back.

"My dear Salvan, we had all but given you up visiting my house," he drawled. "I trust you have spent a pleasant afternoon?"

"A most pleasant afternoon," replied the Comte. He presented the newcomers with a magnificent bow, the long white ruffles of one sleeve sweeping the carpet. He could not even bring himself to look at his cousin such was his distraction with Antonia. He openly appraised her from head to foot allowing his eyeglass to linger longer than was polite at the low-cut bodice that show-cased the high swell of her full breasts. He smiled appreciatively and let fall the glass. "A most pleasant afternoon," he echoed. "I am all joy for your sister and M'sieur Vallentine. It was a shock to me, this announcement, because it was so sudden! I came expecting to find you home. My son, he said you were at home. He was here this morning, yes? To visit you, mademoiselle. He said you were recovered but I had no idea how—how delightfully recovered…" He dared to move closer, but when Antonia shivered her disgust he smiled acidly. "Come now, my dear, have you no kind words for one who has longed to see you up and about and fully yourself again? Your illness has deprived Salvan of your beauty and your so unusual wit."

With a push from the Duke Antonia went forward and reluctantly held out her hand.

"I am well, thank you, M'sieur le Comte," she said and managed a pretty curtsey, but she could not bring herself to smile.

When the painted little man kissed her hand it was Vallentine who grunted his displeasure at the Comte's flowery mannerisms. And when Salvan refused to relinquish his hold on Antonia's wrist and had her sit close beside him on the sofa it was Vallentine who was out of his chair, but a quick dark look from the Duke and he sat down again.

"Maurice has done you justice, mademoiselle," Salvan was saying. "And to see you laugh so prettily with mon cousin the Duke, it fills me with joy. The air at court must not suit. Yet, Paris? Or perhaps it is another ingredient which fires your so beautiful eyes? I was just saying to Estée, Roxton, that the Parisian air does not suit Thérèse Duras-Valfons at all. She was in a mute rage last night, was she not, Estée? And all because you did not attend her soirée. It annoyed her beyond belief, your absence. I think she will go back to court and to the arms of that snivelling lover of hers, you know the one, the English Baron, if you are not careful. But," and he kissed Antonia's hand a second time, "Salvan, he understands the reason for your momentary distraction from the talented and blue-eyed Thérèse…"

"Coffee?" asked Madame in a voice that broke. She signalled to the maid who hovered at the door to come closer. "You both must be thirsty after your adventures. Would you like coffee, Antonia? Lucian, what say you?"

"Splendid idea," voiced his lordship heartily. He sauntered over to where the Duke still stood and whispered near his ear. "Duvalier has it all arranged. Just as you ordered. I enlisted the help of your valet, too."

But Roxton was not attending him. He was staring fixedly at his cousin. His cousin's methods of seduction had always disinterested him. Occasionally he was amused by them. But watching him visually strip Antonia bare filled him with repugnance. Just as earlier in the day so too had the Vicomte's outrageous behavior. It had taken all his self-control not to turn on the youth with violence. As it did now to mask his true feelings with a façade of indifference. Such intensity of emotion was rare in him, but he was not blind to its source which was surprising and more than a little disturbing. When he heard the Comte ask after Antonia's damaged shoulder he thought it time to intervene.

"If you cannot make light conversation which will amuse us I suggest you keep your pretty mouth shut," said the Duke. "Estée, where is the promised refreshment?"

Lord Vallentine sat forward and smiled at Antonia. "So you had a pleasant day, little one?"

Glad to be able to finally turn away from the Comte's penetrating gaze Antonia nodded eagerly. "We had a wonderful day, Vallentine. Did we not, M'sieur le Duc?"

"Very enjoyable."

"Tell us about this fête you went to and about your nuncheon in the village," coaxed Madame.

Antonia was only too pleased to oblige. Anything to forget the Comte's presence. "At this ancient village—it was ancient because there is a road built by the Romans, and a water-wheel we do not know how old, but it is old—we fell in company with a group of travellers whose French tongue was not the best," explained Antonia. "They were from Venice, you see, and all old gentlemen. I do not know what they are doing in France for they did not say. I think perhaps they are just curious and want to see a little of the world. But as not all of them were fluent in French we spoke to them in their own tongue." She looked reproachfully at his lordship. "You must take back what you said, Vallentine, because Monseigneur speaks Italian just as well as anyone I know!"

"What did I say?" stuttered his lordship. "I ain't a mind reader, chit. Don't look at me in that way, Roxton. I don't remember for God's sake! Ask Antonia."

"I will not repeat it now," said Antonia loftily, the dimple showing itself.

Madame smiled at the treatment of her betrothed. "Go on with your story, child. Lucian you can berate over dinner."

"Yes, I am sorry. Vallentine interrupted me—"

"Inter—Oh, I'll be quiet!" mumbled his lordship.

"These gentlemen were so happy to hear their own tongue that we talked with them for almost an hour. And one of them was an artist, for while we conversed he took out his blotter and inks and made a very tolerable likeness of me which he presented to M'sieur le Duc." She turned to Madame and whispered. "You will never guess what this Venetian said to Monseigneur! I thought it amusing, but he was very put out and went to great pains to correct M—"

"That will do, Antonia," said Roxton reproachfully. "Estée is not the least interested."

"I am."

"And if she ain't, I am!"

"If it has amused mademoiselle," put in Salvan, "then we too shall be amused."

"No, Antonia," said the Duke.

"Come and whisper the Venetian's words in my ear," suggested his lordship. "If I think it worth repeating then you may say it out loud."

"Very fair," agreed the Comte.

Antonia leapt up at Lord Vallentine's invitation but half-way across the room she had a change of heart and instead crossed to the Duke's chair. She stood with her back to the Comte and Estée. "I will not tell them if you do not wish it," she said in a low voice. "I thought it amusing only because you were so shocked he mistook you for my father. You were very angry with him I think. But is that such a bad thing? At least he did not have the indecency to suggest you were my lover and I your whore."

The Duke drew her closer. "Believe me, Antonia, I am no fit man for you in either role. Do you understand?"

She frowned, head tilted to one side. "No, Monseigneur. In my heart I do not believe that."

This intimate scene was too much for the Comte. Although he could not see their faces or hear their words their close proximity was enough to have the Comte out of his chair. He jumped to his heels and slammed the end of his cane into the deep pile of the carpet with a thud. "Roxton! Attend to me! We must speak, you and I. *Parbleu*! It is urgent!"

Lord Vallentine who had been regarding the Duke and Antonia with a silly sentimental smile was also on his feet, but it was Madame who intervened.

"Antonia, it is late," she said in a nervous voice. "You must change your travelling gown before dinner. I have had your girl lay out the oyster silk Maurice thought suited you best."

Antonia hesitated. Still holding the Duke's hand she looked from Madame to the Duke, from the Comte to Lord Vallentine, whose fingers stole to where the hilt of his sword would normally rest at his side, and back to the Duke.

"A word, Roxton," stated Salvan shrilly, taking a step closer to his cousin. Lord Vallentine did likewise.

"You won't let him take me, will you?" Antonia whispered in panic. "Promise me you won't give me to him."

Madame put an arm about Antonia's shoulders. She wished her brother would say something but he just sat there looking at Antonia with a blank expression. "Come, child, it is time we were changing for dinner."

Antonia pulled away from her. "No! I want Monseigneur to promise—"

Roxton kissed her hand, a fleeting look at his cousin who hovered at the girl's back. "Go with Estée," he said and stood up to attend to the Comte. "My dear, you really must learn to control such ill humors. I fear for your health. Have you been bled lately? There is your problem, Salvan. A good bleeding would restore your usual good humor. Would it not, Vallentine?"

"Aye," answered his lordship with a grim smile.

The Duke sensed the ladies had not left the room and he turned on them angrily. "*Allons!* Take the girl away," he growled and turned back to the Comte with a cool smile. "Surely, whatever you have to say can wait until I've had my dinner?"

"No! That is—It is very important I speak with you immediately. You know why I am here."

"That ain't very polite, Salvan. Roxton's request is a simple one."

"Yes, but I—"

"The least you can do in consideration of how your son acted this morning"

"Acted, m'sieur?"

"Yes. Not very gentlemanly of him to force his damned attentions on the girl—"

"What!" gasped the Comte. "He told me nothing of this. What did he do, Roxton?"

"It don't bear repeatin'," said Lord Vallentine as he guided the little man to the door. "Just be glad Roxton had the presence of mind to forgive the lad his forwardness. Now, if he'd been in my house, well, I'd not have let him off so damned lightly. But let's not discuss it. We want our dinner and you'll be wanting yours. It'll be a long affair so you needn't be on the doorstep too soon. I'm sure you understand the situation—"

"Understand?" the Comte scoffed. "I only concede because Roxton, he is mon cousin. It is a family matter and so I am a gentleman. As a man I recognise the power of the little mademoiselle's attractions. So, I let him have his last supper!" He laughed at his own wit and allowed himself to be guided down the sweeping stairs to the foyer. "A last supper, eh, Vallentine?"

"I heard and it ain't humorous."

Lord Vallentine pulled the Comte by his great cuff out of earshot of the porter and an attending footman. "Now listen to me, Salvan," he said quietly. "If I had my way you'd not get a greasy paw on that girl. But it ain't my affair, so I don't draw my blade and teach you the lesson you deserve for praying on the likes of innocents. And one other thing I'd like you to remember next time you feel free and easy 'bout spouting my friend's intentions about the place: You've got it all wrong about Roxton. I'll tell you this and you won't repeat it because you're a sensible man, and I'll run you through if I hear one whisper of it: the Duke's only got the girl's best interests at heart, nothin' more or less. He ain't goin' to seduce her, he merely seeks to protect her."

"*Malheur!* A man such as mon cousin not want to seduce a pretty female?" exclaimed the Comte with a swagger to his gait. "With his reputation? That I do not believe! I laugh at the very idea!"

"Remember, one word and I'll run you through."

The Comte de Salvan affected a wounded look. He permitted a footman to shrug him into his roquelaure and another to open the door to his sedan-chair. "Why would I repeat what you have told me because no one would believe me should I say a word. And I will forgive you your great rudeness in threatening me because, although you are a barbarian, you are to marry Estée. It is for her sake I will not be offended. That you are to marry her causes me great sadness. It wounds me but I shall live. You think Salvan cares nothing for what is in the child's best interests. You are wrong, my friend. Mademoiselle will be well cared for once she is my daughter-in-law. My son, I shall see to it, will make her happy. All will be respectable. I give you my word."

Lord Vallentine watched the Comte assisted into his sedan-chair and be carried away. He dragged himself up the stairs to change for dinner. He had no faith whatsoever in the Comte's assurances.

~⁓—⁓~

When the Duke escorted Antonia through to the vast dining room she found Madame and Lord Vallentine already standing behind their respective chairs. The long mahogany table had had two leaves removed to make the meal a more intimate affair. It was set with the best Dresden china and gold plate. Both crystal chandeliers were polished to dazzling brilliance and blazed with light. On the polished table crystal bowls brimming with freshly cut flowers mingled with dome-covered silver dishes of various shapes and sizes. Duvalier and four liveried footmen stood by the sideboard in attendance and awaited the Duke's pleasure.

Antonia hesitated. "Why is Madame not at her usual place at the foot of the table?" she asked.

"Tonight you are to sit there," answered Estée with a bright smile.

Antonia looked to the Duke for confirmation and when he nodded she went to her place, a footman quick to draw out her chair. "You've put the best service out tonight and there are— *Eh bien*!" She saw the wrapped packages tied up with ribbons and her eyes widened. "I thought you had—I did not expect you would know—" She glanced up at the others who had sat down and gave an embarrassed laugh. "You knew it was my birthday all along!"

"Well, sit down and open your gifts," demanded his lordship. "Mine's the one with the big red bow."

Antonia obediently spread out her petticoats and sat down, her embarrassment disappearing at the prospect of opening her gifts. She held up a long flat box tied up with red ribbon and shook it. "There is nothing in this one."

"Hey!" demanded Vallentine. "Have a care!"

She laughed and put the parcel back on the table. "Mayhap I will unwrap that one last." When Vallentine frowned she untied the red bow with a tug. "No, I will unwrap M'sieur le Duc's gifts last and yours first, Vallentine." Inside the parcel was a delicate fan of painted chicken-skin, the sticks of silver, and with a pearl and silver-thread tassel. "It is very beautiful, Vallentine, thank you. I have never had a fan of such—quality and—taste." She opened it with an expert flick of the wrist and fluttered it playfully as she had seen many a lady do at court. "This is how I shall use my lord's fan when I go to Operas and balls. I hold it just like a great lady, do I not, Monseigneur?"

"Just so, *mignonne*."

Vallentine laughed. "A great lady, eh? You'll be that and much more one day, chit! Open Estée's gift. I'm anxious."

Antonia put aside the fan and picked up a rather large soft package and felt its contents cautiously. "What can this be? Do you wish to hazard a guess, Vallentine?"

"Not necessary. I know what's in that one. Open it."

"You are extremely anxious, is he not, M'sieur le Duc? Mayhap I will open the rest of my gifts after we dine."

"If you wish."

"Don't encourage her, Roxton," snapped Vallentine. "You're goading me, minx! I want you to hurry with Estée's gift so we can see what Roxton has for you. He's been damned secretive, I can tell you. Haven't been able to prise it out of him."

"Thank you so much, Lucian," sulked Estée, feigning hurt feelings.

"Damme! I didn't mean anything by it," apologised Vallentine. "It's just—well aren't you curious to know what your brother got the chit?"

The ladies laughed at him and he grumbled something about a female conspiracy and fell silent.

Madame de Montbrail had given Antonia a pair of lavender kid gloves and a ball mask of peacock feathers. She tried on her new gloves and held the mask up by its painted handle and cooed with delight.

"This is a proper mask. Thank you, Madame. Do you think Grandmother Strathsay might hold a masked ball in my honor, M'sieur le Duc?"

"Undoubtedly, once she has seen your mask. How could she refuse you?"

"I have never had such a delightful birthday as this!"

"There are two more parcels to unwrap," Vallentine reminded her as casually as he could manage.

Antonia dutifully put away the mask and new gloves and gave her full attention to the remaining gifts. Each was wrapped in silver tissue and tied up with black ribbons. She chose the larger of the two. "It is a book."

"How d'you know that?" asked Vallentine. "It ain't unwrapped yet."

It was a book, a slim volume of poetry, and she opened the cover and found the Duke had inscribed it for her. Before Madame could ask to see it she covered it in tissue paper and set it aside.

"I hope it is a fit and proper book for the girl," Madame said primly.

"Would I give her any other kind, Estée?" answered her brother and sipped at the claret in his crystal glass.

With the last gift Antonia was very deliberate. When she had finally removed the outer wrappings she held in her hand a long slim case covered in black velvet. She did not immediately open it but set it before her and stared at it with knitted brows.

"For pity's sake, Antonia!" pleaded Lord Vallentine, all self-control lost. "I can't bear this procrastination a minute longer. The damned thing can't open itself!"

She grabbed up the case and hastily prised it open with a laugh. What she saw inside made her instantly snap shut the lid and push it from her. She looked up at the Duke and found it very difficult to speak.

"M'sieur le Duc, are—are you sure this is for me?"

Roxton's dark eyes held hers and he smiled thinly. "To match your eyes, *mignonne*."

"I've had enough of this!" declared Vallentine and leapt out of his chair to snatch up the case.

"No!" commanded Antonia and ran with the case down the length of the table. She held it out to the Duke with a shy smile. "You will put it on me please?"

He put down his glass and beckoned her closer. "Turn about and stand still," he ordered softly. "And be good enough to hold that unruly mop of curls off your neck."

From the velvet case the Duke produced the most exquisite emerald and diamond choker Estée had ever set eyes on; each emerald the size of her brother's smallest fingernail and divided one from the other by a sparkling diamond. She stared open-mouthed as he slipped the heavy string about Antonia's throat and deftly twisted the diamond clasp into place. The precious stones were indeed the color of the girl's eyes.

Antonia felt for the jewelled collar and fingered it gently. "I cannot see it. I must—find a looking glass," she murmured and fled the room.

Lord Vallentine was as struck dumb as Estée and they stared at one another across the table with wide eyes and parted lips.

The Duke signalled for Duvalier to start serving dinner, saying over his shoulder, "No claret for Mademoiselle Moran. Barbados will suffice."

"I should have guessed!" his sister said with a brittle laugh, finally overcoming her amazement. "When I suggested you give the girl a collar I didn't mean for you to take me literally."

"But how perceptive your jest, my dear," answered Roxton. He held up his quizzing-glass to the dish of prepared oysters being offered him and waved them aside. "I can only guess by the swing of your jaw, Vallentine, that you wish to say something to me?"

"I want to know what you've got planned for Antonia," he said. "It's been worrying me for weeks."

"Planned? I never make plans."

"Don't be damned difficult! This is serious. Salvan's got a letter from Lady Strathsay saying she don't care a whit if the girl is married off to that demented boy or not!"

"I know, my dear," said the Duke. "Calm yourself. I suggest we not mention this—er—distasteful topic this evening. Allow Antonia a pleasant birthday party at least."

"I'll not argue with that," agreed Vallentine. "What I'm worried about is her birthdays to come."

"Roxton," said Estée putting down silver knife and fork, "you must know she has put great store in your ability to protect her from the Salvans and their intentions. If you break her heart I'll never forgive you!"

The Duke regarded his sister with a bland expression. "Then let me alleviate some of your fears by telling you that our dear cousin will be unexpectedly recalled to Court tonight by l'Majesty and unavoidably detained there for the next seven days."

"You did that?" asked Vallentine and grinned when his friend inclined his head. "I don't know how you managed it, but I'm just damned glad you did!"

The Duke sipped from his glass with a small smile of satisfaction. "As master of the bedchamber my dear friend Richelieu is very close to his royal master. I merely called in a favor."

"I am very pleased to hear it," his sister said with a smile of relief, yet she was not satisfied. "But seven days or seven weeks, Salvan he will return for the little one as soon as may be. There must have been something more you could have contrived to ensure our cousin cannot come back at all!"

"Now, listen, love, your brother has managed this much," lectured his lordship when the Duke merely rolled his eyes to the ceiling but said nothing. "Have a little more faith, for I'm sure he's got more up his sleeve that he ain't tellin' us just yet."

Madame opened her painted mouth, not at all satisfied with this response, yet quickly shut it again when his lordship hissed out a warning, a nod to the doorway.

Antonia had come back into the dining room and went quietly to her place. She drank from her glass without looking up. It was obvious to the three diners she had been crying so they politely ignored her and carried on a conversation as if nothing untoward had occurred. The Duke was prompted by his lordship to recount an amusing incident that had happened while he was on a hunt in the forests surrounding Fontainebleau. A boast by Lord Vallentine as to his outstanding horsemanship made Antonia look up from her plate with a mischievous grin.

"Don't believe me, aye?" asked his lordship, fork in mid-air.

"Lucian is a master in the saddle," Madame said with pride.

"Can jump fence for fence with Roxton here. Never met a fence yet I can't get horseflesh to jump over, one way or t'other." When Antonia still looked sceptical Vallentine added indignantly: "Ain't you going to ask the Duke if I'm telling the truth? You'll believe him, I know it."

To spite him Antonia gave the Duke a questioning look.

Roxton smiled at her imperious treatment of his friend. "You must not treat Vallentine so poorly, *mignonne*. He deserves most of what you care to dish up at him but not upon this occasion."

"He is as good as you in the saddle?" she asked incredulously.

Estée laughed and shook her black curls. "My darling girl, you think M'sieur le Duc is the best at everything?"

"Why, yes, Madame, I do," she answered simply. "Oh, except with a blade, because everyone knows Vallentine is the greatest swordsman in France."

"An honorable mention!" Vallentine cried out. "Don't flatter me. I'll learn to like it!"

"But Monseigneur is the more elegant in form and wrist," Antonia added seriously, which caused his lordship to roll his eyes and groan.

"Good God!" he said dramatically and clapped a hand to his forehead. "In all your days have you ever heard the like of her? She thinks Roxton here is a damned paragon of male virtues."

Antonia tilted her little nose at him. "You are merely jealous."

Estée and Vallentine laughed, his lordship adding in a paternal voice at odds with the twinkle in his blue eyes, "If it wasn't your birthday, my girl, I'd argue it out with you. But I'll relent just for today."

"One hopes that will allow m'sieur sufficient time to reflect on the folly of his words," said Antonia with a practised sigh. "Tomorrow you will see that I am right."

"You cannot win, Lucian!" Madame giggled.

Lord Vallentine blustered for a response but finding none suitable leaned toward the Duke. "You listening to this, Roxton? Mademoiselle Fire-eater tries to convince us you're a damned paragon of all the male virtues! Been a lot of things in your time, my friend, but a shinin' example you ain't."

The Duke was staring fixedly at the contents of his glass, a heightened color to his lean cheeks. He gave no response and went back to eating what remained on his plate. His friend glanced at Estée to find her as puzzled as he. It was just possible the Duke was embarrassed. A month back Vallentine would not have thought the man capable of such self-effacement. He sat back and picked his teeth with his gold toothpick, an observant eye on the Duke, and with a mental grin as wide as the Seine.

It was Estée who suggested they have coffee and brandy in the adjoining drawing room but Antonia wanted to go to the library. It was a break with tradition but the Duke permitted her to have her way. They sat down to a game of whist until Antonia drew the Duke away to play at reversi and then at backgammon. Lord Vallentine and his betrothed settled on a sofa near the players, but far enough away so as not to be overheard. It was not a very long time before their intimate conversation returned to the couple seated across the room.

"Look at them, Lucian," Estée said stirring her black coffee in an absent manner, gaze on the emerald and diamond choker. "I do not know what is to be done for her. I am very worried. I think she has fallen in love with my brother but is too young to know it. How can she at her age? And the Duke? He spends too much time with her, playing at their silly board games, encouraging her waywardness, and lavishing expensive trinkets on her. Is it a wonder her head is turned? It is wrong of him to encourage her. Where can it lead but to heartbreak. He is too old for her."

"Remember your first marriage to Jean-Claude?" said Lord Vallentine patiently. "You were younger than Antonia, I'll swear, when you married him. He must've been twice your age, too! And you were happy, weren't you?"

"That was different."

"Different in what way?"

"It was an arranged marriage," argued Estée. "Arranged by my mother and my uncle Salvan, and approved by my brother. At first I did not like the idea at all. I cried all the way through the ceremony. But they knew what was in my best interests and yes, Jean-Claude made me very happy."

"And he was twice your age."

"It is ridiculous of you to compare Jean-Claude with my brother! Jean-Claude, he was a widower and knew how to treat a female as a wife. Besides, he could never be branded a libertine. Do you think my mother would have approved such a man for her daughter had he my brother's reputation?"

Lord Vallentine nodded despondently. "You're right, of course. There's not a mamma in Paris, or London for that matter, who'd care to have her daughter wedded to a nobleman with Roxton's reputation. Still, there ain't a law that says a man can't live just as he pleases."

Estée wasn't listening. She sighed and said, "I am worried, so worried, Lucian. You heard Salvan. He has a letter from Antonia's grandmother. Not even she wants the girl. She leaves her to the wolves. I have always despised Augusta and this only makes me detest her all the more. And there is this marriage contract that only requires her grandfather's signature…"

"I'll wager your brother has worked out some plan to get the girl out of this fix. Didn't he say at table he knew about Augusta Strathsay's letter? If he knows that much then he's worked somethin' out."

Estée took her gaze from the girl's throat and viewed his lordship candidly. "And if not?"

His lordship sat back against the silk cushions and sighed heavily, passing a hand down his handsome face. "Look here, Estée," he said. "I don't want to argue this with you any more. I'm ready to put my faith in your brother's ability to protect Antonia from the Salvans. I don't see why you shouldn't either."

Estée smiled hesitantly and rested her head on his lordship's shoulder. "Do not be naïve, Lucian. I do love you for your romantic notions, but it is not the Salvans who are going to break Antonia's heart. Me, I see how it is. She is such a sweet dear little thing and she is going to be hurt by my brother, very hurt by him, and I do not know how to prevent such a thing!"

Lord Vallentine scratched his wig. "Neither do I, damme! But we can't be morose, not tonight, or the chit will guess something is up and hound me until I blabber the lot. I've no defence against her, y'know!"

Madame laughed and pinched his cleft chin.

"Monseigneur and I have given you enough time to court on the couch," announced Antonia, standing by the tray of coffee and brandy. "So now we will make polite conversation, yes?"

The gentleman were greatly amused by this pronouncement but Estée delivered Antonia a stern lecture on her forwardness, that a young lady did not make such unacceptable pronouncements in mixed company.

"It-it was thoughtless of me," stammered Antonia. "I did not realise—I am sorry…"

"Yes, of course you are," said Estée and gave her a crushing hug. "I am tired, that is all." She looked over Antonia's fair head at her brother. "Do not let her stay up too late."

"I'll see you up," said Lord Vallentine and offered his arm to his betrothed. He winked at Antonia. "Don't go away, imp. I want one last try at defeating you at the backgammon board, even if it is your birthday."

"Good night, Madame," said Antonia and smiled. "I am very happy you are to marry M'sieur Vallentine. He will make you a good husband I think, even if he is hopeless at all board games and cannot fence with—"

"Brat!" laughed his lordship and flicked her under the chin.

Antonia waited until they left the library before she turned to the Duke with a puzzled look. "Was I tactless, do you think?"

"Quite tactless. But it is of no consequence. Estée is over-sensitive, as her kind are."

She sat next to him on the sofa and kicked off her shoes. "Mayhap I should not tease Vallentine so much either?"

"He would be disappointed."

She chuckled. "Mayhap I will tease him, but just a little. Do you mind if I sit in my stockinged feet, Monseigneur?" she asked, wriggling her toes to the warmth of the fire.

"Not I. But you must remember it is not polite in—er—respectable company for a lady to take off her shoes. Nor should a lady ever show her ankles."

"No? And yet a lady can display to the world most of her breasts and not an eyebrow is raised in disapproval. I find that rather strange."

"Society's dictates are strange, *mignonne.*"

"Well I do not care at all what society thinks of me as long as you do not take exception to what I do."

"But I am not a respectable gentleman, Antonia," he said flatly and moved away from her to pour out a brandy. "Strive to remember that."

"And if I was not a respectable lady?" she asked lightly, regarding his straight back with a small smile, "would Monseigneur kiss my ankles then?"

The Duke looked over his shoulder at her. "I would not stop at your ankles, you little wretch. Now behave yourself or I will send you off to bed."

This response was all that she'd hoped for but a niggling doubt caused her to frown and be serious for a moment. "Étienne, he said that his father and you are playing a silly sordid game for my virtue."

The Duke set his brandy glass aside and sat down beside her and possessed himself of her hands. "Antonia, look in my eyes and tell me if you honestly believe I could be party to one of my cousin's detestable schemes."

"I do not believe it, Monseigneur," she answered quietly. She glanced down at his long fingers holding her hands and decided there was no better time than the present to find out how much he truly cared for her. "This horrid marriage contract between the Salvans and my grandfather, I am not so naïve that I do not know that when M'sieur le Comte obtains my grandfather's signature I will be compelled to marry Étienne. And with my grandmother also for the union I have not an ally in the world…but for you and Madame and of course Vallentine. But there is something you can do—

"Believe me, *mignonne*, if there was a way—"

"—to help me," Antonia continued, and took a moment to compose herself before saying forthrightly, "I wonder if you would do me the honor of bedding me before I am married—"

"Mademoiselle goes too far," snarled the Duke and let go of her hands.

"—because if you do not, Salvan he will have me first and I do not think I could bear for that to happen," Antonia added in a rush, the dark look on the Duke's face making her less brave with every passing second. "I have heard that if—that if a female's first time with a man is not a pleasurable experience for her, if he thinks only of his own wants and needs and nothing of hers, then every time after that will be equally unbearable for her. And that is what will happen, Monseigneur, if Salvan has his way."

"Antonia, for pity's sake…" Anger was replaced with anguish, for he knew she spoke the truth and he did not know how to allay her justifiable fears. "What you ask… It is not my right… You must understand that I cannot interfere…"

Antonia blinked. "You want Salvan to have me?"

"No! Of course not! And even if I want to I cannot have you either!"

"Because you do not want to bed me?" she asked in a small voice.

"Not want to?" he repeated, as if the answer was self-evident.

Yet, it was the first time since he had helped her escape Versailles that he had allowed himself to contemplate such an eventuality. The realisation that he wanted to make love to her very much was so blindingly obvious that he felt the heat in his face and he looked down at his hands to hide a guilty blush. "*Mignonne*, if there be no harm in it and I could alter time, suspend time for just the two of us, I would do so, all for the privilege of making love to you," he confessed. "But time cannot be suspended. It is not a question of not wanting to bed you, but a question of not doing so because it is not right. It is wrong for a man of my years and position to take advantage of a girl in his care, that would be an abuse of trust."

"But if it is what I want," she asked simply, "then how can it be an abuse of trust as you say?"

He retrieved his brandy glass from the mantle and drank the contents in one, an eye on Antonia who sat as still as a statue on the sofa, petticoats billowing about her, and her small stockinged feet peeping out from under the layers of silk. She was regarding him with studious enquiry, her large, slightly almond shaped, emerald green eyes full of the expectation and optimism of youth. She had such lovely eyes. It caused him to swallow in an aching throat and glance down at the emerald ring on his left hand.

"I cannot do as you ask," he rasped and swallowed again, adding tonelessly, "It—I would be beneath contempt; my morals judged more unspeakable than Salvan's."

"When two people *in* love *make* love what does the judgement of the world matter? Surely all other considerations are unimportant?"

At this simple pronouncement he smiled crookedly. Antonia knew with a sinking feeling that his cynical façade was once again firmly fixed in place.

"An entertaining but exceedingly naïve view of the world, my dear," he drawled and turned back to the fireplace, the smile dropping into a frown of preoccupation as he continued to gaze upon the dying fire in the grate. "It's time you were abed," he said flatly. "Tomorrow Vallentine is escorting Madame to St. Germain to visit some ancient aunts. They will be away two nights at most, so you will not be alone for long."

Antonia came across to the fireplace in her stockinged feet and looked up at his impassive profile. "You are not staying here with me?"

"No. That would be improper," he said to the flames. "At first light I join the King's hunt at Fontainebleau."

"*Bonne nuit*, Monseigneur," Antonia replied and dropped a curtsey. "And thank you for today. I had a lovely birthday. And your gifts..." She lightly touched the emerald and diamond choker about her throat. "I will treasure them always."

At that she quietly retreated to slip on her heeled shoes and was half way to the door when he called out to her, making her heart race and expectation again spark in her eyes.

"Antonia. It is best that our—er—conversation tonight never took place."

"Yes, Monseigneur," she replied obediently and did not linger.

Yet, she went off to her rooms smiling. Ever the optimist, she at least knew now that he did care enough to want her and yet not take her up on her offer. Tomorrow she would prove that her intuition was foolproof. Tomorrow she would suspend time.

$\mathcal{N}$ine

$\mathcal{L}$earning the Duke had departed at first light for Fontainebleau to hunt with the King surprised Estée. Her brother made no mention of his intention to do so, but it meant that she and Lord Vallentine could visit her ancient aunts in St. Germain without needlessly worrying over the propriety of leaving Antonia alone at home with the Duke and no female chaperone. Just as her brother predicted, the Comte had also returned to Court, most reluctantly too said his scrawled note to her. He would now be caught up in Court duties for the rest of the week, which meant he would be unable to carry out his threat and remove Antonia from the hôtel. This gave Estée even more reason to feel comfortable with her resolve to journey to St. Germain.

Yet she wasn't absolutely convinced in the rightness of her decision and so was still in two minds with the carriage loaded with portmanteaux, the driver up on his box and Vallentine pacing the cobblestones under the portico in greatcoat and gloves, proclaiming that if the love of his life didn't get in the carriage immediately they wouldn't make St. Germain in daylight. Antonia was finally fetched, having risen late and breakfasted in her rooms, and Madame's fears were finally put to rest.

Antonia assured Madame that she felt no apprehension at being left on her own, said she was content to spend her time in the library reading with the Duke's two whippets for company. She wished the couple a safe journey. That said, Madame hugged her, Lord Vallentine blew her a kiss and Antonia waved the carriage out of the hôtel's black and gold iron gates onto the Rue St. Honoré. She then went inside and promptly told Duvalier that all the clocks in the hôtel required their springs and cogs be cleaned and to be sure that all the timepieces in the Duke's wing were removed first. They were to be taken down to the servants' quarters where the clockmaker could devote his time to the task without disrupting the household.

By nuncheon all clocks big and small had been removed from the Duke's private apartments and now resided below stairs, the clockmaker and his assistant already busy at work. Duvalier apologised to the little mademoiselle that the task was a painstaking one and would take several days to complete. Antonia looked suitably grave and hid her smile between the pages of Tacitus. She was not smiling when the Vicomte d'Ambert made an unexpected call an hour later.

She had put her book aside and gone out into the main courtyard, with its cobblestone paths, chestnut grove and large square of lawn, to play fetch with the whippets. The Duke's valet, who had disturbed her in the library to take the dogs for a walk, had been unable to resist her entreaties that he join her to play at fetch with Grey and Tan. The capitulation of this haughty little man caused such an uproar of mirth amongst the Duke's army of servants that the housekeeper and Duvalier were forced to order them away from the upper windows for fear the valet would catch them with their noses pressed against the window panes and in retaliation promptly inform the Duke of the lax behavior of his servants in his absence.

Antonia had no wish to see Étienne and Ellicott came to her rescue. He informed the Vicomte that Mademoiselle Moran was not at home. The youth lingered in an anteroom without a fire for thirty minutes before finally departing with a warning to the valet that he would return on the morrow and that Mademoiselle Moran would be at home to him then or he, the Duke's lackey would face the consequences. Tomorrow he would not leave the house until he had seen her. The valet bowed him out solicitously, wondered what consequences the Vicomte could possibly enforce, and returned to the courtyard without repeating the boy's threats to Antonia. The game of fetch continued without further interruption until nuncheon.

Antonia's buoyant mood remained with her until night fall. It was only when she had undressed and prepared for bed, and sat at her cluttered dressing table in her thin cotton chemise that she had her first doubts. Her spirits began to flag. Perhaps her intuition had failed her upon this occasion and the Duke did indeed mean to stay away to hunt with the King? But for how long would he be gone? And would he return before Madame and Vallentine?

Antonia knew that the King's hunts lasted for weeks. And she also knew that Madame had planned to be married by the end of the month and expected the Duke to be party to all her plans and preparations. Reason enough for him to stay away, thought Antonia with a chuckle, but she also knew that he was enough of a friend to Lord Vallentine not to let his lordship suffer such preparations alone. Having cheered herself up she decided she should trust in her instincts. And so she threw a silk flowered banyan negligently over her chemise and slipped out of her rooms with a single lighted taper, and, much to her maid's horror, with her hair left down her back and no night cap.

The hotel was very still as she traversed the countless corridors, rooms and staircases that took her as far from her apartment as was possible in this mansard-roofed mansion. She arrived at the second floor of the south wing that housed the Duke's private apartments via the servant stairwell. She thought herself very clever to have located this private stairwell used only by the valet and a handful of male servants. No one trespassed into these rooms, not even servants, unless honored with their master's implicit trust. Antonia had gleaned this interesting fact and other facts from Ellicott in the middle of their game of fetch.

It surprised Antonia that once she had gained entry to the second floor there were no doors on the cavernous rooms that led one into another. Every room was also surprisingly warm and well-lit, decorated with fine furniture, deep carpets and heavy curtains. Large gilt framed paintings by current artists such as Fragonard adorned every wall and japanned cabinets contained a myriad of ornaments and objects d'art. There were busts of Roman Emperors, statues of naked nymphs and deep chairs to curl up in with a good book. There were plenty of books in floor to ceiling bookcases, much to Antonia's satisfaction, and had she not been growing increasingly nervous with every new room she entered she may well have been tempted to take a moment to read the spines of the leather-bound volumes.

In the second to last room she heard activity coming from the room up ahead and it was only then that she took stock of her surroundings and realised she was standing in the middle of the Duke's bedchamber. The ornate four poster bed of carved mahogany with velvet curtains in blue and gold appeared inconsequential in such a vast chamber. Even more so the chaise longues, sofas, cabinets and occasional tables. There was a massive marble fireplace where blazed a good fire and which had an elaborately carved overmantel that reached to the decorative plaster and gilt ceiling. A long desk with fine spindle legs and matching chair, its inlaid surface covered in parchments, stood by an undraped French window adjacent to the bed. Through the window Antonia could just make out the stars.

Her gaze returned to the four poster and she wondered if the Duke had ever shared this bed with another and guessed he had not. This was his private male domain, free of the responsibilities of his position, of family, friends, retainers, servants, all those who relied on him in one way or another for their existence... and it was free of his lovers.

The thought was a sobering one and for the briefest of moments Antonia almost turned tail and fled, until curiosity led her forward when she heard the splashing and pouring of water and low voiced conversation coming from the next room.

She stood framed in the doorway, hesitant to venture further, not as brave as she thought she'd be upon discovering her intuition had not let her down. The Duke had indeed returned home, and she had wanted to run up to him and throw herself in his arms, but for one all important fact that held her suspended on the threshold.

He was naked.

He had just finished bathing in his plunge bath and stood on the deep Aubusson carpet in front of the warmth of the fireplace unselfconsciously towelling himself dry.

Antonia had considered him a splendid specimen dressed in his customary black velvet and white lace, with all the trimmings of his class and wealth, but naked he was magnificent. A tall, well-built man, velvet and lace had disguised muscle definition and contour in all but his large calves and wide shoulders. His broad back tapered to narrow hips and small firm buttocks that accentuated the flare in his muscled thighs. And his feet were long and just as elegantly formed as his long fingers.

Watching him move, bend and stretch as he dried his well exercised flesh of moisture brought the heat of desire flooding into Antonia's throat and face and she finally permitted her yearning gaze to follow the thin trail of dark hairs from his navel, down the plane of his stomach to where his essential maleness nestled between his thighs. She knew instantly why the ladies at Court had tittered behind their fluttering fans that the English Duke brought a whole new meaning to the expression *too big for his breeches.*

Her gaze lingered in fascination at this the most vulnerable and sensitive part of a man's body, for she had never seen a naked man before and certainly never expected to do so at such leisure. And she shocked herself at her reaction to this new and enthralling experience because her overwhelming desire was to caress him *there* and to see him take pleasure in her touch. She didn't know why but just having such thoughts made her feel weak at the knees and at the same time were strangely pleasurable.

Finally he stopped moving about and stood still, facing her, totally on show and unselfconscious of his nakedness. He had thrown aside the damp bath sheet and was tying a band to the end of his long black braid, having just deftly replated the damp ends. Color and heat deepened in Antonia's face and breasts and she moistened her parted lips as she forced her gaze up to his face.

He was staring straight at her.

Antonia dared not move.

Time indeed was suspended as they stood on opposite sides of the room, neither moving nor speaking.

She willed herself not to take her gaze from his. And if desire had fired her cheeks and throat, trespass and discovery fixed her bare feet to the floorboards and tied her tongue in knots. Yet, the intensity in his black eyes made her realise that just as she had been regarding him, openly and carnally, he had been involved in doing the same to her, and a frisson of desire coursed through her at the thought of him visually stripping her bare.

Antonia had to move. Her knees were about to buckle. She took a step forward.

Then he spoke, and in such an altered voice that again she froze.

"Get out! Damn you! Get out!" the Duke snarled, his whole body tensing. Yet he did not move and his eyes only left her for the briefest of moments to glance to his right.

Had Antonia not noticed that glance she would have turned and fled. A sob caught in her throat, but that glance and the astonishing realisation he had spoken in English made her hesitate. He had never spoken his native tongue to her before. She quickly looked to her left, and there, scrambling across the floor wrestling to hold to his chest the Duke's discarded riding clothes and smalls as he propelled himself out of the room at full speed, was the valet Ellicott.

The servant's antics of abject capitulation had Antonia smiling and brought comic relief to a situation that had reached an intensity that was now beyond hers to control. Yet her smile died watching the Duke turn away and shrug his nakedness into a silk banyan the valet had earlier placed over an upholstered chair back.

"Did mademoiselle like what was on offer?" he asked bluntly, shoving his hands deep in the pockets of the banyan.

"Yes, Monseigneur," she answered truthfully.

"You find this body to your liking then?"

"Yes."

He began to stroll toward her.

"You do not have a virgin's disgust of seeing a man's—er—equipage for the first time?"

Unconsciously Antonia began to back away from him.

"Not at all, Monseigneur. Should I? It is very—fascinating."

"Fascinating? A novel description. Most women admire my size, but for a virgin who would not know one man's packet from another's, I will take fascinating as a compliment."

"It-it is not only *that*," she stammered, confused by his flat voice and unblinking gaze. They were now standing in his bed-chamber. "To look on all of you is-is fascinating. You have a beautiful body."

He grinned, showing even white teeth.

Did he think she was being insincere? Surely, with all his years of experience, he wasn't embarrassed by such honest praise?

"As a rule, women enjoy looking over the stallion before a mount, to satisfy themselves he is worthy of the ride. Do you think me worthy of the ride, mademoiselle?"

Ride? What was he talking about? And if he wasn't embarrassed was he angry with her or was there some other emotion in his voice?

"I did not mean to offend you."

"Offend me...?"

Christ! He had just done his best to offend her so that she might have a disgust of him and choose to flee before it was too late to alter the unalterable, and here she was apologising to him! What was he to do? He knew precisely what he wanted to do, but taking that final stride to close the space between them was not unlike leaping a ravine. Once the leap was taken, there was no turning back in mid-flight of the attempt, one had to jump to the other side.

He had convinced himself that helping her flee Versailles had protected her from his cousin Salvan. He told himself that she did not interest him physically, that she was not ripe enough for his tastes. She had relieved his usual state of ennui and he had grown to have affection for her but that was the extent of it. Or so he had tried to convince himself. But then he had caught the Vicomte kissing her...

Unspeakable anger had welled up within him and he had come within a flea's breath of turning on the boy with violence. But there was more to it than being angry at the boy for taking liberties. Finding Antonia in the arms of another had given him a severe jolt. Then last night she had offered herself to him, and to his shameful surprise he realised he wanted her very much. He hungered to be inside her. He wanted to make love to her more desperately than he had ever wanted to make love to any female.

Yet it was not conquest he craved. He wanted to *make love to her*, not simply bed her. Paramount was a fundamental yearning to initiate her into the pleasures of making love, of wanting to see her joy and satisfaction when he brought her to climax.

And he wanted to be the first and only one to take her to paradise.

But he had always been with experienced women, women who knew what they wanted and how to get it. Pleasuring women for mutual satisfaction, and not merely as a self-congratulatory affirmation of his considerable sexual talents, was what made him a much sought after lover in the salons of Paris and the drawing rooms of London, but guiding inexperience through the same sexual maze was a completely new and daunting phenomenon, and one he was not sure he could perform with the same bravado.

"You do not enjoy being admired?" Antonia asked curiously, at a loss to know why he continued to stand just a few feet away, yet with his thoughts seemingly miles away.

Not enjoyed it? Having her watch him while he dried himself was the most arousing episode he had ever experienced without actually touching female flesh. To be admired and desired so openly and honestly was such a new and powerful aphrodisiac that he had wanted the experience to continue for as long as it was humanly possible for him to remain in control of himself. It had taken all his will power to stand before her and not get a full blown erection. He kept telling himself that here was a girl with no sexual experience, that if he allowed himself free reign she might well have run off in the shock of discovery. The angry embarrassment of Ellicott's untimely intrusion had poured cold water on that imminent occurrence in the nick of time.

"Perhaps it is I who do not please you?" she asked anxiously with a frown of embarrassment to be standing before him in a thin cotton chemise that was shapeless and thus completely obliterated her female curves. "I am sorry, Monseigneur... I-I will go—"

"Antonia, you little wretch!"

Capitulation.

In two strides he closed the space between them and gathered her to him, hands bunching up her chemise as he bent swiftly to kiss her full on the mouth. It was a gentle kiss to which she eagerly yielded, hands up around his neck and breasts pressed against his hard torso. It was her first real kiss and gentleness soon gave way to passion. He had a wonderful way of bruising her lips she thought wickedly as her mouth hungrily clung to his.

Before she knew what was happening she was in the air and he had carried her to the bed where he lay with her amongst the mountain of down pillows. But no sooner had he done so than he broke away. She did not want him to stop kissing and touching her. Confused, she watched him shrug off his banyan but he kept his back to her. So she sat up and pulled the chemise over her head and cast it aside, reasoning that if he was going to be naked before her she should not be embarrassed to show herself to him.

"I am not afraid," she murmured near his ear, arms about his neck. Her hands tentatively worked themselves across his shoulders and down his back, but when she slid them around his torso, he stayed her fingers before they could stray further. Surprise sounded in her voice. "You do not want me to touch you?"

He brought her hand up to his lips and kissed her wrist. "*Mignonne*, I want you to touch me more than anything, it's just... I don't want to *hurt* you. I want very much for you to *enjoy* making love... Do you understand?"

"But... I will enjoy making love...with you."

"It's just that this is your first time and I want it to be pleasurable and I have never... I have never bedded a virgin..."

God, why was he suddenly the gauche one?

Antonia smiled and scampered to sit beside him, her mane of waist-length honey curls her only covering. "Then it will be a first time for both of us," she assured him with a smile and leaned forward to kiss his stubbled jaw.

Startled by such naïve confidence he was slow to respond. He who had always been totally self-possessed with a female in a bedchamber was being reassured by an ignorant girl that everything would be all right on the night! She had unsettled him and held him spellbound at one and the same time and for the briefest of moments he wondered if he would be able to perform at all.

And as he turned and kissed her, drinking in the scent of her skin, fingers tangled in her hair, his paramount concern was to make this night of all nights as pleasurable for her as possible. To do so he must be ever so gentle and tender and take matters slow and—The breath caught in the back of his throat.

"I have wanted to touch you here since you stepped out of your bath," she confessed guiltily, hand between his thighs.

"You are shameless..." he muttered, the rush of blood and heat between his legs at her caress causing him to stiffen to an excruciating hardness. He watched her eyes go very wide before looking at him from under her lashes with a wicked little smile. "*Utterly* shameless."

"Yes, I must be," she confessed. "Though yesterday I would not have thought so." She fell back amongst the feather pillows with a giggle. "Now you will please show me what it is you do with him when he grows to the size of a beast."

They slept. Antonia cradled in the Duke's arms, both snugly tucked up between the mountains of pillows, under the heavy coverlet in his massive four poster bed. Before the sun was up they made love twice more. Not as emotionally fraught as the first time but just as intense, perhaps more so now that the Duke had initiated Antonia into lovemaking. He was more wantonly reverential of her wants and she, now knowing what it was to make love and enjoying it, was eagerly amenable to his tutelage. Finally, the deep sleep of satiated lust overcame them both and they slept past noon.

It was early afternoon when the Duke awoke.

He was alone.

For one moment he thought Antonia had returned to her own rooms. He frowned, not liking the idea at all. But then he heard the unfamiliar, something so totally foreign to his apartment that he wondered if the pleasant sound was coming from somewhere outside in the courtyard, that is until he heard splashing. Singing and splashing and a very pleasing female singing voice; contralto and melodic.

It was Antonia and she was singing in Italian.

He threw off the covers, retrieved his banyan from amongst the assortment of pillows and discarded coverings, and strolled into his closet to find Antonia in his tiled plunge bath up to her shoulders in perfumed bubbles. She had piled her lovely long hair atop her head, but not very successfully as the whole was rather lopsided and a long curl had escaped down her bare back to dangle in the water. He leaned a shoulder against a Mahogany Tallboy and watched her with an indulgent smile.

She saw him almost at once and with a bright smile waded towards him, the bubbles breaking up in her wake, exposing her glistening breasts for his admiration. She leaned her folded arms over the tiled edge of the bath's top step and looked up at him. "I hope you do not mind that I have a bath, Monseigneur," she said with a shy smile. "I felt it most necessary after...after what we... because—" She immediately corrected her slip, taking the sentence in another direction, "—because it is a very interesting bath this one. Almost a small pond. It took Ellicott and the footmen an age to refill it. I am surprised their comings and goings did not wake you. But perhaps you always sleep as one dead after a night of—I was most interested to learn about the mechanism by which it drains," she stumbled on to mask her awkwardness, which only broadened his smile. "Ellicott tells me there is a series of pipes that flushes the soapy water down to the drains below the kitchen. I was thinking it a great pity a similar mechanism could not be worked for drawing clean water up."

"Your thirst for learning is unquenchable, *mignonne*," he quipped, ignoring her two embarrassing slips and retrieving his quizzing glass from the clutter on his dressing table. He sat down on the dressing stool and faced her, long bare legs crossed at the ankles with his heels resting on the tiled bottom step of the plunge bath. "No doubt my valet was only too happy to talk mechanics with you while I was sleeping as one dead?"

"I have always found Ellicott to be most solicitous. And not once did he ask me why I was in your rooms or make me feel at all awkward."

"Not if he wishes to keep his position," murmured the Duke, quizzing glass let to dangle on its silk riband between two long fingers. He looked at her keenly. "You are—well, *mignonne?* You are not in any—er—discomfort?"

Antonia frowned and shook her head. Another curl unravelled and bounced to her soapy shoulder. "No, Monseigneur. Should I be? Why?"

He did not know how to respond to her straight-forward question other than in kind, and he had confessed that to her the night before. "I have heard that sometimes after making love, a female who has never been with a man before may suffer some discomfort," he said slowly, a heightened color in his cheeks. "But not having any—er—previous experience of such a situation, I cannot answer you with any authority." He smiled kindly. "My only concern is for your welfare and happiness, *mignonne.*"

This pleased her very much and to hide her blush she stood up and, taking the small pail of fresh water set aside for this express purpose, she rinsed herself free of soapy bubbles before stepping down out of the bath via the three tiled steps. Covering herself with the bath sheet Ellicott had discreetly provided on the closest upholstered chair, she turned to the Duke, who had not taken his gaze off her for a moment, and said chattily,

"I hope you do not mind, but I sent Ellicott to fetch a few petticoats and necessaries."

"I am relieved to hear my erstwhile valet has had—er— occupation while I slept," he replied, admiring her bare shapely legs through his quizzing glass.

"Yes. I told Ellicott, to Gabrielle he must not say a word about my whereabouts, although I think perhaps she knows."

"You astound me."

"But she must, Monseigneur, because—"

"I believe you, *mignonne,*" he said and gave her bath sheet a tug so that it fell away and left her standing naked before him.

Despite her diminutive stature, her womanly curves were perfection itself and had the power to stop the breath in his throat. For the first time in his life he questioned what he could possibly have done right in the world to deserve bedding such a beautiful woman; this delightful elfin-like creature who possessed a pure heart and untainted soul. He felt curiously blessed and uplifted.

He did not want this day to end.

He pulled her into his arms and cradled her on his lap. "Must you dress?"

Antonia put her arms about his neck but could not meet his gaze, suddenly shy. "If we are to have the nuncheon Ellicott has prepared for us, then, yes, I think we must."

He fondled her breast, thumb gently rubbing across her nipple. "But you are even more beautiful than I imagined possible without your clothes, *mignonne*," he murmured, nuzzling her bare neck. "Indeed, this connoisseur of fine female flesh deems you the most beautiful of all..."

Yet, as soon as he had uttered his compliment, he regretted it. It did not need her head turned into his shoulder to realise she had not taken his open admission with the sincerity in which it was intended, but as a lover's throw away line to a beautiful woman. And thus for the second time in less than a day he, the consummate lover, felt incredibly gauche in this girl's company.

He removed his hand from her breast and pinched her chin.

"You are quite right, *mignonne*," he apologised, brushing a soft honey tendril from her flushed cheek. "Ellicott would be most offended if we did not accord his cuisine the respect it deserves. And he would be unable to serve up his quail in a red wine sauce without dropping the lot if we were to sit at table as we are now. And so I shall bathe, shave and wear a frockcoat befitting my august rank. My very correct valet will approve, don't you think?"

She smiled and felt comfortable again. "He will be very pleased with you, Monseigneur. And when we've had nuncheon I wish you to take me exploring!"

He grinned, a particularly lewd response popping into his head. But he restrained himself. "Exploring? And what does mademoiselle have in mind to explore?"

"Last night coming through your rooms, I noticed a bookcase filled with interesting volumes in all shapes and sizes."

"As only you would."

"Will you show me some of these volumes, Monseigneur?"

A simple request and one he would honor, though he would be discerning in his selection. After all, for all her worldly façade, Antonia remained quintessentially naïve, and he would not change that about her for the world. The bookcase she described housed his most prized collection of priceless erotic writings, and artists' folios of pen and ink sketches, charcoal renderings and watercolours, gathered from all over the known world. There was a particular folio that instantly sprang to mind, from Asia Minor. From India, if memory served him correctly. Beautiful illustrations. Very enlightening. The exploration might be very interesting indeed...

And so settling into a makeshift pattern of domesticity within the confines of the Duke's apartment, Antonia and the Duke spent several daylight hours in the sitting room and study, and the rest of their time in the big four poster bed.

Only Ellicott had any contact with his master over those few days and then it was when absolutely necessary for him to trespass on the couple's time. One morning he entered the private dining room to clear away the remnants of a late breakfast only to realise too late that the lovers had not retreated to the study for their coffee as had become their custom. To the valet's astonishment Antonia was standing upon the surface of the polished mahogany dining table in her petticoats, parading up and down in her stockinged feet in front of the Duke; a rapt audience of one who sat in his shirt-sleeves and black breeches, long legs negligently stretched out to the nearest upholstered chair. The little mademoiselle seemed to be acting out what appeared to be a scene from a play. And as if all this wasn't enough to stun the dapper little valet into incredulous immobility, his master was laughing; laughing so hard his eyes watered. He was laughing at the girl's exceptional mimicry, this final performance that of the Queen of France, Marie Leczinska, Louis' nondescript and very pious, Polish wife.

The Duke was so far removed from the phlegmatic and aloof aristocrat as to be disbelieved and Ellicott was convinced drink was somehow involved. As if the events of the previous few days had not been enough to test the selective blindness of even the most broad-minded of gentleman's gentleman, his master's unrestrained good humor was the last straw and he fled the room in panic, only narrowly managing to escape tripping up on the carpets and gilded furniture. He dared not return until called upon.

It was late on the evening of the sixth day, with Antonia fast asleep on a sofa, head resting on a cushion in his lap, that the Duke put aside the week old English newssheet he'd been perusing and let his gaze wander about the room. Something about this room, in fact all the rooms in his apartment, was not quite right. He'd been unable to put his finger on it. With the leisure to seek out the reason, the answer presented itself. What had happened to all his clocks? There was not a single timepiece to be seen, and he would hazard a guess that when he was at liberty to check the other rooms, he would find the same to be the case. It was baffling.

When Ellicott appeared in the doorway with the coffee things, and his master's customary late-night brandy, the Duke enquired in an under voice if the valet was able to clear up the mystery. Ellicott placed the brandy and a glass in easy reach of his master's free hand, while most reluctantly informing him that mademoiselle had ordered the removal of all the timepieces in the hotel for cleaning and restoration.

The Duke was speechless. Then he smiled to himself.

...if I could alter time, suspend time for just the two of us, I would do so...

He was all admiration for Antonia's cunning.

It was then that he asked not only what was the time of day, but what was the actual day of the week and if there was any news of the outside world of which he should be informed.

Ellicott had been fussing with the coffee things, setting the silver tray on the low table by the sofa, careful not to trip over Antonia's discarded mules, and trying his best to ignore her existence. Yet he failed dismally and found himself openly admiring the girl with a silly sentimental smile, thinking how lovely and unspoilt she appeared in sleep, with her tangle of honey hair and silk embroidered petticoats in disarray, and with a hand still clutching an open book to her breast.

The Duke caught him and inexplicably anger got the better of him.

"You, my friend, remain deaf, dumb and blind until I say otherwise," he hissed and was gratified when his valet staggered back as if from a blow and immediately dropped his gaze to the carpet. He then repeated his demand to know the time, day and any urgent news requiring his attention.

Ellicott handed him a billet he had placed amongst the coffee things. It was from the Comte de Salvan and had arrived two days ago with instructions it be given to the Duke without delay. Ellicott hadn't the heart to do so, despising the French noble nearly as much as Lord Vallentine did. He then informed the Duke that Lord Vallentine had returned from St. Germain the previous day, Madame electing to remain with her relatives the rest of the week to keep company with one of the old aunts who had taken a fall from her carriage and broken her foot. Lord Vallentine had then asked after the whereabouts of the little mademoiselle, for he had been instructed to take her to Madame at St. Germain.

With a poker face the valet told his master he had informed his lordship that the little mademoiselle had taken to her bed with an undisclosed contagion but was confident of her full recovery within the next day or two. He then bowed very low, a glance at his master's face before quickly departing, not at all surprised the Duke seemed to have aged a decade in as many minutes.

For the first time in six days, in the very early hours of the morning and with Antonia tucked up in his bed fast asleep, the Duke left his private apartments with his dogs to stroll alone in his chestnut grove by moonlight; the Comte's billet in his frockcoat pocket.

Ten

Lord Vallentine visited Rossard's on the second night of his return to Paris and loitered about the various gaming rooms hoping the Duke would saunter in at any moment, but he never did. Those gentlemen he fell into conversation with denied seeing the Duke at any of the usual haunts he frequented in the city. Was there not talk of his cousin Salvan seeing him at the King's Hunt at Fontainebleau in company with his latest mistress the Comtesse Duras-Valfons?

As he was leaving, Lord Vallentine then chanced to meet the Marquis de Chesnay in the vestibule and he repeated the rumor, which caused the fat nobleman to go off into a peel of roguish laughter. Of course he had seen M'sieur le Duc de Roxton at Fontainebleau! He had spent an evening of drunken debauchery with four or five cronies, the Duke of that number. Where had Monsieur Vallentine been? Was his betrothal turning him into a mushroom? It was quite an orgy. A pity Vallentine had not cared to disport himself. But de Chesnay quite understood. Marguerite was right again. The beautiful Estée tolerated such excesses in a brother, but not in her future husband. He wished the much embarrassed Vallentine the best of luck, and as an aside, informed him the Oriental had been passed over for a red-haired Cyprian. Roxton, he cooed, was insatiable. De Chesnay tottered away into the early morning light humming the tune of a bawdy melody.

Not ten minutes later the Comte de Salvan, very bright-eyed and full of bonhomie, pirouetted into the vestibule. If de Chesnay made Vallentine feel uncomfortable, seeing the Comte's laughing painted face as he acted the part of the great courtier he deluded himself he was, brought the bile up into his throat. Not only de Chesnay and Salvan, but the whole heady atmosphere of Rossard's sickened him. But it was not his betrothal which had soured such entertainments for him but the knowledge the Duke remained indiscreet and cared nothing that his appetites continued to provide amusement for the nobility.

And what the Comte de Salvan announced to his lordship was so depressingly expected that Vallentine muttered not more than two civil words to the little nobleman before he dashed out into the street needing fresh air and a clear head. It made him all the more determined to discover the whereabouts of the Duke, for he could not believe out of hand what the Comte had told him. He would not believe it until he had heard it from the Duke himself.

On the way home in a chair Vallentine told himself over and over that the Comte's affected display of self-congratulation was merely that, a display. It was inconceivable Salvan should get his way. And so by the time he stepped out under the hôtel's portico he had convinced himself that the Comte's announcement of another betrothal in the family, a betrothal very dear to his own heart and one he Vallentine must keep to himself until he Salvan could inform the little mademoiselle of her great good fortune, was a great pile of horse manure. He didn't want to believe it and he wouldn't believe it, not until he saw the betrothal document with his own two tired eyes.

A sleepy porter helped him off with his greatcoat and sword and he went up to the second landing, candlestick in hand. He was about to take himself off to bed when a footman came out of the library and glanced expressionless from Vallentine to the door and back to his lordship. The servant's wordless look was enough for Vallentine to shove the candlestick aside and quietly enter the library.

He took out his pocket-watch and read six of the clock. There was still a good fire in the grate and one candelabra burned, casting light over the mantle and a couple of chairs close to the fire. The rest of the long room remained in shadow. A silver tray by the Duke's favorite chair held a crystal brandy decanter and three empty claret bottles. Thus, he was not surprised to discover a pair of booted legs sprawled out upon the hearth, one white, ruffle-covered hand slowly swirling brandy around in a glass. What did surprise his lordship was the brooding intensity in the lean face and the glaze to the black eyes that stared unblinking into the flickering light of the fire.

Vallentine thought it best to hail his friend as if it was only yesterday he had seen him.

"Hey, Roxton! I had a run of luck at Rossard's this evenin'. You should've been there. Took ten thousand livres off a greenhorn from London. Don't know what the silly fellow was doing at such a place. But I suppose he's pretty flush. His friend told me the pater owns Northumberland. Name of Harcourt. I'm certain you know his father. Anyway, good luck to him I say! Damme, who'd want such a windswept corner of ol' England. Mind if I join you in a drop?"

He poured out a brandy and leaned his shoulders against the mantle and cast a concerned look at the Duke as he drank. He wondered if his friend had taken ill. He was chalk white, despite putting away three of the best. He decided to play straight.

"Salvan was at Rossard's," he said seriously. "He was mighty pleased with himself, too. He was struttin' about like a prize Dartmouth cock. Where have you been for the last couple of days, Roxton?" Vallentine demanded suddenly. "I've lost shoe leather tramping about Paris like a damned fresh-faced tourist. Damme! And I come home to find you missin' and Antonia struck down with flu. Well, I'm told the poor little thing has flu but I wouldn't be at all surprised if she's just taken to her bed to avoid Salvan and his morose son. Don't it just choke you up that those two circle her like vultures round carrion?"

"Taken on the rôle of brother's keeper, Vallentine?" asked the Duke. "I do as I please when and where I please. I am not accountable to you, my sister, or Mademoiselle Moran. If you must know I have been rather—er—preoccupied."

"I can see that. You're three-quarters foxed!"

"No. Seven-eighths," responded the Duke placidly and raised his glass. "Do you want to know with what, or should that be with whom, I have been preoccupied?"

"If it concerns a female then I ain't interested," his lordship muttered angrily.

"Ah, Vallentine, there was a time when that was all you—"

"Look here, Roxton, this ain't the time to be flippant!"

"My dear, I am being perfectly serious. And I have drunk a goodly quantity of claret to justify the seriousness of a forthcoming celebration."

"Celebration? What celebration?"

The Duke gave a tired sigh. "I am home to an inquisition," he murmured. "The cause for celebration, my dearest Vallentine? A betrothal. But not yours, another's."

Vallentine threw up a ruffled wrist in annoyance and turned to look into the fire. "Well I ain't interested in any of that. I want you to tell me how it is Salvan's got somethin' to crow about."

"Didn't he tell you?"

"He told me a whole lot of pap I don't want to believe. So I'm askin' you for confirmation," Vallentine said quietly.

The Duke took a long time to answer him.

"Antonia is formally betrothed to the Vicomte d'Ambert," stated the Duke. "There is a marriage contract, drawn up by Salvan's lawyers, signed in Strathsay's own hand, and witnessed by two premier peers of France. Even l'Majesty has seen fit to give it his royal blessing. Thus it is legal, it is final and it is irrevocable. Is it Wednesday or Thursday?"

"Jesus!" thundered Lord Vallentine. "It—It can't be true! You've got to get to the old man and make him change his mind. Do whatever you have to. Threaten him if you like. I'll come and lend a hand. He'll see reason, and if he don't, then we'll use a little persuasion—"

"Vallentine, the Earl of Strathsay died four days ago."

Vallentine gaped at him. He had to struggle with himself not to pick up the closest object, be it candlestick or bottle, and throw it at the opposite wall to vent a pent up angry frustration. "What?" he shouted. "What the—what the—"

"Oh do stop these womanly hysterics," the Duke complained.

"She trusted you to set matters to rights," Vallentine said quietly. "She's put all her hopes in her paragon of an English Duke and for what—"

"For pity's sake, Vallentine," whispered the Duke, "do you think I don't know that? Do you think I haven't exhausted all possibilities? Do you think I want to see her Vicomtess d'Ambert? The fact remains there is a legally binding contract. It is what both her grandparents want. She is betrothed to d'Ambert and Salvan has already started to shout it from the rooftops. What would you have me do?"

"I don't know if you've woken up to this," Vallentine said awkwardly, "but you're a man of the world so I dare say it isn't news to you—but just in case you've overlook—"

"I may be foxed but I'm not an idiot! What are you blathering?"

"Antonia is in love with you, Roxton."

The Duke stared at him, pale faced and rigid. "You are a romantic fool."

"Romantic fool, am I? Why? Because I dare tell you the truth. Aye, then so I am!"

Roxton looked back into the fire.

"Well. What d'you say?" demanded his friend.

"She is too young to know her own mind," Roxton said flatly. "To her I am a hero who dared snatch her out from under the claws of my dear cousin Salvan. She thinks I have rescued her. She doesn't know me for what I really am."

"So you think? You're wrong. She's young, I'll grant, but she knows exactly what you are. It don't matter a whit to her."

The Duke laughed softly. "How touchingly pathetic," he sneered.

"God damn Salvan!" burst from his lordship, thumping his fist on the mantle. "God-damn-him! You can't permit this forced marriage. Be damned if the little thing is going to be sacrificed to the likes of that painted, disease-ridden clown, and that morose piece of his flesh he calls son. There's no backbone in the father and the son ain't natural. There's bad blood in that family."

"You forget yourself," said Roxton haughtily. "Salvan blood runs in my veins too."

"I ain't forgetting it! But you and Estée are the best of 'em," said his lordship. "So what's to be done?"

"Worse matches have been contracted."

Lord Vallentine was thunderstruck. "Lord!" he muttered in a broken voice. "How can you say that? She'll wilt."

"My morals are far worse than Salvan's, my dear, and Antonia knows this," said the Duke with a crooked smile. "In London she will find ample distraction, and distance will give her the clarity of perspective. She will be glad to forget me soon enough."

"London?" Vallentine gave a shout of relief. "Damme! I knew you'd not let her down. You've figured a plan!"

"A—er—plan of sorts. Yes. Strathsay's death is an inconvenience to Salvan," the Duke said mechanically. "There must be a suitable period of mourning for the dear departed Jacobite General before the marriage can take place. Even my dear cousin would not fly in the face of convention to satisfy his—er—desires. So, he must wait six months."

"Bravo! How did you get him to agree the girl should be sent to London?"

"Ah, Vallentine, I wish I could tell you it was an easy matter," said Roxton and stood up to stretch his legs. "There is a condition attached. That aside, Salvan forgot the existence of an uncle, one Theophilus Fitzstuart, whom I told you about some time ago. Augusta may not want her grandchild but gallant Theo does. He has put a claim on her and challenged the validity of the marriage contract."

"Got him to do that did you?"

The Duke smiled unpleasantly. "I wrote to him some time back but Theophilus needed no persuasion. Unlike his mother he has a sense of what is morally right and wrong. As Antonia's uncle and the next Earl of Strathsay he has an obligation to the girl."

"Can he challenge a contract signed by his father? On what grounds?"

"If he can prove he, and not his father, was the girl's legal guardian at the time the contract was drawn up—yes."

"That would make the contract invalid," said Lord Vallentine, a sparkle in his eyes. "I don't understand why you think the boy, and not his father, is the chit's guardian, it's all a bit beyond me at this time of the morning, but I'll grasp at anything you care to throw in Salvan's path. I knew you'd not disappoint the little thing! I told Estée as much in the carriage. And you're damned lucid, too, for someone who looks as if he hasn't slept in days, and has got himself three-quarters drunk!"

"Ah, my declining prestige," sighed the Duke and took snuff with a steady hand. "But understand the delicacy of the situation, Vallentine. I would appreciate nothing of what I've told you be said to Antonia. That she is going to her grandmother as promised will suffice."

"You'll take her?"

"I? No. I remain in Paris," Roxton told him. "I am entrusting her to Ellicott's care. How I will manage without him for a few days I know not. The price of playing the hero, I suppose."

Vallentine ignored the flippant manner. "Why ain't you takin' her?"

"The—er—condition, my dear," he answered softly. "My dear cousin won't allow the girl to leave Paris unless he has my word I will not make my bow to her again until such time as she is the Vicomtess d'Ambert. Thus, I remain in France. Oh, do spare me that pained expression! I don't deserve your sympathy."

Lord Vallentine shook his head. "You needn't have agreed to that, surely? It's a greater punishment than either of you deserve."

"Yet, how fitting," mocked the Duke. He nudged an errant log with the toe of his boot. "If nothing comes of Theophilus Fitzstuart's claim then 'tis better for Antonia I remain in—er—exile."

"You think you can sit back with ease and watch her become the Vicomtess d'Ambert? You think your life will go on as if nothing has changed—" asked his lordship then broke off because he sensed an intrusion.

Peering through the blue-grey morning light that filtered through the undraped window at his back he smiled as Grey poked his muzzle around the library door, closely followed by Tan. Spying their master they trotted up to the Duke and demanded a pat. Roxton crouched on a knee to oblige them and scratched one, then the other, under the chin.

"Don't think they're neglected," said Vallentine pulling Grey's ear affectionately. "Antonia spoils them. I am reliably informed that she and your punctilious valet were spied playing at fetch in the courtyard. He's got a tendre for the girl."

"Ellicott?" Roxton was greatly amused by the dark look on Vallentine's face. "Should I have words with him?"

"No. Just warning you."

Roxton grinned.

"What's so amusing?" his lordship demanded darkly.

"Apart from the picture in my mind's eye of my valet playing at—er—fetch, the look on your face, dearest Vallentine. Has it never occurred to you that Ellicott is of a different—er—inclination to you and I."

"Good morning, chit!" cut in Lord Vallentine. "It's a bit early for you to be wandering about. The servants ain't even up yet."

Antonia stood hesitantly in the doorway in her slippered feet. A flowered silk robe was buttoned carelessly over her thin chemise and her hair was a mass of unbrushed curls. She smiled shyly at his lordship and came gingerly into the room.

The Duke looked up from his whippets and wished he had not. He flicked Grey's ear in dismissal, stood up and gave Antonia a view of his back. "I don't recall asking for you," he said coldly in English, which surprised Vallentine because he had never considered it a possibility that Antonia was able to understand or speak that of all tongues.

When Antonia all but ignored him and went straight up to the Duke and whispered something at his back, Lord Vallentine politely retreated to stand half way down the long room in the semi-darkness. He took out his snuffbox for want of occupation.

"When I woke up and you were not there… The truth is I find I cannot now sleep without you," Antonia confessed naïvely in whispered French. She glanced over her shoulder and was relieved Vallentine had had the manners to move out of ear-shot. "Ellicott, he told me you had taken Grey and Tan to the chestnut grove late last night, and that you did not tell him when you would return—"

"I may come and go in my own house as I please, may I not?"

"Y-yes, yes, of course," she stammered, confused by his cold demeanour and the fact he continued to address her in his native tongue. "I only told you because I was worried for you and I presumed—"

"You *presumed?*" he interrupted, glancing down at her with disdain. He took out his snuffbox and tapped the lid. "You presume a great deal too much."

"If-if I have intruded on you and Vallentine I will return to your apartment and wait—"

"You will return to your rooms."

"My rooms…" she repeated, startled. "Why?"

"You are being sent to your grandmother in London—"

"*London?*"

"—while arrangements are completed for your marriage to the Vicomte d'Ambert."

Antonia blinked with incomprehension. "*Marriage?*"

The Duke ventured to take a pinch of snuff, but his hand was trembling so much that he gave up on the attempt and closed the lid, shoving his hand in a frockcoat pocket and hard-gripping the little gold box. "Your maid will have your portmanteaux packed and you and your belongings will depart my house by noon."

"Noon?" she murmured, dazed.

And then it hit her.

Noon.

Time.

Her glance darted to the mantelpiece and she was suddenly wretched. There stood a carriage clock in its gold filigree case, brightly polished and keeping perfect time. She had the presentiment that time had sped forward without her and the dream she had been living, the dream she did not want to wake from, had, without her knowledge and consent, turned into a nightmare. Hot tears sprang to her eyes.

"Please. No. It is too soon," she pleaded in a whisper, and clung to the Duke's great upturned velvet cuff, warm breasts pressed to his arm. She looked up at his profile in angry disbelief. "I do not want to go to London. I do not want to leave you. I will not!"

Roxton forced himself to shrug her off. "Stop this childish display at once. It is unbecoming and vulgar."

"But there has not been enough time for-for *us*," she whimpered, hand still clutching at the lace ruffles at his wrist.

He turned on her, a hard glitter to his black eyes, and pulled her fingers free of the Brussels lace. "I have indulged you long enough and now this interlude is at an end."

"In-indulged?"

"That is not to say your company hasn't been amusing."

"Amusing?" she echoed in a tiny voice. "I—I thought... that with me—"

"—it was different?" he drawled with amused condescension, finishing the sentence for her. "My dear girl, they all think that and eventually they are all sadly mistaken." He chuffed her under the chin and said patronizingly, "In time, you, like those before you, will come to look upon my expert tutelage as a stepping stone to greater things. Your future husband should certainly thank me."

Tears were now coursing down Antonia's hot cheeks and she felt physically ill. She wanted to run from the room, to be a thousand miles from his hateful, cruel words, and yet her legs would not move her feet. "That was beneath the contempt of even such a one as you, M'sieur le Duc," she said in a low voice.

The Duke swept her a formal bow and without daring to meet her tear-filled gaze shouldered past her to the lacquered escritoire. He grabbed up a pile of unopened correspondence, saying to Lord Vallentine as if Antonia was no longer in the room, "Vallentine, be good enough to inform Estée I won't be home until Thursday week. Madame Duras-Valfons is waiting for me to rejoin her at Fontainebleau..."

Too fraught to speak, drained of all prospect of future happiness, and knowing it was not all a bad dream from which she would soon awake, Antonia fled the room at the Duke's mention of his mistress, hand pressed tightly to her mouth to stifle her shattering sobs.

"Jesus! Roxton. That was a wretched piece of work," Lord Vallentine threw at him, coming out of the shadows with the door slammed on Antonia's back. The look of utter despair on her pale and tear-stained face was enough to bring the color flooding into his own. "Was it necessary to treat her so damned brutally?"

"For God's sake, Vallentine," the Duke rasped in a dry throat, the tremble in his right hand threatening to invade his entire body, "not now. Not *ever.*"

"Aye, I'll hold m'tongue," Vallentine said on a long sigh. "I hope for your sake and hers—bless her precious heart—the next few months prove their worth, before any real damage is done."

"My dear, it has been done," stated the Duke. "The damage has been done."

*E*leven

Part Two: The England of George II

*A*ntonia's grandmother, Augusta Mary Fitzstuart, the Countess of Strathsay, had turned fifty-one a month back. Ordinarily this circumstance would not have bothered her. She was still considered a beautiful woman, had not one grey hair in her flaming curls, and her voluptuous figure was not to be scorned. She appeared younger than her years, kept long hours, and never tired of taking a new lover in the long intervals she did not see her one true love. The fact she was grandmother to a beautiful young woman had never crossed her mind, until the girl was thrust upon her.

She lived a lifestyle considered by more than a few of the ton to be outlandish for a woman of her years; the more prudish going so far as to condemn her as a common harlot for fornicating with her widowed brother-in-law, Lord Ely. He was the man she should have married thirty years ago, and now legally could not, the law such as it was. They had been lovers for more than twenty years. He would be in London tonight, in this room, and although she could not wait to see him again after an absence of four months, she was apprehensive of his coming. For that she blamed her grand-daughter. The girl she also blamed for the fault she now found with her face. She wished she had never set eyes on her.

Her incestuous relationship—in the eyes of Church and State— with the Earl of Ely had never caused her a sleepless night. Having Antonia under her roof had caused her more sleepless nights than she cared to remember. It was not that the girl was the slightest trouble. She kept much to herself and spent a good deal of time in the company of her uncle Theo, Lady Strathsay's only son. So there was nothing to complain of in that. She was not vain, or over modest, spiteful or childish. She had a ready tongue and was too educated for her own good, but that was the fault of the girl's father. It was the fact she was not the least nuisance that proved a constant worry. That, and the girl's likeness in form to herself.

She should have been flattered to discover her only grand-child had inherited her unusual emerald-green eyes, famous breasts, and cream complexion. There was no denying such a marked resemblance. Lady Strathsay wished she could deny it, and ignore it. And as if this wasn't enough to send her scurrying to her paint pots and powder, there was the number of gentleman callers who kicked their heels in the foyer of her Hanover Square residence. And not to see her. All came to pay calls on her granddaughter. It gave her the headache. It so reminded her of her own youth. Yet, whereas she had welcomed the attentions of suitors and still did, Antonia was indifferent to them all. It was Lady Strathsay's sinking belief her granddaughter would not have cared in the slightest had no gentleman ever called to see her.

She was about to speculate on the reasons for this odd be-havior when a scratch on the boudoir door disrupted her thoughts and she sat up on an elbow, signalling to her black page to answer it. A footman gave her Mr. Percival Harcourt's card and she shooed him away, ordering the visitor to be sent up at once.

"My dearest lady, as always I am at your feet," exclaimed Mr. Harcourt as he swept into the room and presented the Countess with a magnificent bow. He pocketed a scented handkerchief and kissed the hand she held out to him. "You never fail to dazzle me!"

"You never fail to flatter me, my dear boy," she said. "I like it. The young men of today are not quite as attentive as they ought. It is a shame. A modern tendency I deplore. But you, my dear Percy, are of my generation in thought, though perhaps not in dress. What is that you have about your neck? One hopes it is dead."

Mr. Harcourt tittered and held out the large sable muff which was suspended about his neck from a ribbon, and rested on the silk burdash tied about his waist. "'tis but a muff, my lady. The weather is frightful. Positively dreadful! I am forced to wear cotton gloves to bed all this week for fear of chaffed hands. There is an awful north-east wind and snow is predicted. Theo tells me in a letter I had from him yesterday that the man on the land predicts snow for all this week, and I'd believe the farmer before a Cit any day!"

"Snow? I do hope the boy returns from Treat before that eventuality," said Lady Strathsay and indicated a spindle-legged chair opposite her chaise longue for Mr. Harcourt to perch on. "He's been there a fortnight or more. God knows what he is up to for Roxton. Some building project or draining of a lake or some such nonsense. Why he should bother when there is no indication the Duke is to return to London any time soon, I know not!"

"Very true, my lady. We all expected his Grace at Christmas-time. That is the usual time he opens his house in St. James's Square. But the knocker is still off the door. Not even Theo has had word, well, not in an *informal* way."

Lady Strathsay caught the note of censure in the young man's voice and frowned. "You need not tell me my son is slavishly devoted to that roué. So degrading for a man about to come into an earldom. But he refuses to give up his position as the Duke's major-domo until such time as his claim to the Strathsay title is verified by King and Parliament."

Mr. Harcourt was somewhat surprised. "I thought—that is—there is a will, isn't there, my lady?"

Lady Strathsay smiled thinly. "Let's not fadge, Mr. Harcourt. Of course Strathsay left a will. What papist would not? Nor leave this world without confessing all to his squalid little priest. I suppose he had to make amends for his sins or he'd be denied the last sacrament or rites, or whatever it is priests perform on a dying man's last breath. Throw buckets of holy water on them possibly. That Strathsay could have done with; the water, that is. He was never one to wash or scent his person. God knows I can still remember it all!

"Here is our tea. Sam, pour out for Mr. Harcourt. It's bohea, you know, and blended for me by a little man on the Strand." She shifted to adjust the shawl which had slipped off her white shoulders, her conversation barely lagging. "Where was I?—Oh,

Strathsay! At least he had the decency to put matters to rights on his death. If it hadn't been for his papist conscience I still maintain he'd have gone to the grave denying Theo as his own. Conscience and vanity both. Men are such vain creatures. To leave a son and heir to carry on the name is all-important to them. And after Strathsay proclaiming Theo a bastard for twenty-seven odd years is it small wonder the poor boy's claim is questioned?

"James never did have any other children after Theo was born; not even bastards. I suspect the pox put an end to that. Not that it interfered in any way with his abilities under the covers. Oh, no, Mr. Harcourt. That was the only thing I admired about him in the end. Well, it is the only fond memory I have of him—Oh dear, you've spilled tea on your lovely canary-yellow breeches! Tea too strong, my boy? Sam, fetch a cloth for Mr. Harcourt."

The page dashed out of the room and Mr. Harcourt was glad for the diversion. He fumbled with the tea dish and mopped a knee of his satin breeches with a dainty handkerchief. He should not have been surprised by the Countess's ramblings. Her affairs were legion, her reputation notorious, and her blunt speech legendary. Above all she was the most vain creature he knew and her jealousy of her granddaughter was so blatant as to be pathetic. He had not come to visit the grandmother, but the granddaughter. Yet he was wise to the fact a visit to the younger without first visiting the elder would not have been politic.

"Blended on the Strand did you say? How interesting, and how very good this tea is, my lady," he said frowning at the dark spreading stain on his breeches. "And I shouldn't worry yourself about Theo's claim. The King will put his signature to it without hesitation. Especially with Roxton and the Lords behind him. And he is Strathsay's heir after all. There's no disputing that!"

"I believe you are right," said her ladyship with a sigh. "You can imagine the strain this has put on me. What with this inconvenient period of mourning and having Antonia to stay…" She picked up the hand-mirror to gaze at her reflection. "I will turn positively old I know it!"

Mr. Harcourt did not take the hint, so eager was he to defend Miss Antonia Moran. Thus he did not give Lady Strathsay the reassurances she craved from her gentlemen callers that she was still as beautiful as the first flowering of her youth. It annoyed her, but he did not see this, saying with a little laugh peculiar to him when faced with an awkward situation,

"Miss Moran must be a comfort to you at such a trying time, my lady. To have a granddaughter to give you every attention and to look upon her who is not the slightest trouble must be a blessing."

Lady Strathsay tossed the mirror aside and viewed the young man and his absurd muff with disfavour. "Comfort? Antonia? Mr. Harcourt, it is plain you have not the slightest idea what a trial that girl is to me! To have responsibility for an eighteen-year-old girl who is pursued by every gentleman in London like hounds to a fox can hardly be called a comfort! She may have inherited my great beauty, but she is not like me in the least. She positively shrinks if a man so much as ogles her breasts from a distance. And what is the good of that? It is my belief that inside that beautiful shell is an ugly girl! Ah! I can do nothing with her— Dear me, Mr. Harcourt, my blend of tea certainly does not agree with you. Your face is the same shade as your scarlet frock. Sam, fetch Mr. Harcourt a glass of burgundy."

The black boy left the room as the Lady Strathsay's good friend, the Lady Paget, entered it, almost colliding with the little man. She side-stepped him with a sweep of her hooped petticoats and laughed when he made her a quick clumsy bow and disappeared. Her large brown eyes alighted on Mr. Harcourt's odd attire and the stain on his breeches with the merest flicker of recognition. She held out her hand to him and sat uninvited on the chair opposite the chaise longue. Mr. Harcourt was quick to kiss her fingertips and resume his seat. Lady Paget wondered what the fop was doing ensconced with her friend, and if he shaved his eyebrows to achieve such a perfect arch.

"My dear Gussie," she said sweetly, "I expected to find you with a man, but not one as young as this! Richard given his marching orders, my love?"

"Dear Kate! Out of sorts?" responded Lady Strathsay with a hollow laugh. "Dick was here only this morning. Perhaps I will send him to you. After all, John is down from Ely for the whole of this week, so I really don't know what is to be done with poor Dick. Shall you amuse him for me?"

"Not I! Besides, I told you. He has that young shrew Anne Yarmouth—a mere judge's wife, so I am informed—to keep him occupied. Terrible of him to stoop so low. I feel for you, my dear, I really do. How do you do, Mr. Harcourt? Ready for an evening of theatre and Mr. Garrick? Your pink carriage is absolutely charming."

Mr. Harcourt's mouth had been working for some time, ready to deny any implication Lady Paget might care to throw at him concerning his visit with Lady Strathsay. But with the mention of his pink carriage he beamed with pleasure. "Do you truly think so, my lady? Will Miss Moran be impressed?"

"The whole of town is talking of your carriage, Mr. Harcourt. Do go to the window and have a peek, Gussie. It's attracting quite a crowd in the square. This rôle of chaperone you've allotted me is a new one," said Lady Paget, waving a fan of latticed-worked ivory. "I really have no idea what I am to do with my charge, Gussie. Where is she?"

"Being dressed in a gown I selected, but I doubt it. She will wear one of Maurice's creations as always." Lady Strathsay glanced at Mr. Harcourt who had tottered to the window. "Percy, shall you go to the Theatre Royal with your tea stain?"

"My lady? The tea stain!" he gasped. "No. I must call for a new pair of breeches!" He stumbled to the door in his haste, muttering to himself, "I hope Patrick can ready another pair of canaries..."

Both ladies laughed at his back. Lady Paget saying: "That boy is absurd! I don't know how he came by that stain but it only adds to the effect. I wish you hadn't got him to go and change."

"I do believe he was clumsy with his dish when I happened to mention Antonia's wonderful breasts. Or was it when I confided Strathsay's abilities under the covers? Whatever! Young men of today are so full of affected sensibilities, Kate. It must carry over into their love-making, don't you think?"

"Possibly. You would know better than I. Young men bored me when I was young. I am not likely to think any better of them now. How old is Dick?"

"Too young. They always are."

"Shame on you, Gussie! And with your granddaughter under the same roof, too!" Lady Paget watched her friend frown and look disagreeable. "It still bothers you?" she said in some surprise.

"Not after all these years of living as you pleased."

"A tinge. A sign of age, my dear. John's visit bothers me. The others, they are nothing, as you know. And I am discreet, as always. Morbidly so with Antonia the floor below me. John is different. He won't abide skulking about corridors and whispers and such. Well, he never has had to in twenty years, so why should he start now? And all to protect Antonia's sensibilities!"

"You underestimate your granddaughter, my dear. What little I know of her makes me think she is aware of a great deal more than you give her credit for," said Lady Paget. "Good God, she lived with Strathsay and was left to fend for herself at Versailles, too. And if that wasn't a good introduction to vice in all its forms, there was the weeks spent at Roxton's Paris residence to complete her education."

Lady Strathsay sat up and directed the page to deposit the heavy silver tray at Lady Paget's elbow, and to pour her out a glass of burgundy. She glanced at her slyly. "Jealous, Kate?"

"Of an ingénue," said Lady Paget with a snort. "Do I have reason to be?"

"She writes him every week."

"Still? What a singular devotion," Lady Paget replied caustically. "If you are still vetting such correspondence then I see no reason to care. I am only amazed the girl is not made suspicious as to why he has not had the decency to reply."

"She did ask upon one occasion but I made light of it and pointed out Roxton's carnal habits. She never asked a second time." Lady Strathsay preened herself in the hand-mirror. "It is no easy thing I do, Kate. I must be growing old to worry after that girl. So much so that I am sending her away for the week, to visit with the Harcourt's while John is in town."

"Plain Charlotte's idea?"

"Yes."

"She will make an excellent daughter-in-law, my dear. Your son is very lucky, as are you."

Lady Strathsay chuckled. "Yes. It was fortunate for me he fell in love with plain Charlotte. I will enjoy having her as a daughter. That is, when the boy finally asks for her hand."

"He still procrastinates?"

187

"Theophilus is a bore. He is the antithesis of his divine mamma. He will only ask for her hand once he comes into the title. And after he has spoken to Roxton. He seems to think it correct form to seek the permission of the depraved Head of the Family! Isn't he absurdly boring?"

Both ladies fell into a fit of the giggles.

"My poor Augusta!" said Lady Paget on a gasp. She wiped her watery eyes. "A bore for a son and a nymph for a granddaughter! You don't deserve such ill-luck. I wonder at John's reaction when he sets eyes on the beautiful Antonia."

As casual as this remark was intended it had its desired effect for the smile was wiped from Lady Strathsay's face and she grimaced. "You must be kept wondering, dearest Kate. As will I."

"Oh, yes, I forgot! He isn't going to have that opportunity. She's going to Twickenham, you say?"

"You mustn't think I vet Antonia's correspondence for your benefit," was Lady Strathsay's pettish retaliation. "I did think your affair with Roxton over long before he went to Paris last summer."

"It was," said Lady Paget. "But what female likes to see her place taken by a younger and much prettier object of desire? I have a right to my pride, Augusta. As you do to yours. My only wish is the child not be hurt by him. But she will be, if she hasn't been already. No doubt he was flattered by her adoration. But his head won't be turned by it. His vanity fed, most certainly. His kind always crave that. But his heart will remain his own."

"Dear Kate. My poor *dear* Kate," said her friend with hand outstretched. "I did warn you not to fall victim to the Duke's charms. And he did break your heart, didn't he?"

"Chipped it, Gussie. Just chipped it. But I am glad I didn't heed your warning. My one regret is that he never did fancy you. It would have been so much fun to compare experiences." She smiled with a raise of her eyebrows. "As it stands, you must take my word for it he is as good a lover as is reported in many a lady's boudoir."

The cover of lead cosmetics and rouge disguised a natural and very deep color which flooded Lady Strathsay's cheeks, a stinging retort only held in check by the unexpected entrance of her granddaughter.

"Theo has come home!" Antonia announced in her thickly accented English. "I heard the carriage come into the stable yard. Charlotte went to the window because Gabrielle was putting up my hair. She said it must be Theo, because of all the portmanteaux up on the box. But she wouldn't let me look. I am just pleased he is home in time to go to the theatre tonight. Though Charlotte said—"

"I am very pleased to hear it, and before the snow too," said her grandmother, a glance at Lady Paget. "Still, all this news does not give you leave to burst into my rooms unannounced. I have warned you of it a hundred times, Antonia!"

"There—there was no footman at the door, Grandmère, so I thought..." Antonia faltered.

"And that gown is not the one I selected for you to wear."

"But this is the one I wish to wear," said Antonia stubbornly.

"And very pretty it is too," said Lady Paget and kissed both Antonia's cheeks.

Lady Paget's spirits had fallen the moment Antonia had entered the drawing room. Her careful toilette and expensive gown paled beside Antonia's preparations. She could do little to stop herself staring at the girl. The gown of emerald-green velvet with its petticoats of silver tissue, the bodice pulled into a tiny waist, and with a low square décolletage that showcased a magnificent pair of creamy white breasts, was enough to make her wish she hadn't offered to be her chaperone. The girl's honey hair beautifully arranged in a cluster of curls, adorned with a bunch of silk ribbons and a diamond clasp was merely icing on a beautiful cake. But it was at Antonia's throat she fixed her gaze. One simple and magnificent string of emeralds and diamonds encircled the slender white throat.

Lady Paget was brought out of her trance by a spiteful remark her friend threw at the girl out of sheer jealousy.

"Yes, I suppose it is a pretty enough creation," mused Lady Strathsay. "This Maurice has talent. Yet he might have shown greater tact in the design and cut of the bodice. He certainly shows off your breasts to perfection but he failed to cover your shoulder where that grotesque disfigurement—"

"Gussie! Really!" said Lady Paget with an embarrassed laugh.

She smiled at Antonia who stood rigid, green eyes ablaze with anger. "My love, take a look out of the window. Harcourt's carriage is in the square."

"It is?" said Antonia and scrambled up on the window seat without a thought for her petticoats. "*Mon Dieu*, it is pink! It is unbelievable, is it not, my lady? Oh, and the horses, they have pink plumes. It is a fairy tale carriage!" She looked back into the room and saw Charlotte's powdered head appear around the door. "I cannot wait to see Theo's face. He will not be happy at all to be going to the theatre in a carriage painted pink." When Charlotte whispered in the Countess's ear making that lady get to her feet with a quick glance at Lady Paget, she frowned. "What is it you say so I cannot hear?" she demanded.

"Antonia, go to Gabrielle and have her fix your curls. And collect your reticule," ordered her grandmother. "Mr. Harcourt is waiting downstairs—"

"But Theo—"

"—is dressing and will join you soon," said Lady Strathsay and herded her to the door. "Now do as you are bid."

Miss Harcourt smiled at her coaxingly. "I would hate for us to be late for Mr. Garrick's play."

Antonia looked at the three ladies with a suspicious frown. "I will go. Only because your brother, he is good enough to drive his pink carriage tonight."

"Why did you get rid of the girl?" asked Lady Paget.

Lady Strathsay and Charlotte Harcourt exchanged a glance.

"Mr. Fitzstuart had a passenger with him, my lady," Charlotte explained primly. "I thought it prudent to inform Lady Strathsay before anything is said to Antonia. It is not of immediate consequence for the passenger merely set Mr. Fitzstuart down and went on his way."

Lady Strathsay sighed when Lady Paget stared at her blankly. "Don't be a peagoose, Kate! Must his name be spelled out to you? Or have I misinterpreted that stunned expression. Perhaps you are simply speechless with joy? It's Roxton!"

"Roxton?" exclaimed Lady Paget.

"Yes! And I would be pleased, my dear Kate, if you did not mention the return of your prime bull to Antonia," announced

Lady Strathsay. "What he is doing back in England when he was forced to give his word to the Comte—though that is of no moment to you…" She gave a sigh of annoyance and tossed the hand-mirror on the chaise longue. "How damned annoying! I can only think it the worst piece of news since I was forced to go into mourning!"

The instant Mr. Harcourt's pink carriage swung into Drury Lane and drew up outside the Theatre Royal it became the center of attention amongst a jam of fine and elegant equipages, and the small crowd of theatre-goers still lingering on the pavement. To one side of the double doors a small group of liveried servants kicked their heels. Mr. Harcourt's odd conveyance caused enough distraction for there to be a moment's quiet amongst this group. Then the din started up again, the servants ran to all four corners of the establishment to give the news, and the occupants of the pink carriage found themselves greeted by a noisy reception.

One liveried servant remained at his post. Unlike his fellows, all eager to inform their masters of the color of Mr. Harcourt's carriage—to settle a multitude of absurd wagers—he was not interested in the carriage, but in its occupants. When they had passed on into the foyer the servant disappeared. His distinctive red and silver garments caught Antonia's eye. Looking at the man-servant's face she could not place him or the title, so let the thought slip that she had seen him before and gave her full attention to Mr. Harcourt.

Antonia hardly heard a word of his discourse on the people who crossed their path in the hot and airless foyer, such was the noise and the laughter. She flicked open her fan and was careful not to get herself and her petticoats crushed in the sea of perfume and plumes. Mr. Harcourt held her close, and with Mr. Fitzstuart's tall frame leading the way, he making a path with outstretched walking cane, they were able to pass through the foyer to the stairs without much fuss.

The stairs were not so easy to negotiate. Lady Paget separated from her party and was lost in the crowd. Mr. Harcourt and Antonia were pounced on by the Duke of Cumberland, whose fat fingers curled about Antonia's hand and showed a reluctance to let go, even after a polite introduction. Mr. Fitzstuart and Miss Harcourt who stood the step below, watched in wide-eyed horror when Antonia rapped His Highness on the knuckles with her fan and continued on her way. The Prince looked after her in amazement and before Mr. Fitzstuart could offer up profuse apologies for his niece's outrageous behavior the fat gentleman let out a great guffaw and swept a bow to her departing form.

"Expertly done, Miss Moran," complimented Mr. Harcourt with a sniff. He held out a chair for her. "Cumberland needs to be put in his place."

"Only Antonia could carry-off such a performance," whispered Miss Harcourt to Theophilus Fitzstuart. "I could not be so brave. Do you think me a coward, Mr. Fitzstuart?"

Mr. Fitzstuart's pale green eyes surveyed her lovingly. "That and much more, my dear Miss Harcourt." He settled himself in a chair beside Antonia. "Are you enjoying yourself, imp?"

"Very much," she replied excitedly. "It is as well you came home today or I would not being enjoying myself half as much. *Tiens!* Theo, it is Lady Paget talking to that fat person Cumberland! Who is the third in the box over there? I cannot see him, only his shoes. He must not be as fat to remain in shadow, yes?"

"Pray do not call His Highness fat, my love," said Miss Harcourt with a laugh.

Mr. Fitzstuart tried to divert Antonia's attention from Lady Paget by pointing out the orchestra and those persons seated in the pit, and he was succeeding admirably until Mr. Harcourt let out a cry.

"Oh God! Cumberland is waving his handkerchief at us!" Mr. Harcourt moaned. "Miss Moran, do please come away from the guard-rail or we will have the rest of the young dogs waving at us! The impudence! What—are—you—doing?" he shrieked.

"It is polite to wave in return. I cannot ignore this fat man or he will be a nuisance and wave at us all night!"

"Come and sit down," coaxed her uncle and put out his hand.

"I had hoped you would ignore him," Mr. Harcourt said with a pout.

"Hush, Percy. You are making yourself ridiculous," said his sister Charlotte, and dared to smile at him, which only sent him into a depression. "Perhaps you could send your man for refreshment?"

"Mayhap a cup to be poured over poor Percy to cool his blood?" enquired Mr. Fitzstuart jovially.

"I wish Cumberland would go away!" grumbled Mr. Harcourt folding his arms. "If he continues to stare..."

"Temper, dearest brother," cautioned Charlotte.

"Harcourt, that is ridiculous of you," Antonia scolded him. In a deliberate and public display she handed the fop her handkerchief. "There. Now he will no longer stare at your scarlet frock and the dead thing you wear about your neck—"

"Stare at me? But he—It's at you—Well, I—Thank—" stuttered Mr. Harcourt and brightened immediately. "You do not care for my frock, Miss Moran?" he asked with concern.

"It is a very pretty frock. Though I do not think yellow breeches suit you so well."

"No?" he muttered, crest-fallen. "And my muff?"

Antonia did not give him an answer. She was diverted by the orchestra starting up and the cheers from the pit. "I hope this actor Garrick is good."

"One of the finest actors this country has produced, my dear," Miss Harcourt assured her and sat back to enjoy the performance.

It was well into the first act and Antonia was enjoying herself with all the enthusiasm of one new to Mr. Garrick's acting abilities when she turned to her uncle to make an observation about the female lead and caught him smiling at her with a curious expression on his face. She frowned, but he seemed not to notice she was staring at him so she said nothing until the curtain came down and the audience started to move about to stretch their limbs, partake of refreshment, and pick up conversations with acquaintances.

"I do not know in the least what is wrong with you tonight, Theo," she said at last. "If you keep looking at me like a stunned *mouton* I will become enraged!"

"A sh-sheep, cherie?"

"A-a *mouton*—sheep? Yes, that is what you look like. I do not like this expression at all, so you will please stop."

"If I remind you of a sheep I can understand why!" Mr. Fitzstuart laughed quietly.

"Why do you look at me so?" she asked, peering at him keenly.

"Oh, because you are very beautiful," he said.

Antonia's fan shut with a snap. "That is not an answer I believe!"

"I wonder where Lady Paget has run off to?" he asked casually and scanned the length of boxes to his right then returned to his niece who was still frowning at him. "If I tell you you will think me a great bore."

Antonia dimpled. "Better a bore than a mouton or a rattlepate. Which is what Grandmère calls Harcourt. That is one who is stupid?"

"Mamma has a nice turn of phrase."

"Something happened while you were at Treat," said Antonia. "Me, I can see that. You have a secret! Do you know Theo's secret, Charlotte?"

"Secret?" blurted out Mr. Harcourt, all interest in Mr. Garrick dissolved.

Charlotte shook her powdered head and smiled. "Your uncle and I have not had the opportunity to speak since his return, my love. If he does have a secret he has not confided it to me."

"He's got a silly grin on his face too!" put in Mr. Harcourt. "Dare say it's the country air." He shuddered. "Pigs and cows and sheep. Ugh! Why! Lady Paget! You have finally returned! My feelings were sorely wounded thinking you did not care for our company."

"Did I hear my name mentioned in the same breath as a pack of farm animals?" asked Lady Paget. "What is going on? I wouldn't be at all surprised if this box is receiving as much attention as Mr. Garrick. Poor fellow! Oh, no! That wretched man is waving at you again, Antonia. I did warn him."

"Cumberland!" shrieked Mr. Harcourt and leapt to the railing.

Antonia was not interested in the Duke of Cumberland's antics or in Mr. Harcourt's performance as he growled in the direction of the fat prince. She turned to Lady Paget who stood behind her chair. "Theo has a secret. Charlotte does not know it. My lady, do you think Theo has been acting a great stunned sheep since he returned from Treat?"

Lady Paget chuckled behind her fan. "An apt description, my dear girl!" Her brown eyes widened at Mr. Fitzstuart. "I was somewhat stunned myself. Just now, in fact."

"That so?" replied Mr. Fitzstuart surprised. "I never thought—"

"In the foyer, dear boy," confessed Lady Paget, "Quite by accident. But it gave me a shock."

Antonia looked at both of them. "I do not understand at all what you are talking about! It is very unfair on Charlotte and I for you to speak in riddles."

"Too true, Antonia!" said Charlotte with a ghost of a laugh at Mr. Fitzstuart. "Although, I know the secret. I didn't discover it in the foyer, but in the courtyard at Hanover Square."

This pronouncement angered Antonia and finding the run of conversation baffling she went to join Mr. Harcourt to peer at the audience and ask him what he thought of Mr. Garrick's performance. Lady Paget looked at Antonia thoughtfully then handed Mr. Fitzstuart a scrap of folded paper.

"I am not at all sure what should be done with this so I am giving it to you," she told him. "You decide for me. Your morals are much better than mine. If it was your mother's decision she would dispense with the formality and call me an over-protective hen."

Mr. Fitzstuart's puzzled expression turned to one of mirth as he read the missive. He gave it to Charlotte to read. Mr. Harcourt looked over his sister's shoulder, his quizzing-glass tickling her ear as he strained to read the scrawl. But before he had a chance to make out more than a few words his sister folded the paper and returned it to Mr. Fitzstuart, who joined his niece at the railing and gave her the note.

"I await your instructions, mademoiselle," he said with mock hauteur.

Antonia read the short note and calmly gave it back to her uncle, a dimple in each cheek. "This M'sieur Garrick is a very good actor I think, so he may borrow my fan." She unwound the silver chain from her wrist and put the fan on the cushion a servant had carried into the box behind Lady Paget. "You must warn m'sieur to take good care of my fan because it was a gift from Vallentine who is a particular friend of mine," she said to the servant. "Never would I forgive him should it be damaged."

The servant bowed his way out and Antonia returned to the railing where Mr. Harcourt brooded. His pointed chin was in the air, his arms were folded, and he swung the quizzing-glass on its riband between two fingers.

"Do you want to see this?" asked Antonia waving the note about. "It is from M'sieur Garrick."

When the young man snatched the paper from her hand there was much laughter from his friends, but he ignored them as he scanned the note. He was the only one not to see the humor in it. "Impudent dog! He and Cumberland both! Are your eyes the same brilliant color as your emeralds?' Indeed! Preposterous and-and—forward! It is a wonder you allowed Miss Moran to hand over her fan, Theo—"

"Come, Percy, it is but a piece of funning," said Mr. Fitzstuart.

Mr. Harcourt was not to be placated. "The liberties these actors take—"

"Look at my eyes, Harcourt," demanded Antonia standing on tip-toe before him. "They are the same color as my emeralds. We—Grandmamma, Theo and I—we all have such eyes. And M'sieur le Duc, he especially chose these stones for me because it is so."

"M'sieur le Duc has excellent taste," said a soft masculine voice from the back of the box.

Powdered heads turned to see who had joined them. But Antonia did not turn. She knew who it was and the joy and disbelief of hearing that beloved voice for the first time in two months held her fixed to the railing.

His Grace, the most noble Duke of Roxton, dressed in his customary black, a solitaire in the folds of lace at his throat, and with his raven locks pulled severely off his face, held his quizzing-glass aloft to survey Mr. Harcourt's little party. To Lady Paget he had never looked more at his sartorial best, nor so self-assured. He did not attempt to join the group but stood in the light of a wall sconce, awaiting a response.

Mr. Harcourt was the first to go forward. "It's Roxton! Your Grace, what a surprise! We thought you permanently fixed in Paris. Did we not, Theo? Well! Well! Welcome home, Duke."

"I must admit to a slight deception," confessed Mr. Fitzstuart.

"Yes, so you should," Lady Paget scolded playfully. "It was the Duke you went to see at Treat, I'll swear."

"Did you?" asked Mr. Harcourt. "Is my friendship worth so little to you, Theo, that you must keep secret—"

"Hush, Percy," said Charlotte watching the Duke, who had eyes only for Antonia. She touched Mr. Fitzstuart's arm and he followed her gaze. "Now we know your uncle's secret, Antonia," she said to the girl's straight back. "But why he should keep the news to himself..."

But Antonia did not hear the run of conversation. She was so happy and excited that the English tongue was forgotten in an instant. Before the Duke had a chance to utter a syllable she was there in front of him, pressed against him in a crush of velvet, and looking up expectantly into his face, a hand clutching at one of the silver buttons of his waistcoat.

"It is you!" she whispered, tears in her eyes. "I thought never to see you again. When did you come to London? I have been so lonely without you. And it has been *such* a long time and I have so much to tell you! I had begun to think that you really did mean what you said to me in Paris. You never did answer my letters and—Oh! Mon-Monseigneur, now I am so very, *very* happy!"

The Duke was so unprepared for such an enthusiastic welcome that to receive the one response from her he had so longed for left him utterly speechless. A hundred words rushed from his throat only to be left unspoken. He swallowed hard, but still could not bring himself to speak. Instinctively his arms went about her small waist and he pulled her to him only to instantly withdraw from her and step away, remembering that they were not alone; that they were in a public place and that four interested onlookers in this box, if not in fact the whole world now seated in this theatre, scrutinised his every move.

"Antonia," he whispered hoarsely, black eyes staring unblinkingly down at her, "I beg of you, for the love of God, don't do this to me."

She did not understand. All she saw was an incomprehensible suppressed emotion in his ashen face and she faltered. "But I thought... You are not pleased to see me?" she said with a pathetic catch to her voice. "You did not miss me? You...You did not come for me?"

The Duke's black eyes continued to devour her and he started to speak but again he failed to find words of explanation. Finally, a flicker of movement over her shoulder decided him. He grabbed her wrists and roughly put her away from him, and stepped into the box. A moment, perhaps not a minute, had passed between them, but it was enough to stun their audience into embarrassed silence.

It was Mr. Fitzstuart who was quick to repair any breach and he went forward, dragging Charlotte with him, and introduced her to the Duke. She was self-possessed enough to chatter away at him on an inconsequential topic which required no response. Mr. Harcourt, however, was left out of his depth, and unable to understand the behavior of Antonia or the Duke, yet feeling curiously embarrassed by it, he turned to observe the movements of the audience as they resumed their seats for the second act.

Only Lady Paget seemed affected enough by the emotional scene just witnessed not to ignore it. She could not help staring anew at the Duke, seeing a side to him she had thought he wholly lacked. She was not angry or jealous, nor did she feel the slightest animosity toward Antonia for having won what she had failed to in the year the Duke and she had been lovers. Curiously, she felt closer to the girl than ever before. And it was she who put a comforting arm about Antonia's bare trembling shoulders.

"Shall you sit down, my love?" she whispered soothingly. "Perhaps a glass of burgundy?"

Antonia could only shake her curls. She was so stricken that her head throbbed painfully and all she wanted was to be alone. She had never felt a greater fool, nor more certain the Duke cared no more and no less for her than he did any of his discarded mistresses. Without realising it she blinked tears down her face.

Her uncle came at Lady Paget's signal, leaving Miss Harcourt valiantly discussing the night's play with the Duke.

"I am taking Antonia home," Lady Paget advised him. "Will you call us a carriage?"

"I say! I'll take you!" said Mr. Harcourt. "You can stay here with Charlotte, Theo. I don't care for Garrick, m'self. Remember to collect Miss Moran's fan. I don't like actors and I don't trust 'em either. He's likely to pawn the thing as soon as he leaves the premises. Sorry to run off on you like this, your Grace, but I'm sure you understand how it is. How is it, Theo?"

"Do be quiet, Percy," said Mr. Fitzstuart and shoved his friend toward the door. He took Antonia's cloak from a footman and put it about her shoulders.

Roxton took a step forward, so acutely self-conscious that for the first time in his life he was at a loss at what to do next. He was waylaid by Lady Paget.

"I'd have thought nine weeks ample time to construct a suitable sentence the girl would understand," she said sympathetically. When he could not meet her gaze she squeezed his arm. "Brandy is very good for settling one's nerves. I intend to give Antonia a measured dose. It will do her wonders, as will a visit from you on the morrow. Good night, your Grace."

Twelve

The morning after the excursion to the Theatre Royal was cold and a fog lay low to the ground and threatened not to lift until late morning. Gabrielle woke her mistress an hour earlier than usual. She put the breakfast tray on the table by the window as she always did and drew back the heavy curtains to admit the muted light of a winter's day. A soft-footed chambermaid knelt at the grate to restore the fire and then lit the tapers in the dressing room and the small sitting room. The sounds of an awakening city drew Gabrielle to peer out of a frosted window.

The distinctive calls of the numerous sellers, the rumble of carriage wheels on the cobbles and the cries of herdsmen attending their animals to market made the girl homesick for Paris. But there was more immediate activity in the courtyard below the sitting room window. Stable boys went about their chores with a whistle as they inspected for damage a mud spattered and filthy travel-worn carriage come in the night before from Ely.

Gabrielle hesitated to wake her mistress. She knew she had not slept at all well. But then, ever since they had left Paris, there was not a night that her mistress did not spend part of the dark hours awake, curled up in the window seat, hugging her knees and staring desolately out at the stars. Gone was the infectious, buoyant spirit of youthful optimism. It was as if a great burden had descended upon her mistress's young shoulders, a weight so heavy that it threatened to crush the life out of her.

Gabrielle had a fair idea what that burden was and who had

inflicted it. It saddened her beyond measure. And although she was a good honest God-fearing girl who had always believed that a female who sinned deserved a very public humiliation for the fruits of her sin, she prayed daily that this would not happen to her young mistress. She hoped with all her heart that there was some other explanation why the girl no longer had an appetite, was paler than usual and had not had her womanly courses since leaving Paris. Any reason other than the one Gabrielle feared most.

This of all mornings her mistress slept soundlessly, after a particularly restless night, and if they were not travelling to Twickenham Gabrielle would not have woken her had the King of France been at the door.

She left Antonia to pick at her breakfast alone and went to see to her bath.

Dressing was accomplished in silence. Antonia showed no interest in the choice of a suitable travelling gown nor in the tying up of her freshly washed curls. Gabrielle did her best and chose a simple open-robed gown of velvet with petticoats in a matching shade of lavender. Gabrielle would have liked to apply a dusting of rouge to the girl's high cheekbones, and given her full mouth an application of red lip paint, for the little heart-shaped face in the looking glass was too pale and forlorn. Instead she painstakingly braided the long damp honey hair into very fine plaits, wound several close to the girl's head and the rest she caught up at the nape of her neck in a silver net set with semi-precious stones, affixing the whole in place with long, pearl-headed pins. The result was breathtaking, but when Antonia looked in the hand mirror held up to her she did not see her reflection and mechanically complimented Gabrielle on her work.

A footman called for the portmanteaux and Gabrielle left Antonia seated at the dressing table, placing the slices of bread before her, which she had left uneaten on the breakfast tray. When she returned the bread remained untouched and Antonia was composing a letter at the walnut secretary.

"Have you been to Venice, Gabrielle?"

"Pardon, my lady?"

"I am going to Venice to live," announced Antonia and put the quill back in the standish. "Will you come with me?"

"But, my lady, I—I have never been outside Paris, until we came here to London. I—I cannot speak their tongue and—"

"You cannot speak English, either, but here we are in England," argued Antonia sealing her letter with a wafer. "We cannot go back to Paris because I will be forced into a wretched marriage I do not in the least want. And I might see M'sieur le D—*him* somewhere, anywhere, and that I could not endure... Papa has friends in Venice, and Maria she is there now. She will not mind at all about the b—And I certainly cannot stay here because poor Uncle Theo he would never recover from the shock of my disgrace. If you do not want to come with me, me I will understand and you are free to return to your mother and your sisters."

Gabrielle blinked at this speech but thought it best to agree to anything, such was her young mistress's present unbalanced state of mind. "No, my lady. You cannot go alone. Who would look after you and care for the b—Of course I will come with you." She handed Antonia a sable muff and a pair of lavender kid gloves. "Mademoiselle Harcourt and m'sieur are in the hall."

There was the faintest scratching on the outer door and Charlotte Harcourt came in unannounced.

"Good, you have a muff," she said brightly. "Percy has warmers in the carriage but you will need your gloves and muff. It is cold but I think the sun may just show its face before too long. If only the fog would go away. Then our drive would be perfect. I insisted Percy leave the pink carriage in London so we are to travel in the relative obscurity of a cornflower-blue chaise. Thank goodness I have the good sense in the family!" She glanced at the sealed letter on the table. "Oh, have I interrupted you? Shall I go away..."

"No. I have finished and Gabrielle she will leave my letter for posting with the butler," said Antonia quickly.

"Very well. I hope your girl packed a riding habit," said Charlotte with false cheeriness, for she saw the darkness under the girl's eyes and the whiteness to her cheeks. "I can't wait to show you our house and the grounds. It is Percy's pride and joy. He is still renovating one wing but it is going to be quite Gothic when it is all finished. I hope you will disregard the carpenters and bricklayers and workmen. It all adds to the fun! Come along then, we mustn't keep Percy waiting or—"

Antonia stopped abruptly on the second landing and touched Charlotte's arm. "I apologise for being such—such a-an imbécile at the theatre."

"Don't think on it. We don't regard it in the least."

"But I was an imbécile."

"Nonsense! It was very ill-mannered of him to act so—"

"No," said Antonia firmly and looked down at her muff. "He—He cannot abide bad manners, and it was ill-mannered of me to act like a child in such a public place. It would have made him very uncomfortable, this unthinking behavior of mine."

"Hush, dearest," said Charlotte with a smile. "You mustn't regard it. Whatever your manners, his were no better. Not that we think you the least ill-mannered. It was only natural you would— But there, this is not the way to start our week's excursion! We have left Percy kicking his heels in the hall, poor man."

She took Antonia by the arm and continued down the stairs. But on the first landing Antonia stopped again and would go no further. Charlotte had heard the voices below in the hall, too, and so she peered over the balustrade. Only the butler and a footman were in view.

"It is only Hawthorne," she assured Antonia. "Most likely it is Percy talking to your uncle. He did particularly want to say farewell to you."

"No. It is M'sieur le Duc," Antonia stated.

Charlotte was sceptical but she humored the girl. "So you think? Shall we slip down the servant's stair to the courtyard?"

Antonia shook her head. "I am a fool, but I am not a coward," and followed Charlotte down the remaining flight of stairs to the wide hall.

It was indeed the Duke. He was dressed in a black velvet riding frockcoat with silver lacings and thigh-tight buff colored riding breeches, one dusty jockey-boot on the first step and an elbow on the balustrade in which gloved hand he carried a riding crop.

Charlotte curtseyed and said a 'good-morning', but was barely acknowledged for the Duke's gaze had remained fixed on Antonia since her descent from the top step of the main staircase. Charlotte did not know whether to stay by Antonia's side or step back.

Undecided she hesitated, a glance up at the nobleman's starkly handsome face that was inscrutable as ever. Charlotte might not approve of this arrogant nobleman and his nefariously predatory habits but she saw no harm in his speaking to Antonia in such a public space as a main foyer and so withdrew to a discreet distance to stand by a group of sofas adjacent to the stairs.

Antonia attempted to follow her but the Duke blocked her path. Her gloved hand hard-gripped the banister rail and she felt her pulse quicken, yet she felt curiously numb. She had rehearsed what she would say to him if the occasion ever presented itself and she resolved she would say her piece without emotion. Having Charlotte as a silent witness helped, but nothing could keep the color from her cheeks.

"I must speak with you," demanded the Duke in an under voice. "Alone."

"Good morning, your Grace," Antonia replied calmly, gaze levelled at the diamond pin in the folds of his lace cravat. She spoke in her curiously accented English, though he had chosen to address her in French. "If you will excuse me, I am just going out with Charlotte. So if you would—"

He took a step closer and gripped her elbow. "Listen to me, Antonia. It is important that I explain myself to you—"

She pulled her arm free and dug her gloved hands deep within her muff. "It is quite unnecessary for you to explain anything further to me, your Grace. You made yourself very plain that morning in Paris and I should have heeded your words then—"

"I did nothing of the sort," he contradicted and couldn't resist brushing her cheek with the back of his hand. "I treated you abominably."

"Please, your Grace, the Harcourts are waiting to take me to Twickenham," she stammered, feeling her face flame at his touch.

"Your English pronunciation has come along very quickly since you left me," he complimented, a smile at her blush, "but I much prefer that we speak in French. Will you not allow me five minutes of your time, *mignonne*? The horses can wait..."

Antonia hesitated, glanced up and caught his indulgent smile. She was not only confused by it but it served to make her forget her English and the well-rehearsed lines, repeated nightly in the privacy of her four-poster bed. The sound of voices on the portico, and the fact the butler had come up to Charlotte and both hovered close by, instilled in her a sense of urgency, that she may not get her opportunity again to say what was on her mind and her determination to be unemotional vanished. She spoke in a rush of French.

"You need not feel guilty in the least," she assured him in a low voice. "You did nothing wrong. Nothing more or less than I asked of you."

"Guilty? But I wish to explain my—"

"There really is no need. I understand. I do. When you took me to Paris in your carriage I should have known then that it was merely a small kindness to a distant cousin and not—"

"Kindness? My actions had nothing to do with kindness. It was because even then I—"

"Please, Monseigneur! You must allow me to finish," she said with a moment's imperial aloofness that caused him to suppress a grin. "If you do not I will muddle the lot and that would never do because I have a great many things to say to you."

"Very well. Go on," he said patiently and leaned an elbow on the balustrade.

"I realise now that in Paris you showed me many little kindnesses and I should have treated them as such. Instead, being very naïve and stupid I put my faith in my feelings and dared to hope that you felt as I did." Fleetingly, she bravely met his gaze. "That you do not is hardly your fault and so I forgive you."

He swallowed. "I hardly deserve—"

"Please! Please do not interrupt. It is very difficult for me to say these things," Antonia demanded in a whisper. She cleared her throat, moved a little closer so only he would hear and continued. "I want you to know that whatever happens, you are not to feel obligated to me because of what we—what we—what—*happened* between us. That is in the past, and the consequences are mine entirely. And if you had had the courtesy to give me the benefit of a reply to just one of the many letters I wrote you then me I would not now be standing here explaining myself to you because I would know that you understand... But at the theatre you made yourself very plain to me, Monseigneur, and so I feel we do now understand one another. I will not bother you again.

Now please allow me to pass."

He did not stand aside and she made no immediate effort to go. Despite the activity all around them, it was as if they were the only two people in the vast hallway. The Duke slowly lifted her chin to look in her green eyes. "I am what I am, Antonia," he said gently. "You have always known that. I have never sought to hide my life from you, even the more sordid aspects, and still you believed me a better man. I don't deserve you, not least after the unforgiveable way I treated you. But since we shared a bed I find that I cannot—that I need—What I am trying to tell you is—"

"There you are!" exclaimed Theo Fitzstuart, coming in through the open front doors and striding straight up to the Duke. "Percy's in a devil of a temper over the horses. They won't hold much longer. Charlotte? Antonia? Are you ready? Ah, your Grace! I've interrupted…"

The Duke had turned a shoulder away from Theo to hide a face ablaze with heat and Antonia knew the moment was lost. With her uncle looking at her expectantly, and Charlotte coming across to join her, she quickly picked up her petticoats, bobbed a curtsey to the Duke and fled across the expanse of hall out to the waiting carriage.

⁓⌒⁓

Theo Fitzstuart watched Antonia flee outside, Charlotte close on her petticoats, then turned to the Duke who leaned against the balustrade frowning down at the crop in his gloved hands. "That was ill-timed of me. I should have heeded Charlotte's warning."

"Yes," the Duke said curtly without looking at him and went up the stairs two at a time.

"I apologise, your Grace, but had I known…" Theo Fitzstuart tried to explain, following up behind the Duke.

"Where is your mother?"

"My mother?"

Roxton strode down a passageway and invited himself into the Lady Strathsay's salon, waving aside an agitated footman and causing her ladyship's chambermaid, who stood with an ear to the bedchamber door, to shriek and burst into guilty tears.

"Get your mistress out of bed," he ordered and threw back the damask curtains to look out the window into the square below. "And tell Hawthorne to send up the breakfast I ordered to this room. Fitzstuart, are you joining us?"

"Breakfast, your Grace?"

"Oh, do stop being obtuse! Well, girl, must I break in the door for you?"

"Surely, whatever you have to say to Mamma can wait?" Theo Fitzstuart suggested, as horrified as the maid at disturbing his mother at such an hour.

"No. I have waited long enough," Roxton said bitterly. "However, by all means do not stay if the thought of wrenching your dear maman from the arms of her lover disturbs you. Which Dick is it today? Or did she forget to send this week's list to the Court-Calendar?"

"That was uncalled for!"

"Yet, very true. I make no apology."

"I didn't ask for one. I know my mother's habits well enough," said Mr. Fitzstuart stiffly. "But for you to condemn such behavior when your own has entertained tea-table gossips for almost two decades—"

"Unlike Augusta, I had the decency to conduct my—er— liaisons under someone else's roof," the Duke sneered. "Your mother has the bad manners to flaunt her depravity one floor above her own granddaughter!"

Mr. Fitzstuart could offer no argument. He sat down on an arm of a Chinese carved chair and swung a leg in moody silence. The Duke took snuff and continued to look out the window until the chambermaid reappeared from the bedchamber. She was quaking and had acquired a red welt across her left cheek. Theo grimaced at his mother's handiwork. The Duke merely put up his quizzing-glass.

"How medieval," he drawled. He waved the cowering maid away. "See to your face."

The maid curtseyed and was gone.

"Ah, here is breakfast," said the Duke as the butler and a

wide-eyed footman deposited a coffee pot and a heavy tray on a side bureau. "Hawthorne, pour out for Mr. Fitzstuart. I will be but a moment, Theophilus."

"What do you intend to do?" asked Mr. Fitzstuart in alarm. "My God! You're-you're not seriously going in there?"

"My dear boy, I am at my best in a bedchamber. Any tea-table gossip will tell you so."

The Duke and Mr. Fitzstuart were drinking a second dish of coffee and had requested another plate of rolls when the Lady Strathsay emerged from the darkness of her bedchamber, not unlike a lioness from her lair. Her red hair fell in knotted curls down her back, she had colored her lips a vibrant red, and she smelled of fresh scent. A flowing robe of Chinese flowered silk was thrown carelessly across her shoulders. It did nothing to cover a thin silk chemise and left no doubts that she still possessed a shapely thigh and the figure of a woman half her age.

"How charming. You've put on your face," said the Duke, stretching out his long legs. He glanced at Theo who had scrambled to stand up the moment the Countess had whirled into the room. "Be a dutiful son and pour out for your dear maman."

"I don't want any!" she snarled, squinting in the late morning light that flooded the salon. "How dare you—"

"Spare me your outrage," said the Duke coldly. "I have heard it all before, and your son hardly deserves a taste of your waspish tongue. I suggest you take a dish of coffee. I intend to keep you entertained for some considerable time."

Instinctively she glanced back at the bedchamber door.

"I took the—er—liberty of ordering John his breakfast," said Roxton and smiled crookedly when she glared at him. "Hawthorne will see to everything, even the morning's newspaper and—er—tankard of ale? That is what he prefers?"

"When I think you had the-the *audacity*—"

"Please, no thanks are necessary. It was the least I could do," said the Duke with an arrogant wave of a white hand. "A tankard of ale is small compensation for wrenching you up off your knees. Though I received the impression John thought the episode not without its humorous side. He did laugh when I offered to wait until he'd—But no, let me not embarrass you further. Especially not in front of your son."

Lady Strathsay looked at her son as if seeing him for the first time. "What are you doing here?"

Mr. Fitzstuart pursed his lips. "If you would prefer I was not…"

"You will stay," the Duke commanded. He indicated a chair. "Sit down, Augusta."

Abruptly she stopped pacing the Aubusson carpet and faced her cousin, eyes slits of green light. The Duke took snuff, seemingly unaware he was being defied, and with an air he expected her to do his bidding without argument. Theo thought it possible she would disobey him. When Roxton did care to glance up from under half closed lids there was an end to her mutiny and she sat where directed.

It was not a meek action. It embarrassed her son. He turned away to fuss with the coffee pot and dishes. She slumped in the wing chair, chemise and robe sliding off one shoulder exposing a quantity of rounded breast that she did nothing to cover. She even went so far as to throw a leg over the chair's padded arm, and with one small bare foot with painted toe-nails pointing toward the window she lounged at her ease.

"When Kate said you had changed she failed to mention in what way," she said in a voice heavy with irony. "In fact she was very reluctant to say much at all last night. I was surprised to see her return early from Drury Lane, and with Antonia in tow. But when she mentioned your sudden reappearance I wasn't surprised she fled. Poor Kate—and poor little Antonia! One will recover, she's young enough. As for Kate?" Lady Strathsay shrugged and chuckled. "I used to envy your eternal youth, Roxton. But, no more. I do believe there is a little grey at the temples of those raven locks. And lines, yes, deeper, more pronounced lines about that sneer. A heavy conscience mayhap?"

Theo stuck out a porcelain dish and frowned. "Your coffee, madam."

Lady Strathsay looked up at him. "Dear Theo, are you angry with me? What would you have me say when it was I who was dragged from my bed?"

"A little respect for—"

"—his Grace?" she mocked. "The Duke knows me better than that. We have never stood on ceremony."

"This is not a social visit, Mamma."

"What? Oh! You want me to make my curtsey to the Head of the Family? Good God! Open your eyes, my son. Roxton may be a Duke but he hardly deserves my respect, not when I tell you the latest piece—"

"Enough," said the Duke very quietly. He stood up and wandered to the window.

"That sneer becomes you more than you know," teased Lady Strathsay. "But think, those lines about your mouth! Have a care—"

"You're a fool, Augusta," the Duke drawled. "It is a pity you have never cultivated your mind half as much as you have your vanity. It may have saved you from a lonely old age. Once your beauty fades into insipidity what will you have left to offer a man? 'tis never too late to cultivate a little humility, Cousin."

"Thus spake humility itself!" retorted Lady Strathsay.

Roxton showed her one of his rare smiles. "Arrogance is a male *quality*, my dear. In a female it is a *liability*. But I did not come here to waste my time in playful argument. Theophilus: Go to your mother's escritoire and search the drawers."

"For what, your Grace?" asked Theo Fitzstuart, looking from the Duke to his mother who was suddenly pale. "Mayhap, Mamma, you would care to...?"

"That is where you keep your correspondence?" interrupted the Duke.

"What right have you to order my son to go through my private papers?"

The Duke put out an open palm. "The key, Augusta."

"It is never locked."

"The key to the only drawer you do keep locked."

"Your Grace, I don't understand why this is necessary."

"I want what is mine. And you do still have what is mine, don't you, Augusta?"

The Countess shifted uneasily and would not look at him, or at her son. "I haven't the least idea what I could have which would be of interest to you," she said airily.

"Letters."

"Letters? I burn all my correspondence. It does not do to leave one's little affairs of the heart lying about. You should know that better than I."

"You allowed one to slip through your net. I want the others."

"A-are there any?"

"Your face betrays you. Those letters were written to me. They belong to me. I will have them. *Now.*"

"I—I destroyed the rest!" she said impetuously. "I did not see the point in keeping them. What good were they? Just pages of inconsequential chatterings of a child. Barely comprehensible for the most part, and full of old news—well, it is old *now.*" She teased him. "Did you hope they would contain pages of undying love for yourself? Hardly! Though, there was one, or were there two? written in Italian. I couldn't decipher that. Mayhap it is easier to explain one's disordered emotions in some sort of ordered way in that language, rather than French? After all French is her native tongue and when—"

"My-my—God, Mamma! You-you stole Antonia's letters off the table in the hall?" Theo demanded angrily. "And *read* them?"

"No. Hawthorne stole them. I merely kept them in a safe place."

"I-I don't know what to say, your Grace," apologised Theo Fitzstuart, red-faced with embarrassment. "I never dreamed— That is, had I known—All those weeks—All those letters— Jesus! She thought you chose to ignore her."

Lady Strathsay laughed nervously. "Don't be so shocked, Theo! Surely you guessed? And I did not do it out of spite, so you need not glare at me as if I was a witch fit to be burnt. Whatever you think, I did it in the best interests of my grandchild. So unhealthy for a girl of Antonia's tender years to correspond with a man of Roxton's reputation," she said with distaste. "What would society have made of it had her letters gone astray? God forbid her name should be linked with his in any way."

She watched her son stride to the japanned walnut escritoire, jerk down the folding desk-top, and rummage through the contents of the small drawers. "How dare you touch my private correspondence!"

"Rather late to appear outraged, Mamma," stated Theo. He found what he was looking for and inserted the small silver key in the lock that secured the row of drawers below the desk top.

"Sit down," demanded the Duke when the Countess half rose out of her chair.

"I have a mind to call John!"

"By all means. If you think it will help," answered the Duke. "I very much doubt it. He probably quite sensibly took himself off to White's."

The Countess groped for a suitable retort, then closed her mouth hard, her eyes widening at the change that came over the Duke's features when her son put a bundle of opened letters tied up with ribbon on the chaise longue beside him. She thought he looked almost capable of emotion. Points of color dotted the clean-shaven cheeks and a small private smile hovered about the thin mouth. She smiled crookedly and went in for the attack.

"Such devotion in one so young is a rare thing indeed," she said silkily. "I had supposed, if there was no reply, she would tire of writing you after a fortnight. But no, she persisted. What a darling girl. Delightfully beautiful, sweet-natured, and still young enough to be molded to one's will. A little head-strong, but some men find that attractive. This childish infatuation for you will pass, of course. I shouldn't think the Vicomte d'Ambert has a need to concern himself, do you?"

Roxton looked up from thumbing through the correspondence.

Lady Strathsay smiled sweetly. "I sympathise with you, oh, I do. I always knew that when you finally allowed emotion to get the better of you you would have a very great fall indeed." She sighed tragically. "Possibly you've lusted after my granddaughter from the first moment you set eyes on her lovely face. No small wonder Kate was devastated. But she is a brave soul." She glanced at her son who shuffled his feet by the fireplace, looking very uncomfortable. "Theo? Tell me, Theo: Do you intend to sit back and allow this noble satyr to plunge his rod between your niece's soft virginal thighs? Is it fair on the young Vicomte to receive a bride with a torn veil on his wedding night? Well, is it, Theo?"

In two strides Roxton reached her chair, his face white with speechless fury and an arm raised across his chest. The Countess shrunk back, a hand to her face, expecting him to strike, hoping her son would intervene. Theo Fitzstuart did not move. He did not know what to do. He was saved from decision. The Duke turned away, disgusted with himself and stood at the window with his back to mother and son. He took a moment to collect himself then spoke without turning, his eyes on a sedan chair that turned into the square in the face of an oncoming carriage and six.

"It is time to end this charade, madam," the Duke said in a level voice. "You know as well as I the marriage contract signed by Strathsay and the Comte de Salvan is invalid. And you have known this from the very beginning."

When he received no reply he looked over his shoulder in time to see the Countess shrug a shoulder at her son, as if in bewilderment. "It is pointless to pretend, even to your son. He now knows the truth."

"That's why I went to Treat," explained Theo. "To discuss with his Grace the validity of the Comte de Salvan's claims on Antonia."

"Did Roxton tell you that by setting foot on English soil he has broken his word to his cousin?" responded Lady Strathsay haughtily. "What think you of a man who gives his word then breaks it?"

"Mamma, it is useless to defame the Duke. He gave his word in good faith, but it was extracted under false pretences. Salvan deceived him—"

"Bosh! Roxton promised not to come near Antonia until she was wed to the Vicomte d'Ambert. How was he deceived? It was not an unfair request, given the girl's head has been completely turned by him. Good God, she even excuses his rake-hell behavior; would tolerate it were she to wed him. Thank good fortune she is not about to be wasted on a man such as this. And thank your father's good sense she is to marry another."

"A little late to play devoted wife, my dear," sneered the Duke. "It must be the only circumstance on which you and he agreed. But I excuse Strathsay his part in this because he truly believed he was doing the best for his grandchild. Whereas you, you only promoted such a match because it would keep Antonia out of England and save you the bother of looking after her.

"You never troubled yourself with her mother's well-being, nor did you trouble yourself with the girl's future when both her parents died. And once you saw she was infinitely more beautiful in form and demeanour than you ever were, you certainly didn't want her under your roof. How convenient she was shunted off to Twickenham before John could clap eyes on her exquisite, youthful beauty."

"You make me out to be a heartless creature," said Lady Strathsay with a trembling lip. "But I am not! I, too, only want what is best for her—"

"—granted it does not interfere with what is best for you!"

"I think it preferable she be married to a boy with no past than be infatuated into the bed of a rake-hell with one toe in the grave!"

The Duke smiled unpleasantly. "Infinitely preferable. If that was her wish. Which it is not. And if the Vicomte d'Ambert was of balanced mind, which he is not. And not addicted to opiates, which he is."

"W-What!?" uttered the Countess. "I don't believe you! Theo, you can't believe this nonsense. How convenient for you, Roxton, that the boy be mad! It allows you to step in and take his place without argument. Come, Theo, you can't seriously believe this piece of scurrilous rubbish."

"I do now. At first I thought it fantastic, but when Roxton explained matters—certain particulars..."

"I'm sure you were convincing," she threw at the Duke. "Now you will tell me Strathsay and the Comte de Salvan were well aware of this when they contracted the girl to d'Ambert!"

"No," said the Duke taking snuff. He shook out his lace ruffles and sat crossed-legged on the window seat. "Strathsay had not the least notion. As for my dear cousin, he is not so innocent. Poor Salvan is rather wafer-headed, though he thinks himself a master manipulator. He is aware of his son's addiction to opiates. He has tried to control him upon occasion by—er—regulating the boy's intake, but without success. He next waved a *lettre de cachet* under his nose. This also did not work. It may have, had opiates been the boy's only—er—malady."

"A pretty story," Lady Strathsay said dismissively.

The Duke smiled at her contemptuously. "As pretty as this next one. About nine months ago Strathsay wrote you—"

"I have no memory of—"

"Then allow me to refresh it for you!" the Duke snarled.

"Strathsay's principal concern in his old age was the care of his granddaughter once he departed this world. He wanted to see her settled in life; married yes, and well. The Comte de Salvan approached him. My cousin knew his son to be given to uncontrollable rages, and so did the rest of court. No mother wanted her daughter married to one such as he. If the Salvans had possessed wealth, as well as title, a daughter of the nobility may have been sacrificed. Whatever. Strathsay had no knowledge of the Vicomte's disposition. He agreed to a marriage contract, but only upon a condition. He wanted Salvan to wait a year. He wanted to send her to you because he was dying, and—"

"Strathsay write to me? And what was my reply?" said Lady Strathsay insolently.

"There was none."

"You see!" she said looking at her son. "Why would your father bother to seek my advice? We've not corresponded these thirty years or more! I wouldn't know his handwriting if it stared me in the face. And even if I did, what of that? The notion he would write me is ridiculous!"

Theo looked to the Duke, but he was regarding the Countess with an ugly smile.

"Thirty years?" he drawled. "Mayhap. But you soon fell into bed with him whenever you visited Paris. You never could resist a good tupping. The product of one such cavort stands before you. Don't blush, my boy, you know your mother better than that."

"How—How dare you," breathed the Countess.

"Do your sums and shut up, Augusta," said Roxton. "To continue with my—er—pretty story. No. You did not write Strathsay, but Salvan. You gave the Comte your whole-hearted support for the marriage. Salvan was delighted. He would marry his son to a girl whose only concerned relative was breathing his last. She had no mother, no father, no siblings; she was of concern to no one. Hopefully the marriage would see the Vicomte's rages pacified for a time. If Salvan was very lucky, soon after the marriage, there would be an heir to carry on the name; this before his son's malady became too much of an embarrassment, and he must be locked away for all time. And the girl?

"What becomes of the young bride? Salvan has himself a

daughter-in-law who is not only beautiful and sweet-natured but young. My dear cousin has a penchant for young girls—the younger the better. He is quite disgustingly Persian in his tastes. Oh, do I see surprise register in your eyes, Augusta? Sordid, isn't it? Even more sordid is the fact he has been pursuing your granddaughter for almost a year. He wants her himself. To have her married to his son makes it all the more convenient."

"You-you didn't tell me this," said Theo Fitzstuart with a nervous half-hearted laugh. "It's absurd to think he would—he could—that he—"

"Yes," said the Duke.

"All too cosy," stated the Countess. "Why would Salvan go to so much trouble on his son's behalf when he could very easily re-marry and save himself the bother of arranging a suitable alliance for his son? Why not clap the boy up and forget all about him? He can have another son."

"He could do that," Roxton conceded. "However, producing more off-spring does not help matters. Étienne remains his first-born and thus his heir. Is it not more expedient for the boy to produce an heir, than await the title to be passed on to a half-brother? To—er—clap the boy up is the least attractive solution to Salvan."

Lady Strathsay reached out for the silver hand-bell. "Neatly argued away. Next you will tell us that Salvan meant to dispense with his son's interference in the process all together and intended to impregnate Antonia himself."

"Mamma, really!"

"Don't be a prude, Theo. Surely that inference was obvious, even to you! Hawthorne," she said when the butler trod quietly into the room, "we require more refreshment. Has Lord Ely...?"

"Gone to White's, my lady," answered the butler. "I was informed he would return in time to dine."

Lady Strathsay waved him away and called for her fan which her son instantly fetched from the escritoire. "If Salvan was so clever he cannot have overlooked the existence of my son."

"He did not overlook Theophilus, he merely dismissed his existence as unimportant."

"Well! Indeed!" said Theo Fitzstuart with a huff and folded

his arms. "I find I like your cousin less and less, your Grace."

"Content yourself you will never meet him," said the Duke sympathetically. "But your mother has hit upon the one flaw in Salvan's charming plans. He never doubted for a moment when Strathsay damned you as a—er—bastard off-spring of one of your mother's numerous affairs. Forgive me, my boy, but I do not intentionally offend you. Salvan has never seen you, thus the re-semblance to your dear Pater is of no significance. And Strathsay went on denying you until his last breath. All for spite. It was his one revenge upon his darling wife for—er—bolting on him when he most needed her."

"Rot!" interrupted the Countess. But she flushed in spite of herself. "He chose to support the Stuart claim, not I. It served him to rights for leading an expeditionary force against the Crown. Fool of a man! How anyone could expect me to follow him into exile after such treason—"

"They did, and you didn't. Such *devotion*."

"You're the last person who has a right to sneer, Roxton! And at my morals! When your own are the most atrocious—the most obnoxious—the most horridly insatiable..."

The Duke bowed to her, a gleam in his eye. "My dear Augusta, if I had known then that to refuse your bed would still smart after all these years, I'd have obliged you. But even as a callow youth of fifteen years I possessed enough discernment to resist every trick in your sexual repertoire to seduce me. But I will say no more. Theophilus is looking particularly offended by our—er—behavior. You may slap my face later, Augusta, if it will satisfy an urge. Ah, here is your tea."

Hawthorne set the silver tray on a side-table and when the Duke had settled himself with a dish of coffee, this time in a chair by the fire, he continued.

"It is not Strathsay's will which need concern us. Theo is named son and heir in that document, which was drawn up many years before the Earl's death. You did not know, my boy? Yes, it is so. But Salvan never knew, and possibly still does not. You see why as a—er—bastard you were never a threat to Salvan's plans?"

"Theo's legitimacy doesn't change the fact there is a marriage contract between Salvan and Strathsay," argued the Countess. "Strathsay signed the document before he died. What can Theo possibly do to change it, legitimacy or no?"

"It is Frederick Moran's will which is all important."

Lady Strathsay frowned. "Now I am doubly confused. That eccentric quack died over a year ago. I don't see what he has to do with it at all!"

"My dear, you blush. A heavy conscience, perchance?" taunted the Duke and glanced at Theo who was staring angrily at his mother. "You know my sister recently married Lucian Vallentine and that they honeymooned in Venice and Tuscany?"

"Of course," said Lady Strathsay, growing uncomfortable under her son's watchful gaze. "Why they decided to go through Italy I'll never understand."

"I sent them," said Roxton. "Vallentine was happy to oblige. I had him go to the house of a particular lawyer—Moran's lawyer. It just so happens the signori had a copy of Sir Frederick's will. Wasn't that a stroke of good luck? When one considers the original was somehow mislaid on his death. But Sir Frederick wrote you of his intentions, Augusta."

"If he did, I can't remember it particularly. It must have been a long time ago."

"Five years ago to be precise. He thought it prudent to advise you, as Antonia's grandmother, of his plans for his daughter should he die suddenly. I have the letter—a copy left with his lawyer. It confirms what I thought months back. But I was unable to act upon it." Roxton drank the last of his coffee and continued. "You know as well as I that Strathsay was never named in Sir Frederick's will as Antonia's guardian. Certainly the name Strathsay is written, but the name is Theophilus James Fitzstuart, second Earl of Strathsay. Moran assumed the old Earl would be long dead before himself, and Theophilus to have inherited the title."

"He meant for me to be Antonia's guardian, Mamma, not Strathsay," stated Theo. "Moran told you this in his letter. He also informed you that he was making the Duke the executor of his will."

Lady Strathsay shrugged a shoulder and yawned. "If he did I cannot remember any letter."

"Rest assured, my boy, you are Antonia's guardian."

"What of it?" retorted the Countess. "It does not change the fact Antonia is contracted to marry the Vicomte d'Ambert."

"It changes everything, Mamma," argued her son. "Strathsay had no right to contract a marriage for Antonia. He was never her guardian, thus the contract is invalid. She is not bound to marry the Vicomte."

"So you think, my son?" said his mother airily. "Until your claim is signed by our monarch you are not the second Earl of Strathsay, are you?"

Theo Fitzstuart stiffened, but the Duke laughed softly. "A spark of intelligence, my dear Augusta. There is no need to freeze-over, my boy. Your claim will be signed and this week, so I am told. You will be Earl of Strathsay by deed as well as birth before the week is out. And as such, Antonia's legal guardian. It is then for you to decide her fate."

"Tell me, Theo," said the Countess caustically, "what will be her fate? Is there to be an exchange of suitors? Who is the more suitable think you?"

"Please, Mamma, I have not thought—that is—this role is new and—"

"A young Frenchman of noble birth—we only have Roxton's word for it he is of unbalanced mind—or perhaps you would prefer to see her wedded to this aging bull—"

"—I want is what's best for Antonia," Theo Fitzstuart concluded firmly. "Antonia's wants and needs are of paramount importance. And so I shall ask her—"

"Oh, spare me! Ask a eighteen-year-old girl what she wants?" The Countess's laugh was brittle. "Now that is insane!"

"Eight—*eighteen*?" It was Roxton and he had spoken in a whisper.

The Countess raised her perfectly arched brows at the Duke. "Yes, *eight*-teen," she enunciated with a purr, watching the nobleman's throat constrict as he put a hand to his mouth. "She had the temerity to add two years to her short life, foolishly thinking twenty would be taken more seriously than eighteen. Whoever heard of a female *adding* years to her age?" She shrugged a bare shoulder, a sly glance of satisfaction at the Duke who, for want of something to mask his discomfort, was concentrating on untying the ribbon on the bundle of letters. "Eighteen or twenty, two years is rather inconsequential to a man hurtling towards forty, is it, Duke? Though... it must make the prospect of tasting the cherry that much the sweeter—"

"*Mamma.*"

"Really, Theo," she said with a sigh of annoyance at her son's embarrassment showing in a brick red face and rose to her slippered feet. "I don't know how you can deplore the conduct and intentions of the one without condemning equally the other. It seems to me Roxton's designs on Antonia are no less sordid than the Comte de Salvan's. What would you, Theo?"

"Bravo, Augusta. Bra-vo!" sneered the Duke. "Your hatred and envy of your only grandchild knows no bounds."

The Countess tossed her long red mane over a shoulder as she flounced to the door of her bedchamber. "Take your letters and go away, Roxton. Though why you would want to read them now, but then, I don't care one way or t'other. Just leave John and me in peace for the rest of the week—both of you. Oh, there is one particular I forgot to mention," she said standing in the doorway and smiling sweetly. "As you are now the girl's guardian, Theo, it is your problem. I dare say the Duke will offer his advice seeing he has such a deep interest in our little Antonia. I wonder how you will go about untangling this mess if you decide against the Vicomte's suit? You can at least tell the boy to his face—"

"Pardon, Mamma?"

"Did I not mention it earlier? How shatterbrained of me! Yesterday afternoon, when Charlotte startled me with the news of Roxton's return, I was so surprised and shocked by it that I immediately wrote off to advise the Comte de Salvan—"

"How like you!" Roxton hissed, rising up.

"Itching to use your blade, Cousin?" she teased, though the venom in his voice made her inwardly quake. "At least I had the decency to inform you of it."

"How could you do such a thing?" demanded Theo in exasperation. "What purpose can it serve? Even if Salvan, his son, or both of them, come hot-foot from Versailles, it changes nothing."

"We shall see won't we. After all, I am not convinced the boy is as bad as Roxton makes out. He has written Antonia many charming letters. And she has never said a bad word about him."

"That's just Antonia. She sees the good in everyone," said Theo with a tired sigh, a hand to his forehead. "God, now what am I to do?" He glanced at the Duke who had gone to stand by the window to look out at the traffic of sedan chairs, carriages, and wagons loaded up for market. "Your Grace, I'm sorry— I..."

Roxton bowed politely to Lady Strathsay and it caused her an instant of uneasiness. "I wish you both a good day. Enjoy a pleasant week, Augusta. The one after won't be.

$\mathcal{T}$hirteen

$\mathcal{T}$heo Fitzstuart arrived at Mr. Harcourt's Twickenham retreat to find his niece's baggage and her maid awaiting the carriage in the panelled hall. He was informed Miss Moran was in the library with Mr. and Miss Harcourt. The butler showed him into a long, cluttered room lined with books. Mr. Harcourt was at the very top of a pair of steps searching a shelf. Antonia stood nearby, her head bent over the pages of a thick volume that rested on a rung. Miss Harcourt sat by a warming fire, the needlework in her lap forgotten as she listened to her brother and Antonia arguing over some point of scholarship that left her mystified.

Theo asked not to be announced, thus was able to surprise Miss Harcourt without making his presence immediately known to the others.

"No, don't disturb them," he whispered and sat beside her on the sofa. "I wish to have a word with you a moment." He took her hand and kissed it. "Has Twickenham been an effort without my company to sustain you, Miss Harcourt?"

She smiled. "I hardly know how to answer you without making you frown, Mr. Fitzstuart. If I said I haven't had a moment's peace this past sennight to be anything but entertained, yet, would have preferred to spend such time quietly, you at my side, would you be satisfied?"

"I hope my niece has not been a sad trial."

"Oh no! She is delightful! You mustn't think she has put me to any trouble or caused a moment's worry," Charlotte assured him. "The first two days she was not quite herself, but once Percy got her interested in his library he managed to coax her out of any tendency to brood on—on certain particulars. There are times, quiet moments, when I see she is not far from her thoughts, but Percy has been such a Trojan. He is rather taken with Antonia."

Theo frowned.

"You needn't concern yourself there is anything more to Percy's affection than boyish worship," said Charlotte tidying her needlework into its basket. "All his great loves are atop pedestals. I don't think one has come out of the clouds yet. And now he has put Antonia up there too. Although she is different from the rest. She tells him what she thinks, and none too kindly for poor Percy's sensitive nerves."

"I'm afraid my niece is given to speaking her mind," apologised Theo. "A circumstance her father encouraged. I trust she has not shocked you in any way?"

"No. Not in the least. At first, that is, on our first meeting, I was inclined to think her of your mother's temperament. There is a striking resemblance in form, you must agree. But as to her conduct and her nature she is as far removed from the Lady Strathsay as any stranger. Forgive me if that offends you."

"No. We have always spoken frankly about my mother," he said with a smile. "That is as it should be." He glanced at Antonia who had a satin slipper on the bottom rung of the library steps and was passing a book into Mr. Harcourt's outstretched hand. "Has she been keeping well?"

"In customary good health, Mr. Fitzstuart. Although, her appetite is wanting. I don't believe I have seen her eat more than a morsel or two each meal. That concerns me, as does the fact she is too pale. And she suffers a slight ache in the joint of her damaged shoulder on very cold days. But she is not one to complain," said Miss Harcourt conversationally. When Theo looked at her in a penetrating way she lost the smile in her brown eyes. "Mr. Fitzstuart, that girl is suffering. She and I do not know each other well enough for her to confide in me her innermost thoughts. But upon one or two occasions we have spoken about her life at Versailles, and of her stay in Paris. It seems she has a great deal to be thankful for in the Duke of Roxton's protection. That French Comte sounds positively odious."

"And, Miss Harcourt?" asked Theo. "Please, I hope you will be just as frank about my niece's welfare."

"She has not told me this herself, and I have no wish to alarm you," she explained with a glance at him from under her lashes, "but Antonia is very much in love with the Duke. At first I was incredulous. I thought it nothing more than a girlish infatuation. Yet, that cannot account for it. She knows what sort of man he is and yet... Am I making myself clear to you?"

"Very clear. And...?"

Charlotte looked down at her hands in her lap, to gather her thoughts. "I am ashamed at repeating what Antonia has told me in confidence but I do so because I am worried for her and I know you, as her uncle, do have her best interests at heart. Your niece has made plans to leave for Venice within the month. She would rather flee to the Continent than be forced into marriage with the Vicomte d'Ambert. She has written to your father's mistress, Maria Caspartti, asking her for sanctuary! To think Antonia would prefer to live with your father's whore than remain with her grandmother not only says a great deal about the Countess's lack of feeling, but that Maria Caspartti, for all her immorality, must have a kind heart. I even offered for Antonia to remain here at Twickenham, with Percy and I, but she is adamant she would prefer to live in the relative obscurity of Venice than bring shame on her family and friends.... and the Duke." Charlotte raised her gaze to Theo Fitzstuart's thin-lipped countenance. "I cannot imagine what shame an innocent girl could possibly bring to a nobleman of the Duke's notorious reputation, do you, Mr. Fitzstuart? But it breaks my heart to think she feels she must ostracize herself on his account."

"Thank you, my dear," Theo stated, glad he would finally have the opportunity to speak privately with his niece on the journey to Treat, and abruptly changed the subject by withdrawing a parchment from his frockcoat and handing it to her. "An invitation to Treat for you and Percy. It is for tomorrow. Although it is short notice I hope you will attend the Duke's weekend party, if only to see my mother in a hundred agonies." He smiled. "Can you imagine it, Charlotte? The Countess to spend four days in the country under Roxton's roof, away from London and her suitors, surrounded by animals of the barn and green fields! She will wilt, I know it!"

"I'm sure she cannot conceive of a worse fate. It is a wonder she accepted the invitation."

"She was not so much invited as commanded. She dare not incur any more of Cousin Roxton's wrath. She has stretched his benevolence to the breaking point as it is. It is he who manages her finances, lets her his Hanover address for a peppercorn rent, and maintains her fine carriage and six. It is useless for her to appeal to Lord Ely. He won't support her as long as she remains in London. He wants her with him at Ely. Then his purse would be hers. Yet, she refuses to give up London!"

"Poor Lady Strathsay," said Charlotte without sympathy. "Percy and I must attend if only to see how she copes with the country life. Mr. Fitzstuart—"

"Theo. I demand you call me by my name. Especially now that we are betrothed. Or you may, if you wish to be formal with me until such time as the notice appears in the Gazette, address me as my title warrants—"

"Theo!" Charlotte gasped, and so loudly Antonia and Mr. Harcourt looked over at her at the same moment.

Lord Strathsay jumped up and pulled her into an embrace. "Dear Charlotte, you see before you the second Earl of Strathsay!"

Antonia ran up to them and tugged on the great upturned cuff of her uncle's travelling frock, forcing him to release Miss Harcourt and look at her.

"I do not mind at all that you kiss Charlotte, but I object to wasting time helping Harcourt. You did not announce yourself!"

"Well! I say!" said Mr. Harcourt with a wounded look. He did not bother to greet Lord Strathsay nor did he notice how red was his sister's face. "If you did not want me to help you find this wretched book you shouldn't have asked for it in the first place!"

Antonia tilted her little nose at him. "I only wanted it because Theo was late and I had nothing better to do with my time—"

"Well! Well! Thank you for being so forthright."

"Besides, your French tongue, it is very bad," admonished

Antonia, but with a dimple at her uncle.

"That is unkind of you, Antonia," lectured her uncle with mock seriousness.

When Antonia hesitated to reply Mr. Harcourt stuck out his lower lip, and this made her laugh. "Do not look so hurt, Harcourt. I was only teasing. Your French tongue, it is not so bad as your Italian, which is better than..." She paused to think.

"Better than whose, Miss Moran?" asked Mr. Harcourt eagerly.

"Than—M'sieur Vallentine's!"

"Me cousin?" blinked Mr. Harcourt. "I'm not surprised. He speaks English badly enough!"

"*Bon Dieu.* All you English are related," Antonia said with a shake of her curls. "But I should have guessed you are a cousin to Vallentine. It is in the brain."

"Antonia!" Lord Strathsay said brusquely, but he could not help breaking into a smile.

Miss Harcourt thought it time to intervene and she took Antonia's hands in her own. "Shall you like to have me for an aunt, Antonia?"

"*Parbleu,* more than anyone! I am glad Theo finally proposed. I was about to become annoyed with him."

Lord Strathsay tweaked one of her curls. "Were you indeed?"

"What's that you say? Charlotte! Are you—are you— betrothed," stuttered Mr. Harcourt.

"Is it such a surprise to you, this betrothal, Harcourt?" said Antonia haughtily. "It pleases me very much because I do not have any aunts. And soon Theo and Charlotte will have babies, which will please me even more because I want many cousins."

It was some three hours later, and approaching the dinner hour, when the elegant chaise carrying the Earl of Strathsay and his niece turned in through the imposing black and gold leaf iron gates that proclaimed the entrance to the Duke of Roxton's Hampshire estate, Treat. The mansion stood atop a grassy hill at the end of a meandering mile-long, tree-lined drive. The main building dated back to the Restoration. Yet, with its decades of remodelling, it barely resembled its former self. Buildings swept east and west from this central structure which had a view of the man-made lake, well-stocked with trout, ducks and swans, and dotted with several small islands accessible by punt and bridge. To the east, acres of Ornamental gardens clung to the gentle slope and curved away down to the lake. To the west was a small enclosed Elizabethan garden, ivy walled and crumbling, and beyond this, forest and fields and hamlets; all belonging to his Grace the Duke of Roxton.

The drive through the tree-lined boulevard skirted the lake and Antonia kept her nose pressed to the glass and caught glimpses of templed islands and swans gliding under a stone bridge, of autumnal forest, and undulating pastures newly fallowed beyond where sheep grazed undisturbed. But nothing prepared her for her first view of the house.

When the carriage came to a halt on the gravel drive she could hardly wait for a liveried footman to open the door and fold down the steps. Grooms ran across the crushed stone to the horses heads, baggage was tossed down to waiting lackeys, and the driver jumped down from his box, stripped off his gloves, and accepted the tankard of refreshment offered him. The door was opened by a bowing lackey. But before Antonia could alight Lord Strathsay put out his hand to keep her in her seat. She looked at him enquiringly and waited an explanation.

"You tell me you're determined to make Venice your home," said her uncle, taking her gloved hand in his. "And I will not stop you if… if after this weekend you still wish it. But I ask you to seriously consider my offer: that you make your home with Charlotte and I."

Antonia shook her head, a curious lump in her throat. "Thank you, Theo. That is very kind of you and of Charlotte. But I—I cannot stay in England."

He squeezed her hand. "We have known each other for such a short time and I do not want to lose you so soon. But I do not want you to be unhappy here, and you are. Why?"

"Please-please do not ask me to explain… One day the reason it will be very obvious and I—I cannot bear for you to think me a better person than I am. In truth I am more like Grandmamma than you can ever imagine! So please, now, let us go inside because this journey has made me very ill."

With that astonishing pronouncement Antonia hurriedly bunched up the layers of her quilted petticoats and scrambled out of the carriage with the help of an attentive footman. She walked towards the collection of monolithic buildings stretching to the left and right of her without looking up until hailed by her uncle to wait up for him. It was only then that she lifted her gaze from the crushed rock of the gravel drive and her green eyes widened at the enormity of the aspect before her.

"*Tiens*. Vallentine was right. This place is as monstrous as the palace at Versailles!"

"Not quite on that scale," Lord Strathsay said with a laugh. "But it is certainly monstrous. And growing more so, what with the Duke's latest improvements. He has commissioned the whole of his private apartments be remodelled and refurbished, and of all things to incorporate into the grand vision, a bathing *room*, with tiled plunge bath and running heated water, along Roman lines, if you please!" Theo shook his head as he led Antonia into an Italian marble foyer the size of a Great hall in any respectable house. "Can you imagine it? Ah, Duvalier, you may take Mademoiselle Moran's coat and muff."

Antonia could well imagine a tiled plunge bath along Roman lines, and tears welled up at the back of her green eyes. Quickly, she took in the ceiling, with its blue skies painted with clouds, and golden cupids, and the Gods all staring down from the heavens at her and inexplicably she felt very happy, happier than she had been in weeks. Perhaps fate had not deserted her after all?

Mention of the butler by name brought Antonia's nose instantly down from the clouds and for one horrified moment Lord Strathsay thought she was about embrace the old man. "Duvalier! Oh, Duvalier, it is such a pleasure to see a familiar face," she said happily and shook his hand.

The butler's face cracked and he beamed at her as he took her coat and muff and held them to him as if they were his own. "May I say what a pleasure it is to have Mademoiselle Moran as a guest at Treat."

Lord Strathsay watched in astonishment as the butler and his niece spoke in hushed tones like two old friends. He could hardly believe this happy smiling creature to be the same girl who on the carriage ride through the countryside had looked so forlorn and with the weight of the world on her shoulders, and he dared not interrupt, following them as they mounted the curved staircase.

"Do you have a long way to walk to the front door?" asked Antonia skipping beside the butler, her head turning this way and that to take in the paintings, the furniture, and all the gilt and marble of the vast rooms that lead off the passageway. "How is Baptiste?"

"Who is Baptiste?" asked Lord Strathsay but was unconsciously ignored.

"Ah! Mademoiselle remembers Baptiste!" said Duvalier beaming up to his ears. "He will never drive again, such is his elbow. It is sad for him, but he is not unhappy. M'sieur le Duc gives him the safekeeping of all his carriages and equipages in Paris. It is an important position, a respectable living. Baptiste, he is not unhappy. His wife, she is very proud of him. She is my sister's second cousin. So, Baptiste, he is family."

"Is that so?" said Antonia with interest. "I am glad for him and your sister's second cousin."

"Duvalier," said Lord Strathsay, and was pleased to see the butler's back stiffen to attention. "Where are you taking us?"

"Forgive me, my lord," the butler said tonelessly and without another look at Antonia, who had wandered off to inspect the view from a set of long windows. "M'sieur le Duc directed that you be shown your rooms immediately as dinner is soon to be announced."

Theo waved him on and took Antonia by the hand lest she wander off again. He left her at the door to her suite of rooms with the promise that she not roam the corridors but wait for him once she had changed into a suitable gown so he could escort her to dinner. He was changed and dressed before she was but he was not kept waiting many minutes. She came out of her dressing room in a froth of Venetian red petticoats. The emerald choker was about her throat and her hair was swept up off her face and left to cascade about her bare shoulders. She collected a large fan of carved ivory and her reticule and went down to the Saloon with her uncle.

About twenty guests were assembled in the Oriental drawing room off the Saloon. Not all those invited for the weekend had arrived in time for dinner. Most were unknown to Antonia and she stuck to her uncle's side as he crossed the room in search of his mother. He found her soon enough. She was talking with Lady Paget and looked anything but pleased with her surroundings.

"They did come in time to dine!" announced Lady Paget and kissed both Antonia's cheeks. "How was your stay with the Harcourts, my love?"

"You look none the worse for a week with Percy Harcourt," Lady Strathsay quipped and held out her hand to her son. "Did you bring Charlotte with you?"

"Percy is bringing her down tomorrow."

Antonia curtseyed prettily to her grandmother then dutifully kissed her forehead but could not understand why she received nothing more than a perfunctory welcome.

"Would you care for refreshment?" Lady Paget asked Antonia. "Come, let us sit down and you can tell me all about Percy's unusual house."

"Enjoying your stay, Mamma?"

"Don't be an ass, Theophilus," his mother grumbled. "What is there to do in the country but get one's feet muddy? The child looks particularly radiant. What did you say to her? Or did a week of Harcourt's sickening devotion restore her spirits? It wouldn't be because you happened to mention the Vicomte's visit? You did tell her I hope?"

"I don't see Roxton…"

"He's always late. So you didn't tell her," said Lady Strathsay slyly, peering over the sticks of her fan. "That was unwise."

"The right moment did not present itself. I hardly see that it makes a difference."

"We shall see who is right," she stated and turned a different face to her granddaughter. "Antonia, my love, come see who has just come through the door." She rose to have a better view of her granddaughter's face, and when the girl gave a horrified start she turned back to her son with a smile of satisfaction. "There," she said triumphantly. "Did I not advise you to tell her before she arrived?"

Antonia had interrupted her conversation with Lady Paget to go to her grandmother. She had not heard her words but followed her gaze across the room. Lord Strathsay was looking in the same direction, but whereas the Countess was smiling as she fanned herself, he was frowning through his quizzing-glass. Antonia expected to see the Duke, such was the general hush. But it was not the Duke. Making a slow progress across the room was the Vicomte d'Ambert.

There was a moment's frightened hesitation before Antonia curtseyed and extended a hand to the Vicomte. His bow was very formal and there was no hint of warmth in his pale face. She noted he had taken to wearing a mouche at the corner of his eye and rouge on his close-shaven cheeks. His wig was thickly powdered and his frock, with its stiff gold skirts, outshone even her grandmother's heavy gold petticoats.

As she stared at the top of his powdered head the warm blood in her veins seemed to turn to ice for she felt suddenly very cold. She wondered if the Comte de Salvan had indeed won out after all and this weekend house party was in effect to be a celebration of her engagement to the Vicomte. Her grandmother certainly looked pleased with the young Frenchman, and as surprise had not registered on her uncle's face it seemed to confirm her fears that this reunion had been arranged all along. She felt sick to her stomach, but forced herself to smile at the Vicomte who was staring at her in a fixed way.

Lady Strathsay prodded her with the pointed silver sticks of her fan. "Have you nothing to say to M'sieur le Vicomte, my dear?"

Antonia could only stammer a welcome. The Vicomte turned away to answer a question put to him by Lord Strathsay, but after five minutes of polite conversation with Antonia's uncle and her grandmother he took Antonia by the elbow and unceremoniously led her to the closest unoccupied sofa.

"Ten weeks in England and you cannot utter one word of warm greeting?" he whispered. "Have you lost the use of your tongue?"

"I was so surprised to see you, Étienne. Did you think I would not be?" she countered in an angry whisper and flicked open her fan.

The Vicomte looked about with distaste and took snuff. "How can you bear it in this barbaric country, eh? The English tongue, it grates on the ear. And to hear them speak French? *Parbleu*, it offends me. And there is this dish called—pudding? Yes, pudding. *Mon Dieu*, it is an abomination!"

Antonia wondered if he was jesting, but he looked so serious that laughter bubbled up in her throat. Despite her efforts to be good she started to giggle.

Lady Strathsay turned a smug smile on her son and raised her perfectly arched brows. "Did you expect different?"

"A moment ago you were foretelling doom, Mamma," Theo reminded her, gaze on the young couple. "Both of us must be thankful the reunion went better than anticipated."

"Better for whom?"

Lord Strathsay saw a familiar glint in his mother's eye and frowned. "Don't interfere in this, Mamma. Roxton knows what he is about—"

"Kate!" the Countess called out, ignoring her son. "What think you of our young Frenchman?"

Lady Paget disentangled herself from a discussion with a local gentleman farmer on the cultivation of exotic fruits and followed her friend's gaze to where Antonia and Étienne sat together talking. "He seems personable enough. Too serious for one so young. Why, my dear? You're not thinking..."

"Certainly not!" retorted the Countess and glared at her son who dared to grin. "But for my granddaughter certainly."

"I can see no objection to such a union," said Lady Paget. "But I don't know the boy. But as your son intends to leave the decision up to Antonia, any efforts on your part to push the match will be wasted, my dear. Shall we go into dinner? I see the Duke has arrived."

Lord Strathsay offered Lady Paget his arm and joined the rest of the guests filing through the heavy mahogany double doors. Duvalier stood behind his master's chair at the head of the long table and a footman was consigned to stand behind each of the twenty chairs, their red and silver livery a compliment to the rich Brussels tapestries that adorned the four walls. Three heavy crystal chandeliers cast a shimmering glow from the panelled ceiling, and from up high in the gallery that ran the length of the long room, came the melodic sound of a string quartet.

The Vicomte sat himself beside Antonia with a shake of his head. "He lives better than Louis!" he whispered, as he took in the blaze of wax, the shimmering of crystal, and the mountains of food expertly arranged in priceless porcelain dishes along the table. "It is as well my father is not here. All this magnificence, it would send him into an apoplexy!"

Antonia permitted an attentive footman to fill her glass with burgundy. "Then be sure to tell him of everything you see," she said, and smiled when Étienne was struck with this idea and laughed out loud.

At the far end of the table Lady Paget kept an eye on the couple as best she could through the elaborate arrangements of food, and the movement of powdered heads and footmen. She could not see Lady Strathsay, who was seated at the far end playing hostess to an elderly General and a self-righteous spinster. She considered herself more fortunate seated as she was on the Duke's left with Lord Strathsay beside her.

She awaited the opportunity to speak with the Duke who was listening politely to the inconsequential chatterings of one Susanna Woodruff, a pretty blonde with big blue eyes and the daughter of Sir Jasper—a breeder of Arabians. Susanna knew all the latest gossip. This fact, thought Lady Paget with a wry smile, and her blonde beauty, placed her in such a privileged position on her host's right hand.

Her opportunity came when Miss Woodruff's attention was diverted by the young man at her side who interrupted her flow of scandal with an impertinent observation of his own.

"I wonder if Susanna has any idea she is speaking to the very man she just maligned as Beth Ruthmore's coxcombical lover?" mused Lady Paget and pushed aside the remainder of her pea soup. But when the Duke did not respond, or look her way, she tapped his lace ruffled wrist with her fan. "Roxton! You've just put away a second asparagus tart, and I know you loathe asparagus!"

The Duke stared at his plate and pushed it aside with a shudder.

"Forgive me, Kate. I am a neglectful host."

"And a distracted one; to me, and all your guests," she

quipped. But he did not smile. "Augusta informs me your sister is on her way to London. Do you expect her any day?"

"Not soon enough. I was the unfortunate who experienced the Grand Tour in Lucian Vallentine's company. Thus, I don't expect they will be here when I want them. A regretful circumstance and one that will displease Estée. But I don't intend to sit idly by to await Vallentine's pleasure." He levelled his quizzing-glass at a bowl of fruit offered him by a footman and selected an apple. "I fear that was not all Augusta told you…"

"Oh no," she assured him. "But I don't break confidences." She accepted a wedge of apple from the Duke's pearl-handled paring knife and smiled at him when he frowned. "I have always been discreet, my dear. You, however, have been remarkably lax. Though that never bothered you in the past." When the Duke's gaze travelled half the length of the table and held, the apple consumed in silence, she gave an impatient sigh. "There really is no hope for you. Damn you! There was a time when I, and several others, would've been most offended by such blatant public un-faithfulness."

"It is exceedingly difficult to put into words, Kate… It's as if she's shown me the existence of color," the Duke marvelled and dragged his gaze from Antonia to look at Lady Paget with a self-deprecating smile. "The world is no longer grey."

Lady Paget smiled and squeezed his sleeve affectionately. "You know of course that this means there is no hope of recovery. You must marry her without delay."

"It is not that—er—simple."

"You hesitate because that handsome French boy thinks himself betrothed to her?"

The Duke returned to slicing up the second half of the apple but the hard set of his features told her something of his feelings. She shrugged.

"There is a solution," she said quietly, for Miss Woodruff had ended her discussion with the young man and was intent on recapturing the Duke's attention. "Elope."

"As her mother and her grandmother did before her? And as my mother did also?"

"You have given the idea serious consideration, I see?"

234

"It is a neat solution—for myself. And for the Salvans? My dear cousin's guilt would be absolved and he sympathised with in the wake of the scandal of our elopement. To argue the illegalities of his claim on Antonia after she becomes Duchess of Roxton is petty retribution."

"What is scandal to you? Is not the fact she will be your duchess punishment enough for the Salvans?"

The Duke downed the last of his wine and signalled for Duvalier. "You forget the Vicomte. He is innocent..."

She showed surprise. "But Augusta said..."

"Told you everything didn't she," he said with a crooked smile. "He believes himself betrothed. His—er—condition only makes the situation that much more delicate. Tell me, Kate," he said as he rose to bow the ladies out, "would the Duchess of Roxton be received in polite circles once the elopement became public?"

Lady Paget had an eye on the train of ladies departing for the drawing room. She also noted that Susanna Woodruff hung back by the door waiting for her. "I see your dilemma," she said with a sigh. "You know the answer as well as I. I have never understood why we females, once cloaked in the respectability of marriage, may be as lax as we please with our favors. But to elope? No. I doubt she would ever lose that stigma."

The Duke smiled thinly. "I watched my mother suffer most cruelly from such social ostracism and I will not allow my wife to suffer as she did."

Lady Paget pressed his hand. "Just so, your Grace. But I do believe Antonia does not care a fig for society's dictates. Because of her father she has been a social outcast all her life. Only one circumstance matters to Antonia: being with you."

At that Lady Paget quickly followed the ladies to the Long Gallery where card tables had been set up and tea and coffee awaited them. Three footmen stood in attendance by a lacquered sideboard laden with dishes and plates of sweetmeats. A huge silver coffee urn stood on its walnut stand and a similar one for tea was placed at Lady Strathsay's elbow so she could pour out. The ladies grouped themselves on the satin-striped sofas and spindle-legged chairs arranged about one of two large fireplaces.

Along the exterior wall was a series of French windows

draped in heavy brocade curtains of blues and gold. Beyond the windows stretched a terrace of black and white marble with a low-columned wall on three sides and a set of stairs leading down to the Ornamental Gardens.

Antonia stood at one of these windows watching a footman light tapers that stuck out at right angles to the low wall. She was not in a good mood. Dinner had been a strain. What with Étienne on one side of her with his incessant questioning of everything she had done while in London, and his constant derogatory opinions of the English and all things English; and on her right, Sir Jasper Woodruff, a good humored gentleman, who thought himself doing Antonia a great courtesy by conversing in French. But the kind gentleman's French pronunciation was atrocious. Antonia remained polite and did not request that he speak in English, so struggled through a conversation with the greatest difficulty.

An hour later he again caught her attention. This time, having drunk a goodly quantity of fine French claret, he confided in English that the pretty blonde on Roxton's right was his daughter. He had great expectations of his good friend the Duke offering for Susanna. He misinterpreted Antonia's look of incredulity for one of astonishment that the Duke, so long a bachelor of notorious reputation, would ever consider the married state. He further confided in her that Susanna had been brought up a sensible female and as such would not make demands that the Duke change his lifestyle in any way. She would turn a blind eye to his indiscretions in exchange for the title of Duchess.

As if to illustrate this point, Sir Jasper proudly pointed out his daughter's exemplary behavior, when across the table from her was Kate Paget. Now what other female could so conduct herself without blushing, when there before her was the Duke's mistress of many moons in intimate conversation with her intended?

Antonia wondered if she had heard Sir Jasper correctly, or missed something in the translation. But thinking it over for the rest of a long meal that she only picked at, she knew Sir Jasper was not spreading mere rumor. Somehow it really did not surprise her. Madame de La Tournelle and Madame Duras-Valfons she had dismissed as mere diversions, as she had the Duke's rumored visits to that notorious bordello catering to the French nobility, the Maison Clermont. But knowing Lady Paget and liking her company made this liaison all the more painful to disregard.

These thoughts ran through her mind as she shivered in the breeze of the open window, oblivious to the cold and the imperious loud command from her grandmother that she instantly rejoin the rest of the group about the fireplace. The ladies continued to drink their tea, nibble on sweetmeats, and exchange the latest gossip. But they were not oblivious to the strange girl with the oblique green eyes who spoke English with a thick accent and, it was whispered, was betrothed to the handsome young Vicomte.

Miss Woodruff was the first to ask the question all were thinking but dared not voice. "My lady," she said to the Countess, her blue eyes on Antonia's back, "I could not help noticing that divine collar of emeralds about Miss Moran's throat. Do tell us its history. Is it a betrothal gift, a family heirloom, or—"

"I am sure it will become an heirloom," cut in Lady Paget before her friend had the chance to reply. "It is divine, isn't it? A gift from the Duke for her birthday, so I am told. Would anyone care for another macaroon? They are delicious."

The plate was passed around and Lady Paget drifted over to the French windows and slipped an arm about Antonia's small waist. When the girl looked up, blushed and pulled away, she was a little hurt but did not let it bother her.

"Close the door, or you'll catch your death, my dear," said Lady Paget with a smile. "Your grandmother requires your presence at her tea party. But if you like I will walk the Gallery with you."

"I am sorry—I did not mean…"

"There is a large portrait over the far fireplace I would like to show you, and several others in between you might find most interesting. Or do you prefer to take a dish of coffee first?"

"No."

"Good. Come along then," said Lady Paget and linked arms with Antonia. "This must be the longest room in the house. Or is the library just as long? I can't remember precisely. It has been quite some time since I was last here. Roxton has done extensive modifications to this wing so I am rather disorientated. Huge, isn't it? An Elizabethan mansion burned to the ground by Cromwell—

barbarian! Only the ruins of the chapel remain and part of the wall which enclosed the churchyard. This present structure, or should I say what is left of it after the fourth Duke and Roxton got their hands on it, dates from King Charles's time. It was the largest residence in the kingdom until Blenheim was built." She glanced at Antonia. "Did you think it hideous on first seeing it?"

"Oh no, my lady. I thought it monstrous."

Lady Paget's brown eyes twinkled. "Monstrously hideous?"

Antonia had to smile.

"There," said Lady Paget looking up to a painted canvas in an ornate gold leaf frame above the Italian marble fireplace.

Against a dark painted background of muted volumes and mahogany panelling were four figures in a splendour of vivid colours. The lady was seated, dressed in a blue velvet gown the same shade as the color of her eyes, her dark hair swept off her face but with one long curl over her shoulder. On her lap was a baby of about two or three years in age with the same colored eyes, and with short curly hair. The lady was very beautiful and the baby was in her image.

Standing behind this lady, a hand to the back of the chair, the other resting on the jewelled hilt of his sword, was her husband. He wore the latest fashion in frocks for that time. The skirts were long, wide and made stiff with whalebone and paste, and the large cuffs were turned back and held up with enormous round buttons of engraved gold. His cravat was elaborate and of the finest lace; his wig, full-bottomed and powdered. He had lean cheeks, black eyes and a strong nose. There was that air of calm assurance about him and a smile that was more insolent than friendly. On a long white finger he wore a large square-cut emerald.

The fourth figure was a long-legged youth in oyster grey satin breeches and matching stiff-skirted frock. He reclined on the floor seated on a velvet cushion, an arm resting on his mother's lap, the other about the neck of a sleek white whippet with its paw on a page of an open book. The boy had his father's insolent smile and the beginnings of a strong nose, his mother's delicate, finely shaped hands and a head of thick black curls worn loose about his shoulders.

Lady Paget had no doubts Antonia knew instantly the identity of the members of this formal but domestic portrait, for the girl's gaze was riveted to the canvas in studious silence. She looked back to the portrait and began her monologue.

"Madeleine-Julie de Salvan was considered the paramount beauty of Louis the Fourteenth's court, and great things were expected of her," said Lady Paget. "Her brother, who was the Comte de Salvan at the time, arranged a splendid match for her with the son of the Prince de Parvelle. It was what both families wanted, and indeed, the match had the King's blessing. All was in readiness for a splendid court wedding. No one suspected Madeleine-Julie of other ideas. One day her maid discovered her mistress missing. Not only that but the girl went missing for ten days."

"Where did she go?" asked Antonia, finally taking her gaze from the portrait to stop a stiffness in her neck.

"She had eloped with the Marquis of Alston," Lady Paget answered brightly. "He was an Englishman, a Protestant, and five and thirty. She was barely eighteen, a Papist, and excommunicated for marrying a heretic and for renouncing her faith. Her family was disgraced and shunned at court. The Salvans lost their posts. It took them a decade to win back the favor of the King. The Comte refused to speak to his sister for many years. Lord Alston had been his closest friend.

"Nor was the marriage accepted by his family. The Marchioness was shunned by her husband's English relatives, too. She never set foot on English soil, and her children were considered bastards by the French—"

"*Mon Dieu.* It is all too horrible," muttered Antonia.

"Not at all," Lady Paget countered and gave Antonia a reassuring hug. "You mustn't think Madeleine-Julie's life with Alston was ever sad. They loved each other very much. They had no need for court life, or the whims of society. They were very content and happy, and as long as they had each other all was right with the world. The Marquis was devoted to his wife and children. It was not many years after their marriage, in fact with the birth of their first child, that the Comte de Salvan permitted his family to visit her. I think Roxton must have been seven or eight years old when the Comte finally forgave his sister.

"She was never permitted court again, but what of that when

the members of society came to her house in Paris to dine and visit? Society is very fickle. What is one day considered a scandal and never to be forgiven, is the next ignored and papered over, and all is as if nothing untoward had ever occurred. Life goes on as before. Do you understand, Antonia?"

"I do not care what society thinks or-or how it may act toward me. Besides, I am not so important that it would ever be bothered with me," said Antonia quietly. "I have never been a member of this society. Be it here, or France, or in Italy where my father took me after mama's death." She hung her head and fidgeted with the lock of her hair that had escaped its clasp. "But I do want to be happy, as Madeleine-Julie was happy. And I—I could not bear it if—if after everything… That is—What if the Marquis of Alston had not been so devoted to his wife and family? What if he had re-entered this society without her, and if he had been unfaithful after all she had sacrificed, and if—"

"La, that is a lot of ifs!" laughed Lady Paget. "Discount them all! You have nothing to worry that pretty head about, I promise you. My dear girl, don't you see? Roxton loves you to distraction!"

Antonia stiffened and blushed, and stared Lady Paget bravely in the face. "We were speaking of Madame la Marquise, my lady," she said tonelessly. "Nothing more than that. I may be young, and at times I know I am naïve, in fact, I am very stupid of the world. But I am not blind, nor a complete fool, that I do not see what is thrust in my face. Sir Jasper he confided he hopes M'sieur le Duc will offer for his daughter. He was very proud of her exemplary conduct at table, that she pretended to be as one blind that M'sieur le Duc's English mistress sat across from her, and she did not mind in the least. Well, I would mind very much! And that is a fault in me, I know it, but I cannot help the way I am. So, please, you of all people will not talk to me of M'sieur le Duc's feelings! I will go back now. I am cold and I want my coffee. Thank you for showing me this interesting portrait."

"Oh dear," said Lady Paget with a sigh as she watched Antonia scurry away. "Damn and blast Jasper!"

Fourteen

Roxton's guests were well into an evening of cards and conversation when the Duke finally made his appearance in the Gallery, the last of the gentlemen to rejoin the ladies. He put up his quizzing-glass to survey the commotion and was pleased the evening was progressing to his satisfaction. He was not at pains to join in the amusements. In fact he declined an offer to play at whist and ignored an invitation to sit at Miss Woodruff's side, the blatant movements of her lace fan eagerly interpreted by two hopeful gentlemen who scurried to throw themselves at her feet. Instead he went to warm his hands at the second fireplace.

Antonia did not notice him because he stood at her back, close to where she sat with the Vicomte on a chaise longue. Her head was bent over an empty tea dish, as if reading the signs in the settled leaves. It was not her dish but the Vicomte's. She preferred coffee, but he had insisted she try a sip of tea. At first she had refused, but his persistence made her snatch the dish so he would stop hounding her and make no further fuss. But a heated argument ensued. All because he dared to pass judgement on her choice of gown. He did not like it, he said. It made her look the whore. When they were married he would dictate what he thought suitable for the wife of a Vicomte. She laughed, but when she realised he was in earnest, disbelief made her angry.

"It was a mistake to let you leave France," he whispered with suppressed anger. "You not only dress like a whore but conduct yourself like a cheap strumpet!"

"I have had enough of M'sieur le Vicomte's opinions for one night," she stated and stood up. But he grabbed her wrist and jerked her back beside him. "Étienne! Let go of me!"

"Hold your tongue!" he demanded. "You dare to talk to me— me—the Vicomte d'Ambert, as if I was a mere…a mere—"

"Oh, Étienne, see reason. When you speak and act so you are Salvan," she said in a rallying tone. "We used to be such friends before he put this silly notion of marriage into your head."

"Silly notion?" he echoed, struggling to find a snuffbox in one of his pockets.

"Yes. I will forget what you called me if you apologize."

"Apologize? I?" he said haughtily. "Mademoiselle forgets herself. It is your conduct which needs an apology!"

"I trust you are enjoying the evening?" enquired the Duke in his characteristic soft voice. He had heard the whole of their exchange and thought it an opportune moment to intervene. He offered his snuffbox to the youth and was not surprised when it was refused. "Forgive me, my boy. I forget. The Vicomte prefers his own—er—blend, does he not?"

The Vicomte was on his feet. "Yes, M'sieur le Duc," he replied stiffly. "Mademoiselle and I were talking privately—"

"How charming," interrupted the Duke without a smile. "I regret I must bring your private conversation to an end. You will allow me five minutes alone with Mademoiselle Moran."

"But I—"

"I do not need you to answer for me, Étienne," Antonia whispered angrily and stepped aside to permit a footman to place a backgammon board on the chaise longue.

"You may watch over us if you so wish," said the Duke. He sat down with an outward flick of his skirts and began to distribute his pieces on the board. Without taking his eyes from his task he waved a lace-covered hand at the Vicomte. "From over there somewhere. I prefer to play at backgammon without an audience breathing down by back. Mademoiselle, when you are ready…"

The Vicomte bowed. "As M'sieur le Duc wishes. Mademoiselle, we will continue our discussion on the morrow. Perhaps she will have had sufficient time to reflect on the folly of her words."

"I have nothing else to say, Vicomte," said Antonia without looking up.

She hurriedly put her pieces in position, though she fumbled as she did so, and kept her eyes on the board, feeling awkward and nervous. She knew she blushed when the Duke put an arm over the back of the chaise and tweaked one of her curls in a cavalier fashion. She cast her die and waited his response.

"The luck is with you, petite," he said. "An ace cannot better your point trois."

Thereafter the game was conducted in silence. Only the sound of the card players at the tables occasionally disturbed their concentration. Several of the guests had spread out down the Gallery, with a few seated about the far fireplace. At one stage Sir Jasper wandered across to the Duke, full of bonhomie and too much claret, only to be ignored.

Miss Woodruff drifted up later to divert the game with a fatuous remark and was also ignored. At first she did not take the hint and stood chattering nothings until she noticed the Duke had eyes only for his backgammon partner. It shut her mouth in an instant and she flounced off to console herself with a puppy-eyed gentleman whom she had consistently avoided all evening.

Lady Strathsay, too, tried to disturb the couple and was intent on ordering Antonia to her rooms. But she was prevented from voicing her opinions on the lateness of the hour by her son, who whisked her away to listen to a recital of poetry at the farthest end of the Gallery.

The Vicomte pretended to interest himself in a game of Basset but all the while he watched Antonia. When he finished at the tables and made a move to cross the room he was intercepted by Lady Paget. He was so diverted to hear his tongue spoken in a civilized manner that he permitted her to take him to join the poetry recital.

Antonia saw and heard none of these manoeuvres. To her it was as if she was back in the Duke's private apartments of the hôtel, as it had been before she came to England, and how she had imagined it would be again. They played in silence. The Duke did not once initiate conversation; yet his mere presence made conversation unnecessary. At the conclusion of a fourth game she scooped up the dice and clapped her hands.

"I have won! You could not make the combinations to outrun my men. Not even with your doublets!"

"As we have won two games apiece we must play a fifth to decide the contest," he said and tossed his men back on the board. "You agree, *mignonne?*"

"Did you—You did not deliberately throw that game, did you, M'sieur le Duc?"

Her offended air amused him, but he spoke in a level voice at odds with the look in his black eyes. "That is a sad accusation to make, Antonia. I am surprised at you. Surely you know me better?"

"I-I am sorry. I did not mean—I know you would never do so," she said quickly and cast her die. "It is just that you so rarely lose."

"Rarely is not never. I hope I am enough of a gentleman to admit defeat when such rare instances do occur." He put up his quizzing-glass to consider his next move. "Now you must play at your best. If I am fortunate to win upon this occasion I will demand a reward, as is my right as victor."

"But we did not decide a stake before play commenced!" she argued. "That is unfair."

Her delay at casting the dice made him look up. "Unfair for whom? If you win it is your privilege to extract a reward. I am willing to take the risk. But if you think that it is not sporting...?"

"No! No! I will do it!" she assured him, and without a thought to her surroundings, kicked off her embossed-satin shoes and tucked her stockinged feet under her many petticoats to be more comfortably situated amongst the cushions. "Now, please, we will concentrate on the game because I want so much to win."

From the outset the game belonged to the Duke. He made careless moves which had his men captured many times, but only to mete out the same treatment to Antonia. Try as hard as she might, she could not get herself in a winning position. The end result was a gammon for the Duke. Antonia took the defeat well, though she complained he had prolonged the outcome by allowing her men to escape his inner table only to be recaptured and eventually shut out.

"It will always be the same," she said without complaint. "We could play at backgammon all our lives and you would still be the better player."

The Duke stared at the dice in his hand. "Believe me, *mignonne*, I would like that more than anything in this life."

She hung her head. "Please, M'sieur le Duc. You must not say such things to me because I-I—Oh! I do not know how to tell you how it makes me feel!" She scrambled off the chaise, slipped into her shoes, and smoothed out her petticoats with an agitated hand. "Grandmamma is coming and she will scold me for sitting with you too long."

From the corner of his eye the Duke saw the Countess sweeping towards them with a decidedly firm tread. He smiled crookedly. "Your grandmother sees me as a corruptive influence, *mignonne*."

"Corruptive influence?" Antonia repeated with surprise. "But she is the last person who should point the finger, Monseigneur!" And in the wake of her grandmother's displeasure she dropped onto the footstool by his left knee. The intense look in his dark eyes and the frown of concern sparked within her a tiny sliver of possibility and so she added mischievously, "If you have corrupted me then I am very glad of it. We had six wonderful days together, did we not? And I find that I like making love with you very much. But when I take lovers in future, I will strive to be more like the females you usually bed. Next time I will be sure not to allow my feelings to get in the way of my affairs—"

"Antonia! You are not to say such things! Do you hear me? You are nothing like those women," he whispered menacingly, grabbing her arm and giving her a little shake. "I don't want you to be at all like them! I have never wanted you to be anyone but yourself. As for a next time, there won't be a next time!"

Antonia lowered her lashes and smiled to herself. She sighed her regret. "I know that, Monseigneur," she said sadly. "You made that very clear to me in Paris…"

"With other men, you little wretch," he hissed, pulling her closer to drop a swift kiss on her forehead. "Understand me?"

"Girls of your age should be in their beds!" snapped Lady Strathsay, standing over the couple who reluctantly fell apart. She glared at her granddaughter. "You are making a fool of yourself, my dear."

Antonia rose to her feet, but she ignored the Countess, saying with a smile to the Duke, "You did not ask for your reward, Monseigneur."

He smiled into her eyes. "Tomorrow, while the household are playing at cricket, come to the library and I will have my reward."

"I won't allow it! It would be most improper—"

Antonia slowly looked her grandmother up and down. "You are the last person to lecture M'sieur le Duc on propriety, my lady," she said haughtily.

"How dare you…" began the Countess, so enraged she could not finish the sentence.

"To bed, petite," the Duke said gently, "before your dear old grandmother puts it about I keep females from their beds rather than in them."

The Countess gaped at them both, the color in her face a match for her upswept hair, and she finally turned to the Duke when Antonia bobbed a curtsey and reluctantly took herself off. "You encourage her wilfulness, Roxton! And I won't stand for it."

The Duke chuckled and sat back to polish his quizzing-glass with a corner of a linen handkerchief. "Then you'd best sit down, my dear, for methinks I have a fine duchess in the making…"

The Countess was still out-of-sorts with her granddaughter's behavior of the previous night as she sat in state under a marquee watching the autumn cricket match. Why men had to play at cricket at this time of year escaped her and only served to darken her already black mood. The wicket had been set up on the lower field beyond the Ornamental Gardens; an expanse of low lush grass bordered by ancient oaks and the beginnings of extensive farming lands. The proximity of a flock of sheep, and the fresh crisp air of a sunny autumn day, did little to improve the Countess's irritability.

The little black page fanned her while a footman stood at the back of her chair to attend to her every whim, should she want a glass of canary or of burgundy, or a plate of food to nibble on from the buffet set out on trestle-tables under the marquee. Lady Paget, Miss Harcourt and Antonia, reclined on cushions on a woollen rug spread out across the grass near the Countess's chair. They were busy chattering amongst themselves and the game took second place, especially for Antonia who had never heard of cricket nor seen it played, and could not fathom what the men were doing with the bats and a ball and why they should choose to run back and forth between two sets of sticks.

Those gentlemen not required on the field and not taking part in the match sat with the ladies, in comfort under the marquee drinking, conversing and helping themselves to the buffet. And those servants not absolutely required up at the house, or needed at the marquee, were permitted to enjoy a picnic of their own down by the oak trees; their wives and sweethearts and children making up a boisterous group of cheering spectators.

Lady Strathsay had attempted to engage the Vicomte's attention but after half an hour's stilted conversation he had wandered off to the tables to find a glass of wine. He drank continuously for most of the morning and brooded in silence, kicking at clods of earth and wishing he was back in a civilised country. He had been approached to play in the gentleman's team and flatly refused. It was unthinkable he would consent to lower his dignity and play sport against menials. The English truly were absurd. He could not wait to return to Paris on the morrow, and take Antonia with him.

He watched her laughing and talking with the ladies and his blood boiled to think she could not behave the same way with him. It was his father's fault, his and the Duke's. They would pay, and pay dearly, for turning her against him. A shout near his ear brought him out of such thoughts and he lost the contents of his snuffbox to the grass. It was Miss Woodruff's voice. The Lady Strathsay's blunt answer to a question had made the blonde laugh. He thanked God he could not speak English; it grated so on the ear.

"Ellicott is batting very well I think," said Antonia to Charlotte. "He is a fast runner between those sticks."

"Wickets, my dear," Lady Paget told her kindly.

"Bravo for the valet!" declared Miss Woodruff with a brittle laugh. "Now we know why Roxton keeps him. He is a fast runner between sticks."

Antonia bristled. "That is not so, Miss Woodruff. Ellicott speaks excellent French, is a good shot with a pistol, and expertly dresses M'sieur le Duc de Roxton. He can also cook quail in a lovely red wine sauce. So, he is indispensable, yes? Why do you laugh at me, Charlotte? It is true, I tell you!"

"My love, you have such a charming way of putting things into perspective," said Lady Paget with a chuckle, looking over Antonia's fair head at Miss Harcourt.

"If Ellicott can cook quail I'm not surprised his Grace treasures him," said Miss Harcourt.

"His quail, it is very good," Antonia assured them with a dimple. "One day, he Ellicott, made for us this quail, because Frédéric, that is M'sieur le Duc's chef, was at his brother's wedding in Dijon—"

"I would have thought the valet kept on because he knows too much about the Duke's many indiscretions to be dismissed," said Miss Woodruff and turned an innocent stare on Antonia.

Miss Harcourt thought it time to intervene. "I was pleasantly surprised to see Lord Strathsay captain of the household team. But shouldn't his Grace be leading his men into battle as it were?"

"What? Roxton play cricket?" said Lady Paget with a snort. "He thinks the game damn silly enough in summer so a thoroughly ridiculous occupation in autumn, to quote him."

"No, that is not true Miss Woodruff," stated Antonia, ignoring the turn of conversation. "Why should Ellicott be dismissed just because he knows whom M'sieur le Duc has bedded?"

"Antonia!" said Miss Harcourt.

"*Eh bien*! What is wrong with the truth?" asked Antonia. "Monseigneur has never made a secret of whom he beds. How then can there be any scandal?"

"Touché, my love," said Lady Paget and looked over her shoulder at the Countess. "That says it neatly enough, don't you think, Gussie?"

"Roxton's whores are of supreme indifference to me," shrugged Lady Strathsay. "I think Theo is doing a marvellous job as captain. He always does. It was just as well you arrived early this morn, Charlotte, or he would have been sorely disappointed."

"He is doing an excellent job of it, my lady," agreed Miss Woodruff. "So much better to watch a younger, more athletic, gentleman run between sticks. I dare say his Grace don't play because he is too old for such youthful pursuits. It stands to reason.

My father and he are of an age when men are apt to suffer the gout—"

"Pshaw! That is a great piece of nonsense!" Antonia said hotly.

"Shall we walk in the gardens, Antonia?" suggested Lady Paget. "Theo will be batting awhile so I'm sure we have the time…"

"Nonsense? Dear me, Miss Moran. Had I realised you would take that piece of truth to heart I'd not have ventured an opinion," said Miss Woodruff silkily. "Far be it for me to open your eyes. But I'd have thought any nobleman who had worn his coronet at the coronation of the second George and his Queen Caroline must needs be considered old today. Why my papa was side by side with his Grace in the Abbey."

"Don't be so shatterbrained, Susanna!" snapped Lady Paget and jumped up to follow Antonia, who had rudely walked away to the tables in the middle of Susanna Woodruff's spiteful monologue.

"I don't know why you bother to go after her," was Lady Strathsay's parting shot. "There was nothing in what Susanna said that could possibly offend the girl!" She waved the page away and sent the footman off to refill her glass. "She's as damnably mule-headed as her grandfather—horrid man!"

At any other time Antonia would have found the Grecian Walk in the Ornamental Gardens enchanting. Many of the trees and shrubs had lost their leaves but it was enough just to marvel at the contrived layout of pebbled walkways, follies, grottos and the placement of statuary. A meandering stream twisted its way through this walk in a series of cascades down to an Oriental garden complete with pagoda, Chinese bridge, and lanterns hung in the branches of willow trees. Carefully placed slabs of stone laid across the stream permitted easy access to the Oriental garden. Antonia managed to make the crossing without soaking the hem of her petticoats, and without the help of the Vicomte.

The Vicomte d'Ambert had rushed on ahead of her and jumped across the stepping-stones two at a time. When he had reached the other side he did not offer her his hand. He waited until she was almost to the middle of the stream then blocked her path, dodging this way and that until he was sure she would trip, only then did he step back and see her to safety. When he offered his hand she pushed him off and continued on the walk as if he was merely an apparition.

She had not asked for his company. She had refused Lady Paget's invitation to join her. When Étienne offered to go in this lady's place Antonia was glad Lady Paget kept him detained so she could slip away. But not ten minutes into a serene stroll he caught her up. She had tried to make conversation about the gardens but he was only interested in taking up the argument of the previous evening. When she refused to be drawn, he not only became persistent but a nuisance. One moment he would be dancing by her side and the next go off in front of her, only to jump out from behind a statue or a shrub.

When she stopped to admire a particularly beautiful grotto complete with fountain he jumped up on a marble bench and watched her.

"I wish you would stop trying to frighten me," she said without looking at him. "I am too annoyed to be frightened. If you are determined to keep me company come down from there and look at this fountain. I think it must be of a Chinese Emperor, no? See how the water cascades into little pools by his feet. I wonder where the stream leads. Possibly the lake. I should like to see the lake. There are swans and ducks and—"

"I do not need to understand English to know you were rude to Mademoiselle Woodruff," Étienne cut in. "You walked off when she was speaking to you. That would not be tolerated in France. I had hoped your manners would improve, but they are still atrocious. My father, he may think such antics refreshing, I do not."

Antonia did not bother to answer. She walked away and at an intersection of three paths went off to the left. Up the hill ahead was a small clearing with a rotunda atop a grassy mount. The rotunda would afford her a view of the whole gardens and hopefully she would be able to see in which direction the house lay. She had just congratulated herself, too, on losing the Vicomte when he appeared in the center of the climbing path.

"Did you think to escape me, little Antonia?" he said with a mocking bow. "A very foolish thought! A singularly stupid thought! For all your book learning you are still an ill-educated female. It is as well you have your looks for no man would bother with you. I think Mademoiselle Woodruff's flaxen curls preferable to—"

Antonia side-stepped him. "I am happy you do. You and she would suit admirably."

"She reminds me of a particular little Parisian I have come to know quite well. Very well indeed. But you would not know her. She does not frequent levees and never salons."

"She is your mistress?" asked Antonia. "I hope you are good to her and she is good to you."

This was not what the Vicomte wanted to hear. Nor did he like the way Antonia smiled at him. It angered and embarrassed him. He dug about in a pocket for his snuffbox then remembered it was empty, its contents wasted on the grass under the marquee. "No, I am not good to her!" he shouted. "I do not care a fig for her! It is more than she deserves that I interest myself in such low-life!"

"That is a horrid way to talk!"

"Why? Do you think I should act a gentleman with one who is not fit to drink from my cup? They are nothing these creatures," he said with haughty contempt.

"Yet M'sieur le Vicomte readily accepts their favours...?"

"That is different! I do them an honor. When we are married you will forget these females exist."

Antonia's back stiffened and she stopped to regard the Vicomte angrily. "Étienne, I will never marry you. I do not love you and you, you do not love me. I do not know why you persist with this nonsense, but you must stop it. If ever I return to Paris it will not be as your wife."

He had a foot on the first of the rotunda's six steps and blocked her access with his body. "What say have you in the matter? It is not your place to tell me what to do or—or to make decisions. We have decided your fate. My father and I. It is what we want, what Strathsay wanted, what my father wants; it is what I want!"

"You want your father to bed me?"

"Quiet! That is not important. It is what is in my best interests that is important. Why do you think I came to this barbaric country, eh? For the pleasure of Cousin Roxton's company? I think not. You are returning to France with me and we will be married—"

"*Mon Dieu*, I am sick unto death of this circular argument," muttered Antonia and attempted to go up the steps. "Please allow me to pass. I wish to see the view."

"How dare you interrupt me! How dare you treat me as if I was a-a boy!"

"M'sieur le Vicomte forgets himself," stated Antonia in a voice of controlled anger when he grabbed her arm. "Even were we betrothed it does not give you the right to touch me without permission. Nor to shout in my face. If you cannot behave in a civilised manner I must ask you to go away."

Étienne gaped at her. Such was his astonishment that he let her go. But he soon recovered himself and bounded up the steps with fists clenched in anger. Antonia was standing with her back to him. She was leaning on the balustrade admiring the view of the Ornamental Gardens, and beyond that, the brightly colored marquee and the field dotted with cricketers. Through the trees below she glimpsed several figures walking in the gardens but they were so distant that she could not identify them. She said something to the Vicomte about the view but he did not hear her. Before he knew what he was doing he had pinned her to the balustrade, forcing her arms into the small of her back. The more she struggled the tighter his twisting grip on her wrists.

"Étienne, you are hurting me…"

"*Taisez-vous*. What do I care for that? You will listen to me now! I offer you my name and you dare insult me as if I, a Salvan, was a nobody? You, the daughter of a buffoon physician who disgraced himself—a-a—heathen no less! And granddaughter of a painted bawd? No, do not struggle! I am much the stronger and I would hate to hurt you."

"Stop it! Let me go!"

"It is a wonder I persist with you—"

"A-a wonder indeed!" she retorted with spirit, though she was now very much afraid of him.

"A little humility is what I want from you. I do not want a wife who is bookful of thoughts. It does not become a Vicomtess to act the part of a bourgeoisie. If you are good and obedient and strive to please me, I will not complain and need to beat you—"

"I am never going to marry—" The sentence was left to hang because the Vicomte had grabbed her about the throat and squeezed until she struggled to gulp in air.

"Do not—Do not contradict me ever again," he hissed in her face. "I have heard enough words from mademoiselle's pretty mouth. You and I return to Paris tonight. I will not stay another day under Cousin Roxton's roof, to be humiliated and treated as if I was a mere schoolboy. I have watched the way you flaunt that whore's trinket he gave you! Did you think I did not know? Foolish Antonia! It is a shabby gift. I have seen diamonds about the wrists of his whores which put your tiny stones to shame."

As he spoke he let go of her throat and she shuddered in a great breath of air. "It is his fault you were shot," he sniggered, his long fingers curling about the tight-fitting satin at her shoulder. "What a great pity you had to play the heroic idiot and get in the way."

"You shot at us? You were the one waiting in the forest? How—how could you do such a monstrous thing?" she demanded, her horror at learning the truth of that night's episode greater than any fear of his intentions. "Why—"

"It was not I!" he spat in her face. "Did I say it was? Did I? Did I? My father—he—he could not help himself! He believed Roxton's boast. I never did. He shot at you, stupid, stupid Antonia! I told you not to struggle! He put that bullet in you—disfigured you—Let me see if it is still as hideous as I remember—"

"For pity's sake, Étienne," she pleaded. But in one movement he had stripped bare her arms and shoulders, and exposed the puckered scar at her collarbone. She stared at him with an unspeakable anger, her face scarlet at his touch. It was then she heard the voices floating up from the gardens, calling out her name. It gave her the courage to find the words she knew would push him off-balance, and hopefully allow her to escape. "Étienne, listen to me," she whispered, trying to cover herself with the remnants of her torn bodice. "The night of the masquerade, your father was right to believe M'sieur le Duc's boast, because in the carriage I let him—"

"Liar!" he screamed, his face was now as red as hers. Not having his precious blend of snuff to calm his nerves he had begun to shake uncontrollably.

It was all Antonia needed to duck under his arm and make good her escape. With one hand clutching a bunch of her petticoats and the other trying desperately to cover her nakedness, she ran down the grassy slope toward the Oriental garden. The voices were louder across the stream. She heard her uncle's voice and Lady Paget's, and she knew they could not be far away, possibly just around the next curve in the walk. She lost her shoes almost at once. The pebbled walk was hard under her tender feet but she dared not slow down.

"Cat! Liar! Come back here! I want the truth!" shouted the Vicomte. "You cannot hide from me!"

A hand grabbed at her through the shrubbery, but she slipped in a muddy puddle, and he missed his chance. She picked herself up and ran on, only to be caught in a particularly narrow section of the path by the thorny branches of a wild rose-bush. There was the crunch of the Vicomte's jockey-boots on the pebbles somewhere to her right as she tugged frantically at the snag and tore a rent in her petticoats. Her throat was dry, but she screamed for help anyway, and stumbled on. He could only be a few feet behind her now, and would be on her in an instant. She only waited to feel his hands on her shoulders.

Over her shoulder she saw him; his face contorted with rage. He threw himself at her, caught at her billowing petticoats, and dragged her toward him. She fell to her knees under the weight of the tugs on her gown and was dragged relentlessly backward. She could offer only a pathetic resistance. She forced herself up, started to scramble to her feet and screamed. No sound issued from her dry throat and she collapsed. Just as she gave up the struggle, her legs and arms gone limp with exhaustion she was unexpectedly scooped up by a pair of strong arms.

She fell against the broad chest gasping with relief. There was comfort in the arms of her protector and she buried her face in the soft velvet of his waistcoat, the dull thud of his heart beat almost as fast as her own. She could not lift her head, or speak, or regain the use of her legs for several minutes. Such was her huge relief that she burst into tears. A handkerchief was given her and she dried her eyes, but she was reluctant to leave the protection of the strong arms which held her in such a comforting embrace. She felt foolish and embarrassed and unsure of what to do next. Then all of a sudden there came the sound of voices, the rustle of petticoats and the scrape of shoe-leather on the pebbles. All at once the garden seemed filled with people.

"Oh, Theo! I am so glad you found me," she managed to whisper and finally peeked up through her disordered curls. Her eyes widened. "Oh, it is you."

"Hush, *mignonne.* There is nought to worry you now," the Duke replied and gently brushed the hair from her upturned face. "Did you doubt I would find you?"

"I should have known," she smiled and snuggled contentedly into his embrace, his arms tightening about her.

Lady Paget and Lord Strathsay came upon the scene from the opposite direction, having first gone to the rotunda. Miss Harcourt, who had followed the path the Duke had taken, limped in from crossing the stream and collapsed to sit on a marble bench. All had been brought up short by the sight of Antonia safe in the Duke's embrace. There was a general sigh of relief. But Lord Strathsay had seen the struggle in the rotunda and he strode forward, searching for the Vicomte. He did not immediately see the boy crouching, head bent and breathing heavily by the little cascading fountain of a Chinese emperor.

He took in the state of Antonia's torn petticoats and disordered curls and was unable to control his anger. "Where is he?" he shouted at the Duke. "Where is that miserable cur! Tell me, Roxton! I demand to have his blood for this!"

"Must you shout?" responded the Duke calmly.

"Is she...?" asked Lady Paget and was instantly silenced by the Duke's blank look.

"Can I do anything to help, your Grace?" asked Miss Harcourt.

"No, I thank you, Miss Harcourt. Except return with Theophilus to the cricket match—"

"Damn the cricket match!" bellowed Lord Strathsay. "She should never have been allowed to go off with that monster alone!"

"I fear that was my fault," said Lady Paget guiltily. "I should have insisted on going with her."

"Do not blame yourself, my lady," said Miss Harcourt. "You were not to know the outcome—"

"There you are you miserable worm!" shouted Lord Strathsay and took a step toward the Vicomte who was pulling at the corners of his crumpled waistcoat.

The Vicomte cowered, but smiled nervously. "M'sieur! It was a game only! I assure you! A game of-of—hide-and-seek, *hein?*"

"Damn you! That was no game!"

"Theo, please," pleaded Miss Harcourt.

Lord Strathsay grabbed the young man by the lace of his stock and let him go with a contemptuous push which sent the Vicomte stumbling backwards into the shrubbery. "How dare you lay a hand on my niece, you mealy-mouthed trencherfly!"

"Strathsay," said the Duke in a voice of quiet command. "Allow me to deal with this."

"I mean to have satisfaction of this piece of worthless scum!" declared Lord Strathsay and dragged the Vicomte to his feet. "You're shaking, and in a sweat, M'sieur le Vicomte. The sight of you sickens me!"

"Roxton is right, Strathsay," offered Lady Paget. "Isn't he, Charlotte?"

"Yes! Oh, yes!" agreed Miss Harcourt on the point of nervous collapse. She looked from her betrothed to the Duke and caught sight of the state of Antonia's feet. "Oh, the poor girl's feet!"

Lord Strathsay spun about without releasing the Vicomte and stared at the Duke, whose face was as white as the lace at his throat. "I ask that you take my niece up to the house and send a servant with our swords. I mean to settle this here and now. Charlotte, my lady, leave us."

"No! No!" Charlotte cried out. "Please, Theo, there must be some other way…"

"Unhand me, m'sieur!" demanded the Vicomte d'Ambert, recovered enough of his nerve to appear haughty, though one glance at the Duke caused him to cower. "As I explained, Antonia and I—"

"Don't dare say her name!" barked Lord Strathsay, twisting the Vicomte's cravat a turn.

"As m'sieur wishes. But I point out to him, Mademoiselle

Moran and I have been on the most familiar terms for a very long while."

"Liar! My niece has never given you cause to believe she considers you anything more than friend. And as a friend you have no right to force your attentions on her. Look at her! Look at your disgusting handiwork! You—you—"

"Strathsay," the Duke interrupted softly, but it was enough for Lord Strathsay to release the Frenchman.

The Vicomte loosened his cravat and wiped his hands on his breeches as if he had touched something repellent. "M'sieur, I ask that you be very careful of what you accuse me. I remind him Mademoiselle and I are betrothed. Thus, it is none of his business what I—what we care to do in the privacy of this garden."

"Betrothed be damned!"

"*Eh bien*. Mademoiselle was hardly unwilling."

Lord Strathsay choked with rage. "Why you—you…"

"Theo! No!" screamed Charlotte and promptly fainted when her betrothed slapped the Vicomte hard across the face with the back of his hand.

Lady Paget rushed to her assistance, put the young woman's head in her lap and waved air onto her face with her gouache fan.

"I mean to teach you a lesson. God damn you, d'Ambert!" shouted Lord Strathsay and followed up the slap to the face with a blow to the Frenchman's chin which sent the young man reeling into a clump of bushes. "Stand up! Stand up and fight!"

"This has gone on long enough," sighed the Duke with impatience. He felt Antonia stir in his arms and looked down.

"Monseigneur. Please, you must not let them meet with swords," she said. "Étienne he was best in his class, and he said it was you who taught him how to—"

"Yes, *mignonne*, I know that well enough," he said gently and held her closer. To the two men staring fixedly at each other, one standing over the other who scrambled further in to the bushes holding his tender jaw, he spoke in a voice of contemptuous boredom. "If I desire to watch two cocks fight I lay my money at Dartmouth cockpit. Theophilus, your lack of—er—manners disappoints me. You know well enough what I think of a gentleman who can so lower himself as to come to blows in front of a lady.

See to your betrothed. She has fainted and is proving a burden on Lady Paget."

"Your Grace! I protest! I demand—"

"It is not your place to demand anything," the Duke seethed. "I am master in my own home, am I not?" He held Lord Strathsay's gaze without a blink. "Your silence is gratifying. M'sieur le Vicomte," he said icily, regarding the young Frenchman with such detestation that the young man hurriedly fumbled to his feet, "you will do me the favor of your company in the more dignified atmosphere of my study. Immediately."

"M'sieur le Duc ! I claim the right to meet—"

"You, my very dear friend, have forfeited all your rights."

Fifteen

The Duke re-entered the library an hour after depositing Antonia on a sofa by a fire. He had issued instructions that she remain there, attended by her maid, her feet in a soothing footbath. If she wanted for anything she was to ring the silver handbell for Ellicott, and if she got bored there were enough volumes on the shelves to keep her occupied until his return. But he was not surprised to find the sofa deserted, the coverlet a crumpled heap on the floor, and several opened books scattered about the footbath. He scanned the length of the book-lined walls, and up to the walkway with its Chinese carved banister that ran around the three walls and gave access to the higher shelves, but Antonia was not to be found. He checked the terrace (although he was quite certain she would not leave the warmth of the house without proper footwear), and was about to ring for his butler when he noticed the odd angle of one of the bookcases.

It was not actually a bookcase but a carefully concealed door that hid a private staircase. It gave access to the library via the Duke's private apartments above. No one used the stairs except the Duke, and at odd times, his valet. He wondered if it had been Ellicott's laxness which saw the door left wide, or if Antonia had found it for herself. He was inclined to the latter explanation.

"Inquisitive chit," he smiled to himself and closed the secret door behind him.

The stairs led up to the Duke's closet, a room crammed with the most personal of his effects. A desk on precariously thin legs of gilt stood by a long window, its surface scattered with rolled parchments, gold seals, books, and petitions seeking his patronage; there was a japanned beech cabinet with glass-front doors crammed with bottles of blended snuffs, unusual snuffboxes and a collection of small objects picked up on his travels; and a long mahogany table was up against one wall and held busts of Roman Emperors and Greek vases.

The panelled walls displayed landscapes, portraits of friends and ancient relatives, and of favored animals—all subjects fit for the discriminating eye. Only one set of engravings—eight in number, and a limited edition by the artist Boucher—could be considered unfit for the eyes of young ladies, maiden aunts and priggish gentlemen parsons. Their subject had a recurring theme; of a satyr of familiar face indulging in various sexual acts with nymphs in wooded settings. The nymphs, of recognisable face and form, were all known for their breathtaking beauty, high birth and notorious reputation.

When first published the engravings had caused an uproar in polite circles; were bought up faster than they could be printed, and so enraged the Duc de Richelieu that he had quit court for a month in a fit of jealous pique. All because it was Roxton's face and not his that breathed life into the satyr. This particular set had been presented by the artist himself and it had pride of place above the snuff cabinet.

The Duke chanced to look at this series and rolled his eyes at fate. He strode through to his dressing room on an oath, and went into the large bedchamber beyond. Here was a good fire in the grate. The heavy velvet curtains had been pulled to shut out a late afternoon light, and only those candles absolutely necessary to cast sufficient glow to see had been lit in their sconces. The four poster was untouched.

Antonia was curled up asleep on the sofa by the fireplace, Grey and Tan huddled at her bare feet. She was dressed in one of his yellow silk banyans, her torn petticoats a discarded heap on the floor beside a basin of scented water and a tray holding the remnants of an afternoon tea.

Without waking her he returned to his dressing room and sat down heavily in front of the looking glass on his dressing table.

Damn all Salvans! he sighed, addressing his reflection, elbows on the table and fingers in the thick hair at his temples. I'm too old for her, he told the reflection, yet it dared to smile back at him. Don't be a fool. Marry her and be damned what society thinks of the match. And Étienne, what of him? The reflection frowned. Yes, I'd run him through as soon as let him touch her again. What? The reflection dared to raise its brows at this. You would go as far as murdering your own flesh and blood for her? The reflection continued to stare at him, as if willing him to confess aloud what he had never confessed to another living soul. He was saved the confessional by the unfamiliar in the reflection of the looking glass and the Duke swivelled about to better view the settee.

Expertly laid out on the settee was a collection of female attire: an open-robed gown of embossed damask, the color of old gold; a bodice and stomacher and several petticoats of similar color, but of a lighter fabric, possibly silk; a pair of white clocked stockings folded neatly in half; satin-covered garters laid on top of these; several ribands, the color and fabric of the underskirt; and a small velvet box containing an assortment of pearl-headed hairpins and clasps, and a pair of diamond shoe-buckles he knew well enough. A domed hoop of whalebone sat on a Turkey rug beside the sofa. The only piece of raiment missing was a pair of shoes.

The collection was so incongruous to his apartments as to be disbelieved. And as if to assure himself they were of this world he picked up one of the garters. He inspected the rest of the garments as if they were all new to his experience, for he had certainly seen an array of female underclothing in his time, but never so neatly laid out. It made him smile for it brought back memories of those six wonderful days spent with Antonia at his Parisian hotel. There was something comforting in her clothes thus arranged, as if time had again stood still and not an hour had elapsed since he had been forced to send her away. They could now continue on as before, as if the ten weeks of separation had simply never happened and this was but day seven for the two of them.

He was peering at the construction of the domed hoop, absently running one of the stockings through his fingers, when the panelled servant door to his left opened silently and in marched his valet carrying a pair of damask-covered slippers.

Neither master nor servant acknowledged the other, and Ellicott went about his business as he had in Paris, as if the room was unoccupied. He placed the slippers by the settee, picked up the stocking the Duke had unceremoniously flung to the floor, folded it neatly, and put it back with its twin. He then set to straightening brush, tortoiseshell comb, etui, ribands, and patch boxes laid out on the dressing table. His back was to the Duke who, for want of something to cover his embarrassment, unfobbed his snuffbox.

"I took the liberty of procuring mademoiselle a change of clothing," the valet said conversationally. "I also took the liberty of making mademoiselle as comfortable as possible on the sofa in Monseigneur's bedchamber; mademoiselle finding her way to these chambers via the stair-well."

"You seem to have taken quite a few—er—liberties," the Duke replied in English.

"Yes, your Grace," Ellicott answered stoically. He ran an eye over his master's riding habit and dusty jockey-boots. "I have laid out a fresh outfit for your Grace and trust you will be comfortable in my quarters. I have prepared mademoiselle your Grace's hipbath, on account that the workmen have not finished with the mosaic work in the bathing room." He stood on the threshold to his room. "If your Grace would care to come through...?"

"Thought of everything haven't you?" the Duke murmured crossing into the valet's bedchamber.

Ellicott patiently waited on his master, fussed over a crease in the sleeve of a white linen shirt, and all conversation was carefully avoided, except the commonplace. When the Duke was sufficiently decent in black velvet breeches and white shirt they returned to the dressing room so the valet could braid his master's long hair into a que with benefit of the looking glass on the dressing table. He affixed a satin bow to the braid. It only remained to shrug his master into a velvet frock adorned with silver lacing, but the Duke waved this aside, to be put on later, and had the valet secure the diamond shoe-buckles in the leather tongues of his black shoes. Ellicott's duties completed for the afternoon, he stood up and bowed slightly.

"If your Grace permits I will see if mademoiselle has completed her toilette."

Roxton looked up from polishing the nails on one long white hand. "Oh resourceful Ellicott, do you intend offering your services as a dresser to mademoiselle?"

"No, your Grace. That is—"

"No doubt it will please your moral sensibilities that I will deny myself the enjoyment of watching mademoiselle bathe and dress until after we have exchanged our vows?"

The valet blinked and thought he had misheard. "Your Grace?"

The Duke tossed the file amongst the clutter on the dressing table and stood to stretch his muscular legs. "I must be growing moral in my old age." He sighed. "I will exile myself to the closet and occupy myself answering correspondence while mademoiselle bathes and dresses. Does that meet with your approval?"

The valet dared to smile. "Yes, your Grace. Thank you, your Grace."

The Duke watched him go to the servant's door, then called him back. "A moment. If you please."

"Your Grace?" said Ellicott with surprise.

"Remind me, if you will, how long you have been in my employ."

"Fifteen years, your Grace."

"Good—God. Has it been that long?"

"Yes, your Grace. My father was the fourth Duke's butler and I—I was an under-footman until your Grace asked me to be valet."

"Is that so?" mused the Duke. "I wonder what induced me..." he said more to himself, though the valet heard and answered him.

"Your Grace said I was the only member of your grandfather's household who had a civilised tongue in his head. My mother was a French Huguenot. I'm sure your Grace won't remember her. She was the housekeeper."

"Indeed?" said the Duke, twisting his emerald ring to catch the light of a candelabra standing on the small bureau. "Tell me: in the years you have been in my service have my—er—exploits ever decided you to reconsider your employment?"

Ellicott's face lost its healthy glow. "I don't understand, your Grace."

"There is to be a change in present—er—arrangements," said his master in an unsteady voice. "I thought you should be told."

263

"Your Grace need not explain," said the valet with polite rigidity. "I will remove myself at—"

"No, no, you oaf!" said Roxton with an embarrassed sigh. "By all means leave, if that is your wish, though I would prefer you stay."

"Thank you, your Grace. I am gratified my services are appreciated. I always strive to do my best and will continue to do my best in the future, so that your Grace need never—"

"Do stop blathering on at me. I am trying to tell you something of the upmost importance and you are running on at me like a fishwife!" scolded the Duke. He caught the smirk that crossed the valet's face and frowned. "Tread warily, friend. No doubt I have provided endless entertainment in the past, but Mademoiselle Moran—she is not—is not like all the others."

"No, your Grace."

"For what it is worth—and I don't know why I need tell you this—I love her. We are to be married this afternoon."

"I know that, your Grace."

"Do you indeed?" said the Duke in something of his old manner. "Then you had best attend to mademoiselle's bath."

"May I be the first to wish you happy, your Grace?"

"You may. Now go away! Oh, and, Martin... thank you."

The Duke was composing a third letter, and Ellicott had just returned with a tray of refreshments, when Antonia tiptoed shyly into the closet. She had finished her toilette, but for the satin slippers and her hair, which she had brushed free of tangles and let fall to her waist. The valet quickly absented himself, disappearing into the dressing room to tidy up, but Antonia's smile and thanks as he passed her so disconcerted him that he almost tripped over his own feet.

She did not disturb the Duke, although he glanced up from the parchment several times to see what she was doing. She was content to wander the room, careful not to disturb anything, but interested in everything it contained. She took particular interest in the contents of the snuff cabinet and knelt to have a better view of the boxes on the second shelf. All were made of precious metals or semiprecious stones, and such exotic materials as lapis lazuli, tortoiseshell, pearl and ivory; one was made from the lava found at Herculaneum. The third shelf displayed a number of Chinese fans, painted in gouache on paper leaf. Many were of silver or gold gilt and enamel, or inlaid with mother-of-pearl. One was black lacquered with filigree worked sticks.

"Are these fans very old, Monseigneur?" she asked, and was surprised to find him standing beside her. "Oh, did I disturb you?"

He opened the cabinet with a key he took from the fob pocket of his breeches. "I think most of these fans date from the early sixteenth century. They are of Dutch-Chinese origin. I have others in the cabinets in the library that are older." He selected the lacquered fan and with an expert flick of the wrist opened it out to flutter it like a woman. He gave it to Antonia. "I presume you know how to take care of a fan."

She scrambled to her feet.

"But it is much too old and too beautiful to use," she protested. But he had gone back to his desk and poured out coffee in two dishes. "I will take very good care of it," she assured him.

"Better care than you did poor Vallentine's birthday gift," he said. From a drawer he produced Antonia's birthday fan.

"*Parbleu!* Vallentine's fan. You had it all the time!" she exclaimed with a clap of her hands. "Poor Harcourt, he spent a day wandering the Theatre Royal boxes looking for it. And he confronted M'sieur Garrick who assured him it had been returned. But Harcourt, he did not believe him in the least, I know it."

"Let that be a lesson to you, *mignonne*. It is not customary for young ladies to offer their fans to members of the acting fraternity. Such actions only cause—er—unnecessary speculation. Nor do they wander about in bare feet," he added, running his quizzing-glass down to her stockinged toes. "You'll catch your death, chérie."

"But I am wearing stockings, Monseigneur," she assured him with a lift of her petticoats.

"So I see," he said. "I hope you will not make a habit of showing your lovely ankles to the world."

Antonia frowned self-consciously. "I have never shown any person. Except you, Monseigneur. Did I offend you?"

"Not in the least," he smiled and beckoned her to sit beside him on the window seat. "Do you feel better for your bath?"

"Very much," she said. "My feet, they are still quite tender.

But the footbath Ellicott prepared was very soothing. He is very thoughtful, Monseigneur. And just as in Paris not once did he ask an impertinent question or-or look at me askance for being in your rooms. I like him."

"Ellicott would turn pink with pleasure to hear you say so," he said. "I am only sorry you did not have the benefit of your maid's assistance to dress. And by the pinning up of that stomacher her services were sorely needed. Stand there and let me look at it."

Antonia put aside her fan and dish and dutifully stood before him. She tried to inspect the sit of the stomacher, her chin on her shoulder. "I was good at dressing myself when I lived with Grand-papa. He never did find the time to engage a maid. Sometimes Maria's tire-woman would help. But since you gave Gabrielle to me I have become very lazy I think. The trouble is, I never can do anything looking at a reflection. My fingers become thumbs and more often than not, if I am affixing a brooch, I will prick my skin rather than gather up the fold of fabric."

When he had secured the hooks of the stomacher into the correct eyelets on either side of the bodice she held out a diamond and pearl brooch. "Thank you. Could you please now pin this on at the shoulder here. It helps hide the scar, you see."

"I will try," he said softly and waited for her to brush the hair off her shoulder. Yet, when he attempted to slip the point of the pin into the damask near her breast he fumbled at the touch of her warm skin, and the brooch fell with a clatter to the floor. "Antonia, I—I am sorry. I—"

"It is not important," she responded cheerfully and scrambled to pick up the brooch. "As it is only you and I, I need not worry about it. Would you care for another dish of coffee? I find I cannot abide tea. I have tried it but it does not agree with me." She took his dish and refilled it and came back to the window seat. "Some persons are persuaded tea-drinking leads to immoral behavior, so they will not indulge themselves in the habit. That is a silly notion, *hein*? How is tea different from coffee? One comes from China; the other is from Persia. I would have thought the Persians far more immoral than the Chinese. You only have to read Herodotus to know that."

"Antonia, listen. What I said the day I made you leave me—I

did not mean a word of it," he confessed, gaze on the contents of the porcelain dish he held. "My conduct was appalling. I am not proud of myself. But circumstances such as they were... I felt compelled to get you away from France... Every day since then I have bitterly regretted sending you from me..."

"But you wanted to protect me from M'sieur le Comte."

"Protect you? And such a fine protector you must think me!"

"I am glad you did not call Étienne out, or allow Theo to do so. Étienne is not very well in his head, is he, Monseigneur? And he is addicted to opiates."

The Duke's eyebrows went up. "You know that?"

"But of course. I've known almost from the first. Papa he took a measured dose every night. Sometimes, when he was too ill to administer it himself, I would give it him. But Étienne, he takes vastly too much. But I do not think it is only opium which causes his attacks of rage."

"No, chérie. He has his mother's affliction."

"Madame de Salvan was considered a great beauty in her day, was she not, M'sieur le Duc?" she said in a small voice, watching his profile intently. "Madame your sister confided that at one time you hoped to marry her."

"Did she indeed? Estée has ever been the polite one in the family. No, I never offered Claudine-Alexandre my name, only my bed. I am sure that does not shock you."

"No. I much prefer to be told the truth."

"However much that may hurt?"

"Yes, M'sieur le Duc."

He kissed her hand and stood up. "What else did Estée tell you of Claudine-Alexandre?"

"N-nothing. Étienne he told me a little. I know she poisoned herself when he was only a boy, and that somehow he blames you because you and she were lovers."

"The boy has the situation confused. He blames me because my affair with his mother was well known. But that happened before he was born."

"But your letters to her..."

"Fabricated by my dear Tante Victoire and my cousin Salvan," he said dryly. "It is so much nicer, and far less complicated, to blame Claudine-Alexandre's suicide on a broken heart than on a broken mind. And convenient to lay the fault at my door. Claudine-Alexandre never made a secret of her—er—infatuation for me. After our affair ended she continued to write to me. I returned her letters unread. It does not do to put ink to paper. I am not so foolish. What is it, *mignonne?*"

Antonia shook her head. She was thinking of her own letters to him, and it angered her that she had been just as foolish. He seemed to read her mind.

"Your Grandmother, in her misguided wisdom, kept your letters from me," he said, and smiled crookedly when she looked up quickly. "I have them now, and read them all. You must not condemn her too harshly. She did not think it—er—healthy for you to correspond with one of my reputation."

"She is a fool!" said Antonia angrily and dismissed her grandmother from her mind. "When I was at Versailles and knew you only by sight and reputation, Maria Caspartti warned me—"

"Your father's mistress was concerned for your welfare, *mignonne.*"

Antonia ignored the sarcasm. "No, it was not that she worried about me, Monseigneur. She never thought you like M'sieur le Comte de Salvan. But it concerned her that if it was discovered Étienne was in truth your son there would be a big scandal and you would again be banished from the Court as happened when the Comtesse de Salvan died. And then you would not be able to help me at all—Monseigneur, Étienne he looks nothing like Salvan. At first I did not believe Maria, until one day I saw you giving Étienne a fencing lesson in the Princes Courtyard and then I truly began to wonder if you were his father. I am certain Étienne wonders too. He has your sister's blue eyes and there is something about him that reminds me of you… And then when Lady Paget showed me the family portrait in the Gallery and I saw your father I was certain Étienne he is your son."

The Duke took a long time to answer her. "You forget my mother was a Salvan, thus Salvan blood runs in both our veins. That is an adequate explanation."

"But he is not Salvan's son. He has Hesham blood," she persisted. "Claudine-Alexandre she wrote and told you the truth just before she died, did she not? That is why Salvan and his mother hate you so. That is why they have conveniently blamed you for her death."

"Yes. Such is the sordid reputation of the women at Court, and Claudine-Alexandre was no exception, that their children can only ever be certain of their mother," he said to dismiss the subject, and she did not push him further.

She watched him shuffle papers on his desk and after a silence between them said, "May I ask a question, M'sieur le Duc?"

"Ask anything you care to. I cannot guarantee you will be pleased with the response."

"I have never understood why Lady Paget—Lady Paget and Grandmamma are such good friends," said Antonia as casually as she could manage. "I love Grandmamma because it is my duty to do so, but I do not like her, Monseigneur. But Lady Paget I like. She is not selfish and vain and she does not always want her own way. She is sensible and kind and rather handsome in a majestic way. I like her very much."

He turned to look at her. "That is not a question, Antonia."

She held his gaze. "Do you—Do you like her?"

"Kate and I are very good friends," he answered, and had to smile to himself when she frowned and looked down at the twisted lock of hair between her fingers.

"She reminds me a little of Madame de La Tournelle. You and she were also very good friends."

"Come here, ma belle," he coaxed. "I don't know what you have been told, or by whom, but I tell you this in good faith. Kate and I have not been lovers since before this last visit to Paris. As for the divine Tournelle, she was a passing interest; someone to relieve the tedium of court for a little while. Does that ease the mind of my grand inquisitor?"

"What of the Maison Clermont?" she asked flatly.

In a blink the smile was wiped from his face and he left her to stand by a window. She knew at once she had pushed him too far.

"They are nothing these females of the Maison Clermont, I know that. Nothing. Nothing at all," she said in a rush, clasping and unclasping her hands. "All the French nobility go there. What man of fashion does not? It is expected. It is tolerated by wives and mistresses alike. I should disregard the existence of such women and I know it is wrong of me to even mention such a place. And I tried very hard to ignore your visits to this place and your mistresses. I told myself that these women mean nothing to you beyond a temporary satisfaction. After all, the wives of noblemen accept such unfaithfulness in their husbands as part of their duty but… But ever since we shared a bed and you showed me how wondrous it is to make love I find that the thought of you pleasuring other women—of you being pleasured by them— makes me so very sad. I do not think I could ever come to terms with such an arrangement. That is my great failing, I know it, but the idea that you could prefer their company to mine, that you would need to frequent such a place because I bored you, or did not please you—"

"I need not justify my—er—past to you or to any other," he interrupted tonelessly. "Nor do I offer up my apologies for how I have spent my life. I can't change the past, Antonia, but I have no desire to, could I do so." He looked down at her with a crooked smile. "I can only offer you the future, such as it is, with a no-bleman who has a past that is beyond redemption. *Mignonne*, you deserve so much better than I."

"I do not want better," she said simply. "I have never wanted any man but you. I love only you." She smiled tremulously. "We are fated to be together, Monseigneur. I knew that from the moment I first saw you."

These words, spoken with quiet simplicity, shattered the last vestiges of the Duke's reserve and in two steps he had her in his arms and stooped to kiss her with that light in his eyes she had seen at the Theatre Royal. "Fate, is it?" he admonished her lov-ingly, looking down at her upturned smiling face within the circle of his embrace. "Then I will blame fate for causing me many a sleepless night from the day I clapped eyes on you at Versailles. I did my best to ignore you, to forget you, to rid you from my thoughts, by attempting to find consolation in the arms of others. But you—the mere thought of you, you little wretch—made this—made this old roué incapable. You see, there has been no one, no one else, since that day you fled with me from Versailles." He kissed her forehead and carried her to the window seat where he deposited her standing up before him. He made her a sweeping bow. "And since we shared a bed I find that I've a mind to become respectable. You, my darling girl, will never have cause for a single doubt. That I pledge on my honor. So, there is your confession, mademoiselle." When this was met with tearful happiness he smiled nervously and took her hands in his. "No more playing with time. If you truly are eighteen years of age and not twenty, then so be it, though I shudder at being so cruelly used..."

Antonia hung her head to hide a guilty blush. "But, Monseigneur, you would never have made love to me had you known my true age."

"You calculating little wretch!" he said with a laugh and lifted her chin. "And no more nonsensical talk of fleeing to Venice," he said darkly, looking into her eyes. "You are staying with me."

"Yes, Monseigneur. I should like that very much." She dimpled and mimicked her grandmother's voice and sour demeanour. "Will you inform Lady Strathsay of her granddaughter's fall from grace, or shall I?"

At that the Duke laughed out loud and pulled her to him, arms encircling her small waist. "You really have no idea how much I love you, do you? I *love you*. I want you for my life's partner, not my mistress, *mignonne*. I am asking you to *marry* me."

Antonia's green eyes widened and at first she could not find the words to express her happiness. "Yes, M'sieur le Duc, I should like that more than anything in this world."

"And that must stop," he scolded playfully, taking from his frockcoat pocket a small gold band set with emeralds and diamonds and slipping it on a finger of Antonia's left hand. For good measure he then kissed this her betrothal ring. "To seal the bargain... No more M'sieur le Duc. It is a wife's privilege to call her husband by his Christian name... in and—er—out of bed..."

"Yes, Mon—*Renard*. I will try and remember," she said with a shy smile, arms around his neck. "That is, it would be much easier for me to remember if you were to kiss me again..."

Sixteen

A carriage and four driven at a cracking pace rounded a sharp curve in the deserted country lane and narrowly missed colliding with a shepherd tending his flock. The driver of this elegant equipage shouted abuse at the shepherd. But the man seemed without a care in the world. He had no intention of hurrying his charges toward the grass verge that bordered the imposing entrance gates to his master's estate. Thus the driver was forced to manoeuvre the bays around this obstruction with all the skill of his twenty years' handling of the ribbons. The carriage then swept through the gates and on up the winding drive. The shepherd had never heard the French tongue but he was quite certain he would know it if ever it was hurled at his head again.

Inside the speeding vehicle a gentleman and his lady wife viewed the tree-lined drive, and the expanse of scenery beyond, with not much more than a blink of interest because they were in a heated argument that had no end.

"If Roxton ain't here I give up!" the gentleman declared and attempted to take snuff. The pinch fell on his lap. "Damme!"

"Where else could he be, Lucian? I do not believe at all those lackeys who say he is not at home. The house in St. James's Square is empty save the housekeeper. And our message to this place? It went unanswered. He is angry with us I tell you!" Estée Vallentine gripped the leather strap above her head with a gloved hand. "This driver, he goes too fast. What is the point of it now when we are weeks late? It was you who wanted to go up to London when I said we should come here first!"

"Now listen, my love. If you recall it was you who was eager to see London, not I! I admit I didn't think another sennight would make much of a difference to Roxton. He's waited this long. I wasn't to know we'd get caught in a damned avalanche in Switzerland. Confound the wretched place!"

Estée pouted. "At the time you said it was a romantic interlude you would never forget. And now you damn it. The honeymoon, it is truly over!"

"Now, Estée, don't cry!" pleaded his lordship. He threw himself to sit beside her and took her free hand in a firm clasp. "You can't show your brother tears. What would he think of me, his brother-in-law, eh?"

"He would think you what you are! An unkind and unfeeling—*brute.*"

Lord Vallentine gave up any attempt to stem the tide and merely handed her his handkerchief. He thrust his hands in the pockets of his frock and frowned. "Know what confounds me: the Countess. You think she would know the whereabouts of her grandchild. But no. She acts like the child ain't even hers! I told Roxton at the time no good would come of sending the chit to that woman. Did you notice the amount of lead on her face? Can't be healthy, can it?"

"That woman is a harlot."

"Look here, Estée, I ain't disagreeing with you, but don't say so in front of the child. The woman is her grandmother after all."

"Her face, it was as painted as a whore's. And to think she admitted us to her boudoir dressed only in a thin chemise and her robe all open! I did not know where to put my eyes!"

"Disgusting," muttered his lordship and pretended to search in a pocket to hide a grin at the memory of the Countess's enticing figure. "I wonder where I put that damned etui."

Estée was not fooled. "I'll wager you cannot tell me the color of her robe! Your eyes, they did not leave her large breasts the whole interview!"

"The robe? It was a yellow. A primrose yellow!"

Estée laughed and pinched his square chin a little too hard.

"It was a cinnamon with ghastly flowers embroidered on the cuffs and hem; lilies, I think."

Lord Vallentine slapped the side of his silken breeches. "If only we had come straight here!"

"It is too late to say that now."

"What if they ain't here, eh? What then?"

"M'sieur le Duc my brother is here. I know it," said Estée Vallentine with conviction. She gave her hand to the lackey who opened the carriage door and dropped down the steps. "You must trust my instinct, Lucian."

"When don't I?" said his lordship with a smile and followed her across the gravelled drive. "What do you think of your ancestral seat? Impressive, ain't it."

"It is on a scale I find incomprehensible!" gaped Estée, craning her neck to take in the sweep of buildings, then swirling around to look out across the velvet green lawns to the lake. "Now I understand a little better my brother's great arrogance. Here he is his own king! It is no wonder he was never dazzled by Versailles and Fontainebleau. Poor Maman. Never did she see Papa's estate."

"A person would get lost in this place if it wasn't for the army of lackeys he keeps. Got lost m'self once. When the servants were off at a local fête. Took me over an hour to find Roxton."

His wife laughed. "He was hiding from you, foolish Lucian!"

Vallentine grinned. "Know that now, don't I. What do you think of the setting? Quaint, ain't it. All Brown's work. But you'd never guess it was artificial. That's the man's trick," he said, pointing out the lake and then the Ornamental Gardens. "Glorious weather! Glorious country! And no better place I know to spend time in the country than here at Treat."

An under-butler had informed Duvalier of the carriage's arrival, which caused the old man to roll his eyes and sigh. He straightened his waistcoat and frock and began the long walk to the front entrance, the under-butler close on his heels. He had the servant repeat the well-rehearsed lines as they went, and counselled him to set his features in an expression that would give nothing away to the uninvited guests. If the intruders proved obnoxious or persistent, as a few had been in the past, they were usually satisfied once shown the Blue drawing room off the foyer, with its furniture under covers and the windows shut tight. The butler permitted himself a private smile. The west wing told an altogether different story.

Duvalier stood well back in the foyer and the under-butler signalled to the footmen to open the doors. He stepped out into the light and made a customary short bow to the figures coming across the drive. The well-rehearsed speech tumbled effortlessly forth as he straightened to meet the visitors' gaze one for one.

"Don't give us that twittle-twattle, man! Damme! Where's Duvalier?"

In an instant the butler pushed aside the blabbering underling. "M'sieur Vallentine! Madame!" he stammered and ushered them into the hall. He helped his lordship out of a coat and took his sword, and pushed these onto a footman. "We have been expecting you this past fortnight, m'sieur. May I say how glad I am to see you and Madame safe in England."

"Thank you." Vallentine grinned. "If you gave all the others that haughty put-off I ain't surprised no one believes M'sieur le Duc ain't here. The place looks like a mausoleum! Why the covers and lack of wax? Roxton ain't economising, is he? Things must've taken an awful turn. Or is this some sort of game he's playing? What is it? I'll wager it's the latter!"

"Don't be so mean to poor Duvalier!" scolded Lady Estée. She smiled at the old retainer. "It is a comfort to see a friendly face and one whose French is not appalling. These English they are exactly as I always thought them; so much phlegm."

"Aye! That'll do, Estée. Duvalier ain't interested in your opinions. Show us to the Duke."

The butler stiffened and some of his hauteur returned. "I will have you shown to your apartments and then, perhaps, you would care for refreshment."

Lord Vallentine was looking at the pearl face of his gold pocket-watch. "Roxton ought to be at his breakfast. It's gone the hour." He smiled down at his wife. "A quick change and we'll join your brother, Estée. It will be like old times in Paris! What think you, Duvalier?"

The butler declined to comment. Nothing, he thought, could

be further from the truth. He instructed a footman to show the Vallentines to their apartments and took his leave of them, returning in half an hour to escort the new arrivals to the west wing.

"I hope Roxton is pleased to see us," whispered Estée nervous with anticipation. "He did tell you in his letter it was urgent and that we make all speed and we are two weeks late."

"I don't doubt he'll be as mad as hell-fire, my love," replied Vallentine cheerfully, and let his wife go before him across the passageway. "We are so overdue it don't matter any more, and he don't care to be disobeyed. But he'll want to see us. I have that confounded will. And I didn't go all the way to Rome to search out some damme Italian lawyer to be turned away at Roxton's door! That would have been a wasted trip."

"Wasted?" said Estée shrilly.

"Now, don't you be gettin' me wrong, lovedy. Wasted only in the sense we could've travelled to St. Petersburg for our honeymoon as go to Rome. We enjoyed Rome, didn't we? And Venice! Now there's somewhere I'd like to return to one day."

Lady Estée giggled behind her fan. "Don't be absurd, Lucian. Venice gave you dysentery."

"Did it?" said his lordship unperturbed. "I must be thinking of Florence. Or was it Milan? Damme if I can remember one Italian city from t'other! Was the same when I went on the Grand Tour with your brother." He took in his surroundings with interest. "This is more like it! Light and no covers! Been doing a bit of redecorating too. A bit sparse on the furniture but it ain't bad just the same. Liveable at least."

Duvalier brought them up short at a door attended by an alert footman. He turned and asked them to wait, saying, "I will enquire if M'sieur le Duc is ready to receive you." He scratched on the door, and summonsed within, waved the footman to turn the handle.

<hr />

The Duke sat at breakfast alone. Duvalier could not approve his master's want of dress. The long black hair fell unrestrained about the lean face, and a banyan of red flowered silk was tied loosely over a white shirt that gaped at the throat. The butler wondered what Ellicott thought of this new-found laxness, amongst other matters.

The latest edition of a London newssheet was spread across the table, a dish of coffee to one corner of the page. The Duke slowly lifted his gaze, identified his butler, and returned to scanning the printed page. His expression was as inscrutable as ever; but his want of dress said everything.

"Unless my memory is failing, I do not recall requesting your presence."

"No, Monseigneur."

"Did Madame la Duchesse ask for you?"

"No, Monseigneur."

Roxton afforded his butler a second look, a rare twinkle in his black eyes. "You thought, perhaps, to see if we were still—er—alive?"

"No, M'sieur le Duc," answered the butler stoically.

"I saw the carriage. Whom won't go away?"

"It is M'sieur le Duc's sister—"

"Indeed? Acquit me. When were Lord and Lady Vallentine due to arrive?"

"The Vallentines are a fortnight overdue, Monseigneur."

The Duke lifted his eyebrows at this. "I wasn't aware—that is, the days..."

"Yes, M'sieur le Duc," the butler answered indulgently, a hint of a smile at his master's awkwardness.

Roxton returned to his reading. "Admit them. Have covers set and inform the cook."

Duvalier was not given the opportunity to formally announce the guests. Lord Vallentine, followed hot-foot by his wife, strode into the room and pushed past the butler with hand outstretched. He had the broadest of smiles. "Roxton! Damme! It's good to see your insolent face!"

The Duke was out of his chair and had pulled the banyan tighter about his shoulders. He met his sister across the carpet and received her crushing embrace with a smile and a kiss dropped on the top of her black curls. "The pleasure is all mine," he said and disentangled himself to hard grip his friend's hand. "You are both well after such a long journey. No tears, I beg you, Estée," he said gently.

"Jesus! But you're looking mighty fine yourself!" exclaimed his lordship. He ran a critical eye over his friend's appearance and whistled low. "What's with the undress? Don't tell me you've just crawled out from under the covers at this hour. I'll not believe it! You?" He shook his head and laughed. "Never known you to sleep late. It's the country air, ain't it. And what's with the loose locks? Tryin' to put a younger man to shame, eh? Damme if your hair don't rival Estée's!" He looked down at his wife and winked. "Dear brother here ain't himself. I think you and I stayed away too long."

Roxton pushed a hand through his hair and for want of something to cover his self-consciousness, went to the sideboard and peered under several of the domed-covered dishes. "Have you breakfasted?" he asked. "I am told there are several excellent courses. Devilled kidneys, potted venison, and I think—yes—trout. We caught a score on the lake yesterday. Oh, and there are of course hot rolls and coffee. Or would you prefer chocolate, Estée?"

Lord Vallentine glanced suspiciously at his wife but she was peering keenly at her brother. He scratched his wig and addressed his brother-in-law in his customary blunt way. "Not ill, are you, Roxton? Lord Strathsay wouldn't say where you were. Not that I think he had the foggiest notion. But there was a rumor you're recovering a bout of influenza—Influenza! You've never been ill a day in your life!" He put up his quizzing-glass. "If you don't mind me saying so, you're acting mighty strange. We've been gone months, not years, and I've stayed under your roof enough times to know you don't eat more than a roll for breakfast. Speaking for m'self, that's not what I consider a gentleman's portion, but you're not one to change a life-long habit. Never will! Estée, do you think your brother is looking slightly flushed? Don't tell me some plaguey physician recommended—"

"Do be quiet, Lucian!" snapped his wife. She put a hand on her brother's sleeve. "Something—something has happened. What is it, Roxton?" she asked softly.

"Don't need to ask the man what's obvious!" blustered his lordship. "Eh? What—what the—who's that?"

The Duke smiled and blushed in spite of himself. "Can't you guess?"

"Eh? Who?" asked Vallentine in mystified accents and turned puzzled eyes on his wife.

"Lucian! Sometimes I cannot believe you're as dull-witted as you pretend! Don't be a blockhead. You know very well who it is! You do!" She squeezed her brother's hand. "You didn't wait for us. That offends me. But me, I understand completely. I— we—are so very happy for you."

The Duke kissed her hand. "Thank you, my dear."

"You've gone and married the chit without us!" his lordship declared in amazement. "Of all the tricks to serve! Couldn't wait another day longer! Just had to up and do it just like that! Well! Well! That explains it all. No wonder you're lookin—"

"*Lucian,*" said Estée in an under-voice of fury and embarrassment. "If—you—please."

"Er, yes. Forgetting m'self," mumbled his lordship sheepishly and kicked the carpet with the toe of his shoe. "Damned awful tongue I've got, Roxton. Must wish you happy," he said and clasped the Duke's hand again. "And we are happy for you! Damned happy! Time you settled down and started your nursery. At your age—"

"Lucian!" whispered his wife angrily. She tugged at his sleeve. "Dysentery wasn't the only malady you came down with in Venice."

"It was your decision to marry him," said Roxton and offered his friend snuff. "Careful, my dear. My mix might be too strong for your senile nostrils."

Lord Vallentine shrugged in resignation and gave the Duke back his gold box. "It ain't madness," he said, "it's marriage that's done it to me."

Lady Estée gasped. "Of all the cruel remarks!" And then she laughed.

Vallentine executed her a splendid bow. "I am yours to command, Madame! So," he said to the Duke, "when do we get to see the minx—Madame la Duchesse?"

Estée sighed. "It has been an age since I've seen her. We were all so sad to see her leave Paris, were we not?"

"You, my love, were in floods for weeks," agreed his lordship. "I've missed her. Can't say when I've missed verbal abuse so much. A good deal has happened since Paris. I hope she hasn't changed."

"Not the least little bit, my dear," the Duke responded and turned to the bedchamber at the sound of his wife's voice.

"Renard?" called Antonia. "I am very sorry to keep you waiting. It is in such unbelievable chaos the dressing room. All is a jumble! I tell you I will be glad when the workmen put everything to rights. But I did manage to bathe without dripping water from the bathing room to the dressing room, unlike the last time. But as you were just as wet and chasing me upon that occasion I feel it was not entirely my fault."

She chuckled as she came through the doorway, head to one side, concentrating on affixing the small pearl buttons at her wrist. She was dressed in a morning sacque of delicate silk embroidered with sprays of bright flowers and vines, and wore matching slippers. Her hair was brushed but left undressed, tied loosely halfway down her back with a silk riband.

"I do not know what we are doing today," she said. "So I told Gabrielle, do not lay out anything until we decide. I should like to stay undressed in this way all day! I have become used to going without those horrid corsets and hoops and—" She looked up with a mischievous smile. "*Bon Dieu*," she stammered and blushed. "Val-lentine and-and—Madame!"

Roxton went to meet his wife and led her further into the room. "I don't blame you for thinking them an apparition, *mignonne*," he said dryly. "We expected them half a lifetime ago, did we not? Estée, my lord, I wish to make you known to my wife—Madame la Duchesse de Roxton."

"Did you think we would never come, little one?" said Estée, who was the first to go forward. She embraced her new sister with tears in her blue eyes. "You have made my brother very happy, child. I can see it in his eyes!" she whispered in Antonia's ear and kissed both her cheeks, saying in her other ear, "When you left us for England I knew then that this could be the only outcome. We-we are so very happy for you both!"

"Thank you, Madame," Antonia murmured shyly. "I cannot explain how I feel. But you must know how-how wonderful it is to be a married lady. It is bon, yes?"

"You can whisper all you want to the chit later!" said Vallentine impatiently. He grinned at the Duke. "Females!" He pushed past his wife to unceremoniously sweep Antonia off her feet in a crushing embrace. "It's good to see you again, minx! We missed you and Roxton while we were away. Too damned much I can tell you!" He put her back on her feet and turned to his friend, an arm still about Antonia's waist. "If you hadn't married her I'd have had you clapped up! You're the luckiest of men, Roxton, and I'll wager you don't realise the half of it!"

"My dear Vallentine, I assure you, I most certainly do," Roxton drawled.

Antonia recovered enough of her composure to say haughtily, "Monseigneur, now I am a duchess it is not right of Vallentine to call me chit and minx, and to pick me up in the air so."

"Quite irregular," said Roxton and took her back in his arms. "Travel has made his lordship lax. He forgets the manners of a gentleman. A duchess demands the highest regard."

"Aye? I didn't mean—You can't think I—Well, it's just that—"

"Oh, Vallentine!" laughed Antonia and looked up at the Duke. "He has not changed in the least! He still looks like a great John Dory fish!"

"I will ignore that comment, your Grace," said his lordship with a sniff and went to the sideboard to peer under the covers. "I'm famished! Let's eat!"

"Yes," said Antonia at his side. "Marriage gives me an appetite, too."

His lordship's plate fell with a clatter to the floor and he gaped at Antonia.

"Did I say something terribly wrong, Renard?"

"Nothing your brother-in-law should not expect to hear from your sweet mouth, *mignonne*."

"Good." She handed Lord Vallentine a fresh plate with a smile. "I am quite an outrageous duchess, I think."

"Outrageous! Jesus! That's a fit description! It won't do. Won't do at all to be so-so outrageous once Roxton takes you into society," lectured his lordship. "It is all very well to be a bundle of mischief as Mademoiselle Moran, but now Roxton has made you his duchess you will have to conduct yourself with a modicum of—"

Antonia gave a sigh. "Poor Vallentine." She filled half her plate and sat at the table on the Duke's right. "I fear marriage has turned him old in the head, Renard."

"Old?" spluttered his lordship and straddled a chair opposite the Duchess. "Did you hear what the chit—what the chit—Did you hear that, Estée?"

"Yes, my dearest one," soothed his wife, though her eyes were brimful of laughter. She accepted a dish of coffee from her brother, addressing herself to him. "I have so many questions to ask."

"And so do I!" stated his lordship waving a forked slice of ham at bride and groom.

"First you must tell us all about your travels," Antonia demanded. "Did you go to Florence, and to Venice, and Milan, too? How was your crossing of the Alps? Oh, tell us everything!"

Lady Estée looked to her husband who swallowed up the rest of the ham and graciously consented to be narrator. He leaned back in his chair, a dish of coffee in his hand. "We did so many things I hardly know where to begin, Madame la Duchesse."

"*Parbleu.* How formal it sounds to call me that! I feel very important of a sudden."

"You are, chit!" nodded his lordship. "And don't you forget it."

"Now that is Vallentine," Antonia said with a gurgle of laughter. She put her hand on the Duke's who raised it to his lips. "Must Vallentine call me Madame la Duchesse?"

"If that is your wish," Roxton told her and kissed her fingers a second time. "But you may condescend to allow him the use of your name as a brother-in-law's privilege."

Lord Vallentine gave a forced, deprecating cough and glanced at his wife. "When you have quite finished I'll go on with my story!"

Antonia flashed him an imperious look. "This is not Paris, m'sieur! As Monseigneur and I are now married you cannot be offended in the least."

"Well met, my love!" applauded Estée and ignored the frowning look from her lord.

"Look here, Estée. In Paris it was you, and not I, who disapproved this pair's match!"

"And you know very well why that was, Lucian. I admit I was wrong but I—"

"Oho! My wife admits she was wrong!"

"Please, Vallentine, will you not go on with your story?" Antonia coaxed.

"Our travels? Yes! Firstly, I must tell you we've carried with us all the way from Venice a damned enormous trunk of your belongings. Confound the thing!" said his lordship without heat. "It's from Strathsay's palazzo and the Caspartti assured us your grandfather would want you to have its contents. Be bound it's full of books! Rare editions and such, and there are some jewellery pieces too. Whatever, it weighs a blasted elephant!"

"Maria!" interrupted Antonia excitedly and put down knife and fork. "She is well? She did not go to a nunnery after all? She is residing at the palazzo you say?"

"In high style. Strathsay left it to her in his will, and a goodly sum for its upkeep. A nunnery?" snorted Vallentine. "Banish the thought! She has four, or was it five? attentive suitors. But my money's on Count di Marchesin. Slippery customer is the Count. But the Caspartti has a mind to become respectable at last. You know the type, Roxton," he said as an aside, a knowing look at the Duke.

"That will do, Lucian," said his wife anxiously. But Antonia's next words made her wonder why she bothered to try and shield the girl.

"I hope this count is good to her," said Antonia. "She suffered much when Grandpapa fell ill. I am glad she decided against becoming a nun. It is not in her nature to be chaste. Her talents, they would have been greatly wasted in a nunnery. Would they not, Monseigneur?"

"I cannot speak from—er—experience, my love. But, yes, she has that reputation."

"She sent you a letter," continued Vallentine and pushed aside the plate and refilled his coffee dish. "She made me promise you will write and tell her how you get on."

Antonia clapped her hands in delight. "She will be so surprised at my news!"

"Without doubt," commented the Duke with a crooked smile. "If I recall she was not particularly favourable of my—er—involvement in your flight from Versailles."

"She does not know you as I do," Antonia said firmly. "I will write and tell her everything."

Roxton's mouth twitched. "I trust, not—er—everything."

"If—you—please!" Vallentine said primly. "Estée, it is as well we came when we did. Someone must uphold certain standards in this family."

The Duke mocked him. "God forbid, Vallentine."

Before his lordship had an opportunity to respond Estée told him to go on with his story.

"Aye. The Caspartti proved useful in helping locate that damme lawyer. She enlisted Di Marchesin's assistance and he got onto the fellow pronto."

Roxton laid aside his coffee dish in its saucer. "All is as I anticipated?"

"Couldn't be better," said Vallentine with pride. "I think you will be well satisfied with Moran's original will."

"The guardianship?"

"As I told you in my letter. Moran left his daughter in the care of the second Earl of Strathsay. Names the fellow. Damme awful name Theophilus. But I like the man. Stolid disposition, but I like him. Got your eyes, chit," he said with a grin at Antonia.

"Then the Comte de Salvan can no longer threaten…"

"He has no claim on you, my love," said the Duke soothingly and caressed her cheek. "There is no power on earth that can drag us apart now." He turned to his sister. "You stayed in Paris on your way to London. What is being said?"

Lady Estée hesitated and the Vallentines exchanged a hurried glance that did not go unnoticed by the Duke.

"You know Paris as well as any, Roxton," said his lordship in an off-hand manner. "What isn't being said, eh? Don't regard it m'self. I'll tell you soon enough, but first I want to know why you couldn't wait until our arrival to wed the minx. I think you owe us that much for trudging all the way to Venice and back."

Roxton raised an eyebrow. "I thought that obvious, Vallentine. And my butler informs me you are some—er—two weeks overdue."

"Two weeks and four days," Antonia corrected. "And that makes it a little over twelve weeks since I left Paris and last saw Madame and Vallentine."

The Duke looked at her in some surprise. "I was unaware you were counting the days, petite."

"I have not—I mean—females just know—know these things," she answered haltingly and went back to drinking her coffee.

"That long, eh?" mused Vallentine. "Though, don't try and tell us you haven't preferred the delay! Driving off friends and relatives from your door; not sending word to London. I think you owe all of us an explanation of what you've been up to down here. Well, not precisely—that, so you damn well needn't pretend to be shocked by my meaning, Roxton! Just tell us about the ceremony and have done grinning at me in that macabre way of yours!"

"I will tell you," Antonia volunteered. "Monseigneur and I were married in the Elizabethan Garden. There is a ruin that was once a chapel, oh, many hundreds of years ago. King Henri, he had it torn down when he broke with the church in Rome over his divorce from the Spanish woman—"

"Ain't she marvellous!" his lordship declared with a crack of laughter. "I ask for details of her bridal and she launches into a history lesson! I expected a monologue on the gown you wore, chit. Most females give you that, but a hist—"

Antonia waved an impatient hand at him. "*Eh bien*! What has my gown got to do with anything? Renard, Vallentine's brain, it is full of trivialities just like Grandmamma's."

"Eh? Now don't start casting me in the same mold as that titian-haired termagant!"

"Will you please permit Antonia to tell her story," said Estée. "What did you wear, child?"

"Charlotte, she tried to have me wear the oyster silk gown Maurice made for me. But I chose the petticoats of gold tissue and the open-robed gown of embroidered damask. And Monseigneur gave me a wondrous string of pearls that once belonged to his maman."

"I know the ones—the Alston pearls."

"I knew we'd get to the gown in the end," muttered Vallentine.

"The Elizabethan Garden, chérie?" prompted the Duke.

"Oh! Yes! This fat little clergyman from the parish married us. He was very nervous I think. For he sweated considerably and he bowed too many times to M'sieur le Duc. That only made you angry, did it not, Monseigneur?" Antonia's eyes sparkled mischief. "But I think Monseigneur was only angry because he was even more nervous than m'sieur the clergyman."

"I can understand that," said Vallentine sympathetically. "Wouldn't be natural if a man ain't nervous on his wedding day. Don't get married everyday; don't want to. Damned harrowing experience! Gives me the goose bumps to think back on the whole business."

"To listen to you one would think it was the hangman you stood before, not a priest," Estée chided. "Go on, Antonia. We won't interrupt again."

"Please do not, or the telling will be longer than was the ceremony," said Antonia loftily. "It was held in the afternoon when all the guests had gone away exhausted from playing all the cricket. But Grandmamma would not go. She did not want to leave without Charlotte and Theo, who acted as the witnesses. But Monseigneur would not have her. So she went away in a temper, and in an unbelievable dramatic display. It truly was unbelievable. I have never seen Monseigneur so angry with anyone as he was with her."

"Antonia. I believe my sister and Vallentine have been given an adequate picture of my—er—condition," interrupted Roxton with a self-conscious frown.

Lord Vallentine gave a low whistle. "That nervous, Roxton."

Antonia shrugged. "There is nothing else to tell. Charlotte and Theo returned to London after the ceremony, and Monseigneur and I eloped to the west wing. That was very clever of us! We have been here ever since. Simple, yes?"

"Simple and effective," agreed Lord Vallentine. "Half Paris has wagered you're in the south of France, Roxton; and t'other half think you've gone into Italy."

"No one believes you are still in England," added Estée encouragingly, her brother's expression telling her nothing of what he was thinking. "And when we left London we told no one our destination, so you need not worry that we were followed."

"Need I be worried, Estée?" asked the Duke.

"This ain't the time to go into all that," said his lordship brusquely, and pushed back his chair. "Plenty of time to discuss everything! What say you to a ride about the estate, Roxton? The two of you could benefit from a good dose of fresh air. Cooped up in here, sleeping your days away, can't be good for anyone— honeymoon or no!" He dragged Estée up from her chair and headed for the door before the couple could say anything to the contrary. "Meet you down at the stables!"

"Lucian, you cannot put off telling them. My brother, he will want to know the news of Paris," whispered his wife as she was escorted from the room by a firm hand.

"Not in front of the girl," counselled Lord Vallentine with a hard set to his mouth Estée knew only too well, so she said nothing further. "This ain't the time or the place to discuss the Salvans. I'll speak to Roxton privately, after our ride. Can't get his attention with Antonia about." He smiled down at her. "Pair of lovedy-birds, ain't they. Never thought to see your brother besotted. Acts like a young blood! Just like when we were all in Paris together. Can't keep his eyes off her, damme! I don't blame him. Never seen her so ravishingly pretty." He frowned at a sudden thought, "Jesus! Those Salvans need to be taught a damned good lesson once and for all time! I've a notion—"

"No, Lucian. It is not for you to do anything. My brother, he will know what to do. He always does."

Vallentine nodded. But at the door to their apartments he stopped and looked at his wife with a frown. "Do you think she's turned him soft?" he asked with a significant jab at his temple.

"Soft? The Duke?" Estée uttered in alarm. "Antonia was right. You are old in the head!"

Seventeen

The Duke was being helped into jockey-boots when Antonia entered the dressing room and sat down on the settee. She had not changed her sacque for a riding habit but wore a velvet day gown of apple green striped petticoats. She carried a parasol and gloves and fiddled with these until Ellicott had completed his tasks and was waved away. Roxton did not immediately get up from the dressing table but sat regarding Antonia's reflection in the looking glass, a deep crease between his dark brows.

"Chérie, you are not unwell?"

She looked up swiftly. "N-no. Why do you say so? I thought I would take Grey and Tan for a walk to the lake to see the swans," she explained. "I promised them yesterday, and I do not much feel like riding out today. But Vallentine, he would be disappointed if you did not go. Do you mind that I do not ride?"

"Only that you will not be with me," he said with a smile as he picked up his black leather riding gloves and put out a hand to her. "Walk with me to the stables. If the weather holds we could have nuncheon on the island."

"I should like that. We have not been there since you rowed me across on our wedding day. But promise me you will not take them into the temple. That is our place."

"If you wish it so. But how I am to keep Vallentine on a leash is another matter. Mayhap if I tell him why…" He stopped to allow her to step out before him into a sunny courtyard that led to the stables. "Perhaps he will guess?"

"You are teasing me!" she said and caught the laughter in his eyes. "Not even Vallentine could guess our wickedness."

He laughed softly and caught her to him. "But I have always claimed him to be omniscient, *mignonne*. But yes, it will always be our special place. Now kiss me and I will leave you to your walk."

Lord and Lady Vallentine were already in the saddle and awaiting the Duke's pleasure. A groom held the reins to his master's mare and when his lordship spotted the couple across the cobbled square he sent the servant across to him.

"Told you, Estée," said Vallentine with a jerk of his head. "Gone soft. It's the broad light of day and look at 'em."

Estée shook her head in disbelief and cantered off to join her brother. "Antonia does not ride with us?" she asked, gaze on the Duchess who had stopped to give directions to a lackey.

"Er—no," answered Roxton pensively. "She prefers to take a walk to the lake."

"That is unlike her. In Paris I was forever forbidding her the saddle because her shoulder had not mended. And it did not please her at all. She—she is unwell?"

The Duke looked frankly at his sister. "She tells me she is well."

"If the girl don't want to ride, she don't," interrupted his lordship, catching the last of this conversation. "Come on, Roxton! Race you to wherever! Just point the way and I'm with you! Estée, don't try and catch us up. Just follow and we'll meet you down by the lake, and be careful 'cause—Hey! Damme! You devil, Rox!"

The Duke had put his knees hard into the mare's flanks and was gone. Lord Vallentine was left far behind, calling out such a string of good-natured abuse that his wife was glad her English comprehension had not progressed to the extent that this outburst could turn her ears very red. Those grooms lingering about grinned appreciably but were quick to disperse when Estée glared at them significantly. She turned her bay mare to the open field and cantered off.

She caught them up down by the lake and spent the next two hours in a leisurely tour of part of the estate. When the gentlemen turned the discussion to farming techniques and the agricultural pursuits of the Duke's tenants, Estée lost interest. She was content to drop back and admire the woods and try and catch sight of the herd of deer her brother kept in the park. And by and by she was left at the edge of the lake under an old oak while her husband raced her brother to the furthest fence on the horizon. Here she hoped to meet up with Antonia. But there was no sign of her so she returned to the house.

She was anxious to have a private word with the Duchess. If Antonia proved disinclined to confidences she would try and take aside her maid to see if her suspicions could be confirmed. But when she arrived back at the stables and asked direction to the Duchess not one of the servants could oblige her. She threw up her hands in disgust at their lack of understanding of her language, and when a servant was finally found who knew enough French to answer her questions he directed her to her own apartments and not to those occupied by his mistress.

Estée gave up the attempt and put herself in the hands of her dresser. She sent a footman to find Duvalier. She had changed into a day gown of flowered silk, her hair was patted into place, cosmetics re-applied, and a fresh mouche affixed to the corner of her mouth, and still the butler did not show himself. Thus she was forced to leave her rooms and go in search of him herself, but without the faintest idea of the layout of the many rooms; whether she was travelling down a corridor which took her east or west.

After a few wrong turns, locked doors, rooms draped in covers and dark corridors she stumbled into the Saloon. Here was a new-ly lit fire, refreshment set out on the polished sideboard, and chandeliers casting a warm glow over the crystal decanters and glasses arranged on a silver tray. A footman stood at the side-board arranging the silver cutlery. He said he had no idea of the whereabouts of the butler, and no, the Duke had not come within doors. He then returned quietly to his task.

With that Estée flounced out of the room mouthing an oath about barbarians and ready to do battle with the next unfortunate who crossed her path. This happened to be Duvalier, in the ante-chamber off the Saloon. He was deep in conversation with one who belonged in the field and ought not to be standing in a room of fine Italian marble in shabby pants of faded leather and heavy boots which had never seen polish.

Estée's nose went up and she grimaced at the rustic who pulled his cap and deferentially stepped aside when she approached.

"Where is Madame la Duchesse?" she demanded without preamble. When the butler hesitated she flicked shut her fan and pointed the sticks at him in a threatening manner. "You think perhaps because M'sieur le Duc is newly married he is not aware that behind his back his servants play idle good-for-nothings? It is not so! And now I am here all will be as it was in Paris. You understand me? Good. So. Tell me. Where is Madame la Duchesse?"

"I have not seen Madame la Duchesse for sometime, Madame," answered Duvalier truthfully, acutely conscious of the shepherd's scrutiny, and thankful the peasant knew no French.

"Has she returned from her walk?"

"I could not say, Madame," he said lamely.

"Tell that stinking peasant to go away!" she ordered and turned her back until the butler had shuffled the shepherd out. "What was he doing in here? Never mind! I do not care in the least! So, you have no idea where your mistress could be?" When the butler could not look up from his hands and seemed to breathe heavily, Estée's anger turned to fear. "What is it? She has taken ill? Something happened on her walk? She sprained her ankle—what?"

"I am sorry, Madame, but I cannot answer you. The last I saw of Madame la Duchesse it was before her walk, and she was on the terrace talking with the valet Ellicott."

"But that was many hours ago! She has not been seen since?"

"No, Madame."

"Did you send the lackeys to look for her?"

"Yes, Madame. It is a mystery."

The butler's tone caused Estée to become furious. "A mystery is it! Have you searched Madame la Duchesse's private rooms? Questioned her maids? Searched the rest of this monstrosity? What? Tell me what you have done to find your mistress!" She stopped pacing and fluttered her fan on her heated bosom. "*Mon Dieu*," she muttered to herself. "I hope the little one is not hurt— Where is my brother? She must be found…"

Duvalier saw his chance to escape and bowed. "If you will excuse me, Madame."

"No! You are not excused! Stand where you are. You know

of something," said Estée shrewdly. "I do not believe at all that you have told me the truth!"

The butler bowed respectfully. He stood his ground and was stubbornly silent. Estée knew she could not force him to speak, whether she stamped her foot in rage or shouted at him. It was useless to detain him, so she waved him away, privately cursing her brother for having such close-mouthed servants. What to do?

She sank down on the nearest chair up against one wall, trembling and close to tears. There was that uneasiness of mind which had followed her from Paris; since last she had spoken to her cousin the Comte. She had wanted to tell her brother of that interview immediately upon arrival, but Vallentine had cautioned restraint. Now she was not so sure he had made the right decision. Her brother should have been warned from the first of the gossip and slander circulating Paris. Now she was inclined to think there was some truth in the rumor.

The best thing to do now was to search out Antonia's maid, but Estée had not the slightest idea of how to reach her. In fact there was no need. The girl found her. She scuttled into the antechamber with a tear-stained face and red-rimmed eyes, twisting a bunch of her petticoats in her hands. When she saw Estée she fell on her and burst into fresh tears.

"Where is Madame la Duchesse?" Estée demanded, holding the girl off and giving her a shake.

"There are four men in the library with swords and pistols, and I do not know them in the least!" Gabrielle blurted out. "And there is one with them I have seen at the hôtel, often. But I do not know his name. They demand Madame la Duchesse! What do they want with her? The valet he is also missing—"

"Him I do not care about in the least!" snapped Estée. "When did these men come? You think then that they are French? Where is your mistress? Speak girl! Tell me!"

"I-I do not know when they arrived, Madame. They are French, yes. The one I have seen before ordered Duvalier not to speak to anyone of the household because he wants only to speak to M'sieur le Duc. He-he threatened things and waved his sword about like a madman!"

"*Mon Dieu.* And where is your mistress?"

"I do not know where she is—"

"Do not know where she is?" repeated Estée.

"M'sieur le Duc's valet, he is with her, I think. I saw them together on the terrace with Monseigneur's dogs. Oh, many hours ago now, but he too is missing. That is strange is it not? But what can these men want?"

"How should I know, girl? Do not ask me stupid questions! What—what am I to do?" she said distractedly, looking over the girl's head to the far wall. "I must find my brother and Lucian and—" She stood abruptly and dragged the maid to her feet, bringing her face close to hers. "There is a question I want answered. And do not try and be insolent with me or you will feel the sting of my hand! Has your mistress confided in you of a certain matter since—since her marriage?"

Gabrielle lowered her eyes.

"Well?" demanded Estée. "There is no need for you to be coy with me. Answer!"

"No, Madame, she would never—that is we—we have never spoken of that," said the maid quietly. "But M'sieur le Duc he has made her very happy. Oh, very happy! And from the first. But no, she would never mention—I hardly see her—They are rarely out of each other's arms—"

"Not that you idiot!" said Estée with an embarrassed sigh. "The Duchesse's health. How is her *health*?"

"Health? I do not understand, Madame," Gabrielle stammered. But when Estée Vallentine opened wide her eyes the maid understood at once. "Oh! No, Madame, the Duchesse has not said a word to me—But I know. I have five older sisters and know the signs. She—the Duchesse—she has had no one to tell her about such things. She is so very young. But there is no doubt about her condition."

"No doubt?" whispered Estée. Her blue eyes narrowed. "But surely it is too soon?"

"I—I could not say... I-I—It is best you speak with Madame la Duchesse, Madame," Gabrielle replied and curtsied, waiting to be dismissed, her tell-tale blush indication enough that she knew more than she was letting on.

The Duke's sister seemed to have forgotten her existence;

such was the far away look in her eyes. Possibly the woman would have made her stand there for some time if not woken from her trance by voices in the Saloon. She was finally waved away, and Estée ran into the adjoining room calling her brother's name. The door slammed in the maid's face just as she caught a glimpse of M'sieur le Duc de Roxton carrying a decanter and glasses to the table.

⌇◦⌇◦⌇◦

The last jump saw Lord Vallentine fall from the saddle, much to the delight of his friend. It was this wound to his pride which prompted him to challenge his Grace to a bout of fencing before they joined their wives for nuncheon. Roxton was not the least bit perturbed. In fact he welcomed the opportunity to loosen up his wrist, not having had any fencing practice since coming down from London.

"Took a round with a Signori—? Now what was the confounded fellow's name? Damme, if I can remember one Italian from the next!" confessed his lordship. "They all look the same to me!" They were sitting on a low wall regaining breath and life in their tired limbs. "The man's credited as having the best manoeuvres in Rome. Pretty foot work, but I soon showed him that his wrist ain't up to it. Wiped the smile from his swarthy face, too!"

"I sympathise with the nameless signori," said Roxton. He beckoned to a lackey who held their frocks and cravats. "I was a poor adversary, my dear. I apologise."

"Not at all. You're a worthy opponent at any time! Damme, I have to have the better of you at something!"

"Believe me, Vallentine, you do," said the Duke. He gave over his sword into the servant's hands. "Since your departure from Paris I've not had a decent opponent. Édouard Flavacourt lacks the experience and Du Barrie, the talent. I see I must concentrate a little more or you will have the better of me at every turn."

Lord Vallentine laughed and shook his head as he rolled down his sleeves. "I don't blame you. You're mind is on other matters, and that's understandable, ain't it. Between you and me,

294

and with all due respect to my lovely wife your sister, you're a damned lucky man, my friend! Damned lucky!"

"Luck, my dear Vallentine?" the Duke drawled, a glint in the black eyes. He threw the cravat about his neck but did not tie it, and left the white linen shirt gaping at the throat. When the lackey offered him his frock he waved it aside. It was a fine cloudless day and he was still warm from the exercise. He had the servant follow them within doors. "What were you so eager Antonia should not know?" he asked Vallentine.

"Don't want to alarm the girl unnecessarily," said Vallentine with a sudden heavy frown. "The news ain't pleasant."

"So I presumed. Go on."

"Had the story from my cousin Harcourt, who had it from a friend of his staying with the De Chesnays in Paris," said his lordship. "Of course we had heard it before then. Our first night back in Paris and who should come scratching on Estée's door but Thérèse Duras-Valfons! She whispered the whole in Estée's little ear. I took m'self off to Rossard's to hear the story from the mouth of a gentleman. Can't trust a female tongue to stick to the facts. And not one dripping with jealous spite."

"Go on," said Roxton, ignoring a significant side-long stare from his friend.

"Well, when I walked into Rossard's I swear they expected to see you at my back. What an unholy uproar! And do you think they believed me, your brother-in-law, when I told 'em I'd no notion of your whereabouts? Jesus! You could've heard the scuttle of a cockroach when I told 'em that!"

The Duke stood aside to allow his lordship to go up the stairs before him. "The news?" he prompted.

"Aye. I'm getting to that. It won't surprise you to know that when Salvan announced the cancellation of his son's nuptials all Paris was stunned. Only topic of conversation for days. Not only Paris but at Versailles, too. King Louis had Salvan up before him to explain himself. He ain't been back at court since. Got leave of absence from his duties, so he says. Though it's whispered he's in disgrace."

"And the explanation given for the cancellation of nuptials?"

Lord Vallentine paused by a long window in a passageway

that had up on its walls ancient members of the Hesham family. "You ain't going to like it one bit, my friend. The rumor in Paris is the Vicomte is in a state of total nervous collapse because you robbed his prospective bride of her—virtue. He ain't been seen for weeks. Rumor has it he's in the country, but De Chesnay is adamant he saw him in Paris just a week or so ago. And there's another thing…"

"Yes?"

"Madame de Salvan is dead."

"Is that so?"

"Thought that would surprise you. She died the very day her grandson was to be married."

"How unfortunate."

"For whom?" said Vallentine dryly. "Salvan's been shouting from the rooftops the old woman died of a broken heart, or some such absurd notion, all because of the shame you've brought upon the family name—kidnapping and seducing Antonia, and ruining his son's future happiness. You know Salvan's style. I reckon that damned little gnome is as pleased as can be that his mother up and died on that of all days."

"Naturally."

"Naturally," spluttered his lordship. "Now listen, Roxton. All this don't go well for you and your bride. Especially so for her. That cur didn't tell the world you up and married the chit. And of course it don't matter a whit to your reputation one way or t'other. In fact not an eyebrow was raised concerning your conduct. As for Antonia—all Paris frowns on her because she allowed herself to be seduced by you! Jesus! The girl is being blamed for it all! Even the death of old Grandmother Salvan. Truth be told the old hag choked on a fish bone. But that don't fit the tragedy, do it? And one other thing—"

Roxton looked bored. "There is more?"

"Aye!" said Lord Vallentine and leaned against the wood panelling. "The court harpies have lapped up this scandal like sweetened cream. Duras-Valfons, de La Tournelle and the rest. How do you think Antonia is going to be received by the likes of them, eh? And when they discover she is Madame la Duchesse de Roxton, what then? Tell me that!"

"Oh do spare me the lecture," the Duke said with bitterness.

"Can't stay at Treat forever, dear brother," Lord Vallentine announced, catching the Duke up in the Saloon.

Roxton had the lackey deposit their frocks and swords on a chair and leave them. He came away from the sideboard with a decanter and two glasses. "I do not wait on the world, Vallentine; it waits on me."

Vallentine accepted a glass with a grin and a shake of his head. "You're so damned arrogant."

The Duke raised his glass in a toast. "It is my most endearing quality."

They both laughed and some of the old easiness returned. But the smiles were wiped from their faces when Estée ran into the room crying, and cast herself against her brother's chest. Roxton held her off with a frown. But Lord Vallentine gathered her up in a comforting embrace and patiently coaxed her down from a high passion.

"What has happened to bring this on, lovedy?" said Vallentine in a soothing voice. "We didn't mean to leave you like that, but y'know what your brother and I are like when we get together. You didn't lose your way, aye?"

"Forgive me. I did not mean to—to be so foolish," Estée sniffed. "But I am frightened for the child."

"Antonia?" the Duke said sharply.

"No! Yes! I do not know what is happening!" she said on a dry sob and put out a hand to clutch her brother's sleeve. "You must be careful with her. She must not have an upset. She is delicate, and in her condition the slightest—"

"What condition?" asked Lord Vallentine and released her, looking from brother to sister.

The Duke snatched at his sister's sleeve. "She has spoken to you?"

Estée shook her curls at her brother's enquiry. "We have not had the opportunity to speak. But something she said at breakfast alerted me to the possibility and then her maid, she assured me it is so."

"Damme! What are you babbling about, Estée? What condition? What's wrong with the chit? Eh?"

Brother and sister ignored him.

297

Estée kissed the Duke's hand and smiled through her tears at his look of total confusion. "Did you never consider such an eventuality?"

"I never suspected… She hasn't said a word. She—she can't be, can she?" he asked. But when his sister smiled and burst into joyful tears he quickly turned away and refilled his glass.

Lord Vallentine gave a low whistle. "Look here, Estée," he said near his wife's ear. "You're not seriously telling us that the girl—that Antonia—is with child? *Already*? Well! Well!" he exclaimed and slapped the Duke's back "Trust you to make quick work of it! Damn your impudence!" he laughed. "If that ain't the devil's own luck!"

"Lu-cian!" scolded his scowling wife, her cheeks burning with embarrassment.

"Where is Antonia?" asked the Duke.

"I do not know," she said in a small voice and avoided looking at him. "Your lackeys, they are insolently stupid! And Duvalier, he is just the same. He refuses to tell me. He will speak only to you."

Lord Vallentine grinned. "She's playing a game with us, I'll swear! And I'll wager Duvalier is in on it. Crafty old fox! If he was thirty years younger I'd warn you against him. He and your valet both. They've got a soft place in their hearts for your wife, Roxton. Damme if the chit isn't playing hide n' seek with us."

The Duke did not smile. "What did Duvalier tell you, Estée?"

"Nothing! The maid Gabrielle, she came to me with some tale of intruders in the library with pistols and swords—"

"What is going on here?" exploded his lordship.

"Do not shout at me, Lucian!" shouted his wife and burst into fresh tears. "How do I know what is going on in a house where the lackeys are-are insolent and closed-mouthed, and do not have a civilised tongue in their heads? Since I returned from our ride all has been upside down in this place! I got lost, and no one will speak to me of the Duchesse, and oh-oh—" She fell into her husband's arms. "Lucian, Lucian, I am very worried for the little one."

"Hush now. I'm certain it's all a pack of flim flam."

"But do you not remember what is being said in Paris? We should not have gone to London but come straight here!"

"That was Salvan merely raving on!" argued Vallentine. "It's too fantastic to be believed. You know your cousin better than I, Estée, and I say he's as mad as the rest of his family." He refilled the Duke's glass but it was not taken. Roxton had turned to the large looking glass over the sideboard and was tying his cravat, a tremble in his right hand prolonging the task. "Roxton," he said kindly, mindful of the shake, "I wish you'd drink this. It will help y'know."

The Duke drained the glass and put it aside, then shrugged himself into his riding frock. "Estée. What did Antonia's maid tell you?" he asked quietly.

"It was a jumble, all of it! She-she said there are four men in your library with another, their leader, and they have swords and pistols and were waving them about threatening Duvalier! And she does not know Antonia's whereabouts, and somehow the valet, he is mixed up in all of this too!"

"Jesus! Who are these fools? Hey! Where are you going with that sword?"

"Excuse me, my dear. I—er—must greet my guests."

"Not without me! Wait up!" cried his lordship, struggling to put on his sword and follow his friend at one and the same time. "I'm coming with you."

"No. I go alone. Madame, you will wait outside."

"You ain't going to face a pack of damned ruffians without me!"

Roxton strode through one antechamber then the next, and disappeared down a long dark corridor. Lord and Lady Vallentine followed him.

"You'd be lucky to steady a pistol least of all a sword!" called his lordship close at the Duke's back. "So you won't argue with me! Do you hear? Besides, you can't deny there's sport in two on five, eh?"

"Lucian! Lucian!" called his wife, unable to keep up the pace and cursing her high red heels. "You must be careful! Oh! Will you not slow down! I will lose a heel!"

"Wait outside as Roxton says," he bellowed over his shoulder. "There's nought for you to worry about. We're a match for any pack of scum Salvan cares to throw at us!" He gave a crack of laughter. "And I ain't braggin', damn it!"

Estée stumbled and decided to give up the chase. She

299

slumped down on a hard-backed settee and tried to regain her breath. "*Mon Dieu*, do not kill him!" she shouted shrilly as husband and brother stormed through a set of doors which had been locked from the inside.

The Duke had traversed half the length of the library when he checked himself. Lord Vallentine cursed and pulled up short, tripping himself up and almost crashing into his friend's broad back. Swiftly his hand went to his sword and stayed there, the knuckles white as he gripped its hilt hard. But the Duke did not move or go for his sword. He stood quite still, his face masked of emotion, the errant hand thrust in a breeches pocket.

The Comte de Salvan, in heavy jack-boots and travel stained riding frock, stood by a dying fire in the grate of the big marble fireplace, a heel on the hearth. To his right four musketeers, similarly attired, kicked their heels. They lounged on the furniture and stared absently out of the long windows that had a view of the velvet lawns. They looked the pack of ruffians Lord Vallentine had branded them, and just as dangerous as the maid described. All wore swords; two carried pistols. Yet it was not this that had caused the Duke to stop mid-stride. In the Comte de Salvan's gloved hand was Antonia's parasol.

Salvan pointed the parasol at the closest musketeer and spoke a sharp sentence the Duke did not catch. The man responded with an oath and his fellows laughed at his expense. The Comte did not laugh. He frowned and swore at them and thumped the hearth with his heel. He was about to bark out something else when he sensed a presence and swirled about to stare into the face of his cousin. His frown dissolved, replaced by a smile that broadened his painted face.

"Mon cousin! At last we are reunited!" he declared with out-stretched arms and a sweeping bow. "It has been an age since last we met—at the Maison Clermont was it not? Yes! I am sure of it! You with the fair flower of the Orient and I? Poor Salvan to content himself with one of the less accomplished bawds—"

"Where is my wife," the Duke asked softly.

The Comte gave a short, bitter laugh. "Ah, yes, your *wife*," he said caressingly and dropped the parasol as if it was something unclean. "Your so lovely, and very young, wife."

The gesture was too much for Lord Vallentine. In a blind rage, and within not more than a blink, his sword was out of its scabbard, its sharp point thrust up under the Comte's throat to gently tickle the ravaged skin.

"Where is Madame la Duchesse, you disgusting trencherfly!"

No sooner had Lord Vallentine drawn his blade than there was the sing of polished steel on steel as four blades were instantly unsheathed and pointed in his direction. Vallentine's sword did not waver. Instead he twisted it a turn, but so swiftly and skilfully that the movement went undetected. Its sharp tip pricked the soft underside of the Comte's chin, causing the little man to smile in panic. The musketeers held their ground. One dared to glance at the Duke who was seemingly unperturbed at the prospect of either gentleman's demise and was warming his hands by the fire.

"Ah, M'sieur Vallentine, Salvan is offended at the reception he receives," whispered the Comte in a constricted voice, his eyes on the murderous weapon. He dared to move his head and shuddered at the feel of the cold metal. "Roxton, your brother, he is not himself. You must calm him or I fear my men—"

"You're a damned coward, Salvan! I don't fear you or these scum at my back. Give the order! But this blade will be well up into your brain before I fall! You followed my carriage here, didn't you, eh? Well, didn't you!"

"Vallentine, if you will permit—" began the Duke, but was interrupted.

"I had a mind to run you through in Paris! I should have! Where is the Duchesse?"

"Remove your blade, m'sieur," said the Comte in his most haughty voice. But the sweat that glistened on his upper lip told the lie of his calm. "I am here only to collect what belongs to me—"

Vallentine gave a snort and twisted the Comte's skin a turn. "Yours? Damme that's rich! She's the Duchesse de Roxton and that's all there is to it! You have no claim on her!"

"Put the blade away, Vallentine," said the Duke in English, his eyes still on the grate. "The four—er—gentlemen at your back are not Salvan's serfs, you fool. They wear the King of France's insignia."

Lord Vallentine's eyebrows went up and he pulled a face. "Musketeers?"

"Exactly so."

His lordship gave a faint whistle. "Jesus."

"In fact, one is your old sparing partner, the brother of your wife's first husband," Roxton told him. "I am certain it is only the esteem in which they hold your skills that has prevented them up to this point from engaging you in a—er—bloody struggle. They will, however, dispatch you if my very dear cousin gives the word."

"I want to kill him, Roxton," said Vallentine with choked rage and reluctantly sheathed his blade with a flourish. "By Christ I wanted so much to spill his guts all over this floor!"

"My desire to do just that is no less strong," responded the Duke calmly and looked back at the mantelpiece. "But we must think of Antonia."

Vallentine bowed his head. "Aye, it was for her I..."

Freed from the threat of imminent death the Comte tried to regain command of the situation. Some of his artificial urbanity returned. He ordered his men to put away their swords and smiled broadly at his cousin. But the musketeers had seen his fear and noted the sweat on the little man's upper lip and forehead, and although they did as he commanded, they had nothing but contempt for this son of France. All four men acknowledged the Duke and Lord Vallentine with a stiff bow, and the one known to the Duke saluted him. It was a slap in the face for the Comte whose pitted cheeks turned red under the lead cosmetic.

Roxton regarded his cousin with an expression Vallentine found impossible to fathom. He wondered what would happen next. One never knew with his friend. Yet, the next moment he was forced to blink. In one stride the Duke had the Comte about the throat and had pushed him up against a wall. The little man laughed nervously and choked. His eyes flew to the musketeers. They stood to attention, a hand on the hilt of their swords.

"What an incompetent fool you are!" snarled the Duke and threw Salvan off. "My instructions were plainly written. You were to meet the boy at Calais and return him under guard to Paris. What are you doing here?"

"M-mon c-cousin! It was not as simple as you suggest," the Comte explained, gasping air into his deprived lungs. "My mother, she would not hear of his incarceration!" He adjusted his cravat with shaking hands. "Parbleu. Think of the shame—the gossip—the sc-scandal! I-I did as you ordered. I went to Calais and waited. But she—my mother—she would have none of it and she got to him first—"

"Spare me the petty details. I hope for your sake you managed to right matters."

The Comte looked confused. "But... He was not at Calais! He's disappeared! No sooner was he set down on French soil than he immediately boarded a return packet for England. We followed and at Dover were told he had asked directions to this your estate." He glanced at Lord Vallentine and pulled a face. "Though why he would return here..."

"Sweet Christ," escaped from the Duke, and he wiped his mouth with a trembling hand. "You think he is here, *in my house?*"

"Eh? What's this?" demanded Lord Vallentine. "Don't Salvan know where Antonia is? Ain't he got her?"

He was ignored.

The Duke addressed the musketeers. "He is still inside my house?"

"We believe so, M'sieur le Duc," answered their leader. "We thought we had cornered him here, in this room, but unfortunately it was a false lead. Although we did find—"

"Yes?"

The musketeer crouched by a bookcase. "Here there is much blood on the carpet."

Vallentine stooped and pressed a finger to the soiled Aubusson rug. The dark stain was large, wet and sticky. "Oh God, Roxton," uttered his lordship with a shudder, "it's a damn bad injury."

"No! That I do not believe," stammered the Comte. "It is impossible! A cut! Nothing more than a cut. I am sure of it!"

Roxton went to a panel in the wall, pushed on it, and the bookcase near where Vallentine and the musketeer crouched swung inwards to reveal a darkened recess. There were a few drops of blood even here. His lordship scrambled into this void, while the musketeers stood back and awaited the Duke's instructions. He immediately dispatched three of them via the main staircase to his private apartments above. Their leader was told to follow the Duke and Lord Vallentine up the secret stairwell. Not wanting to be left behind, the Comte trotted after his cousin and forced his way forward to grab at the Duke's sleeve.

"What are you going to do to him?" he asked the Duke in a whisper.

The Duke shrugged him off and went up the stairs. "What do you think? If he has dared to lay a finger on her..." He looked over his shoulder at the little man's upturned painted face. "Salvan, she is with child."

"*Eh bien*," hissed the Comte in wide-eyed disbelief. "With child? You are certain of it? Jesu, if he discovers this..."

The Duke turned away and gestured for the others to follow quietly at his back, the Comte only too happy to allow Vallentine and the musketeer to pass him on the stairs. He had shown his cousin a face full of concern and sympathy, yet in the darkness of the stairwell he permitted himself a leisurely grin; he almost sniggered.

There was an eerie silence in the first of the rooms above. Nothing had been over-set in struggle and all was untouched. The Comte turned up an envious nose at so much comfort and opulence, as he had done on first seeing Treat, but he could not help an interested glance at his surroundings. He was careful to stay well back. Lord Vallentine and the musketeer were blind to everything except the urgency of the situation and finding the closet deserted they were eager to press on to the dressing room. The Duke stopped them.

"Let me go first." Vallentine whispered. "Quiet, ain't it?"

"Trying to spare me, my dear?" said the Duke with a crooked smile. "No. I go. Stay here with the others. If the boy sees a regiment he might panic and—"

"Look here, Roxton," lectured Vallentine. "There's a pitcher-full of blood on that carpet downstairs! That boy ain't in his right head. He's dangerous. Understand? You can't expect to reason it out with one such as he. Christ! Who knows what he'll do when he sees you? I only pray he doesn't know the full story—that she didn't tell him—" He broke off seeing a look of deep pain cross the Duke's pale face and he gripped his friend's arm. "Insensitive brute, ain't I. You go on. I'll wait. But give me that pistol." He took it and cocked the trigger. "If anyone is going to do any firin' it's me!"

The Comte, who had picked up off the writing desk a lady's fan, sat down and crossed his stockinged legs with all the calmness of one waiting an appointment. He fluttered the fan like a woman and sighed. Lord Vallentine glared at him, confused by the bland look on the Frenchman's face, when not five minutes before he had been a quacking mass of nerves and sweat.

"You're mighty cool for a man whose maniac of a son is runnin' amok and has possibly caused someone a grave injury, ain't you, Salvan?"

The Comte raised his eyebrows. "But, M'sieur Vallentine, I am all devastation, I assure you."

The musketeer grunted.

"If Roxton gets his hands on him he'll kill him. You know that, don't you?"

The Comte continued to fan himself. The musketeer rolled his eyes. He thought this nobleman as mad as his son, and wondered what wrong he and his fellows had committed to be sent secretly on this equally insane adventure into a country that was at war with France, and where all men, save the phlegmatic Duc de Roxton, spoke a harsh tongue and possessed no manners.

"Your lovely wife, she is resident in this great lump of a house, too?" asked the Comte, looking about the room with interest.

Lord Vallentine's brow darkened. "What of it?"

Salvan shrugged a padded shoulder. "Do not look at me with such a jealous passion. I only want her advice. She is my cousin, enfin."

"Advice?"

"But of course," replied the Comte and threw the fan aside. "I am about to remarry and I need Estée's advice on what I should do ab—"

"You're fit for Bedlam!" hissed Vallentine "Your son is a maniac on the loose, damme! And he's got the Duchess holed up, and someone's bleeding all over the rugs and you—and you talk to me about your damned notion to remarry? What's the trick, Salvan?"

"Trick, m'sieur?" asked the Comte and offered his snuffbox. "I do not think I understand you."

Vallentine waved the pistol menacingly. "Get away from me you trencherfly, or I'll end the whole Salvan line here and now!"

Eighteen

The Duke found the dressing room similarly deserted but he did not call for the others to come through. He was about to cross into the bedchamber alone when he was confronted with his valet. Ellicott came out of the bedchamber holding his left arm above the elbow; blood oozed from between his fingers and was smeared down the front of his shirt. When he saw his master framed in the doorway, a hand on the hilt of his sword, all the fight drained from him and with shoulders slumped he hung his head. When he dared to glance at his master's ashen face it was to blink away tears.

It was enough to send the Duke to the edge of madness.

He was barely able to speak.

"The Duchess?" he asked huskily.

The valet dared to hesitate and wished he had not for the Duke's face took on a deathly hue. "No! No! She—the Duchess is unharmed," he assured him in a rush. "When you see her there is blood on her petticoats but it is not hers, it is Grey's blood. He—the Vicomte—he slit Grey's throat—"

The Duke shut his eyes.

"—in front of her. In the library. A madman's act. The Duchess fainted. When I attempted to go to her the Vicomte came at me with the knife but I managed to fend him off. It's nothing serious, your Grace," he said when the Duke glanced at his bloodied arm and before the question could be asked. "I—I made the mistake of trying to interfere in his plans. And in his present frenzied state he—he has the strength of ten men."

The Duke glanced at the bedchamber door. "He is in there with her now?"

The valet nodded. "Yes. He thinks I have gone to fetch a footman to help with the bags. He is taking the Duchess with him to Paris. We thought it best to humor him. The Duchess is doing her best to fall in with his plans. She even packed her bag herself. And now—"

"And now?"

"She is sitting with Tan on her lap in the window seat." Ellicott looked at the drops of blood on the polished floor. "He has threatened to slit Tan up too if she does not do as he asks. Your Grace…"

The tone in the valet's voice made the Duke look at him. "You had best see to your arm, Martin. I will deal with him now."

"Yes, your Grace, but I…"

The Duke waited. His valet swallowed.

"I think you should know that the Vicomte has no idea of the present situation; that you are married and that her Grace is with—" He swallowed again. "I only know about the child because when she came round after her faint she feared the blood on her petticoats meant she had miscarried. But I assured her that everything was as it should be. That her child was safe. Your Grace, the Vicomte is insane—"

"I am well aware of that, Martin," the Duke said quietly.

Ellicott looked his master full in the face. "So insane that he will not hesitate to kill her should you interfere."

Antonia huddled in the window seat with the tan and white whippet curled up in her lap. Somehow having him to protect made her feel less fearful. She must keep calm for Tan's sake. She must continue to be pleasant and agreeable for as long as it took the Duke to find her. She prayed that Ellicott had found him by now because the Vicomte was becoming increasingly agitated.

But this creature was not the Vicomte d'Ambert she had known. He could not be called anything else in his present state, what with a full beard disguising his face and his natural hair grown back to stubble on his head. Dressed in the leather pants and woollen shirt of a shepherd he could easily be mistaken for the most ill-kept peasant. A peasant who snorted such quantities of opium that his nostrils had festered and openly wept and his hands shook so violently that he was incapable of picking up any object without dropping it, except when enraged, then he seemed to have the strength of a regiment.

Antonia watched him now, through a tangle of hair that hid her face, and prayed that he had forgotten her presence. He was pacing the space between the bed and the window seat, arguing with himself and gesticulating into thin air. His movements frightened the whippet and it attempted to stand up in Antonia's lap. She quickly coaxed Tan down again and stroked his muzzle. But the Vicomte had heard her soothing words and turned on her with violence.

"You laugh at me!" he spat out, sticking his face close up to hers. The smell of him was enough to make her stifle a heave. He grabbed her hair and jerked it back off her face. "I should cut this all off! Then you could not laugh at me! Shall I cut it off? Shall I cut it all off?" He pulled out a bloodied knife from inside his boot and with his other hand twisted a handful of her long hair about his wrist. Then he hesitated. Antonia dared not move or speak. She kept her eyes lowered and prayed that some other flight of fancy would divert him. "If I cut it off I could make a rope," he said to himself and nodded with satisfaction. "A rope to hang you with if you dare disobey me." But as soon as this idea took root he just as suddenly put the knife away and sat down beside her, pushing her round so that her back was to him. He began to braid her hair. "Such beautiful curls. I think I will not cut them off after all." He caressed her neck. "Remember when you would let me braid it for you in the Caspartti's apartments?"

Antonia tried not to shiver with repulsion at his touch. "Y-yes, Étienne. I do. We had such good times then, did we not?"

He continued to braid and unbraid her hair, his shaking fingers in her curls. "Yes. Such good times," he murmured. Then, just as quickly, his fingers convulsed violently and became tangled in her hair, as if caught in a web. Her cry of pain as he tried to disentangle himself only made him shout. "Stop it! Stop it! I'm not hurting you! You do not know what you have done! You do not know! Come here!" He pulled her up off the window seat with a jerk, which sent Tan sprawling to the floor with a yelp, and dragged her toward the bed. "I have waited long enough. I have been patient long enough."

"No, Étienne! No! *Please.*"

When she tried to pull free he slapped her across the face. Instantly a red welt appeared on her cheek.

"Do you know what hell I have endured since you left Paris? Eh? Do you?" he demanded, dragging her across the room. "Poor Grandma Salvan died of a broken heart all because of you, you selfish little bitch! And I barely escaped Salvan's thugs to come back and fetch you!" He kneed her in the small of the back, pushing her against the bed, tearing the back of her bodice as he did so. Her sobs fell on deaf ears. "Do you know how long I have been skulking about this place waiting to find you alone? Two weeks! Two weeks of eating the scraps from the kitchen and the bones left out for his hounds." He hoisted her effortlessly up onto the bed and then climbed up beside her. "M'sieur le Duc is in for a surprise—

"Étienne, no!"

He slapped her across the face again, and this time so hard that the blow split the corner of her mouth. "How dare you interrupt me! Do you know who I am?" He sniggered in her face, but seeing blood at the corner of her mouth he put out a finger to tenderly wipe it away. Antonia recoiled and wished she had not because it sent him into a frenzy. He began to pull up the bed clothes, and to tear the stuffing out of the pillows. As quickly as it had begun his fit ceased and he fell back amongst the feathers and ripped cloth to regain his breath. When Antonia dared to shift he caught her wrist and squeezed it painfully, pulling her down beside him. "Do you know who I am?" he enunciated in a whisper.

Antonia shook her head.

"Look at me!" he snarled. "Whom do you see?"

She stared at him and felt nothing but fear and loathing. "Who are you, Étienne?" she asked politely.

He put his hands behind his stubbled head and smiled. "I am M'sieur le Duc de Roxton's *bastard* son."

Antonia covered her face with her hands and began to cry. It was not the response he wanted and he sat up, confused and a little stunned. "You do not believe me?"

"Yes, I believe you, Étienne."

"My mother became M'sieur le Duc's whore just after her marriage to Salvan. Grandma Salvan told me that my mother knew from the first that the child she carried was not her husband's but belonged to M'sieur le Duc d'Roxton. She told me this just before she died. She said my mother confided the truth to M'sieur le Duc in a letter and then took her own life," he said in a conversational, almost rational, tone. "Salvan thinks it was my mother's madness which made her name M'sieur le Duc as my father. But M'sieur le Duc knows my mother spoke the truth because my mother she told him as soon as she knew she was with child that she carried his child and that is when he cast her off like some used broken thing! M'sieur le Duc he laughs at Salvan and at me his son—"

"No! He—"

"Do not interrupt! Do not ever interrupt me," the Vicomte said through gritted teeth. "Or I shall be forced to punish you." He smiled and patted her hand and stared up at the silk pleated canopy. "Is this not the bed in which he made you his whore too?"

Antonia bit her lip. How she wanted to scream for help. Instead she kept her silence. The Vicomte scrambled up and shook her.

"Well? Is it? Is this the bed or is it not?"

"No! No! It is not! Please, Étienne, you are hurting me."

"Liar! Whore!" he screamed in her face. "You are his whore, are you not? Just as my mother was his whore. Well, we shall see what tricks he has taught you!" he snarled, and started to bunch her petticoats up over her stockinged knees. "I want you to—"

"No! I beg of you! Please! Étienne, for God's sake, have pity on *my* child!"

The Vicomte stared at her, puzzled, and dropped her petticoats. "What? Child? What are you talking about, eh?" He seemed unable to grasp her news. It was as if she had spoken to him in a foreign tongue. It gave her a moment to scramble off the bed.

She made a dash for the door that led into the private dining room.

The Vicomte was mesmerised. He was staring at the gold

threaded coverlet as it slithered off the bed along with Antonia and his lip curled with distaste.

"His child? Another *bastard* for M'sieur le Duc? I think not!"

He looked up, saw what she meant to do, and let out a great guttural cry as he sprung down off the bed with all the energy of an animal pursuing its prey.

Antonia saw the knife flash before her eyes as her knees buckled under her. She slid down the wall, certain that he meant to slit her throat.

Something tickled her face and made her open her eyes. She smiled and said the Duke's name. But it was not the Duke who bent over her but the Vicomte, and catching the stench of his breath she knew the nightmare was not over. She wanted to cry out but was too exhausted to do even that. She was still lying on the floor where she had collapsed, while her captor knelt over her, tracing patterns on her bodice with the point of a knife that shook so violently in his hand that it was only a matter of time before he put a rent in the fabric.

"I wonder where it is in there?" the Vicomte murmured, his free hand carefully smoothing out the many layers of Antonia's dishevelled striped petticoats. "Do you hope for a son, little Antonia?" Then he laughed gleefully and shook his head. "We will never know now, will we?" and he stopped tracing imaginary patterns to press the point of the knife into the velvet. "You know you cannot have this child. You do know that?" he said seriously, looking down into her face, his smile almost serene. "It would not be kind of me to let it live. Not another bastard to suffer the hell I have suffered."

"Étienne, listen to me," she pleaded, fingers inching across her body, hoping to distract him so she could knock the knife out of his trembling grasp. "I love this baby as your maman loved you."

"Maman? Yes, Maman loved me," he said as if this fact had just dawned on him.

"Yes, she loved you and cared for you and—"

"Why are you talking about her?" he growled. "I do not want to talk about her."

"She would not want you to do this terrible thing."

"Terrible? It is not terrible to put a bastard out of its misery!"

he argued. "She would see that. She must!" he muttered to himself. "It cannot live."

Suddenly he lashed out and grabbed Antonia's wrist just as her fingers had managed to brush the ornate hilt of the dagger. He twisted and squeezed her flesh, burning it, causing her to cry out with the pain, and then slammed her hand back against the floorboards. "You scheming little bitch! I was going to spare you! I was going to be quick. Now I shall take my time to be rid of it! Oh! Oh! Tears! Crying will not help you now!"

Instinctively, Antonia tried to roll on her side to shield her belly but he threw her shoulder back and pinioned her arm with his knee. Her tears turned to aching sobs as he started to rent the many layers of her petticoats, laughing down at her like some grotesque gargoyle.

"For pity's sake, Étienne!" she screamed. "Think what you are doing! *Please!*"

Then, through a haze of tears, she saw him, standing over them, just a little to the left, his whole being tensed and focused on the Vicomte. And as she closed her eyes with the sheer relief of his presence he raised his right arm and struck.

The Vicomte was hit so hard on the side of the head that his body pitched sideways. Instantly he lay completely still, the knife falling with a clatter beside his paralysed form.

The Duke had come into the room without his sword and hoping to reason it out with the mad Vicomte. Reason with him enough to get Antonia to safety. Now it did not matter. He had struck him with a force fuelled by such rage that he did not know if he had killed him or not; and now he did not care.

Certain that the Vicomte would be unconscious for many hours he finally turned his attention to Antonia. Entering the bedchamber he had forced himself to ignore her until such time as she was out of danger. He had put out of his mind that a madman stood over her, knife poised, in what looked like a ritualistic ceremony of death. He knew that if he had not acted at once the Vicomte would have plunged that knife into her; and he guessed why. Now it did not bear thinking about.

He saw the blood on her apple green-striped petticoats, the great rents in the delicate fabric from her struggles, and when she looked up at him, he saw the blood at the corner of her mouth and the beginnings of an ugly bruise to her cheek. Yet he shut his eyes and thanked God she was very much alive. For what seemed an eternity of minutes he could do nothing but stare at her as if she was an apparition. Yet when she smiled and Tan nuzzled his hand in greeting he was down beside her in an instant.

He gathered her up in his arms and held her so tightly to him that she felt the tremors of relief that shook his whole being. It was as if a tightly bound cord twisted suffocatingly about his throat had finally been cut and he was only now able to breath. And with relief came unspeakable fury at what had been done to her, and a frustrated anger that he had been impotent to stop such an attack. Sensing his anguish Antonia was quick to reassure him she was only a little hurt. She had been terrified and yes, very much shaken, but she had escaped before any serious harm was done.

"It is just a cut," she said with a teary smile when he brushed her cheek with the back of his hand. "And I am certain to have a few bruises to my back, but I am all right otherwise. It—it looks worse than it is, truly. He hit me when I argued with him. I should not have done that." She looked up and saw his eyes flicker to the blood on her petticoats. "It is not mine. No. It—it is Grey's. He kill—"

"I know, *mignonne*. In the library."

She nodded. "Ellicott and I—He, Étienne, slit Grey open in front of us and left him to bleed to death." She swallowed and sniffed back tears. "Ellicott wrapped him in a blanket and took him outside. I think he must have put him out of his misery, Monseigneur. It was for the best because he was bleeding to death; the poor little thing."

"Ellicott would have done what was best," he assured her.

"Yes. It was for the best."

He cradled her gently on his lap, her head in the crook of his neck. "Do you want to tell me what else happened, chérie?"

"Étienne—but it is not Étienne—He is truly mad, Renard."

"Yes, *mignonne*, I think he must be."

"I did not recognise him without his wig, and with his beard all grown on his face, and his clothes soiled and tattered. At first I thought it was one of the shepherds who had lost his way into the house. Next thing I knew I saw him running along one of the corridors before he—before he found me in the library." She shuddered at the memory and shifted a little in his arms. "Ellicott tried to-to protect me and shield me when Grey was killed in that horrible way. He threw his coat over him, but I could not help but see all the blood and I fainted... I did not mean to faint but seeing all that blood, and Étienne such a madman, made me feel very sick. I truly could not help it."

"Hush. No one would blame you," he said, stroking her hair. "So my valet was very gallant?"

"Yes, Renard," she confessed shyly. "I awoke to find all this blood on my gown and Ellicott reassured me it was not mine. Which of course it could not be when I think about it, it was Grey's, but I did not know that at the time." She gave a tired sigh. "I am a coward."

The Duke smiled softly and gently kissed the top of her head. "But a very brave coward."

Antonia looked up from snuggling into the warmth of his black velvet frockcoat. "Monseigneur, I am sorry, but I think I am about to be very ill."

"If you must. But Ellicott will be furious. It's a new riding frock."

She gave a gurgle of laughter and felt better for it.

Yet her smile disappeared when the door to the bedchamber burst open and a musketeer rushed in brandishing his sword. The valet followed him, but at a sedate walk, and with his nose elevated at the impetuous Frenchman. His arm was newly bandaged and he wore a fresh shirt, although in his haste and worry he had neglected to wipe the dried blood off his face and hands. When he saw his master seated on the floor beside the bed with the Duchess safely curled up in his arms his mouth quivered; this the only sign of emotion he would permit himself.

The musketeer showed his confusion. He saw the body of the Vicomte d'Ambert lying very still beside the bed but there was no blood and there appeared to be no wound. And seated on the floor not two feet from the body was the Duc de Roxton with a very beautiful girl on his lap. He openly stared at them. Roxton felt Antonia turn in toward him and sensed her embarrassment. A sharp word at the gaping soldier and the sword was put away and he retreated to stand at a discreet distance, his eyes cast elsewhere.

"I apologise for this intrusion, your Grace," said the valet calmly, all his old hauteur returning to him now that the Duchess was out of danger. "This—this *Frenchman* did not believe me when I said there was only one maniac on the loose and he now in your custody."

"Indeed?" said the Duke in English, taking his valet's lead. "I did not tell you before, the—er—situation as it was, but I am greatly indebted to you, Martin."

"Please, your Grace," Ellicott said hurriedly, flushing. "I merely did my duty to you and the Duchess, and your—" He stopped himself and made a quaint little bow. "If your Grace permits I will see to a wrap for the Duchess."

Antonia turned to look at him through a tangle of hair. "Thank you, Ellicott," she said with a soft smile. "I think you are very brave."

The valet bowed to her with great courteousness and hurried into the dressing room. When he returned with a silk banyan he found the scene unchanged. The Vicomte's body still lay very still where it had fallen. He asked the question the musketeer itched to have answered. "Your Grace, may I be permitted to know what you did to him?"

The Duke told him. He had knocked the Vicomte out cold; possibly he had fractured his skull; he may even have caused deafness to one of his ears. But he certainly had not killed him. No, a worse fate was to befall the Vicomte and the Comte de Salvan. The valet could be certain of that.

Satisfied, Ellicott took his leave, informing the Duchess that he would find Gabrielle to prepare her a bath and to set out a change of clothes. With that he left the room with his nose a little higher than when first he had entered it.

In the next moment Lord Vallentine came storming into the room with two musketeers at his back; all brandishing swords and hoping to do battle. They had grown impatient. Hearing voices and expecting the worst they had decided to storm the apartments. The Comte de Salvan did not exert himself and entered the bed-chamber at a leisurely pace when he thought it safe to do so.

At the same time Estée swept into the bedchamber from the private dining room with the fourth musketeer. She saw her husband and the musketeers with their glinting swords before they saw her, and her scream of alarm made them jump, spin about, and almost cross blades with one another.

As they rushed forward Lady Vallentine swooned and was caught by a musketeer. When his companions had orientated themselves they laughed at his chivalry. Lord Vallentine did not think it humorous and he quickly relieved the soldier of his burden. Estée said she had not fainted and demanded to be set upright. She had seen her brother and Antonia seated on the floor and all she cared for was to reassure herself the girl was unharmed.

The antics of these performers provided the Duke and Duchess with some comic relief. Yet when the Comte de Salvan appeared their smiles vanished. Antonia turned her head away, and the Duke stood up and shielded her, his features carved of stone. He was no less cold to his sister when she gave a startled cry at the Vicomte's handiwork. The blood splattered across Antonia's petticoats made her jump to the worse possible conclusions.

"*Bon Dieu!* My darling girl! Has no one attended to your hurts?" cried Estée. "Are you in much pain? And the—the blood—"

"Please, Madame, it is nothing—nothing," murmured Antonia as the Duke helped her to her feet. She retreated behind her husband, acutely conscious of the stares of the soldiers and the Comte de Salvan.

"How can you say it is nothing? Look at what that *fiend* has done to her, Lucian! Where is he? What have you done with him?"

"Calm yourself," ordered the Duke. "The Vicomte is lying under your feet, but he is perfectly harmless."

Lord Vallentine stepped in. "This ain't the time, Estée," he said firmly and stooped to pick up the bloodied knife that still lay beside the motionless body of the Vicomte d'Ambert. "You can see she is unharmed—"

"Unharmed? You call her condition *unharmed?*" said Estée shrilly. "I hope that monster is dead! *Dead* I tell you!"

"Dead? My son is dead?" exclaimed the Comte in melodramatic accents. He looked from one to the other with a dramatic sweep of his arm. "No! My son, he cannot be dead!"

Estée glared at him with hatred in her blue eyes. "You are no better than he! What do you care if he is dead? You do not give an *écu* for that mad son of yours. If the truth be told it is you who sent him mad, with your stupid schemes and feeding of his addiction! Oho! Yes, it is common knowledge you fed him opiates to keep him in your control. I felt so sorry for that poor boy. You—you turned him into a monster. A *monster.*"

Lord Vallentine put his arms about his sobbing wife to comfort her as best he could with a room full of persons looking on in embarrassed silence.

The Comte's smile did not waver. He signalled to the musketeer closest the dining room door. "Fetch wine for your Tante Estée, Paul."

Estée broke free from her husband's embrace. "Paul? Paul de Montbrail?"

The musketeer bowed with a nervous smile and disappeared to find the butler. Duvalier came quickly. He had been hovering in the next room and now set a tray of glasses and bottles of burgundy and claret on the table. The musketeers were left to guard the Vicomte, their leader the only one to follow the others into the private dining room. Estée took Antonia in hand to bathe the bruise to her cheek with lavender water while the gentlemen drank burgundy. The Duke declined. He set his shoulders against the mantle and watched his wife with a concerned frown.

Lord Vallentine had a hundred unanswered questions but he refrained from opening his mouth. He sipped his wine in angry silence, a smouldering eye kept on the Comte. Finding Antonia relatively unharmed slackened his desire to run the little Frenchman through the belly but his thirst for revenge was far from satisfied. He did not even know if the Vicomte was alive or dead.

The Comte de Salvan looked less the mournful parent and more the invited house guest. He drank his wine in smug silence and smacked his lips in private satisfaction. "Ah, Roxton, you have a fine cellar. One of the best! But you do not drink? You must. I insist! It has been a trying day for all of us, but we must go on! I am full of apology that we did not catch that monster before he set upon your wife." He shook his head sadly. "Yes, my son, a monster! But it is over! Never again will we be troubled. I blame myself entirely. Estée was right. Poor Salvan, he tried to do what he thought best but—Ah, who can predict the future, eh?"

Slowly the Duke turned to look at his cousin. "I am pleased you find my cellar to your liking," he said softly and in a voice that made Lord Vallentine sit up and take notice. "Finish the bottle. I insist."

The Comte refilled his glass. "You are too generous!"

"Because it will be the last you consume in my house."

"Mon cousin! What is the meaning of this hostility?" laughed the Comte. "Have we not both suffered enough today? Indeed I am so very sorry for the attack on Madame la Duchesse. It was unfortunate. But think of my loss. My son! My heir!"

"Salvan," stated the Duke, "the Vicomte is not dead. He is not even greatly injured."

"*What*. Not dead?" exploded the Comte up on his feet. "But I thought… His attack on your wife… Did you not kill him? Is his body not lying dead in the next room? He is dead I tell you! I saw his lifeless form with my own eyes! Estée, she said he was dead!"

"Sit down, Salvan," ordered Lord Vallentine, and pushed the Comte onto a chair.

"His skull may be cracked, but he will live," said the Duke. "In fact," and he grinned unpleasantly, "he will live a good many years yet. Given the proper care and every attention I should think he will live long enough to inherit the title."

"*Bon Dieu!*" Salvan mopped his glistening brow.

"He don't sound too thrilled with the idea, Roxton," said his lordship, enjoying the Comte's discomfort. "Why is that do you think?"

"I do not understand at all why you did not run that monster through!" Estée said with a shudder.

"He is too mad to kill, Madame," said Antonia a little sadly.

"But he deserves to—"

"Hush, Estée," ordered her husband. "I want to hear what your brother has to say."

The Duke held out a small key to the hovering musketeer. "If you would oblige me. In the top drawer of the desk in the library you will find a certain—er—document. You won't mistake it. Bring it to me." When Paul de Montbrail departed he continued. "I will be brief, lest our friend returns too quickly. The night my wife was shot on the Versailles road it was by your hand, Salvan."

"W-What!" gasped Estée.

"It was a mistake," continued the Duke. "You aimed at the man on horseback who tried to wrest the Duchess from the chaise. You missed your mark. In your anger at my—er—pronouncement your aim went awry and the bullet struck my wife."

"A wild assumption! Why would I bother to shoot a highwayman who held up your carriage? Preposterous! I was at a masquerade I tell you. You have no proof." The Comte sniffed. "I am insulted by such a ridiculous accusation."

"That highwayman was your son," said the Duke. "There was ample time for you both to contrive a road block and enlist the aid of a couple of your more—er—brutal servants. You saw that my carriage waited until the Duchess's belongings had been fetched from her lodgings. Mayhap you planned for such an eventuality, should she finally be successful in gaining my help to get her to Paris. She had told your son she had approached me should he be unwilling to aid her escape from your unwanted attentions. Whatever, that is unimportant." He took a pinch of snuff and glanced at Lord Vallentine. "You waited out of sight. Your son and his accomplices were braver. You hoped to kill d'Ambert and thus implicate me in his death. A pity your neat little scheme did not work. A pity for both of us."

Salvan gave a snort and waved a hand in dismissal. "Preposterous."

"The snuffbox!" announced Vallentine. "That's our proof, ain't it, Roxton? Damme, if I didn't think of it earlier."

The Duke's eyebrows shot up. "My dear, I applaud you. Yes, the snuffbox."

Estée shook her head. "Me, I am lost."

"Your brother and I went to Rossard's that very night," explained Vallentine. "All Paris was there and talking of nothing else but the hold up of Roxton's carriage. Well, Salvan was there too. And d'Ambert storms in creating a damned fuss, shouting at his father it was his fault Antonia was shot and—well, it's all rather complicated. Anyway, Roxton here passes the boy a snuffbox and says to him he dropped it. Well, d'Ambert thanks him and pockets the thing! Don't you see?"

"And did he drop it?" asked Estée.

"Of course he dropped it!" blustered his lordship. "He—"

"Allow me, my dear," the Duke intervened. "He did drop it. But not at Rossard's. But in a puddle on the Versailles road. I cannot take the credit for its discovery. I was—er—otherwise occupied. I sent a party of men under my valet's direction to scour the countryside at the scene of the crime. It was they who found the Vicomte's snuffbox."

"Good man Ellicott," said Vallentine with a firm nod. "I've always said so. I like the man."

"Oh, I like him very much," said Antonia sweetly and glanced mischievously at the Duke.

Lord Vallentine's brow furrowed. "I'd watch him all the same, Roxton," he said darkly, with a glance at the Duchess.

"Lucian! What are you implying?" demanded his wife.

"It is nothing, Madame," said Antonia airily. "Vallentine is merely jealous of M'sieur le Duc's valet. Is that not so, Monseigneur?"

Roxton smiled at her but Lord Vallentine was far from pleased and he groped for a suitable response. Just then the Comte stood up, but his sudden movement had his lordship's sword drawn on the instant.

"M'sieur! Put away that blade," demanded Salvan. Yet he decided to resume his seat when Lord Vallentine poked the tip closer his throat. "This snuffbox business I find infinitely *de trop*," he said haughtily. "Why would I want to kill my son when I had arranged such an advantageous marriage for him? Why would I go to such lengths to secure him mademoiselle's hand and then want to kill him, and have all my plans a ruin? Estée, I appeal to your good sense in this! You must believe poor Salvan."

"It was never your intention to marry your son to Mademoiselle Moran," said the Duke. "You planned to marry her from the start. You offered Strathsay your son because the Earl rejected your suit, though you still had every intention of killing the boy. Strathsay said you were too old for his granddaughter."

"Too old for her?" scoffed the Comte. And for the first time since entering his cousin's house he let down his guard. "As are you, mon cousin," he sneered, "Strathsay must turn in his grave knowing it is you who mounts her every night."

"That'll do, Salvan," growled Lord Vallentine.

"It fills me with disgust I tell you. When I think of you and her as one; you filling her with your seed—"

"Enough I said! Shall I slit his throat for you, Roxton?"

"No," answered the Duke quietly. "That would be too easy. I have a much neater solution."

Lord Vallentine removed the point of his sword. But he was careless and nicked the Comte under the chin. He made no apology and symbolically wiped the blade clean with his handkerchief. He smiled as Salvan dabbed at the stinging cut with a sweaty handkerchief, and, for good measure, trained a pistol on him.

Paul de Montbrail came back into the room carrying a sealed parchment. He handed it to the Duke with a reverential bow. His respect for this English Duke had increased tenfold within as many minutes. The seal was the royal seal of Louis, King of France. The parchment, a royal warrant.

"Montbrail! Tell this fool to put away his pistol!" commanded the Comte.

The musketeer looked at Salvan but did nothing.

"Where is my son? I demand to see him!" shouted the Comte. "Roxton tells me he is alive but this I do not believe! Montbrail! I say arrest this man! Him! The Duc de Roxton! He has killed a nobleman of France! My son! Did not the King send you with me to bring back my son to France alive and unharmed? What do you think will happen to you and the others when His Majesty learns the truth of your treason? And when I tell him you disobeyed my orders, what then?" When the musketeer continued to stare at him, immobile and blank-faced, nervousness showed in his voice, it was almost hysterical. He began to sweat. "My son had his head turned by that—that whore over there! If he is mad it is only because she made him so. He loved her. And this pox-ridden rake defiled her! It is true I tell you!"

"I await your orders, M'sieur le Duc," said the musketeer calmly.

"The Vicomte d'Ambert will be attended to in the Blue drawing room," the Duke told the musketeer. "Once he awakens he is yours to escort back to France with all speed. I am entrusting you with his safe return. It is imperative he is incarcerated in the Bastille, alive."

"I understand perfectly, M'sieur le Duc," said de Montbrail. "And M'sieur le Comte?"

"Treason! This is treason!" screamed the Comte on his feet but wary of the pistol. "It is you who will be clapped up, Montbrail! Executed, if I have my say!"

The musketeer was shaken by this threat but he remained steadfast. "And M'sieur le Comte de Salvan?" he repeated in a steady voice. "What does M'sieur le Duc require I do with him?"

Roxton turned the warrant over in his hands several times, as if considering his answer. When he looked up it was to stare at Antonia; at the state of her dress, the cut to the corner of her beautiful full mouth, and at the deep green of her eyes.

"Nothing," he whispered.

The musketeer blinked. "Pardon, Monseigneur?"

The Duke looked at the musketeer. "I said do nothing with him. I only ask that he be escorted off my land and out of my country immediately. Once in France he is free."

"Aha! I knew you would come to your senses!" said the Comte with a grin. "Put that pistol away, Vallentine. I am famished! Let us eat, yes?"

"Roxton," Vallentine said in English, "I don't understand. You can't leave it there. You can't! Jesus! You had him! You had him and you're going to let him go? Not on my life! The moment he steps off your land I'll meet him and kill him. I swear it."

"Show a little brain, Vallentine. Death is too good for him. *Think*." Roxton sighed at his friend's blank face and addressed the Comte in his own tongue. "You may eat whatever you wish, Salvan. But not at my table. Nor will you take another drop to drink. Put down that glass."

"I do not understand," said the Comte flustered. "We are cousins! All is forgotten. My son, he will be locked away. He will not bother you again. He will be taken care of. I give you my word!"

"Your word?" drawled the Duke. "When you leave England

I never want to see your face again. When I desire to go to Versailles, or to Paris to Rossard's, to the Comédie Française, to take a stroll in the Tuileries with my wife, you, my friend, will simply disappear. If ever you approach the Duchess for any reason I will kill you. If you ever cause her the slightest distress, be this the mere mention of your name in connection with my family, or you cause a rumor of any description to reach my wife's ears, I will kill you." He held up the warrant. "If your son should have the misfortune to die before he reaches the Bastille you will live out your days at the Castle Bicêtre." With that he bowed to his cousin with exquisite politeness and turned his back on him forever.

The Comte was choked with such terror that his whole body trembled, and when the Duke held up the *lettre de cachet* his face drained of all natural color. The silence that followed the Duke's bow was broken only when Lord Vallentine started to laugh loudly. He was still laughing as the musketeer marched Salvan from the room and the door was closed on their backs.

"I still say you should have run him through here and now!" complained her ladyship with a pout. "Both of them!"

"Oh, no, my love," said his lordship wiping tears from his eyes with the lace of his sleeve. "This is much better. Much, much better. Don't you see it? With his crazy son and heir locked up in the Bastille he'll be a laughing stock at court. It don't matter a tester if he remarries and has ten more sons 'cause d'Ambert's his heir and that's that! And he ain't going to shout it to the world the boy's insane. No, not Salvan! He's too proud. And if that ain't enough to turn his hair white, there's the prospect of Roxton sneaking up on him and making good his threat. It'll be a living hell for a man like Salvan. I wouldn't be at all surprised if he don't retire to his estates or end it all with a bullet. He might as well. His life is over. Damme, if you ain't a cunning fox, Roxton!"

The Duke bowed. "I will accept that as a compliment, my dear." He sat beside Antonia on the settee. "What is it, *mignonne*? Did you hope I would—er—run him through?"

She shook her head but the frown still lingered. "No. He is

not worth your energy. He will kill himself I think. It is the only honourable thing left for him to do. Monseigneur," she said quickly and grabbed suddenly for his fingers, "I have something of importance to tell you."

The Duke tried not to smile. "Yes, you do," he said softly, raising her hand to press it to his lips.

"But I do not need to tell you because you know, do you not?" she asked hesitantly, peeping up at him.

"Do I? You think me a mind reader, *mignonne*."

"No. I think somebody has already told you my great surprise for you," she said with a pout. "I do not know who because—because oh! My surprise, it is all spoiled because *everyone* knows it!"

"Why do you think that is?" the Duke asked gravely, although he was fast losing his composure.

"How should I know," she grumbled, plucking at the lace at his wrist. "I have known for some time now but me I did not believe it could happen so soon, so I waited until there was absolutely no doubt." She glanced up to find him smiling down at her. "You are laughing at me because you are thinking how can someone who reads so much be so ignorant of such worldly things. But how could I recognize the signs when this is my first... I have never been... I mean, how could I know for certain what was happening to me? It seems it is I who am the last to know!"

"Know what?" interrupted his lordship, and received such a scold from his wife that he grinned sheepishly. "Aha. Sorry! Not my business..."

The Duke and Duchess ignored them.

"Why didn't you tell me earlier?" the Duke asked gently. "Must needs my valet know before me?"

She blushed. "Oh! That—I could not help. I was very afraid, you see, when I saw the blood—but all that does not matter now."

"Is this the reason you foolishly decided to flee to Venice?" he asked softly.

She frowned and could not look at him. "I did not want to be a burden."

"*Burden?* My poor misguided darling." He kissed her forehead then whispered near her ear, "You conceived in Paris, *mignonne?*"

She nodded and finally met his gaze. "*That* is the one thing I am very sure about." She smiled shyly. "You are pleased, yes?"

"Beyond words," he murmured and added at an audible level, "And I not the only one."

"Glad that's all sorted out!" said Lord Vallentine with an impatient sigh. "Now perhaps we can all talk about the baby, eh? Here," he said, and handed each a glass of wine. "It ain't champagne, and we'll get Duvalier to fetch up a bottle pronto, but I'm parched at the present. And I want to propose a toast here and now! A toast to—"

"But, Vallentine," Antonia interrupted, "I do not find it at all convenient Renard should do this to me so soon."

Lord Vallentine blinked and wondered if he had heard correctly. "Did-did you hear what the—what the chit just said, Estée?" he blustered. "You needn't laugh about it! You either, Roxton! She can't go about saying such—saying such—Damme! Am I the only one with any sense of the proprieties? It's damned—it's damned—"

"Outrageous?" suggested the Duchess of Roxton raising her glass in a toast, a smile at the Duke and with a mischievous twinkle in her green eyes. "Me, I am quite an outrageous duchess, yes?"

$\mathcal{T}$o be continued ∼

The Roxton Series continues in Book 2 *Midnight Marriage*, the story of Roxton and Antonia's son Julian, Marquis of Alston and his bride Deborah Cavendish.

CPSIA information can be obtained
at www.ICGtesting.com
Printed in the USA
BVHW071005020621
608627BV00001B/36